Freidrich Max Müller

Auld lang syne: Second series

My Indian friends

Freidrich Max Müller

Auld lang syne: Second series
My Indian friends

ISBN/EAN: 9783337303662

Printed in Europe, USA, Canada, Australia, Japan

Cover: Foto ©Andreas Hilbeck / pixelio.de

More available books at **www.hansebooks.com**

AULD LANG SYNE

SECOND SERIES

MY INDIAN FRIENDS

BY

THE RIGHT HON. PROFESSOR F. MAX MÜLLER

AUTHOR OF "THE SCIENCE OF LANGUAGE" ETC.

LONGMANS, GREEN, AND CO

39 PATERNOSTER ROW, LONDON
AND BOMBAY

1899

PREFACE.

HERE follows the second volume of my *Auld Lang Syne*. In some cases my recollections go back very far, and, after a lapse of nearly seventy years, they may not always be so fresh as they ought to be. It is very strange, on looking back to the various stations through which we have passed in our journey through this life, to find how much our own fate has depended on our surroundings and on circumstances over which we ourselves could not possibly have had any control. Our friends, nay even our enemies, seem to form part of our life, and thus it has come to pass that instead of writing my own life, I have almost unconsciously come to write about my friends rather than about myself. As to enemies, if indeed I ever had any, I prefer to be silent, for it is difficult to be quite fair in speaking of them, and we seldom know, till it is too late, what real benefactors they have been to us. Scholars, who on questions of scholarship differ from us as we differ from them, should never be counted as personal enemies, if only they are

truthful and straightforward, and if otherwise, is it
not best here also to follow the old rule, *De mortuis
nihil nisi bonum*? But with regard to my friends
and acquaintances, the older I grow, the more I feel
how much I have owed and still owe to them, nay,
how often the whole stream of my life has been
turned East or West by a word or two spoken by
a friend at the right moment, just as a whole train
may be turned by the mere touch of a handle by
the pointsman.

The first volume of my *Auld Lang Syne* contained recollections of musicians, poets, crowned
heads, and beggars, such as had not entirely vanished from the *camera obscura* of my memory.
The present volume is chiefly devoted to my *Indian
Friends*, and to certain events that first led my
attention to India. Though I have had but visions
of the rivers, the mountains, the valleys, the forests,
and the men and women of India, having never
been allowed to visit that earthly paradise, I have
known for many years the beauties of its literature,
the bold flights of its native philosophy, the fervid
devotion of its ancient religion, and these together
seem to me to give a much truer picture of what
India really was, and is still meant to be, in the
history of the world, than the Bazaars of Bombay,
or the Durbars of Râjahs and Mahârâjahs at Delhi.
Of course, I shall be told that my picture of India
is purely ideal, but an ideal portrait may sometimes
be truer than even a photograph, and, though I
trust that my facts on the whole are right, I shall

always feel most grateful, if any facts are pointed out to me which either contradict or modify my own judgments.

India has never had full justice done to it, and when I say this I think not only of ancient, but of modern India also. And though it can easily be seen that my chief interest lies with ancient India, it should be remembered that in no other country is the past still so visibly present as in that southernmost home of the ancient family of Aryan speech. There may be more historical monuments, reminding us of the past, in Greece and Italy. But life, with its religion, philosophy, and literature, has completely changed there, and we look in vain for a Socrates or Plato on the steps of the Parthenon, or for a Cato or Caesar among the lonely columns of the Forum. In India, on the contrary, the religion of the Veda is by no means entirely extinct. Not long ago even one of the old magnificent Vedic sacrifices, the Agnish*t*oma, was performed at Benares with all its pristine array. The old epic poems are still recited by the Pâ*t*hakas of the country, and some of the old philosophies are flourishing in native Colleges, such as Nuddea, so that men of the present day, such as Gaurî-sa*m*kara, the Prime Minister of Bhavnagar, and the Yogin Râmak*ri*sh*n*a, bring back to us in full reality the Rishis and Yogins of a thousand or two thousand years ago.

What seems to me to prevent a full appreciation of the intellectual achievements of ancient and medieval India is that they are mostly looked upon, as we look on the prodigies in our exhibitions, as simply curious. Now, we should never say that Plato and Aristotle were curious. We take them far more seriously. We look upon them as our equals, nay as our teachers. It cannot surely be the brown skin that keeps us from feeling the same sympathy and paying the same homage to the poets and philosophers of ancient India, and that prevents even at the present day any real friendship between the best sons of India and England? That brown skin may at first cause a feeling of strangeness, but I know how easily that feeling can be and has been overcome, and, judging from my own limited experience, I can truly say that there is behind that warm and almost Italian colour of the Âryas of India the same warm heart, the same trust, and the same love as under the white skin of Europeans. Real friendship between the rulers and the ruled in India ought to be no impossibility; it has existed again and again; only it should no longer be the exception, but the rule.

If the account of my Indian Friends which I give in this volume, should serve here and there to overcome that feeling of strangeness and lead to real trust between the two most distant members of the noble family of Aryan speech, I should indeed feel amply rewarded.

I could not well pass over, as belonging by right to the circle of my friends and acquaintances, the ancient Rishis of the Veda, call them Dîrghatamas,

Vasish*th*a, or any other name, and in order to show what these ancient poets were really like, I have ventured to add metrical translations of a few of their hymns, celebrating the matutinal procession of their bright Devas or gods. For these I have to crave the indulgence of my critics. These poets were the first to call me to India, and I have never regretted having followed their call, as far as other calls allowed me to do so. They have revealed to me a whole world of thought of which no trace existed anywhere else, and they have helped me to throw the first faint rays of light and reason on perhaps the darkest period in the history of religion, philosophy, and mythology. That period, which I should like to call the *Etymological*, will, I doubt not, become illuminated hereafter by a flood of light from the same source. The work of the present generation of Vedic students could naturally be that of pioneers only, but they may fairly say *In magnis et voluisse sat est*, or in Sanskrit, Yatne k*ri*te yadi na sidhyati, ko*tra dosha*h*!

F. M. M.

OxFORD, *May* 1, 1899.

CONTENTS.

—◦—

	PAGE
I. MY INDIAN FRIENDS	1-46
My first acquaintance with India	1-5
Dvârkanâth Tagore	5-14
Debendranâth Tagore	14-23
Râjah Râdhâkânta Deva	23-46
II. MY INDIAN FRIENDS	47-112
Nîlakantha Goreh	47-65
Keshub Chunder Sen	65-90
Chaitanya	66
Nânak and the Sîkhs	69
Râmtonoo Lahari	90
Dayânanda Sarasvatî	93
Vedânta Philosophy	102
Râmakrishna	105
III. MY INDIAN FRIENDS	113-166
Behramji Malabâri	113-121
Râmabâi	121-129
Ânandibâi Joshee, M.D.	129-134
National Character of the Hindus	135
Indian Theosophy	148
My Indian Correspondents	153-166
IV. MY INDIAN FRIENDS	167-234
The Veda	167-234
Hymn to the Asvins, Day and Night	194
Hymn to Ushas, Dawn	200
Hymn to Savitri, Sun	210
Hymn to Agni, Fire	216
Hymn to Râtrî, Night	228
Hymn to Varuna	230
Hymn X, 129, on Creation	232
V. MY INDIAN FRIENDS	235-268
A Prime Minister and a Child-wife	235-268
INDEX	269-271

AULD LANG SYNE.

MY INDIAN FRIENDS.

I.

My first Acquaintance with India.

How I fell in love with India is a very old, and
a very long story. We have all read of young
knights who in a dream had a vision of a beautiful
princess, and who did not rest until they had found
her, delivered her, and, after many hard fights with
giants and monsters, carried her home in triumph.
I had such a vision of India when I was not yet
ten years old. It may seem passing strange that
a little boy in a small town of Germany should as
far back as 1833 have dreamt of India. Few
people would know that small town in which he
lived. However, if they will look on the map of

Note.—In Sanskrit words an italic *k* should be pronounced like
English "ch" in church, italic *g* like "j" in join. Thus, mle*kkh*a,
or, as some used to spell it, mlechchha, should be pronounced
like mlêcha. Proper names, however, and Oriental words that
have already a recognised spelling in English, have mostly been left
unchanged.

II.   B

Germany, somewhere between the 12th and 13th degrees of longitude and the 51st and 52nd degrees of latitude, they will find *Dessau*, the capital of the Duchy of Anhalt. It lies on the road from Leipzig to Magdeburg, and in these days of railways people often pass it on their way to Berlin. I have never been a very superstitious man, and have never believed in ghosts or spirits, in table-turnings or spirit-rappings, in visions or apparitions; in fact, in anything that can strike the material senses, and yet pretend to be immaterial, and has nothing to strike with. This is the whole problem of ghosts in a nutshell. If ghosts are immaterial, they cannot strike our eyes, or tickle our ears. They could not even have a sulphurous smell. If, on the contrary, they are material, they are not ghosts. But this by the way. But though an unbeliever in ghosts, I have not been able to withhold my belief from coincidences, strange coincidences, which we have to accept in the course of our life without any attempt to account for them. I well remember when I was at school, one of my copybooks had a large picture of Benares on the outside. It was a very rough picture, but I can still see the men, women, and children as they stepped down the ghats to bathe in the waters of the Ganges. That picture caught my fancy and set me dreaming. What did I know of India at that time ? Nothing but that the people were black, that they burnt their widows, and that, in order to get into Paradise, they had first to be mangled under the wheels of the car of Juggernâth. On my picture, however, they were represented looking tall, and, as I thought, beautiful, certainly not like niggers; and the mosques and temples visible on the shores of the river impressed me as even more beautiful and majestic than the churches and palaces at Dessau. Boys will dream dreams, and as I was sitting idle at school dreaming and seeing visions of Benares, instead of doing my copy, I was suddenly taken by the ear by our writing-master, and told to copy several pages containing such names as Benares, Ganges, India, and all the rest, because I had been so idle and had made a very bad copy. This was my first and somewhat painful acquaintance with India, and it led to nothing else at the time. It simply left the memory of a kind of vision, and, if I had not later in life become devoted to the reality of that vision, I should probably never have thought of my copybook again.

It was when I had left school, and had gone to the University of Leipzig in 1841, that my vision, like a *revenant*, appeared again, and assumed then a more tangible and permanent form. I was getting a little tired of Greek and Latin, and the warmed-up cabbage, the *crambe repetita*, of Homer and Horace, when I heard of the foundation of a new Chair— a Chair of Sanskrit—and saw lectures on Indian literature advertised by Professor Brockhaus. Here my curiosity was roused at once; I had already had a slight flirtation with Arabic, but now I fell seriously in love with Sanskrit, and became more and more faithless to my first classical love. Pro-

fessor Brockhaus was an excellent, kind-hearted,
and helpful teacher. I began Sanskrit with a will,
and, after I had attended his lectures for several
semesters at Leipzig, and had read with him such
ordinary books as Nala, *Sakuntalâ*, and even a
little of the Rig-Veda, I went to Berlin to study
under Bopp; and then proceeded to Paris, attracted
by the fame of Eugène Burnouf.

At that time my desire to see India, as I had
seen it in the visions of my schooldays, became
very strong. As classical scholars yearn to see
Rome or Athens, I yearned to see Benares, and
to bathe in the sacred waters of the Ganges. But
at that time such a thing was simply out of the
question. At that time to go to India seemed to
be the privilege of Englishmen only, and it took
half a year to get there, and a great deal more
money than I could command. The dream of my
life to see India face to face has never been realised.
When I was young enough, I had not the where-
withal to go there, and when, later in life, I was
invited again and again by my Indian friends to
go there, I was too old and too much tied down
by duties from which there was no escape. Besides,
unless I could have stayed in India at least two
or three years, could have learned to speak the
languages, and come to know the few native scholars
still left, it was nothing to me. My India was not
on the surface, but lay many centuries beneath it;
and as to paying a globe-trotter's visit to Calcutta
and Bombay, I might as well walk through Oxford

Street and Bond Street. But, though I never stood
on the ghats of Benares, and never saw the men,
women, and children step down from them into the
sacred waters of the Ganges, I have had the good
fortune of knowing a number of Indians in Europe,
and no doubt some of the best and most distinguished of the sons and daughters of India.
I have often been told that I have been misled
by these acquaintances, and have taken far too
favourable a view of the Indian character; that
I had seen the best of India only, but not the worst.
But where is the harm? I have seen what the
Indian character can be, I have learnt what it
ought to be, and I hope what it will be, and though
we cannot expect a whole nation of Rammohun
Roys, of Debendranâth Tagores, of Keshub Chunder
Sens, of Malabâris and Râmabâis, we ought not to
neglect them in our estimate of the capabilities of
a whole nation.

Dvârkanâth Tagore.

Indians did not travel so freely fifty years ago
as they do now. The crossing of the black water
and all its consequences had not then lost its
terrors. When, therefore, in the year 1844, a real
Hindu made his appearance in Paris, his visit
created a great sensation, and filled me with a
strong desire to make his acquaintance. He was
a handsome man, and, as he took the best suite
of apartments in one of the best hotels in Paris,
he naturally roused considerable curiosity. I was

then attending Professor Burnouf's lectures at the
Collège de France, and, as the Indian visitor had
brought letters of introduction to that great French
savant, I too was introduced to the Indian stranger,
and soon came to know him well. He was the
representative of one of the greatest and richest
families in India, Dvârkanâth Tagore, the father
of the Maharshi Debendranâth Tagore, who is still
alive, and the grandfather of Satyendranâth Tagore,
the first successful native candidate for the Indian
Civil Service, whom I knew as a young student in
England, and who now, after serving his country
and his Empress with great distinction for many
years, has retired from the service.

Dvârkanâth Tagore was not a Sanskrit scholar,
but he was not unacquainted with Sanskrit literature. The first time I saw him was at the *Institut
de France*, when Burnouf presented him with a copy
of his splendid edition of the Bhagavat-Purâna.
On one side was the Sanskrit text, on the other
the French translation, and it was curious to see
the Indian placing his delicate brown fingers on the
white page with the French translation, and saying
with a sigh, "Oh, if I could read that!" One
would have expected that his wish would have
been to understand the ancient language of his
own country; but no, he pined for a better knowledge of French.

He was not an antiquarian, nor a student of his
own religion or of the language of his own sacred
books. But when he was told by Burnouf what

my plans were, and how I had actually copied and collated the MSS. of the Veda at Paris, he took a lively interest in me. He invited me, and I often spent the mornings with him, talking about India and Indian customs. Strange to say, he was devotedly fond of music, and had acquired a taste for Italian and French music. What he liked was to have me to accompany him on the pianoforte, and I soon found that he had not only a good voice, but had been taught fairly well. So we got on very well together. After complimenting him on his taste for Italian music, I asked him one morning to give me a specimen of real Indian music. He sang first of all what is called Indian, but is really Persian music, without any style or character. This was not what I wanted, and I asked whether he did not know some pieces of real Indian music. He smiled and turned away. "You would not appreciate it," he said; but, as I asked him again and again, he sat down to the pianoforte, and, after striking a few notes, began to play and sing. I confess I was somewhat taken aback. I could discern neither melody, nor rhythm, nor harmony in what he sang; but, when I told him so, he shook his head and said: "You are all alike; if anything seems strange to you and does not please you at once, you turn away. When I first heard Italian music, it was no music to me at all; but I went on and on, till I began to like it, or what you call understand it. It is the same with everything else. You say our religion is no religion, our poetry no poetry, our philosophy no philosophy. We try to understand and appreciate whatever Europe has produced, but do not imagine that therefore we despise what India has produced. If you studied our music as we do yours, you would find that there is melody, rhythm, and harmony in it, quite as much as in yours. And if you would study our poetry, our religion, and our philosophy, you would find that we are not what you call heathens or miscreants, but know as much of the Unknowable as you do, and have seen perhaps even deeper into it than you have!" He was not far wrong.

He became quite eloquent and excited, and to pacify him I told him that I was quite aware that India possessed a science of music, founded, as far as I could see, on mathematics. I had examined some Sanskrit MSS. on music, but I confessed that I could not make head or tail of them. I once consulted Professor H. H. Wilson on the subject, who had spent many years in India and was himself a musician. But he did not encourage me. He told me that, while in India, he had been to a native teacher of music who professed to understand the old books. He had expressed himself willing to teach him, on condition that he would come to him two or three times a week. Then at the end of half a year he would be able to tell him whether he was fit to learn music, whether he was in fact an Adhikârin, a fit candidate, and in five years he promised him that he might master both the theory and the practice of music. That was too much for 'an Indian civilian who had his hands full of work, and though he learnt many things from Pandits, Professor H. H. Wilson, then, I believe, Master of the Mint and holding several other appointments besides, had to give up all idea of becoming apprenticed for five years to a teacher of music. Dvârkanâth Tagore was much amused, but he quite admitted that five years was the shortest time in which any man could hope thoroughly to master the intricacies of ancient Hindu music, and I too gave up in consequence all hope of ever mastering such texts as the Sangîta-ratnâkara, the Treasury of Symphony, and similar texts, though they have often tempted my curiosity in the library of the East India House.

There is another member of the Tagore family, Râjah Surindro Mohun Tagore, a very liberal patron of Indian music, who has published a great deal about it, but he too has kept aloof from touching on the old science of music that once existed in India, though we know as yet so little of its literature. If we could accept a tradition that has been repeated again and again by Sanskrit scholars, even by men of great learning, such as the late Professor Benfey, we should have to believe that Guido d'Arezzo (about 1000 A. D.) borrowed his gamut from the Arabs, and that they had adopted it from the Persians, who had been the pupils of the Hindus. In itself such a borrowing has nothing incredible in it, for we know that our figures, not excluding the nought, travelled on the same road, from the Indians to the Persians, the Arabs, the Spaniards, and the Italians. It is true also that one of the Indian gamuts consisted of seven notes, and that these notes went by the names *sa, ri, ga, ma, pa, dha, ni,* which were the first syllables of their Sanskrit names. So far, therefore, there is some plausibility. But if it is maintained that these seven syllables were changed in Italian to the well-known *do, re, mi, fa, sol, la, si,* we require some more of real historical evidence of such a change before stating as a fact what is, as yet, a guess only. Gladly as I should claim any merit for the people of India, it seems to me that the differences between the names of the notes of the two gamuts are greater than their similarities. All we can say is that it is possible that we owe our gamut to India, but until more evidence is produced, we cannot say more. If we remember that we owe the nought to that country, mathematicians will be ready to confess that this was one of the greatest discoveries in the history of mathematics and of all the sciences that depend on mathematics, one of the greatest benefits, in fact, that the East has conferred on the West. Whether we owe to India Beethoven's symphonies is another question, that has yet to wait for an answer.

My Indian friend Dvârkanâth Tagore, though not learned, was very intelligent, and a man of

the world. He rather looked down on the
Brâhmans, and when I asked him whether he
would have to perform penance, or Prâyaskitta,
after his return to India, he laughed and said,
" No. I am all this time feeding a large number
of Brâhmans at home, and that is quite penance
enough!" The real penance was, of course, the
Pañkagavya, the five products of the cow which
the penitent had to swallow before he could be
readmitted to his caste; and these products were
not only milk, sour milk, and clarified butter, but
likewise other products, such as Mûtra and Gomaya.
That penance still exists, and many of our Indian
visitors have had to undergo it after their return,
though at present the five products of the cow are
reduced to infinitesimal proportions and swallowed
in the shape of a gilded pill.

But if he took a low view of his Brâhmans, he
did not show much more respect for what he called
the black-coated English Brâhmans. Much as he
admired everything English, he had a mischievous
delight in finding out the weak points of English
society, and particularly of the English clergy.
He read a number of English newspapers, political
and ecclesiastic, and he kept a kind of black book
in which he carefully noted whatever did not
redound very much to the honour of any bishops,
priests, or deacons. It certainly was a curious
collection of every kind of ecclesiastical scandal,
and I have often wondered what could have
become of it. His son, the saint-like Debendranâth

Tagore, the head of the Ârya-Samâj, would hardly make use of such weapons ; but his father delighted in the book, and brought it out whenever the question turned on the respective merits of the Indian and the Christian religions.   All I could say was that no religion should be judged by its clergy only, whether in Italy, in England, or in India.

Dvârkanâth Tagore lived in a truly magnificent Oriental style while at Paris.   The king, Louis Philippe, received him, nay, he honoured him, if I remember right, by his presence and that of his Court at a grand evening party.   The room was hung with Indian shawls, then the height of ambition of every French lady.   And what was their delight when the Indian Prince placed a shawl on the shoulders of each lady as she left the room !

When in England, Dvârkanâth fulfilled a sacred duty to the memory of Rammohun Roy, the great religious reformer of India, by erecting a tomb over his ashes in the cemetery at Bristol, little thinking that he would soon share his fate, and die like him in a foreign land.

I believe it was his doing also that a new interest was roused in India for the study of the Veda.   It was certainly a curious and anomalous state of things that in a country where the Veda was recognised as the highest authority in religion, invested with all the authority of a divine revelation to a greater degree even than the New Testament is in England, this Bible of theirs should never have been printed,

and should have been accessible to a small class
of priests only, who knew it by heart and possessed
a few MSS. of it. Still, so it was; nay, so much
had the study of the Veda become neglected that
when a prize was offered by the late J. Muir to
any one who would undertake an edition of it, not
a single native scholar was willing or able to undertake the task. When, therefore, Dvârkanâth saw
that I was quietly preparing an edition of the
most important, in fact, the only true Veda, the
Rig-Veda, and that I had copied and collated
the MSS. which existed in the Royal Libraries
at Paris, at Berlin, and elsewhere, and was going
to finish my collection in London, he seems to
have informed his son, Debendranâth Tagore,
of what I was doing at Paris, who, full of interest
for religion and religious reform, dispatched about
the same time four young native students to
Benares, in order to enable them to study the
Veda under the guidance of the Pandits of that
sacred city. One was to learn the Rig-Veda,
another the Sâma-Veda, a third the Yagur-Veda,
a fourth the Atharva-Veda. To judge, however,
from a letter of Debendranâth Tagore himself, this
may have been a mere coincidence. Unfortunately
not one of these young Pandits seems ever to
have done any independent work in the direction
suggested by Debendranâth Tagore.

I may as well state here that I never claimed
nor received the very substantial prize offered by
J. Muir. Such vague and exaggerated accounts

have been spread and even published as to the magnificent *honorarium* paid to me by the late East India Company that I may as well state that, even if I could have carried through the press one sheet per week, after copying, collating, and adding all the references to Sâyana's commentary, I should never have earned more than £200 a year for a work which during more than twenty years of my life occupied nearly all my time. I do not grudge that time, and I shall always feel deeply grateful to some of the Directors of the old Company for having taken so active an interest in what seemed at the time a very useless undertaking. I do not think that the financial position of India has greatly suffered on account of the printing of the Rig-Veda, nay, the expense incurred for it must have been amply recovered, considering how largely the six large quartos have been used for presents to the Râjahs in India and to the Universities and Museums in Europe. Of course it is impossible to make presents without having to pay for them. If people will invent and exaggerate, I may as well tell them that I believe the youngest clerk in the India Office would have declined to work for twenty years at such a salary as I did. And yet I was as happy as a king all the time.

Debendranâth Tagore.

Though I have never seen the son of Dvârkanâth, Debendranâth Tagore, I have had several most interesting letters from him, and I have always felt the deepest sympathy for his noble and unselfish efforts to purify the religion of his countrymen. He was the patron and friend of Keshub Chunder Sen, and, though he was too conservative to be able to follow his young friend in all his reforms, his love for his enthusiastic pupil never ceased. When Keshub Chunder Sen had been forsaken by nearly all his friends, because he allowed the marriage of his daughter with the Mahârâjah of Kuch Behar, when she was a few months under age, the old man remained true to him to the last, and mourned over him at his death-bed as a father would mourn over his only son.

Here is at least one of Debendranâth Tagore's letters to me. I am always ashamed when I print any letters from my Indian friends. They are far too kind, far too complimentary. I know how to make allowance for their warm heart and for their exuberant language, but I am afraid that to people unacquainted with Eastern skies and Eastern hearts, it will naturally seem that such letters ought never to have been published. But what gives so true a picture of a man as a confidential letter?

"CHINSURA, via CALCUTTA,
    December 27, 1884.

" My Dear Sir,

I was very glad to receive your letter. It will always give me pleasure to hear from the Pandit of the Far West who has done so much for the language and literature of my country. There

are branches of knowledge and art in which the
East is deficient, and which she must learn from
foreign sources.   But there are other things all
her own, and even your enlightened countrymen
may turn with pleasure and profit to a leaf or
two out of the books of the East to learn something new, to get a glimpse of vistas of thought
with which they are not familiar.   And you, Sir,
have done not a little to open out before the
world treasures of Oriental wisdom which only
the diligence of scholars like you could unfold.
By the publication of the Rig-Veda and the
Upanishads you have brought within the reach
of European scholars the thoughts and aspirations
of our ancient Rishis, hitherto hidden in inaccessible
manuscripts.   And it is to be hoped that the dis-
semination of the knowledge of our ancient literature will help to cement the bonds of union
between the two peoples who, brought up under
a common roof, parted from each other and
scattered over distant quarters of the globe, again
to be brought together under the mysterious decree
of Almighty Providence.

"You are perhaps not quite right in taking me
for a Sannyâsin in the sense of one who has wholly
renounced the world.   To be in the world, but
not of it, is my *beau idéal* of a Sannyâsin, and in
that sense I am one.   My sons are settled in life
and working before my eyes.   I take a keen
interest in all that goes on far and near, in my
domestic circle and outside.   My infirm health,

however, does not permit me to take an active
part in the affairs of the world.   So I have settled
down for the present in a country house by the
banks of the Ganges, far from the din and bustle
of the town, and yet not too far to be out of its
reach, and my life glides smoothly along like the
waves in winter, resigned to His will and ready
to quit its mortal coils at His call.

"The schism in the Brahmo Samâj is a thing
to be regretted, perhaps it may do present harm
to the cause.   We should have been stronger, if
united, but there is no cause for despondency.
The seeds have been sown, and they will bear
fruit in God's own time.   We are but humble
seekers of the Truth and humble workers in her
cause.   We must work and labour each in his
own sphere and according to his own light, regard-
less of consequences.   The crowning and fruition
of our work rests with God alone, and we may
repose our trust in Him for success.   Truth will
triumph in the end.   Satyam eva gayati.

"Accept my best thanks for the copy of your
Biographical Essays you have so kindly presented
to me.   It is a very interesting book, and I have
read it with the greatest delight.   The charitable
feeling which you have shown in judging of
Keshub Chunder Sen is worthy of your liberality
of thought.   I received no intimation from my
father regarding the publication of the Rig-Veda.
It was my own idea to send Pandits to Benares
to study the Vedas.   The project entirely originated

with me, and had no connection with the work you had taken in hand.

Yours sincerely,

DEBENDRANÂTH TAGORE."

Whatever may be thought by others of such a letter, to me it seems a most instructive and characteristic page in the recent history of India. Let us think, first of all, whether there is a single man living in Europe, a man of wealth and high position in his own country, who could have penned such a letter in a foreign language, whether German or Sanskrit. There is hardly a word in it that would have to be altered, and as to the spirit pervading it, no bishop need be ashamed of it. And yet how many people are there even among members of the Indian Civil Service, who would look upon this man as their equal, not to say, as their better? What he says about the new lessons which even we in England might learn from India, more particularly from the Rig-Veda and the Upanishads, is by no means a mere phrase. He knew quite well what he meant. He was quite sufficiently acquainted with our language, our literature, our philosophy and religion to have a right to say that there are things in those books which are new to us, and might be truly helpful to everybody who strives to solve for himself the many riddles of this world. Let us remember, first of all, that the Rig-Veda is the oldest book of the world. It is

older than anything in Greece and Rome, older,
as a book, than any book in China, older than
the old Persian Avesta, older than Buddhism and
its sacred canon, older also than the Old Testament. I know that this last statement will make
many people shake their heads, as if the truth
and value of a book depended on its age. Is
the Old Testament truer than the New, because
it is older? Truth is neither young nor old, it
is eternal, and history teaches us that the older
a religion, the more has it been exposed to
deterioration in the hands of priests and no-priests.
Ancient ruins are, no doubt, venerable and impres-
sive, but for dwelling in them and for the daily
work of life new buildings are better.

No one would say that because the Rig-Veda
is the oldest book of the human race—we cannot
call cuneiform or hieroglyphic inscriptions, however
large they are, books in the ordinary sense of the
word—it is therefore the best or the truest. It
is on the contrary a record of the childhood of
our race, full of childish things, but full also
of such unexpected sparks of thought as occasionally startle us from the minds and mouths of
babes. The more childish the words of the Rig-
Veda are, the more instructive they should prove
to us. Where are we to study the origin of
religion of the Aryan race to which we ourselves
belong by language and thought, if not in the
Rig-Veda? Nor does it require much study.
Whoever runs may read it on every page. No

one doubts now that the gods of the ancient
Âryas were representatives of the great phenomena
of nature, conceived in the only way in which, in
the then state of language and thought, they could be
conceived, that is as active and personified. What
we should have anticipated, and what in fact was
anticipated by philosophers, was fully confirmed by
the hymns of the Rig-Veda, which were found to
be addressed to the Dawn, the first miracle and
the greatest revelation the world has ever seen,
though we have learnt to look upon the light of
the morning as a matter of course. They were
addressed to the morning Sun, the bringer of light
and life, to the blue Sky, the gatherer of clouds,
the giver of rain and fertility, to the Earth, the
Rivers, the Fire, the Storms, and many more.

During the period reflected in the songs of the
Rig-Veda, the poets had already made the step
from the worship of many gods, the Devas, or
the Bright Ones, as they called them, to the
recognition of one, but still personal God above
all gods, nay, they had purified the concept of
that Supreme Being from all that was implied
in a male or female personality, and had acknow-
ledged it as neither of the one nor of the other
sex, as untrammelled by what personality means
with us, as the true, free, and eternal Godhead
of which the other gods were but human renderings more or less perfect. We can watch in the
Rig-Veda how all these thoughts and conceptions
of the Deity arose naturally in the human heart,

and there is no other literature in which the
genesis of the Divine in the human mind can be
so fully and so clearly watched and studied.
A record of this theogonic process is surely
worth having, and though it naturally holds true
of the Aryan race only, it is after all the race to
which we ourselves belong, not merely by blood
and bones, but, by what is far more important,
by language and thought.   If we can observe
this theogonic process among other races also,
whether civilised or uncivilised, a comparison of
the different roads that led to God may become
most important.   Care, however, must be taken
not to mix what is heterogeneous.   The religions
of uncivilised races, whether ancient or modern, but
mostly modern, should be studied by themselves,
and of course by scholars only, or by those who
have at least a knowledge of the grammar of the
language in which the religious ideas of such races
lie embedded.   A beginning in this direction has
been made, and much may be expected from ethnological studies in the future. . Hitherto they have
mostly proved amusing only, and without much
scientific value, for which the scarcity of materials
is answerable far more than the credulity of some
of our ethnological students.   What is the true
value of the theogony of the Aryan race is its
historical character, and its continuity which enables
us to watch the growth of the concepts of the
gods and of God in an unbroken chain till we
arrive, chiefly in the Upanishads, at that true

conception of the Godhead, free from all limitations, even from that of personality, in the human
sense of that word, a stage that had been reached
by Greek and Jewish thinkers at Alexandria in
the first centuries of Christianity, but was soon
afterwards hidden again in the clouds of theological
anthropomorphism.

It makes no difference whether we ourselves
consider this religious development of Aryan
thought of the Godhead as true or mistaken. Its
real interest is that it has historical reality, and
that at all events we can learn lessons from it
which we can learn nowhere else. It was my
desire to gain a direct knowledge of what is
preserved in the Rig-Veda of the earliest religious
development of our race, and thus to fill a gap
which had been felt for many years and deplored
by all true scholars, that made me conceive the
idea of publishing the text and native commentary
of the Rig-Veda ; a task not without its difficulties,
both scientific and material, for it would otherwise
have been undertaken long before.

I have a letter dated August, 1845, now before me
from the late Professor Roth, the editor with Professor Boehtlingk of our great Sanskrit Dictionary,
where he says, "It is a truly youthful boldness
to undertake an edition of the whole of Sâyana's
commentary by yourself alone," and he proposes
that I should allow him, Dr. Trithen, Dr. Rieu
and others to take each a part of the work. In
some respects I am sorry now that I did not

accept this offer, for the Veda would have appeared sooner. But there were difficulties in this combination, as in most combinations, and being then very youthful and bold, I took the whole work on my own shoulders.

But if my edition of the Rig-Veda helped to usher in quite a new period in Sanskrit scholarship in Europe, it naturally produced an even greater commotion all over India. After all, it was their Bible, and had never been published before during the three or four thousand years of its existence. Attempts were made in various quarters to taboo it, as having been printed by a Mlekkha and with cow's blood; but the book proved itself too strong, it was indispensable, and was soon accepted even by those who at first had placed it under their interdict. The late Dr. Haug sent me a full account of a meeting held by the Brâhmans at Poonah, who, though unwilling at first to touch the book, called an assembly in which a man, not a Brâhman, read out my edition, and all the Brâhmans corrected whatever MSS. they possessed, according to the text as settled in the distant University of Oxford.

Râjah Râdhâkânta Deva.

This brought me into correspondence with many of the leading men both among the conservative and orthodox, and among the progressive and enlightened party in India. At the head of the conservative party stood then a well-known man,

Râjah Râdhâkânta Deva, a kind of Indian Lord
Shaftesbury. He had distinguished himself by
publishing a large thesaurus of the Sanskrit language
in seven large quarto volumes, called the *Sabda-
kalpa-druma*, the paradise-tree of words. I was
highly pleased when I received so valuable a present
from the Râjah, and deeply interested in a letter
which accompanied it. People in India, even intelligent people, were evidently very much puzzled,
how a Mle*kkh*a, as they called all barbarians, or
all not twice-born men, could have got hold in the
libraries of Germany, France, and England of the
disjecta membra of their sacred book, how he could
have made it out, and actually corrected it. The
reforming party naturally rejoiced in the publication
of the Veda. But some even of the old orthodox
believers in the Veda were highly pleased when
I presented to them their venerable Bible. Strange
as it may seem to us, such is the power of a long-
continued tradition that even the more enlightened
among the Hindus, at least at the time of which
I am writing, had no kind of doubt as to the divine
origin of the Veda. They looked upon it not only
as a revelation granted to mankind thousands of
years ago, but they believed that it was pre-
mundane, that it had existed in the mind of the
Supreme Being from all eternity, and had been
breathed forth before the beginning of the world.
They thought of it, not as a book, but as a revelation
handed down from teacher to pupil in an uninterrupted succession. There existed manuscripts of it, •

but not very many, and the only way recognised
in India of learning the Veda, without destroying
its sanctity and efficacy, was to learn it by heart
from the mouth of a qualified teacher. Every
word, every letter, every accent of the Veda had
been settled by authority as far back as about the
fifth century B.C., and from that point of view the
authority of oral tradition was, and is still considered much higher than that of a mere manuscript.
Formerly, as in the time of the Laws of Manu,
it was even forbidden to write the Veda or to sell
copies of it. That so sacred and more than sacred
a work should have been published for the first
time by a barbarian, and that hundreds of copies
of it should suddenly be for sale in the streets of
Benares, Bombay, and Poonah, was at first a very
great shock to the orthodox. Still, though there
were protests, and though all sorts of doubts were
thrown on the genuineness of the printed text, even
the most bigoted opponents of everything European
had at last to give in, and to confess that the printed
text was really their true Veda, and that it was
more complete and more correct than any manuscript
then in existence.

We must never forget that the ancient literature
of India was entirely mnemonic. This may sound
almost incredible, yet there are few Sanskrit scholars
who would any longer doubt it. In their recognised
system of education the imprinting of the ancient
books on the memory of the young was the most
essential feature. Boys, not girls, had to spend

years and years of their youth, while staying in the house of a Guru, in learning by heart line after line of certain books, and nothing else. Thus only can we account for the wonderful capacity and tenacity of their memory. They at first learnt their sacred books, as I have known children to learn poems in a foreign language, without even attempting to understand a single word. Children of good Brâhman families were simply treated like sheets of paper, on which the teacher impressed letters, syllables, words, and sentences by sound only. Later only came the time for going over (Adhyayana) what stood thus imprinted on their memory, and for understanding, under the guidance of qualified teachers, its real purport. This, too, may seem almost incredible to us, but in the absence of writing and printing, what else could have been done? Every boy who passed through the orthodox system of education (Brahmakaryâ) became a copy of whatever text he was made to learn, and this copy had to be kept in good condition by constant repetition. Unless we keep this clearly before our mind, we shall never understand the state of ancient literature in India, with all its changes and chances, before the introduction of writing. When we consider, for instance, the enormous bulk of the ancient Sanskrit epic, the Mahâbhârata, a poem of more than 90,000 couplets, four volumes quarto, we hesitate before accepting it as a mnemonic poem. And yet we have what amounts to almost positive evidence of the poem having existed before the

introduction of writing into India, in the fact that
there is an episode, added at the beginning of the
poem, in which we are told how the whole poem was
reduced to writing by the god Ga*n*e*s*a, and that this
episode is absent in many MSS., particularly those
of the South of India. And even after the introduction of writing every precaution was taken to keep
certain sacred texts from being written down, so as to
force each rising generation to learn their literature,
sacred and profane, from the mouth of a teacher,
and not from a manuscript. Even to the present day
this old system of imprinting whole books on the brain
has not been allowed to become entirely obsolete,
and the mnemonic achievements which in several
cases I have witnessed myself in young men when
they come to Oxford are almost unbelievable.

A printed edition of their sacred Rig-Veda was
therefore, even under the changed circumstances
of the nineteenth century, a kind of monstrosity.
Among the first to recognise my edition of the
Rig-Veda was the Râjah Râdhâkânta Deva, and
his recognition was all the more important to me
as he stood at the head of the strictly orthodox
and conservative party in Bengal. He himself
had no doubt that the whole Veda was really
the eternal word of God, and that an unswerving
faith in it was the *sine quâ non* of a religious
and pious life. Even such highly esteemed books
as the Laws of Manu, the Mahâbhârata and the
Purâ*n*as had to give way before it, if there should
ever be any difference between them and the Veda.

We can hardly imagine how people in India could
live in such an atmosphere, but it evidently agreed
both with those who thought for themselves and
with those who thought as they were bid.

My friend, Râdhâkânta, however, made some
reservations. The Rig-Veda, he said, though far
the most important, is only one out of four Vedas
which, though all founded on the Rig-Veda, have
each certain portions peculiar to themselves. This
no one would have denied, but what are the
hymns of all other so-called Vedas put together, if
compared with the Rig-Veda? They are mere
sacrificial prayer-books, most of their hymns being
taken from the Rig-Veda, and the Atharva-Veda
being confessedly a later collection, though it
contains curious remnants of Indian popular poetry,
incantations, medical formulas, and the like. If all
had been lost, except the Rig-Veda, the loss would
not have been very great, at least so far as the
study of ancient mythology and religion was concerned. Of course I had studied the Yagur-Veda,
and had actually copied the whole of it with
Mahîdhara's commentary at Paris. This was published afterwards by Professor Weber from my own
copy which I had presented to him. I could also
tell my Indian friend that we possessed in Germany
an edition of the Sâma-Veda by Benfey, and were
expecting an edition of the Atharva-Veda by
Roth. These were editions of the hymns of the
four Vedas, but I could assure him that even
the Brâhmaṇas, on which he laid great stress as

being the highest authorities for sacrificial rules, for traditions, and ancient customs, were no longer hidden from us, but ready to be published by scholars such as Haug, Weber, Aufrecht, and others. But even then he would still make his reservations. We might know one _Sâkhâ_, or text, he said, of each of their sacred books; but, in conformity with the highest theological authorities, he maintained that there existed formerly many more of such texts which had become extinct; but which nevertheless must be admitted as the original authority for any doctrines or customs not sanctioned by the Vedas, such as we possess them now. The first part of this argument I readily granted, but I had to demur to the second, because anything, even the most degrading customs, might thus have been invested with a divine sanction.

And so it was, as is well known by this time, in the case of Sutti, or the burning of widows, a custom which, though it had long ago been abolished by law, gave rise to a long and animated controversy between the old Râjah, Professor Wilson, and myself.

To show what kind of man the Râjah was, I shall here give some specimens of his letters. It is difficult to do this, because, as I stated before, the style adopted by Hindus in writing letters, whether in Sanskrit or in English, is so flowery and ornate that, particularly when it is addressed to oneself, it seems very conceited and egotistical to publish any of their laudatory remarks. Allowance must be made for Oriental phraseology, and all super-

lative expressions have to be considerably reduced
in English before they reach the level of reality.

In November, 1851, the Râjah, when sending me
his Thesaurus, wrote :—

"When I ventured to assume the character of
a lexicographer, my most ambitious wish was but
to revive the study of Sanskrit in my own country,
where it has been on the decline; but I should
not dissemble that love of fame stimulated my
exertions through worldly tribulations, where
patience must have failed and perseverance wearied.
I devoted the greatest portion of my life and no
inconsiderable amount of labour and expense to
the execution of the work; and though as an
encyclopaedist I have no claim to originality, or
to the merits of genius, yet, I trust, my industry
and application will, at least, be applauded when
I may be considered as a humble pioneer of Sanskrit
learning.   I have endeavoured to obtain the appro-
bation of those whose good opinion one cannot but
be proud of and solicitous to secure ; nor is it an
inconsiderable reward of my labour that it has
deserved the commendation of a Müller and a
Wilson, who have won golden opinions by their
profound scholarship in Sanskrit."

To be named by the side of Wilson was a com-
pliment highly appreciated by a young man of
twenty-eight, as I then was, and I may be pardoned
for having felt flattered at the time more than was
perhaps quite right, by the old Râjah's well-turned
phrases.

Then, turning to my edition of the Rig-Veda, my correspondent continued :—

" I have lately been honoured by the Honourable the Court of Directors with the present of the first volume of your noble and excellent edition of the Rig-Veda, published under their patronage. Some time ago when I received your specimen copy of it, which you had so politely desired Dr. Roer to send me, I read it with eagerness, and, although I was obliged to return it sooner than I could have wished, I saw enough to convince me that you would go far beyond all expectation, and your present publication has confirmed this opinion.

" Arduous and novel as is the undertaking you have entered on amidst a variety of disadvantages, the able and masterly manner in which you have begun to execute it displays your profound erudition, critical acumen, and unparalleled industry of research ; you stand forth a very illustrious example of uncommon ardour and undaunted perseverance, such as is not to be cooled by discouragement, nor obstructed by difficulty ; your labours will furnish the Vaidik Pandits with a complete collection of the Holy Sanhitâs of the first Veda, only detached portions of which are to be found in the possession of a few of them, and enable the student of antiquity 'to snatch the veil that hung her face before,' supply materials for the history of the ancient East—nay, ancient world, and rear up for you a monument more durable than brass."

I confess I feel somewhat ashamed of copying

this panegyric, but no one will suspect me of having believed a word of it. It seemed to me, however, that a letter so well conceived and so well expressed was worthy of being preserved as showing a phase through which the Indian mind had to pass, and which by this time it has left behind. If we consider how different the trend of native thought really is from our own, we shall have to confess that few, if any, European scholars have ever mastered any Oriental language to the same extent as the writer of this letter has mastered English, or have adapted their thoughts so cleverly to English models as this old Râjah.

Let us see now how he arranged the facts of the case, so as to satisfy his own mind :—

" It is surely," he continues, " a very curious reflection on the vicissitudes of human affairs that the descendants of the divine Rishis (prophets) should be studying on the banks of the Bhâgîrathî (Ganges), the Yamunâ (Jumna), and the Sindhu their Holy Scriptures as published on the banks of the Thames by one whom they regard as a distant Mlechchha, and this Mlechchha, the descendant of the degraded Kshattriyas (noblemen), according to our *S*âstras, and claiming a cognate origin with the Hindus, according to the investigations of the modern philologists, who will ere long rise to the rank of a Veda-Vyâsa (arranger and revealer of the Veda) of the Kaliyuga.

" Though our *S*âstra is deemed the grand and primeval fountain from which the present streams of knowledge that run through the civilised countries of the globe have taken their rise, yet it has not been considered as defiled by receiving into it a foreign tributary. As Yavanâchârya (a Greek teacher) gave to the Hindus his system of astronomy many centuries ago, so the German Bhatta (Doctor) is now giving them his edition of the Rig-Veda, and will, as he promises, furnish them with his commentaries upon them."

If we wish to understand and to appreciate the effort made by this highly educated Indian nobleman, to digest what must have been a hard morsel to his orthodox mind, the edition of his own sacred book by a German or an Englishman, let us try to imagine what it would have been to us if the New Testament, never printed before, had been published for the first time, not by a Dutch scholar, such as Erasmus, but by a Hindu at Benares. We know how great was the commotion when, after the invention of printing, Erasmus published the first critical edition of the New Testament. We must not imagine that the feelings of awe and reverence for their Veda were different from our own for the Bible. To have this book, which few only had ever seen before in India, sent to them from London and offered for sale, proved indeed a great shock to the Hindu conscience, nor was it easy for many of their priests to take the same dispassionate view as this enlightened Râjah. He had by no means broken with his religious convictions or national prejudices, and in his eyes, in spite

of all his kindness and politeness, I was and could be
no more than a Mle*kh*a, that is a barbarian.   As
I had never been in India and could never, like so
many other scholars, have availed myself of the valuable assistance of native Pandits, it seemed to him
impossible to account for my knowledge of Sanskrit,
particularly of the obscure and difficult Vedic
Sanskrit, unless he made me a descendant of certain
noble or Kshattriya families who, according to the
Purâ*n*as, had been exiled from India many centuries
ago.   And, as if to quiet his own conscience in
accepting my edition of his sacred book as un-
defiled by the foreign hands through which it had
passed, he reminded himself that after Alexander's
conquests in India certain Greeks or Yavanas had
acted as teachers to the astronomers of India, and
had even been accepted as inspired, so long as they
taught what was true.   All this shows a most
interesting crisis through which the Hindu mind
had passed in former times, and had to pass once
more, a crisis which, though it has not yet finished,
is at all events preparing a religious reformation in
India, by assigning to the Veda its true historical
position, as the best that the Hindu mind could
have produced four thousand years ago, and that
to the present day has retained a certain vitality
among the true leaders of the people of India.

I have always been a bad correspondent, finding
it quite impossible even at that early time to answer
all the letters of my many unknown friends.   India,
from a very early day in my career, has been

smothering me with letters, many of them in Sanskrit or in local dialects which I do not even understand. Now it seems that in this case also I waited
for some time before acknowledging so interesting
a letter as that of the Mahârâjah. However, I find
the draft of a letter to him among my papers, and
I may as well give an extract from it here :—

"The letter which you addressed to me in 1851
on receiving the first volume of my edition of the
Rig-Veda reached me so late that I had nearly
finished the second volume of my Rig-Veda, and
I therefore postponed writing to you, because
I wished at the same time to send this my second
volume, if only to show you that I meant what
I said, and was determined to carry out my undertaking—namely, to publish in time the whole collection of the sacred hymns of your Rishis, together
with the commentary composed in the fourteenth
century by the learned Sâya*nâkâ*rya. I have stated
in my Preface how much I owe to your valuable
Thesaurus, a work which will make your name
not only revered by your own countrymen, but
respected among all the scholars of Europe. Tathâ
*k*a *s*ruti*h*, Yâvad asmi*n* loke purusha*h* pu*n*yena
karma*nâ s*rûyate, tâvad ayam svarge loke vasatlti.
And thus says your Scripture : 'So long as a
man is known in this world by a good work, so
long does he dwell in heaven.' . . . How happy
I should be if I could spend some time at Calcutta
or Benares, and discuss with you and your learned
Pandits your ancient religion, your sacred writings,

your traditions, and the future of religion in India.
It was not mere idle curiosity that led me to a
study of the Veda, but a wish to know a work
which has been for so many centuries the foundation on which millions and millions of human beings
have built up their religious convictions. However
much we may differ from the old forms of faith and
worship, it is our duty, it seems to me, to approach
every religion with respect, nay, with reverence.
The vital principle, the original source of religion,
is the same everywhere; it is faith in a Higher
Power, and a belief that our moral life should be
such as to please Him to whom we owe our being
and to whom we feel bound to ascribe the highest
perfection which our limited human faculties can
conceive. Nor have I been disappointed by the
Rig-Veda, though it is different from what I and
others expected. There are large portions in it
which have hardly any connection with religion at
all, but they are interesting all the same as relics
of antiquity, such as the song of the gambler, the
dialogue between Lopamudrâ and Agastya, between
Yama and Yamî, between Purûravas and Urvaśî.
Other prayers for health and wealth are appropriate
in their simplicity to a very primitive state of
society. But there are passages which show a
truly religious spirit, such as 'Eka*m* sad viprâ ba-
hudhâ vadanti'—'The sages speak in many ways
of the One that exists'; 'Yo deveshu adhi deva
eka âsît'—'He who alone is God above gods.'
Simple moral sentiments also occur in it which

deserve to be treasured; such is 'Vi ma*k* *kh*rathâya rasanâm ivâga*h* '—'Loose from me sin like a rope'; 'Dâmeva vatsâd vi mumugdhy a*m*ho, na hi tvadâre nimisha*s* *ka* ne*s*e'—'Loose from me sin like a rope from a calf, for away from Thee I am not master of a twinkling of the eye.' Though their number is small in the Sanhitâ, yet there is so much more simplicity and purity in most of these old hymns that I cannot understand how they could ever have been superseded by the Purâ*n*as, works which from a moral, religious, and intellectual point of view do not seem to me worthy to rank as the Bibles of a nation so highly gifted as the inhabitants of Âryâvarta.

"If my edition of the Rig-Veda could help towards bringing the people of India back to the study of what their ancient writers unanimously considered as the highest authority of their religion, it would, I think, be an important step forward, not backward, though I hope that the future has even greater things in store for them than a mere return to their ancient form of belief and worship. We must not forget that, like everything else, religions also grow old and can seldom defy four thousand years. The antiquity of a religion which is often appealed to as a proof of its truth, seems to me to tell in the very opposite direction. The older it is, the more likely it is to have become effete in human hands, and unfit for new times, and to require either reformation or entire abolition, to make room for a new and better form of faith.

"I know you are bound to consider me as a
Mle*kkh*a, but allow me to say that I do not enter-
tain the same exclusive feelings towards you and
your countrymen. And remember that one of your
Vedic Rishis says that all the castes, the Sûdra as
well as the Brâhma*n*a, came from Brahman, and
participate, therefore, in the same nature and substance, the Divine in man. We believe that all
men are equal before God, and with that feeling
and in that spirit I remain, with great respect,

Yours sincerely,

F. MAX MÜLLER."

I shall, with the same caution as before, add one
more letter, though I know I shall be very much
blamed for doing so. The Râjah in expressing his
own sentiments, expressed no doubt the sentiments
of the society in which he moved, and the crisis
through which the conservative and orthodox party
passed at that time, unimportant as it may seem
to us, was full of vital problems for the future of
the religion of the cultivated classes of India. On
March 5, 1855, Râdhâkânta Deva wrote :—

"I have lately received through the Bengal Government a copy of the second volume of the Rig-Veda,
as a present from the Honourable the Court of
Directors, and I can ill express the feelings of
mingled joy and admiration with which I grasped
this most precious gift. Our Pandits are startled
out of their wits, and scarcely credit their senses,
when they are told that the sacred volume before
them has been edited by a distant European scholar

who had no opportunities of consulting with a
Vaidik Pandit, who had to collect, copy out, and
collate various manuscripts of texts and commentaries, mutilated and corrupted, and to refer to the
scanty and almost inaccessible sources of information on the subject for the purpose of ascertaining
their genuine reading, and then with aching eyes
to revise the proof-sheets.

"Great is the obligation under which you have laid
the learned world. By your successfully embarking
on such an arduous undertaking, you have done to
the Hindus an inestimable benefit, supplying them
with a correct and superb edition of their Holy
Scriptures. Accept therefore my most grateful and
sincere thanks, which, in common with my countrymen, I owe you, and my special acknowledgments
for the very kind and obliging manner in which
you have noticed my name and work in the preface
to the second volume of the Rig-Veda. At the
conclusion of this preface is to be found a truly
poetic touch, a noble, frank, and irresistible gush
of feeling for the irreparable loss sustained by the
literary world and you personally, on the termina-
tion of the earthly career of Eugène Burnouf.
I wish I could find terms adequate to respond to
your sympathy; we cannot be too lavish of eulogies
for his merits, or weary of dirges for his loss. In
the few letters he has written to me I find a noble
trait of humility and simplicity in his character
which is the invariable exponent of a great mind.

"In 1833 on the occasion of acknowledging the

present of the *S*abda-kalpa-druma he says : 'Ce n'est pas à un Européen qui est à peine sur le seuil de cette vaste science de l'Inde, qu'il appartient de juger une composition de ce mérite et d'une telle étendue. Des hommes comme les Colebrooke et les Wilson, qui ont puisé la grande partie de leurs connaissances à la source des entretiens brahmaniques, sont les juges les plus dignes d'un aussi beau travail.'

" In 1840, when he had the kindness to send me a copy of his fine edition of the Bhâgavata Purâ*n*a, he—the first decipherer of the Cuneiform inscriptions—the first Pali scholar and historian of Buddhism—the first editor and interpreter of the Zend-Avesta—and the great Sanskrit philologist—thus speaks of himself : ' Mais, vous songerez que c'est l'œuvre d'un lointain Mletchha qui ne fait que commencer à balbutier la langue des grands et vénérables Rishis . . .'

" Wishing you a long life to crown all your undertakings with success, and requesting you to offer my best regards to my learned friend Professor Wilson, I remain with great respect,

Yours sincerely,

RÂDHÂKÂNT, RÂJA BAHADOOR."

I repeat once more that I must decline all the undeserved compliments paid to me by my Indian correspondents, who, though they show so perfect a mastery of English, are hardly aware that in the North our language is less warm and less sunny than in the South, and that we leave many things

unsaid which must bring a blush to the cheeks of
any one who knows himself, and knows how very
imperfect his knowledge really is, and how far below
his ideals the execution of the work of his life has
remained. If Burnouf said that he was only
beginning to stammer Sanskrit, what shall I, his
unworthy pupil, say? But the letters themselves
are important as showing the attitude assumed by
the conservative orthodox party in India, when the
first edition of their Sacred Book fell among them
like a bombshell. For years, for centuries, nay for
thousands of years, this Veda on which their whole
religion was founded had been to them a kind of
invisible power, much as the Bible was in the early
centuries of the Papacy, when the privileged only were
supposed to know it and were allowed to interpret
it. In discussions between Brâhmans and Christian
missionaries, this Veda had always been the last
stronghold of the Brâhmans. Whatever was held
up to them as a doctrine peculiar to Christianity,
was met by them with the ready reply that it had
been taught long ago in the Vedas also. But this
Veda itself was never produced when they were
asked to point out chapter and verse. Long after
the MSS. of other Sanskrit texts had been freely
communicated to English students, the MSS. of the
Veda were kept apart, and the touch, nay the very
look of an unbeliever was supposed to desecrate
them. And now the book was there, handled by
everybody, and spelt out more or less successfully
by anybody acquainted with Sanskrit. The Brâh-

mans always accept the inevitable, but we shall see
how, with a better knowledge of the Veda, there
sprang up discussions as to its divine or revealed
character, and how these discussions led gradually
to the formation of a new religious sect, which,
though at present confined to small circles, will no
doubt in the end stir the millions, and produce a
reformation in a country which seemed to be unchangeable. Of this I shall have to speak later on,
when I gather up my reminiscences of Keshub
Chunder Sen and his fellow-workers. Movements
in which we are interested and engaged ourselves
from their beginnings seem generally much smaller
to us than they really are in the light of history.
When Luther was translating the Bible in the castle
of the Wartburg, he little dreamt that he was laying
the foundation of a new Church in Germany and
in all Teutonic countries, nor did Rammohun Roy
on his death-bed at Bristol foresee what would grow
up from the few hints he had thrown out as to
the possibility of a reform and a revival of the
ancient national religion of his country. But Debendranâth followed, Keshub Chunder Sen followed,
and if the fire they lit does not at present burn
and shine so brightly as it ought, it will certainly
not die, but burst out again; for the way which
those heroes pointed out is the only possible way
leading from the past to the future, from ancient
to modern religion, from darkness to light. Many
who have lived in India and who imagine that they
know India, because they know Calcutta or Bombay,

are inclined to shrug their shoulders and to look down with superior wisdom and pity on those misguided dreamers, as they call them, who imagine that they can guide millions to a higher and more truly religious life. We may not live to see the hopes of Rammohun Roy or Keshub Chunder Sen realised; but, as certainly as the sun rises in the morning, the new light for India will break forth from that East to which those prophets and martyrs pointed in the last moments of their life.

The Râjah Râdhâkânta Deva was a conservative of the purest water, not touched as yet even by that conservative liberalism which guided Debendranâth Tagore and made him sympathise with, though it kept him for a time aloof from, his bolder pupil and friend, Keshub Chunder Sen. He himself seems to have never doubted the divine authority of the Veda, and in a curious controversy which I had with him on the Burning of Widows he held his ground firmly as a defender of the old ways. As we became better acquainted with the Veda, it became perfectly clear that the verse from the Rig-Veda which was cited by the Brâhmans as the supreme command for the burning of widows, had been tampered with. The Brâhmans themselves seem to have felt that so barbarous and murderous a custom as the burning of widows, whatever its origin may have been, could only be defended by an authority that was admitted to be infallible and superhuman. Such was the Rig-Veda, and they did not shrink from altering

a verse which occurred in a funeral hymn of that
Veda, so that instead of conveying a command
to the widows to return to their home after
having performed the last duty to their departed
husbands, it came to mean that they should enter
into the womb of fire to follow their husbands
to a better world. How such a falsification could
have been committed is difficult to understand,
when we consider that at first the falsification had
to be made in the thousands of memories which
represented the real copies of the Rig-Veda. It
must have taken place at a very early time,
because cases of Sutti do occur, if not in the
Rig-Veda, at least in the ancient popular tradition
of India, as represented to us in the Mahâbhârata.
Even Râdhâkânta Deva seemed inclined at last
to agree with me that in the Veda, as we possess
it, there is no direct command for this terrible
custom; but he took his stand on the old tradition
and maintained that we did not possess the whole
of the ancient Vedic literature, and that the
authority for the old custom may have existed
in one of the lost Sâkhâs or branches of the
Veda. This was a favourite argument with Indian
casuists, but Indian casuists had likewise found an
answer to it. They called it the "skull argument,"
and reasoned that as little as a skull could be
accepted as a witness in a court of law, could
a lost Sâkhâ of the Veda be appealed to as an
authority for a custom like the burning of widows.
All this gives us an insight into the thoughts

that rule Indian society, of which even those who
spend their best years in India have hardly any
suspicion. That an educated Hindu should defend
the burning of widows seems strange ; still, if Popes
and Cardinals could defend auto-da-fé's or the
burning of heretics, nay, even of witches, because
the fire would purify and save their souls which
could not be saved otherwise, why should not
an Indian Râjah have been convinced that the
burning of widows could not be wrong, believing,
as he did, that it was enjoined by a lost Sâkhâ
of the Veda, and that the poor women could not
be saved unless they followed their husbands on
their heels into another world? These are ingrained feelings, and every Hindu would at once
recite the popular verses, "Accompanying her
husband, she shall reside so long in Svarga
(Heaven) as are the thirty-five millions of hairs
on the human body."

A loyal wife is defined as "she whose sympathy
feels the pains and joys of her husband, who mourns
and pines in his absence, and dies when he dies."

In theory this is all very beautiful, and that
there may have been cases where a widow wished
to be burnt on her husband's pile, can hardly be
doubted [1]. It is well known that this custom of
widow-burning, or of widows dying with their
husbands, was by no means confined to India ;
but it is known also, now that the pages of the
Veda are open to us, that the Veda certainly

[1] Chips from a German Workshop, Vol. IV, pp. 35-9.

does not countenance it. The custom seems to have arisen with the warrior caste, and I still feel inclined to think that in its origin it was voluntary, and arose from blind, passionate love, and a strong belief in an immediate meeting again in a better world. The idea that its object was to deter wives from poisoning their husbands is simply preposterous, and though it may be quite true that at present the life of a widow has been rendered so miserable that many would willingly prefer death to so wretched an existence as that of a widow, that too could not account for so ancient and so widely spread a custom. In our own ancient Teutonic mythology, when Baldur had been murdered and his body had been placed in a ship to be carried out to sea, his wife, Nanna, died of grief, and was burnt with him on the same pile[1]. And Gudrun (Brynhild) also, after Sigurd had been slain, had but one wish, to be burnt with him on the same pile, two servants at their head and two at their feet, two dogs also and two hawks, and the biting sword between them, the same sword that lay between them when they slept together on the same bed, like brother and sister[2]. There is humanity in all this inhuman barbarism, if only we try to discover it. The strange part is that this human feeling should have manifested itself in the women only, and never in the men.

[1] Edda, Gylfaginning, 49.
[2] Sigurdakwida, III, 64; Helreidh Brynhildar, 12.

MY INDIAN FRIENDS.

II.

Nîlaka*nth*a Goreh.

IF I knew the Râjah Râdhâkânta Deva by correspondence only, the next son of India whom I came to know, and for a time very intimately, as one knows and loves a friend, had travelled all the way from India, having come to England with Dhulip Singh. While I was sitting in my room at Oxford copying Sanskrit MSS., a gentleman was shown in, dressed in a long black coat, looking different from my usual visitors, and addressing me in a language of which I did not understand a single word. I spoke to him in English, and asked him what language he was speaking, and he replied with great surprise, " Do you not understand Sanskrit ? " " No," I said, " I have never heard it spoken, but here are some MSS. of the Veda which will interest you." He was delighted to see them, and began to read, but he had soon to confess that he was not able to translate a single word. When I expressed my surprise—though perhaps I ought not to have done so—he told me that he did not believe in the Veda any longer, but had become a Christian.

His countenance was most intelligent, and almost
heavy with thought, his language and his manners
most winning, and we were soon deep in conversation.   His name had been Nîlaka*ntha* Goreh—
Nîlaka*ntha* being a name of *S*iva (the Blue-neck)—
but had been changed into Nehemiah Goreh, when
he became a Christian.   I have tried to find out
more about his birthplace and his parents, but in
vain ; and, after all, who cares for all these monotonous details with which biographers generally
fill the first chapters of their books ?   Nor did
I care much for them myself, except to know that
he came from a highly respected Brâhman family,
and that his father had been an educated man and
a Sanskrit scholar.   What I really cared for was
the man himself, such as he stood before me, a
man, I should have guessed, of about five-and-
twenty, glowing with youthful enthusiasm, and
evidently brimful of thought.   I must leave it to
others to supply the year of his birth and all the
details of his paternal and maternal genealogy.

   It was not long before I discovered a sad and
perplexed tone in his conversation, and, though
he assured me that nothing but a deep conviction
of the truth of Christ's teaching had induced him
to change his religion, he told me that he was in
great anxiety and did not know what to do for
the future.   What he had seen of England, more
particularly of London, was not what he had
imagined a Christian country to be.   His patron,
Dhulip Singh, had placed him at some kind of

missionary seminary in London, where he found
himself together with a number of what he considered half-educated and narrow-minded young
men, candidates for ordination and missionary work.
They showed him no sympathy and love, but found
fault with everything he did and said. He had
been, as I soon found out, a careful student of
Hindu philosophy, and his mind had passed through
a strict philosophical discipline. Hindu philosophy
is in many respects as good a discipline as Plato
or Aristotle, and, Christian though he was, he was
familiar with the boldest conceptions of the world,
as found in the six systems of Hindu philosophy,
and he could argue with great subtlety and accuracy
on any of the old problems of the human mind.
The fact was he stood too high for his companions,
and they were evidently unable to understand and
appreciate his thoughts. He did not use words
at random, and was always ready to give a defini-
tion of them, whenever they seemed ambiguous.
And yet this man was treated as a kind of nigger
by those who ought to have been not only kind,
but respectful to him. He was told that smoking
was a sin, and that he never could be a true
Christian if he abstained from eating meat, particularly beef. He told me that with the greatest
effort he had once brought himself to swallow a
sandwich containing a slice of meat, but it was
to him what eating human flesh would be to us.
He could not do it again. When he thus found
himself in this thoroughly uncongenial society, and

II.   E

saw nothing in London of what he had supposed
a Christian city to be, he ran away, and came to
Oxford to find me, having heard of my interest in
India, in its religion, and its ancient literature.
He had evidently dreamt of a Christian country
where everybody loved his neighbour as himself;
where everybody, if struck on the right cheek,
would turn the other also; where everybody, when
robbed of his coat, would give up his cloak also.
All this, as we know, is not the fashion in the
streets of London, and what he actually saw in
those streets was so different from his ideals that
he said to me, "If what I have seen in London
is Christianity, I want to go back to India; if
that is Christianity, I am not a Christian." This
sounded very ominous, and I hardly knew what
to say or what to do with him. He was not a
man to be smoothed down by a few kind words.
I tried to find out first why he had given up his
native religion, and the more I heard, the more
I was amazed. He began life as a worshipper of
Siva, had then chosen Krishna as his deity, and,
dissatisfied with this form of worship also, had
proceeded to study the Korân. All that time he
had kept carefully aloof from Christian missionaries
and Christian converts. But when he saw that
the Korân also was full of contradictions and of
things which he could not approve, he began to
study by himself both the Old and the New Testaments. Saturated as he was with philosophical ideas,
he soon found that these books also did not satisfy

his yearnings, and he wrote, as I was told, two
essays in Sanskrit, one against the Old, the other
against the New Testament, both directed against
a book written by my old friend, J. Muir, the
Mataparîkshâ (Examination of Doctrines). Those
who knew him at the time in India say that his
answer to the Scotch scholar was in flowing and
melodious Sanskrit, and was "alike most classical in
diction and irrefragable in reasoning." Christianity
in India, even as represented by so enlightened
a Christian as J. Muir, was supposed to have received its death-blow by it. But the fact was, that
in studying the New Testament and trying to refute
it, he had become a Christian unawares.

When I asked him to tell me how in the end he
succumbed, and was satisfied with the religion of
Christ, he shook his head and said, "I can explain
everything, I can explain why I rejected Siva, and
Krishna, and Allah, and tell you everything that
kept me back so long from Christianity, as preached
to us in India, and made me reject the New as
well as the Old Testament as unsatisfactory to
a thinking man. But why and how I became a
Christian I cannot explain. I was caught as in a
net, and I could not get away from Christ." This
did not quite satisfy me, and I pressed him hard
several times to find out whether there had not
been any other inducement, perhaps unknown to
himself at the time, that might have influenced him
in taking this momentous step. But it was all in
vain. So far from there being any worldly motives

mixed up with his conversion, all outward circumstances, on the contrary, were strongly against his
professing himself a Christian. He could not tell
me of any missionary or teacher whose personal
influence might directly or indirectly have told on
him.

No one was more surprised than the clergyman,
to whom he wrote that he was a Christian, that
he required no instruction or persuasion, but simply
wished to be baptized. His mind was like a crystal,
perfectly bright and transparent. He held nothing
back from me, but the answer which I most cared
for, he could not give. · His father, a learned man,
holding a high place among the Brâhmans socially,
a kind of bishop or dean, as we should call it, owed
it to his position, not only to disown, but to dis-
inherit, nay, publicly to curse, his son. The loss
of his fortune was nothing to the son; but when
it came to the curse, the father himself shrank
back. He loved his son, and it is hinted that to
a certain extent he may have shared his feelings.
So, in order to evade the necessity of the curse,
he retired from the world and took upon himself
the vow of perpetual silence (Mauna-vrata). We
wonder at the Trappists and their silence, but they
at all events live in company with other Trappists.
But to be silent among friends who speak must
be a greater trial still. These men generally retire
from the world altogether. Nehemiah Goreh's
father, after he had retired into the forest, never
uttered a single word again to any human being.

He disappeared altogether, and, though for several
years his son and his friends hoped that he would
return, he never came back.   He probably went
out of his mind, and died, as many Sannyâsins die
in the forests of India.   There are more tragedies
in heaven and earth than are dreamt of in our
philosophy.   Nor was that all.   Even his wife was
taken away from the new convert, though she really
was devoted to her husband.   Timid as Hindu
ladies are, his young wife had been frightened when
asked before a judge whether she would remain
with her apostate husband or return to her parents.
This is what the law enjoins in case of a husband
becoming a Christian.   But after she had taken
refuge in her parental home she repented, and
wished to join her husband again.   And here a
curious scene occurred.   The husband actually had
to elope with his own wife, and carry her off by
main force.   After that the law allows a new appeal;
the guilty couple were brought once more before
a judge, and when the young wife (she was only
thirteen) was asked what she wished to do, she
declared publicly that she would remain with her
husband, and was then allowed to return to him and
to her home.   What more could a man sacrifice
for his religious convictions?   All I can say is that
in the whole of my life I have never seen so true
a Christian, so true a martyr, as Nehemiah Goreh.
Few Christians, not even bishops, would have
passed through such ordeals unscathed.   And with
all that, he was a philosopher, he knew what

philosophy could say and had said on the possibility of revelation and of religion, and yet he was
perfectly satisfied with Christianity in its very
simplest form. One thing he said sometimes, to
account to me for the momentous step he had
taken, and for the sacrifices he had made to retain
his inward honesty. "Christianity is so pure," he
said. One can quite understand how this purity
must have told on a mind that had waded through
the impurities of the sombre worship of Siva, and
the lascivious innuendos of the legends of Krishna
and the shepherdesses, however much they may be
explained as a mere allegory. Even as an allegory,
the story of a god who carries off the clothes of
the shepherdesses while bathing, is not edifying.
If it is meant for devotion without guise or disguise, the meaning is too much hidden for ordinary
mortals. We may be able to account historically
or mythologically for many excrescences of religion,
but we cannot dispute them away, nor can we
wonder that a pure mind, sickened by them, should
turn with a delightful relief to the pure and fresh
atmosphere of Christianity.

There was for a time real danger of Nehemiah's
falling into utter despair, and all that his friends
could do was to send him back, as soon as possible,
to India, and to find him some occupation there as
a teacher and Scripture reader. There, what seems
almost an innate tendency of the Indian mind soon
developed itself in Nehemiah, namely, asceticism
and a complete renunciation of the world. For

a time he was attracted by outward ceremonial and symbolism, and found comfort in it; but when that also failed to satisfy him, he became, to all intents and purposes, a Christian Sannyâsin (hermit). For himself he wanted nothing, even controversy had no longer any charm for him; though, in the essays which he was induced to address to his countrymen on the insufficiency of the six systems of native philosophy, he proved himself a subtle critic of Hinduism, and a powerful defender of Christianity. These essays, originally written in Hindi, have been translated into English by Dr. Fitz-Edward Hall, under the title of "Rational Refutation of the Hindu Philosophical Systems," Calcutta, 1862, and they are extremely interesting and useful.

Judging from letters which I received from him from time to time, he never quite recovered the balance of his mind. His trials had been too much for him. Not only had he lost his father and his wife, but he became separated even from his children, so that no cares of this world should disturb his peace with God and in God. But to give up a religion—the religion of our father and mother, the religion of our childhood and of all our friends, however imperfect it may be from our own point of view, inflicts a wound that heals but slowly, and is apt to break open again and again. Why should missionaries fail to see this, and expect from their heathen pupils sacrifices which they themselves would shrink from by a natural instinct of self-preservation? It is no answer to say that the

religion of those whom they wish to bring over to
Christianity is antiquated, vulgar, hideous, and false.
The religion in which a man is born, the religion of
a man's father and mother, has always something
sacred in it that ought to be respected. Is there
a single missionary who, if he had been born a
Hindu or a Parsi, would have embraced Christianity
without a struggle? When we consider how unimportant the differences are between the religion
of reformed and unreformed Christians if compared
with the treasures that both share in common, why
should it be such a wrench for a Roman Catholic
to become a Protestant, except that his father and
mother were Roman Catholics? The points of
difference between them are all, without exception,
the work of men, and often of men who have no
very high record in the pages of history. Yet to
give up the mass for the eucharist, the wafer for
the bread, the mixed for the pure wine, has often
been too much even for a truly Christian heart, and
has separated those who were meant to be brothers
in Christ. I say all this only in order to make
people understand what trials and tortures Nehemiah Goreh had to undergo before he could take
that step which, from a missionary point of view,
seems so easy and natural. To be torn away from
all our friends, to think that they are all wrong and
we alone are right, was too great an effort to a
sensitive mind, such as his was, and left a wound
behind which it required a very strong and healthy
nature to bear and many years to heal. That he

should have become a kind of Christian Sannyâsin, or anchorite, was natural; that he should have been attracted for a time by childish ritualism was a pity. This, however, was chiefly due to personal influences, and, if it in any way soothed his broken spirits, no one would grudge him such anodynes. I was much touched when, in one of his later letters, after expressing his perfect satisfaction with what Christianity had given him, he added, " Yet, I often feel like a man who has taken poison." He was for many years a useful member of a Christian brotherhood at Sigra, founded by the Rev. R. M. Benson, whom I remember meeting often in old days in the cheerful common-room of Christ Church. They were very kind to him, and he was most grateful to his brothers. Yet I feel doubtful whether even they understood him fully, and made allowance for all his troubles and all his sacrifices.

When Nehemiah Goreh was in England for the last time, and staying at Oxford, he was not allowed to come to see me, except on the very day of his departure. This was unkind to both of us; he was in no more danger from me than I was from him. I know that in his early days he had used the wings of his mind with great freedom, that he had tried to soar to the highest abodes of the Divine, and to fathom the deepest abysses of human nature, fearless of all consequences. He reminded me in that respect of Dr. Pusey, who often declared that he had studied more heresy than anybody else; but, having seen the horrors of utter darkness on

every side, he felt it his duty to warn others, and
to keep them from seeing what he had seen.
Strange only that Nehemiah, brought up as he
had been in the doctrines of the Vedânta, should
not have seen how even the highest heights and
the deepest depths which can be reached by the
human mind are lighted up by the omnipresence
of Brahman, the Indian name and concept of what
we mean by the omnipresent Father, or, if you
like, of that ineffable Godhead of which even the
Father is one person only. He had become tired
of his lifelong search, and had long closed his eyes
to this world of seeming. When at last his heart
ceased to beat, he felt satisfied that all was well, and
that he was safe in trusting in Christ.

It is curious that he should not have drawn more
of his countrymen to follow him. His original
conception of Christ's teaching was such that many
an excellent Hindu could honestly have accepted
it. If anywhere, the harvest is ripe in India, and
the labourers are many. Unfortunately his philosophical Christianity became more and more ecclesiastical, nay ritualistic in time, through influences
which he was too weak to resist. He might have
done a great work in India; but what India wants
is the young and vigorous Christianity of the first
century, not the effete Christianity of the fifteenth
century, still less its poor modern imitations. Much
the same opinion was expressed by an Indian correspondent, Mr. Brojolall Chuckerbutty, a personal
friend and admirer of Nehemiah Goreh. In one of

his letters to me he said: "Years ago I had
a long discussion in my own house with Nehemiah
Nîlakantha Goreh concerning the Christian religion.
He, of course, tried hard to convert me to his
faith. But we arrived at a conclusion in which
nothing was concluded. I really could not understand how a man of Mr. Goreh's intelligence and
learning, who had discarded Hinduism, could accept,
in its stead, popular Christianity which stands on
the same level with popular Hinduism. By popular
Christianity I mean the Christianity of the Church,
as contra-distinguished from the Christianity of
Christ."

His friends have sometimes found fault with
Nehemiah Goreh for having during the latter part
of his life so completely withdrawn himself from
the world and its social obligations. But here too
we must learn to make allowances for the old
Indian leaven. He longed for rest. It was a
recognised thing in India—I speak, of course, of
ancient India—that a man who had fought his
fight might retire from the world, shake off all
shackles, and become free, even here on earth.
Many left their homes and lived in forests—a most
delightful way of life in India. These anchorites,
fugitives from the world, wanted very little to
support life, and that little, so far as we know,
was either supplied by nature or given them readily
by the members of their family, or even by
strangers. There was no lack of family affection
in India, but higher than all worldly affections stood

the ideal of Vairâgya, freedom from all desires and
passions, freedom from all worldly attachments,
freedom from all that must perish, real happiness
in the Eternal, in the Self, that is, in God who
changes not. Some of the most beautiful poetry
of ancient and modern India was inspired by that
sentiment of unworldliness, the very opposite of
that passionate love and attachment which forms
the constant theme of European poetry. Love, so
far as it means passion and desire, or exclusive
attachment to one person, was considered as of
this world, and everything belonging to this world
was perishable, and therefore not worthy of our
highest affection. The Buddhists adopted the same
doctrine, but, while condemning love, they preached
pity—a splendid substitute. Father and mother,
wife, husband, and children were not excepted.
They, too, should never be passionately loved or
idolised, but they should always be pitied. That
pity means a great deal, it may mean all that is
best in love. The very relation in which husband
and wife, father and mother, parents and children
stood to each other could be of this life only, not
of that life in which they neither marry nor are
given in marriage, the life that underlies even this
life on earth. We find it difficult to enter into
these ideas, they are so entirely absent from our
own literature, particularly from our poetry; which
deals mostly with passionate love, but they were
quite familiar to the Hindus. We call them strange
and curious and extravagant, and then we have

done with them. But the subject is not so easily disposed of, and in a country such as India, it is difficult to say who has chosen the good part. There the man at rest with himself and with his God, the man free from all worldly fetters, was a recognised character, and was allowed to live up to his ideals without let or hindrance. How those ideals were realised we may learn from Indian poetry, from the Vairâgya-Sataka, for instance (the century of dispassionateness) ascribed to Bhartri-hari, and from many similar works. There we read [1] :—

" A hermit's forest cell, and fellowship with deer,
    A harmless meal of fruit, stone beds beside the
        stream,
    Are helps to those who long for Siva's guidance
        here,
    But be the mind devout, our homes will forests
        seem [2]."

A more literal translation would be :—

" Dwelling in a hallowed forest, nay fellowship with deer, pure diet of fruit, and stones for beds from day to day, such are the requirements of those who desire to worship Hara ; but for those whose minds are entirely fixed and pacified, forest or house is alike." (No. 33, ed. Gopinâth.)

[1] Metrical translation by C. H. Tawney, *Indian Antiquary*, November, 1876.
[2] That is, if only our mind is quieted, we shall enjoy peace in our own home as well as in a forest. Siva is here looked upon as the symbol of the Supreme Spirit.

I give a few more verses in prose translations, as more faithful, though less perfect than poetry :—

"The earth has been dug by me in hope of treasure, the ore of the mountains has been melted, the ocean has been crossed, and princes have been zealously served, nights have been passed among the graves with a mind bent on propitiating by charms; yet have I not obtained a doit. O Desire, leave me now!" (No. 4, ed. Gopinâth.)

"Even if they have longer remained with us, the objects of sense are sure to vanish. What difference is there in the separation, that man should not forsake them himself? If they pass away by themselves, they cause the greatest pain to the mind, but if we forsake them ourselves, they cause endless happiness and peace." (No. 16, ed. Gopinâth.)

"When pride is failing, when our wealth has departed, when the beggar has gone away disappointed, when our kinsmen have vanished and our friends have disappeared, and youth is slowly waning, one thing only befits the wise man—to dwell somewhere in the arbour of a cave in the valley of a high mountain where the rocks are sanctified by the milk (waters) of the daughter of Gahnu (Gamgâ)." (No. 31.)

"In health there is fear of disease, in family-pride fear of a fall, in wealth fear of the king, in silence fear of disregard, in strength fear of an enemy, in beauty fear of old age, in knowledge

fear of blame, in virtue fear of calumny, in life
fear of death; everything on earth is surrounded
by fear; freedom from desires alone gives us
freedom from fear." (No. 116.)

"Where before there were many in the house,
there is left only one; where there was one,
there are now many, and in the end there is
not left even one; thus does Kâla (time), shaking
the day and the night like two dice, play cleverly,
together with Kâlî (death), with mortals as with
figures on a board." (No. 38.)

"Delights are unsteady like lightning, flashing
from the midst of a veil of clouds, life is fleeting
like a shower from a mass of clouds that have
been torn asunder by the wind; the caresses of
youth enjoyed by man are fickle. O ye wise,
when you have pondered this, set your heart
quickly on Yoga that can be gained by perfection
of meditation and firmness." (No. 53.)

"You are I, and I am you, such was formerly
our mind; what has happened now that you are
you and I am I?" (No. 63.)

"What good is there in the Vedas, the Smritis,
the reciting of the Purânas, and all the tedious
Sâstras, or in the trouble of performing sacrifices
which are to reward us with an abode in the
arbours of the gardens of Svarga? If we except
only the compassing of an entrance into that
place where there is bliss in oneself and which
is like the fire at the end of the world which
destroys all that produces pains by means of the

fetters of existence, everything else is a mere
matter of bargain." (No. 79.)

"O mother Earth, father Wind, friend Light,
kinsman Water, brother Sky, I fold my hands in
adoration to you. I, with whom the burden of all
ignorance has been cast off by means of bright
and spotless knowledge; I, shining with increase
of good works produced through contact with
you, I now melt away in the Highest Spirit
(Brahman)." (No. 85.)

Ideas like these, very beautiful when clothed
in the beautiful language of ancient India, seemed
never to be absent from the mind of my friend,
though modified by the Christian atmosphere in
which he had learnt to breathe. He too would
have been happiest in the forest, on the banks
of the Ganges—a stone for his couch, the deer
for his friends, wild fruits for his food, lost in
his God, who was more to him than a mere
Jehovah, more also than the Brahman of the
multitude. He might have called him Brahman,
hidden under the features, or under the Pratîka
(*persona*) of a father. He himself, however, had
soared higher and discovered the true Brahman
in himself, and with all these exalted ideas he
had found rest and happiness in the humble
faith of a Christian. With him Christianity
would have been perfectly compatible with Indian
philosophy, particularly the Vedânta, if only properly understood. Men such as Dr. Henry More
were Christian Platonists at Cambridge; why then

should there be no Christian Vedântists, such as Nehemiah Goreh was in the beginning of his career? Later in life the bold eagle became tired, his pinions faltered, and he yearned for his nest. He is at rest now from all his doubts and earthly troubles. His name is known to few only, and will soon be forgotten altogether, like the names of many who were martyrs to their convictions on earth. He had the true courage of his convictions, and in my memory he will always retain his place very near to Stanley, Colenso, and a few others who shall remain unnamed. If he changed later in life, I feel sure that he changed honestly, and that he was as true in his ecstatic adorations (Upâsanâ) as he had been in his philosophy (Gñâna).

Keshub Chunder Sen.

While through Râdhâkânta I came in contact with the rigid conservative elements of Indian society, and in Nehemiah Goreh was able to witness the first real conquest achieved by Christianity and its concomitant powers over the Indian mind in its highest excellence—for I doubt whether, if left to itself, the Indian mind could reach a higher degree of intellectual vigour than it did in Nehemiah Goreh—a new phase of Indian life was opened to me through my long friendship with Keshub Chunder Sen. That contact with Christianity would sooner or later produce a fermentation in the religion of India might easily have been foreseen. It was the same when Mohammedanism reached India. Both Mohammedanism and Christianity were modern religions compared with Brâhmanism, they belonged to a more advanced state of thought and culture, and were free from many of the childish ideas almost inseparable from an earlier stage of religion in the history of mankind. But, strange to say, the very antiquity of the Vedic religion was looked upon as an argument in its favour, and it certainly made its surrender more difficult to its followers. Nânak, Kabir, Chaitanya, and other reformers, near contemporaries of our own reformers, tried to effect a compromise between the two religions by eliminating the glaring imperfections of the ancient national faith of India, such as idol-worship, animal sacrifices, &c., but retaining its sublime moral and philosophical spirit, which, in some respects, was purer and higher than even the doctrines of the Korân. It may be useful to glance at some of these reformers, if only to show that Keshub Chunder Sen was not without his predecessors.

Chaitanya.

The most important among these reformers about the beginning of the sixteenth century was Chaitanya (1485–1527). At all events he had the largest following, and has so even to the present day. He did not perhaps go quite so far as Keshub Chunder Sen, but in many cases this modern reformer seems certainly to have been influenced by the spirit of Chaitanya, nay, in some cases, to have used almost the same words. The followers of Chaitanya, whether they are called Gosains, Bhâgavatas, Vairâgis, or other names, are said to form even now one-fifth of the whole population of Bengal. Whether for rules of life or for doctrine they still appeal to Chaitanya and to his two fellow-workers, Advaitâ-nanda and Nityânanda, as their highest authorities. They are outwardly worshippers of Vish*n*u in his form of K*r*ish*n*a, but by the more enlightened among them, K*r*ish*n*a or Vish*n*u is conceived as Brahman or the Supreme Spirit. The social impor-tance of this reform consisted chiefly in the complete ignoring of caste. " The teacher of the four Vedas," Chaitanya used to say, " is not my disciple, but the faithful *K*and*â*la (outcast) enjoys my friendship." Even Mohammedans were received as brothers in the faith, in fact the union of Hinduism and Islam was one of the leading ideas of the time. Every true disciple of Chaitanya had the right of begging for alms, and was expected to lead an ascetic life. At the same time there is a verse quoted as coming from Chaitanya, which leaves the impression that his ideas of asceticism were not very strict. " Let all enjoy fish, broth, and women's charms, be happy and call upon Hari (Vish*n*u)." But if he saw no harm in the enjoyment of life, resembling in this another honest reformer, Luther, he protested and warned his disciples against all worldly pleasures that would draw away their thoughts from K*r*ish*n*a. According to an article lately published in the "Journal of the Buddhist Text Society," 1897, Vol. V, Part 4, p. 87, Chaitanya taught, and his followers continue to teach

that the original cause of all things was Wisdom.
That Divine Soul was believed to vivify all, and
to be the Lord of all and the Protector of all.
He is called spiritual, pure, and full of ecstasy.
The Vedas chant His praises unceasingly.   It is
this Being, he taught, whom we call Kr*i*sh*n*a.   This
Supreme Being has three phases : (1) Brahman, the
light of the world that gives vitality to all.   The
sages try to reach Him by wisdom.   (2) Paramâtman, he who is sentient, omnipresent, and omniscient.
The sages go to Him through contemplation or
Yoga ; and (3) Bhagavat or the Personal God,
who manifests Himself in the material world.   Men
try to reach Him through Bhakti (devotion).

Some ascribe creation to matter : but this, according to Chaitanya, is impossible.   What power has
inert matter, he asks, that can produce so grand
a creation, filled with wisdom and beauty ?   It is
the will of an Almighty Being that brought this
universe into existence.   It is impossible for man
even to think of His greatness.

The human soul, the *G*îvâtman, is, according to
Chaitanya, an infinitesimal portion, like a ray,
of the Divine Being.   God is like a blazing fire,
and the souls are like sparks that come out of it.
Deluded by Mâyâ, i. e. the attractions of the
world, the *G*îvâtman forgets its own nature : but
when it has recognised the transitory nature of all
things, it goes up again to its Maker.

Many ascribe to this *G*îvâtman the attributes of
God.   But this, according to Chaitanya, cannot be,

because it has an individual character. *Sruti* (revelation) says that he who thinks that he has found out the nature of God knows nothing of Him.

Chaitanya says that it is the duty of every man to adore K*ri*sh*n*a and to perform good deeds without any expectation of rewards. Bhakti (devotion) is the channel that carries man to K*ri*sh*n*a. When a devotee says, "O Lord, I am yours," it is then only that he can attain K*ri*sh*n*a.

Lastly, it must be the aim of every man to gain K*ri*sh*n*a's love, and Bhakti is the way that leads to it. Chaitanya defined Bhakti as an uninterrupted tendency of the heart towards God, just like the flow of a river towards the sea.

It is difficult to understand how the followers of Mohammed could ever have been induced to use the name of K*ri*sh*n*a for that of Allah, but we know that it was so, and the same religious amalgamation between Hinduism and Islam was attempted by Nânak, the contemporary of Chaitanya. The Sîkhs, though much changed in time, are the followers of that reformer.

Nânak and the Sîkhs.

It is a pity that we possess so little trustworthy information about the original Sîkh reformers. Their sacred book, the Granth, exists, nay, it has even been translated into English by the late Dr. Trumpp. But it turns out now that Dr. Trumpp was by no means a trustworthy translator. The language of the Granth is generally called old Penjâbi, and it was supposed that a scholar who knew modern Penjâbi might easily learn to understand the language as it was four hundred years ago. But that is not the case. The language of the Granth is said to be full óf local dialectic varieties and forgotten idioms, so much so that it has been said to be without any grammar at all. That is, of course, impossible, for there is method even in what we might call grammatical madness, and we may hope that such a method may in time be discovered. Mr. Macauliffe, who has spent many years among the Sikhs, and has with the help of their priests paid much attention to their Granth, has given us some most interesting and beautiful specimens of their poetry which form part of their sacred book. Though Nânak was the chief founder of the new religion of the Sikhs, that is of the Sishyas or disciples, other well-known poets, such as Amgada, Râmdâs, Râmânand, Kabîr, Farîd (a Mussulman), and Mira Bir, a queen, are mentioned as his helpers and as contributors to the Granth. Râmânand, a Brâhman, or rather a Sannyâsin who had renounced many of the old ceremonial restrictions, on being asked one day to attend a Hindu religious worship, wrote the following lines :—

"Whither shall I go? I am happy at home,
  My heart will not go with me; it has become
      a cripple.
  One day my heart desired to go;
  I ground sandal, took attar of roses and many
      perfumes,

And was proceeding to worship in the temple
  of Brahm;

But my spiritual guide showed me God in my
  heart.

Wherever I go I find only water and stones (for
  bathing and worshipping);

But thou, O God, art equally contained in everything.

The Vedas and the Purânas I have all seen and
  searched.

Go thou thither, if God be not here (in the heart).

O true Guru, I am a sacrifice unto Thee,

Who hast cut away all my perplexities and doubts.

Râmânand's Lord is the all-pervading God,

The Guru's word has cut away millions of acts
  (sins)."

Another and perhaps the greatest among the disciples of Nânak was Kabîr, i. e. the Great. He was
strongly opposed to idol-worship. " If God is a
stone," he used to say, " I will worship a mountain."
Idol-worship was, of course, the greatest stumbling-
block in the way of a reconciliation between Hinduism and Islam. Still the defenders of idol-worship
and the iconoclastic Mohammedans managed to come
to a certain understanding. They agreed to speak
each his own language, but to feel that they meant
the same. Why cannot Christians and Hindus do
the same, particularly when the best spirits among
the Hindus at least, have adopted a language
which shows that they are very near the Kingdom

of God, nearer, I believe, than thousands who are baptized and call themselves Christians? It is most interesting to watch the compromise made between Hinduism and Islam four hundred years ago and to compare it with the compromise between Hinduism and Christianity that is now so eloquently advocated by the followers of Rammohun Roy and Keshub Chunder Sen.

Kablr said :—

"What availeth devotion, what penance, what fasting and worship,
To him in whose heart there is worldly love?
O man, apply thy heart to God :
Thou shalt not obtain Him by artifice.
Put away covetousness and regard for what people say of thee.
Renounce lust, wrath, and pride.
By the religious ceremonies (of the Hindus) conceit is produced,
That if they join and worship a stone (they shall receive salvation).
Saith Kablr, by serving Him I have obtained the Lord.
By becoming simple in heart I have met my God.

How many wear the bark of trees as clothes!
What if men dwell in the forest?
What availeth it, O man, to offer incense to idols and drench thy body with ablutions?

O my soul, I know that thou shalt depart.

O silly one, know God!

Wherever I look I see none but those who are entangled in worldly love.

Men of Divine knowledge and meditation, great preachers, all are engrossed in this world's affairs.

Saith Kabîr, without the name of the One God, this world is blinded by Mammon.

By the favour of the Guru the slave Kabîr loveth God,

O Brethren, the Vedas and Mohammedan books are lies, and free not the mind from anxiety.

If for a moment thou restrain thy mind, God shall appear before thee.

O man, search thy heart daily, that thou mayest not fall into despair.

This world is a magic show which hath no tangibility.

Men read falsehood and are pleased; they quarrel over what they do not understand.

The truth is, the Creator is contained in the Creation. He is not of a blue colour, like Krishna."

Nânak himself expresses his devotion to the true God in the following words :—

" Were a mansion of pearls erected and inlaid with gems for me,

Perfumed with musk, fragrant aloe, and sandal, so as to confer delight—

May it not be that on beholding it I should
    forget Thee and not remember Thy name!
My soul burneth without God.
I have ascertained from my Guru that there is
    no other shelter than thou, O God.
Were the earth to be studded with diamonds
    and rubies, and my couch to be similarly
    adorned,
Were fascinating damsels, whose faces shine with
    jewels, to shed lustre and diffuse pleasure,
May it not be that on beholding them, I should
    forget Thee, and not remember Thy name!"

The following verses will show what was in the
mind of Nânak and of his followers, and we know
from history how well their labours for conciliation
between Hindus and Mohammedans succeeded, at
least for a time, and how what seems to us impossible
at present was fully achieved by them. Rammohun
Roy and Keshub Chunder Sen would gladly have
joined in the following words of the Granth :—

"Some men are Hindus and some Musalmans.
    Among the latter are Rawazis, Imams, and Sufis;
    know that all men are of the same caste.
    The Creator and the Beneficent are the same ;
    the Provider and the Merciful are the same,
    there is no difference, let no one suppose so
    even by mistake.
    Worship the One God, He is the one Divine
    Guru after all; know that His form is one,
    and that He is the one light diffused in all.

The Temple and the Mosque are the same, the
 Hindu worship and the Musalman prayer are
 the same; all men are the same; it is through
 error they appear different.
Allah and Alekh are the same, the Purânas and
 the Korân are the same; they are all alike,
 it is the One God who created all."

No wonder then that Rammohun Roy and
Keshub Chunder Sen should have been hopeful
that their endeavours also might be crowned by
the same success as Nânak's, and that their new
Church would have included not only the believers
in the Vedas and the Korân, but the believers in
the Bible also. They both tried very hard to
come to an understanding with the representatives
of Christianity in India. It is the same even now.
There are men who can speak in the name of the
Indian people at large, and whose example would
tell on the masses who in every country have to
be led by their own men of light and leading.
Mozoomdar, the natural successor of Keshub Chunder Sen, would not recede a step from the position
which his great predecessors took up with regard
to Christianity. The idea that his Samâj was in
any sense opposed to Christianity or jealous of it
would be scouted by him as it was by Keshub
Chunder Sen. "Woe unto me," Keshub wrote, "if
ever I harboured in my mind the remotest desire
to found a new sect, and thus add to the already
accumulated evils of sectarianism! Woe unto us,
if I ever conceived the project of setting up a move-

ment against the Church of Christ! Perish these
lips if they utter a word of rebellion against Jesus.
And let the genial currents of my life-blood be
curdled at this very moment, if I glory in the hate-
ful ambition of rising against my master. A new
sect! God forbid. We preach not a new sect, but
the death of sectarianism and the universal reconciliation of all churches. But the very idea of an
eclectic church, it will be contended, is anti-Christian.
To mix up Christ with the hundred and one creeds
of the world is to destroy and deny Christ. To mix
Christ with what? With error, with impurity?
No. Mix Christ with all that is Christian in other
creeds. Surely that is not un-Christian, far less
anti-Christian. In uniting the East and the West,
in uniting Asiatic and European faith and character,
the Church of the New Dispensation works faithfully upon the lines laid down by Christ, and only
seeks to amalgamate the Western Christ and the
Eastern Christ. It is not a treaty of Christ with
anti-Christ that is proposed, but the reconciliation of
all in Christ. It is not the mixture of purity with
impurity, of truth with falsehood, of light with darkness, but the fusion of all types of purity, truth, and
light in all systems of faith into one integral whole.
It is the expurgation of anti-Christian elements from
the so-called Christian and heathen creeds of the
world, and the amalgamation of the pure Christian
residuum left. Such is the pure Christian electicism
of the Church of the New Dispensation."

Men of the type of Rammohun Roy could not,

and did not, shut their eyes to the superiority of
Christianity from an ethical point of view. They
despised in their heart the idols, as worshipped by
the vulgar, they saw through the pretensions of their
priests, and had long learnt to doubt the efficacy of
their sacrifices.   But their social institutions were
so intimately interwoven with their religion that it
required no small amount of moral courage openly
to break with it, and to lose caste, that is, to become
estranged from all relations, friends, and acquaintances.   But while they clearly perceived that their
religion was behind the time, and, as a social institution, could not stand long against Christianity, they
were by no means inclined to admit that from
a philosophical point of view also it was inferior
to Christianity.   Then was the time when Christianity might have stepped forth in its strong
armour and gained its greatest victories in India.
Rammohun Roy and his friends were ready.   He
himself spoke with the greatest humility of the
ancient Hindu religion ; nay, in conversations with
his English friends, he used language far too
depreciatory, as it seems to me, of the religious
and philosophical inheritance of India.   Then was
the time to act, but there were no Christian am-
bassadors to grasp the hands that were stretched
out.   Such missionaries as were in India then,
wanted unconditional surrender and submission, not
union or conciliation.   In many cases they were
themselves fettered by superstitions which men of
the type of Rammohun Roy had long discarded.

We keep religion and philosophy in different com-
partments, while with men such as Rammohun Roy
the two were one, and the religion of the Veda led
naturally on to the philosophy of the Vedânta, which
became in turn the firm foundation of their religion.
The Vedânta philosophy was so broad that it could
well have served as a common ground for religions so
different as Hinduism and Christianity undoubtedly
are, both in the form of *Gñâ*na (knowledge) and
of Bhakti (devotion). Rammohun Roy went so
far that, when he was in England, it was doubtful
whether he, in his mind a Vedântist, was not in
his heart a Christian. He spoke with the highest
respect and enthusiasm of Christianity, he carefully
studied the New Testament, and he willingly joined
in Christian worship. Though after his death the
Brâhmanic thread was found on his breast, this does
not prove that he would not have been willing to
surrender that also, if he had met with a real
response from his Christian friends on more important subjects. We shall see that some of his
followers surrendered even that outward badge of
Brâhmanism, but they could not surrender that
ineradicable belief in the substantial identity of the
eternal element in God and in man. A man like
Athanasius might easily have brought them to call
this consubstantiality the divine sonship of man, if
that expression had been fully explained to the
Vedântists. But no one was there, nay, no one
seems even now bold enough to speak out, and
to separate the vital kernel from the perishable

crust of religion. That vital kernel was more clearly seen by Rammohun Roy than by many of the missionaries who came to convert him. In Rammohun Roy's translation of the Upanishads we can clearly see that in his view of the Deity and of the relation between the human and the Divine he had never yielded an inch of his old Hindu convictions, though his practical religion was saturated with Christian sentiments. The same mixture of Christian and Hindu thoughts and Christian sentiments may be seen in nearly all the recent reformers of the ancient Hindu religion. The history of these attempted reforms has been so often written that I need not enter more fully into it, beyond repeating my conviction that great opportunities were lost then for planting Christianity on the old and fertile soil of India.

As to Keshub Chunder Sen he was more of a true Christian than many who call themselves Christians, and who are Christians in the ordinary sense of the word. And he knew it and did not deny it. Only he thought that Christianity should not be confined to a small sect, but should comprehend all religions. As Nânak had declared that what was wanted was a religion in which there were all religions, Keshub Chunder Sen also held that Jesus and Moses, Chaitanya and Buddha, Mohammed and Nânak should all become one before God. His New Dispensation was to embrace and unify all religions, all scriptures, and all prophets in God, and India was to be the birth-place of that all-embracing religion, because it was the birth-place of the Vedic and the Buddhist religions, and the meeting-place of Christianity and Islam. In one of the last numbers of the " New Dispensation," the organ of the followers of Keshub Chunder Sen, we read :—

" Who rules India ? What power is that which sways the destinies of India at the present moment ? You are mistaken if you think that it is the ability of Lord Lytton in the cabinet or the military genius of Sir Frederick Haines in the field that rules India. It is not politics, it is not diplomacy that has laid a firm hold of the Indian heart. It is not the glittering bayonet nor the fiery cannon of the British army that can make our people loyal. No. None of these can hold India in sub-jection. Armies never conquered the heart of a nation. Muscular force and prowess never made a man's head and heart bow before a foreign power. No. If you wish to secure the attachment and allegiance of India, it must be through spiritual influence and moral suasion. And such indeed has been the case in India. You cannot deny that your hearts have been touched, conquered, and subju-gated by a superior power. That power need I tell you—is Christ. It is Christ who rules British India, and not the British Government. England has sent out a tremendous moral force in the life and character of that mighty prophet, to conquer and hold this vast empire. None but Jesus ever deserved this bright, this precious diadem, India, and Jesus shall have it."

Is it not time to lay hold of these outstretched hands, and not reject them any longer with a cold *non possumus*?

After Rammohun Roy's death there was a pause, for nothing moves in India without a leader, and, though there were followers of the enlightened Râjah, there was for a time no leader of sufficient strength to inspire enthusiasm and to command respect. What happens generally to religious re-formers happened in India also. They all agreed in wishing for reform in general, but when it came to settling special reforms, some of no importance whatever, they soon diverged in different directions.

Those who are acquainted with the Vedas, I mean with the hymns and Brâhmazas, find it hard to understand how people of enlightened intellect could have hesitated for years and years before deciding against their revealed character. These hymns are not only old, they are antiquated and effete, they have no right, like megatheria of old, to hover about in the strata in which we live. We are ready to give them a place of honour in our museums, but we cannot allow ourselves to be swayed by them any longer. This may seem a harsh judgment, especially as coming from one who has devoted the best years of his life to the publication of the Rig-Veda, and who certainly has never regretted having done so, as little as he would regret having been the first to unearth the bones of the oldest of all megatheria, or the ruins of Babylon or Nineveh. I am not unaware that there are sparks of profound truth in some

II.   G

of the Vedic hymns, but they form a small portion
only of that large collection, and have been brought
into focus in the Upanishads and in the Vedânta-
Sûtras. With these neither Rammohun Roy nor
Keshub Chunder Sen nor Mozoomdar would be
willing to part, but to break with anything called
Veda was by no means an easy task, even for men
of enlightened minds, nor can there be any doubt
that the surrender when it took place at last, in-
volved an enormous sacrifice. All that Keshub
himself tells us in one of his Lectures is that there
was a terrible strife, the strife of conscience against
associations of mind and place; duty against pre-
possessions; truth against cherished convictions.
But conscience triumphed over all; the Vedas were
thrown overboard by Babu Debendranâth Tagore;
and the Brâhma-Samâj bade farewell to their Bible.
This step was particularly painful, because all these
struggles had to go on before the eyes of foreign
observers. In their controversies with the advocates
of Christianity, who claimed all the privileges of a
revelation for their own Bible, the invariable answer
of men like Rammohun Roy had been for a long
time " that the Veda also had for thousands of years
been considered as divinely inspired." And who
could prove that it was not ? Arguments in support
of the revealed character of the Veda were quickly
at hand, for they had been carefully prepared by
the ancient theologians of India. And, if the truth
must be told, the ideas which missionaries connected
with revelation were mostly not very different from

those familiar to the Brâhmans. "What argument is there," the Indian apologists asked, "in support of the revealed character of your New Testament which is not equally applicable to the Vedas?" The Buddhists had already said the same to the Brâhmans, though for the sake of argument only, hundreds of years before. "If your Kapila is inspired," they said, "why not our Buddha?" In the same spirit the Brâhmans now said, "If your Christian revelation is claimed as infallible, why should not the Vedic revelation be the same?" The fact was that on one side, as well as on the other, the idea of revelation had lost its original and true meaning; had become purely mechanical, a mere name to conjure with. But the more revelation had become something miraculous in the eyes of the people of India, the more creditable was it that the members of the Brâhma-Samâj, founded by Rammohun Roy, after becoming better acquainted with their own sacred writings than they ever had been before, should solemnly have declared in the year 1850, that the claim of being divinely inspired could no longer be maintained in favour of the hymns and Brâhmanas of the Veda. I know of no other instance in the whole history of religions that equals the honesty and self-denial of the members of the Brâhma-Samâj in their throwing down and levelling the ramparts of their own fortress, and opening the gates wide for any messengers of truth. Their honesty will appear all the more creditable when we remember that they were by no means inclined

to discard the Vedas altogether, but only declared
that reverence for the Deity prevented them from
claiming any longer anything like divine workmanship or penmanship for the whole of it. It is a
pity that we know so little of the mental struggles
through which men like Keshub Chunder Sen and
his friends had to pass before they could bring
themselves to let go the chief anchor of their
religious faith. But Hindus keep their agonies to
themselves. No doubt they lose thereby much
of that human sympathy which we feel for others
who lay open their inmost hearts before us, while
slowly surrendering their old for a new, a purer,
and a better faith. It is very rare that we are
allowed an insight into the home-life and heart-
life of eminent Hindus. The female members of
their families, the mothers, wives, and sisters, who
with us take often so prominent a place in religious
struggles, are excluded from our sight altogether.
But we know that in India also their influence as
mothers and wives is very great. I have several
times heard from my more enlightened friends in
India that they would like to come to England, or
would like to do this or that, but that they shrink
from offending their wives or mothers. Women in
India, ignorant as they may be, wield great power
in their own homes, and it is a common saying that
it is easier to defy H. M.'s Secretary of State than
to defy one's own mother-in-law. Though mothers
and wives are much less enlightened than their
husbands and sons, it is for that very reason that

they feel the apostasy of their beloved all the more deeply. It is everywhere a more severe trial for a woman than for a man to lose caste, and to lose caste means more in India than it does with us. When now and then we catch a glimpse of what is going on in the sanctuary of an Indian home, we learn that human nature is the same everywhere. Thus we read of the old mother of Keshub Chunder Sen, who must have felt her son's discarding of his old religion very keenly, standing by his deathbed and lamenting that she, poor sinner, should be left behind, while the dearest jewel of her heart was being plucked away from her! And the dying one answers, " Don't say so, dear mother. All that is good in me I have inherited from you ; all that I call my own is yours." So saying, he took the dust of her feet and put it upon his head.

When Keshub Chunder Sen arrived in England, he was received with open arms, particularly by the Unitarians. Wherever he spoke or preached, he attracted immense audiences, and his command of the English language, nay his real eloquence pro- duced a deep impression on the religious public in London and elsewhere. I regretted that there was no opportunity of his addressing the young men when he came to Oxford. I was very anxious also that Dr. Pusey should see him, and the kind- hearted old Doctor, friendly as he always was to me, was willing to receive him and to hear what he had to say. Though Dr. Pusey was a scholar, and, as such, above many of the prejudices of his followers, he was not particularly pleased with the speeches made by Keshub Chunder Sen, nor was his close relation with the Unitarians to his theological taste. Still he received him with friendly sympathy, and some very serious questions of religion were discussed by the two men with great freedom. I never kept memoranda even of such important meetings and discussions at which I happened to be present. I thought they would remain engraved on my memory. But now, after the lapse of so many years, I find that it is not so. I have indeed the general impression remaining in my mind, but I cannot trust myself to repeat the actual words that passed, and it would not be fair to give what one thinks was said by such men as Dr. Pusey and Keshub Chunder Sen, when brought face to face, as if it were what was actually said by them. In conversation I have often repeated what passed between them, and this very repetition is apt to mislead a poor memory like my own. I know I cannot trust it as to minute details. I remember, however, very distinctly, how at the end of their conversation, the question turned up, whether those who were born and bred as members of a non-Christian religion could be saved. Keshub Chunder Sen and myself pleaded for it, Dr. Pusey held his ground against us. Much of course depended on what was meant by salvation, and Keshub defined it as an uninterrupted union with God. "My thoughts," he said, "are never away from God;" and he added, "my life is a constant prayer, and

there are but few moments in the day when I am
not praying to God." This, uttered with great
warmth and sincerity, softened Dr. Pusey's heart.
"Then you are all right," he said, and they parted
as friends, both deeply moved.

I must say for Dr. Pusey, much as I differed
from his views, and much as I regretted some of
the steps he took at Oxford, where his influence for
a time was very great, he always tolerated me, and
befriended me on different occasions. We had a
common ground as scholars, and whenever I seemed
to go too far for him, I well remember his looking
up to the clouds and saying, "Oh, I see you are
a German still." When my friends first submitted to
the Delegates of the University Press at Oxford my
plan of publishing, whether at Oxford or at Vienna,
translations of all the Sacred Books of the East,
Dr. Pusey, being a Delegate and a very influential
Delegate, strongly supported my plan, only stipu-
lating that the Old and New Testaments should not
be included. In vain did I explain to him that these
two books could never have a better setting than in
the frame formed by the other Sacred Books, and
my firm conviction that the time would come when
the gap thus left would be greatly regretted; but he
remained unshaken. I had to give up a wish that
was very near to my heart in order to save the rest,
but I still hope that hereafter these two, the most
important of the Sacred Books of the East, will
find their proper place in my collection. Nothing
will serve better to show the difference between

these and the rest of the Sacred Books, and to make us see both what they share in common with the rest, and what it is that has given to them the overwhelming influence which they have exercised on the highest destinies of the human race.

When Keshub Chunder Sen was staying with me at Oxford, I had a good opportunity of watching him. I always found him perfectly tranquil, even when most in earnest, and all his opinions were clear and settled. He never claimed any merit for the sacrifices he had made, he rather smiled at what was past, and seldom complained of his opponents, except when they accused him of having been a traitor to his own cause by allowing his daughter to be betrothed and married to the Mahârâjah of Kuch Behar, before she had reached, by a few months, the marriageable age which he and his friends had themselves fixed for all members of the Brâhma-Samâj. This is too long and too complicated a story to be told here; but, whether the father had shown any paternal weakness or not, there was surely no cause for his former friends to separate from him on so paltry a ground, to insult him and to break his heart, and in the end to produce a fatal schism in the Brâhma-Samâj. When Keshub Chunder Sen introduced new reforms, surrendering the Vedas, abandoning the Brâhmanic thread, sanctioning widow marriages, and forbidding child marriages, his society, hitherto called the Brâhma-Samâj, assumed the new name of the Brâhma-Samâj of India (1861), while the more conservative Brâhmas[1] under Debendranâth Tagore, were distinguished by the name of Âdi Brâhma-Samâj, or the first Brâhma-Samâj. Those who later on separated again from Keshub Chunder Sen, because they disapproved of the marriage of his daughter, and objected to his claiming, or seeming to claim for himself the gift of inspiration and a higher authority than was right for any human being, assumed the new name of Sadhârana Brâhma-Samâj or the Catholic Society of Brâhmas. These different sections carry on the same work, each in its own way. Some see in these divisions signs of healthy vitality, others regret them, as impeding the more rapid advance of a powerful army. The points of difference are so few and so insignificant that it only requires a strong arm to weld them together once more. Protâp Chunder Mozoomdar seemed pointed out for this, and it is to be hoped that he may still succeed in the great work of conciliation.

Many of those who bore the burden of the day,

[1] Brâhma is the same as Brâhmo ; the former Sanskrit, the latter Bengali. Thus, Debendranâth called his book on the Upanishads "Brâhma-dharmah," though Brâhma also is a faulty name in Sanskrit.

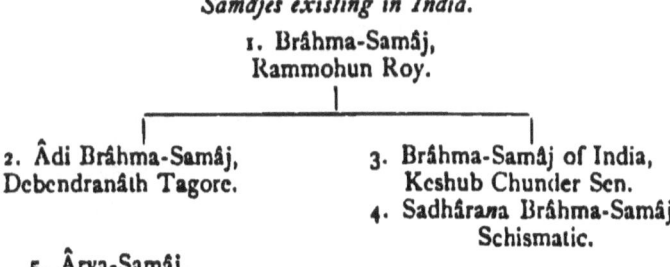

Samâjes existing in India.

1. Brâhma-Samâj,
   Rammohun Roy.

2. Âdi Brâhma-Samâj,
   Debendranâth Tagore.

3. Brâhma-Samâj of India,
   Keshub Chunder Sen.

4. Sadhârana Brâhma-Samâj,
   Schismatic.

5. Ârya-Samâj,
   Dayânanda Sarasvatî.

and without whose ready help Keshub Chunder Sen would hardly have been able to achieve what he did achieve in his short life, are by this time dead and forgotten. Even Debendranâth Tagore's constant help and patronage are seldom recognised as they deserve to be in the history of the Brâhma-Samâj. The memory of Hurrish Chunder Mookerjee has lately been revived by the republication of his Three Lectures on Religious Subjects (Calcutta, 1887); and it was his recent death (August, 1898) that reminded the friends of India of the sacrifices made by Râmtonoo Lahari and others in support of the reforms initiated by Rammohun Roy.

Râmtonoo Lahari.

Râmtonoo[1] was born in 1813, and must therefore have been older than Debendranâth Tagore, who is generally considered as the Nestor of the Brâhma-Samâj.

He was a pupil of David Hare, who had undertaken the philanthropic work of educating native youths, and after spending a few years at his school, he was admitted into the Hindu College at Calcutta, which was established in 1817 as the first fruit of the annual vote of £10,000 for educational purposes insisted on by the English Parliament. The teacher who chiefly influenced the young men was D. Rozario,

---

[1] Râmtonoo is probably meant for Râmatanu, body of Râma, but when a name has once become familiar in its modern Bengali form, I do not always like to put it back into its classical Sanskrit form.

who, though branded by the clergy as an infidel
and as a devil of the Thomas Paine school, was
worshipped by his pupils as an incarnation of
goodness and kindness.   It was Christian morality,
as preached by D. Rozario, that appealed most
strongly to the heart of Râmtonoo and his fellow-
pupils, many of them very distinguished in later
life, the fathers and grandfathers of the present
generation of Indian reformers.   Râmtonoo became
a model among his friends in all matters per-
taining to morality and conscience, penitence and
sincerity being the watchwords of his early career,
vice and hypocrisy the constant objects of his de-
nunciation, both among his equals and among those
of higher rank and authority.   Even the founder
of the Brâhma-Samâj did not escape his reproof,
on account of what he considered want of moral
courage to act up to his convictions.   As to himself,
he denounced caste as a great social and moral
evil, and silent submission to superstitious customs
as reprehensible weakness.   In order to shame
those who denounced beef-eating as sinful, he and
his friends would actually parade the streets with
beef in their hands, inviting the people to take it
and eat it.   The Brâhmanical thread which was
retained by the members of the Brâhma-Samâj as
late as 1861, was openly discarded by him as early
as 1851.   And we must remember that in those
days such open apostasy was almost a question of life
or death, and that Rammohun Roy was in danger
of assassination in the very streets of Calcutta.   It is

true that European officials respected and supported
Râmtonoo, but among his own countrymen he was
despised and shunned. However, he continued his
career undisturbed by friend or foe, and guided by
his own conscience only. Poor as he was, he
desired no more than to earn a small pittance as
a teacher in public and private schools. Later in
life he was attracted to the new Brâhma-Samâj, and
became a close friend of Keshub Chunder Sen.
When he saw others who spent much time in
prayer he considered them as the most favoured
of mortals, for pure and conscientious as he was,
he felt himself so sinful that he could but seldom
utter a word or two in the spirit of what he considered true prayer before the eyes of the Lord.
While cultivating his little garden he was found
lost in devotion at the sight of a full-blown rose,
and while singing a hymn in adoration of God, his
whole countenance seemed to beam with a heavenly
light. One of his friends tells us that one morning
early he rushed into his room like a madman
and dragged him out of bed, saying that when the
whole nature was ablaze with the light and fire
of God's glory, it was a shame to lie in bed. He
took the sleeper to the next field, and pointing
his fingers to the rising sun and the beautiful trees
and foliage, he recited with the greatest rapture—
what? Not a hymn of the Veda, but some verses
from Wordsworth. When his end approached, his
old friend Debendranâth Tagore went to take leave
of him, and when he left him, he cried : " Now the

gates of heaven are open to you, and the gods are
waiting with their outstretched arms to receive you
to the glorious region." Did the old Vedântist
really say "the gods"? I doubt it, unless he used
the language of Mâyâ, as we also do sometimes,
knowing that his friend would interpret it in the right
sense. I see, however, that Mozoomdar also speaks
of his spirit reposing in his God—showing how the
old habits of thought and old words cling to us
and never lose their meaning altogether.

Many more names might be mentioned, but to
us they would hardly be more than names. Debendranâth Tagore is the only one left who could give
us a history of that important religious movement
in India, and of the principal actors in it. But he is
too old now to undertake such a task. The others,
to use the language of their friends, have, like
the stars that rise in the Eastern sky, after com-
pleting their appointed journey, sunk below the
visible horizon of death, to pass from the hemisphere
of time to that of eternity! But though their names
may be forgotten, their good works will remain, for
" Good deed," as they say in India, " never dies."

Dayânanda Sarasvatî.

One more Samâj should be mentioned here to
prevent confusion, namely, the Ârya-Samâj. This
movement, which was inaugurated by another man,
of the name of Dayânanda Sarasvatî, was proclaimed as a revival of the ancient Vedic religion.
Dayânanda held fast to his belief in the Veda as

a divine revelation, though he understood by Veda
the hymns only, and admitted that the Brâhma*n*as
showed clear traces of human workmanship. The
followers of Dayânanda are quite aware that the
Vedas were composed long before the art of writing
was discovered in India, and they strongly object
to the Veda being styled book-revelation, which
they evidently consider as an inferior kind of revelation. They say, what they have no doubt learnt
from European scholars, that the Vedas were not
received in the form of books, but were revealed
to the four principal Rishis. But their antagonists
of the Brâhma-Samâj rejoin that, because the Vedas
were committed to paper only a few thousand years
back, it does not follow that they do not partake
of the nature of book-revelation. They ask point
blank whether Dayânanda and his followers believe
that the very words and combinations of words
forming the hymns of the Vedas as we now find
them in MSS. were uttered by God Himself? As
long as they hold to this belief, the followers of
Keshub Chunder Sen accuse them of being believers
in book-revelation, quite as much as if they held
that the bound volumes of the Veda had tumbled
down from heaven. Their discussions on that point
are often very ingenious, and may prove instructive even to our own apologists. Dayânanda himself and his followers disclaim any indebtedness to
Western ideas, and they have gained many ad-
herents, chiefly on the ground that, though pervaded
by a reforming spirit, their Samâj has always re-

mained thoroughly national. Dayânanda denounced idolatry and polytheism, he even repudiated caste, and allowed widow marriages. This required great courage, but, being a liberal-conservative, he was naturally attacked both by liberals, for not going far enough, and by conservatives, for going too far. His followers believe that he was actually poisoned by his enemies. I am told that, at present, this revival of the ancient national religion has gained and is gaining far more support in India than the reforms initiated by Rammohun Roy and Keshub Chunder Sen. National feelings are strong in religious matters also. But though his doctrines may be more popular, there is more real vitality, more real reasonableness in the ideas of the other Brâhma-Samâjes. If they would only combine under a strong leader, they would, I believe, soon carry with them the wavering followers of Dayânanda; for in India whoever has once taken the first step, and surrendered his belief in the revealed character of even a part of the Veda, will easily be driven to take another step and adopt human reason as the only guide to human truth.

We know little of the personal character of Dayânanda, and what we know sounds very apocryphal. Though I was told soon after his death that he had been poisoned by the Brâhmans, who were afraid of his sweeping social reforms, I am now told by an Indian friend of mine that it is supposed that his death was caused by the dancing-girls who, at the instigation of Dayânanda, had been placed under strict *surveillance* by the Mahârâjah of Jayapura. Their stipends had been stopped, and they are supposed to have enticed a young Brâhman cook to poison their enemy. The cook is said to have afterwards committed suicide. This though only a rumour among rumours, would certainly put a different aspect on Dayânanda's sudden death. He must have been a powerful man, and he knew how to be a leader of men. His ignorance of English deprived him of much that would have been helpful to him, and would have kept him from some of his wild ideas about the Veda. He maintained that all wisdom was to be found in it, down to the discovery of the power of steam and its application to steam engines for railways; and this thousands of years B.C.! He was still more unfortunate in falling, for a time, an easy prey to Madame Blavatsky's spiritual fascinations.

For some time he understood her as little as she understood him, and that is saying a good deal. But when at last they came to understand each other, there followed a breach that could never be healed. The life of Dayânanda, published under the authority of the so-called Theosophists, which I accepted formerly as genuine, has been discredited, and we shall probably never have a real biography of the man, for biography in India seems to share the fate of history; either it tells us nothing, or what it tells us is fact and fiction so mixed together that it is impossible to separate the one from the other.

We can see clearly, however, that a strong and healthy fermentation is going on in the religious life of India, and if we consider the geographical extent of that country and the influence that it has always exercised on the intellectual atmosphere of the East, we can hardly treat that religious movement, which was inaugurated by Rammohun Roy, as indifferent to ourselves. What is wanting in it at present is the personal element, which is always very important in India. People are ready to be led, but they expect a leader to lead them.

I should never have understood the real motives and the true objects of these Indian reformers but for my personal intercourse with Dvârkanâth, years ago, and more recently with Keshub Chunder Sen. Though I did not know Rammohun Roy personally, I knew several of his friends who had known him at Bristol, and though I had no personal intercourse with Dayânanda, I learnt something of him also from some of his personal friends and followers. Still, we want to know a great deal more of the chief actors in a reformation which affects a far larger number of human beings than did the Reformation when it reinvigorated the whole of Europe in the sixteenth century. Some of the questions now being agitated in India are just the same as the questions which led in the end to the reformation of our own Church. If with us the chief question was that of the authority of the Bible replacing that of Pope and Councils, with them it is the authority of the Vedas. And if it was the

first printed edition of the Greek New Testament
by Erasmus that gave the strongest impulse to
our Reformation, it was the first printed edition of
the Veda that gave the most powerful incentive
and the strongest weapon to the founders of the
Brâhma-Samâj in India. Let us hope that India
may be spared a Thirty Years' War before it can
consolidate the work so courageously begun by
Rammohun Roy, and so valiantly carried on by
my departed friend, Keshub Chunder Sen.

It may very naturally be asked, but what is to
become of the religion of India, and more particularly of the religion of Keshub Chunder Sen
and his friends and followers, after the very foundation of their ancient faith has been withdrawn, or,
at all events, has been deprived of its sacred and
infallible character? What would become of us if,
say, by the discovery of ancient papyri in Egypt,
it were suddenly placed beyond the reach of reasonable doubt that the Old and the New Testaments
had been composed by some well-known Rabbi or
philosopher in Egypt? Keshub Chunder Sen himself might have thought that all was gained after
the heavy incubus of the Vedas had once been
removed from his conscience; but some even of
his best friends thought, not unnaturally, that all
was lost. The idea that whatever truth was contained in the Vedas remained the same, whether
with or without supernatural credentials, and that
its acceptance without any such credentials required
even a greater amount of honest conviction or faith

than its acceptance on the ground of an assurance of its superhuman authorship, and that assurance given by human individuals like ourselves, seems never to have been entertained by the former believers in the Veda. To most of us the Bible would probably remain the same, whoever might be proved to have written it. But it was not so, as far as I can see, with the members of the Brâhma-Samâj. And yet it was felt that their Samâj or Church, if it was to strike root, required some kind of sacred code after the momentous decision had been taken to give up the Vedas. It must not be supposed that these reformers were without religion; on the contrary, they had more of the true religious spirit in them than those from whom they differed and from whom they had separated; and it was only the strength of their religious convictions that emboldened them to throw away their crutches and to stand without any inter-mediary, whether human or divine, before the highest object of their faith and veneration.

The first step they took was to explore some of the great religions of the world, and to select from their sacred books the most important and most convincing passages. This was very carefully done by Keshub Chunder Sen himself, but this inter-national Bible failed to appeal to the hearts of the people of India. In religion anything that is not homegrown, or has become familiar to us from our childhood, cannot easily be divested of a strange and almost grotesque sound. When

Bishop Colenso published an English translation of a beautiful prayer addressed to Vishṇu, it produced nothing but merriment among his English readers, and why? Because Vishṇu was addressed in it by his well-known popular name of Hari, and the invocation "O Harry" was too much for the risible muscles of John Bull.

The same effect was produced on the Hindus when they were told of a God that had made the world in six days, and rested the seventh day, or when they heard Christ invoked as *Agnus Dei*, or Vatsa Devasya. Language is a very important element in religion, and the slightest incongruity is sometimes fatal. It is well known that Dr. Arnold had to part with an excellent French master at Rugby simply because he had spoken of the Holy Ghost as a pigeon, instead of a dove. The boys could never forget or forgive it.

Then there was also the national sentiment, which asserts itself, even when it seems to be most out of place. The people of India wanted to have a national religion, and they did not see why they should have to borrow their prayers from Jews, Christians, Parsis, or other infidels. I strongly advised Keshub Chunder Sen, when he was staying with me at Oxford, to have a good translation made of the New Testament in Sanskrit, and in the more important vernaculars of India, only leaving out the historical passages, which conveyed no meaning to the large masses of the people in India, and any other chapters or verses which he considered inap-

propriate for influencing the Indian mind. Keshub
himself was quite ready to adopt such a course, for
he was really in his heart a true follower of Christ.
Once when I had asked him why he did not declare
himself publicly a Christian, he said, in a very
grave and thoughtful tone, "Suppose that thirty
years hence people find out that I was a disciple
of Christ, what would be the harm? Only were
I to profess myself a Christian now, all my influence
would be gone at once." Whether any steps were
taken by Keshub to carry out the idea of a New
Testament for India I cannot tell. Something of
the same kind had been done in English by
Rammohun Roy himself. The book has become
very scarce, and I doubt whether it ever influenced
even his own followers.

Debendranâth Tagore, the paternal friend of
Keshub Chunder Sen, adopted a different course.
He would never declare against the whole Veda, but,
discarding the hymns and the Brâhmanas, he made
a careful selection of important passages from the
Upanishads, and published them, with an explanation in Sanskrit, under the title of " Brâhma-dharma,"
the Law of the Brâhmas. This became for a time
the new guide of the Brâhmas, even before Keshub
Chunder Sen published his selections from the
Bibles of the world, and will probably in time
become their Bible, or at all events their Book of
Meditations. The primitive religious doctrines
of the Upanishads were reduced to an elaborate
system of philosophy by Bâdarâyana, probably long

before the Christian era, though after the rise of
Buddhism (fifth century), under the title of Vedânta-
Sûtras, and a most wonderful system it is, though
difficult to describe in a few pages. It is generally
supposed that the Vedânta philosophy denies the
reality of the whole world. But this is not so; it
only declares, and even more consistently than we
do, that the world is phenomenal. It is not what
it seems to be, but it would not even seem to be,
unless it reposed on the Divine, which alone is
really real. That Divine, in order to be what it
is, or what it ought to be conceived to be, must,
according to the Vedânta, be free from all limitation,
it must therefore be one, with nothing beside it, it
must be subjective, not objective or perceptible by
the senses, devoid therefore of all qualities. But,
instead of calling the world a mere nothing, the old
Vedântists held, on the contrary, that there could be
nothing objective or phenomenal, unless there was
something real beneath it, in comparison with which
anything else might be called unreal, that is, phenomenal. Thus, even our unreal world could not
exist unless there was at the back of it a something
real; and, if we claim any reality for ourselves,
we can only do so after surrendering all that is
phenomenal in ourselves, all that is changing,
perishing, and mortal. Only then can we find and
recover our true being, where alone it can be
found, namely in the divine, invisible, but ever-
present, absolute Power, the uncreate, the eternal
and never-changing Being whom we call God. This

was that ultimate Reality which they called Brahman, and this was, in fact, but another name for what European philosophers have called the Ultimate, the Unknowable, the Great Reality, the Hidden, the Abyss, the Silence, the Fullness, the Eternal Life — names all meaning the same, or meant for the same, though powerless to reach what is beyond the reach of words.

Then came the very natural question, whence comes the change from the Real to the Phenomenal, or what we call the creation? Whence the phenomenal in place of the noumenal world? The Vedânta answer is, From Nescience. This has been called the weak, the human, the vulnerable point in the Vedânta; but we should remember that, in some shape or other, that vulnerable point can never be absent from any system of philosophy. I doubt whether there are many founders of philosophies who have disguised it better than Bâdarâyaṇa and his predecessors in the Upanishads. Nescience, they say, is neither real nor unreal. It is, but it cannot be called real, because it can be destroyed, and is to be destroyed by Vidyâ, science, i.e. the Vedânta philosophy; yet it cannot be called unreal, for we see its effects in all the phenomenal world. This nescience must not be taken for the ignorance of the individual man, or for his unacquaintance with the Vedânta philosophy. It is something inherent in human nature. Brahman itself is affected by it indirectly, but not directly. Brahman, as conceived by us, may be said to be for a time under its sway.

A power such as this nescience was sure to yield
to the mythopoeic influence of language, and to
become *she*, as it did under the name of Mâyâ
(illusion, magic), or even of *S*akti, *potentia*.
But whether that impulse which produced the
phenomenal world is called Avidyâ (nescience),
or Mâyâ (illusion), or *S*akti (*potentia*), it was and
is the aim of Vidyâ or the Vedânta philosophy
to dispel it, and thus to destroy the illusion that
there is any real difference between man and Brahman.   It then becomes clear that this phenomenal
world in its endless variety is but an ignorance,
a dream that will pass away, if once our eyes are
opened.   Whatever is known by us, becomes, *ipso
facto*, objective and phenomenal, and to know this
is the first step towards the truth.   It may seem
difficult to understand how such a philosophy could
be treated as orthodox, and go hand in hand with
the popular religion.   But we must remember that
Brahman, the first and the only real Being, as soon
as perceived or conceived as an object, becomes at
once a phenomenal being.   Thus Brahman (neut.)
became to human intelligence Brahmâ (masc.), and
was recognised and worshipped as phenomenalised
under such popular names as *S*iva, Vish*n*u, K*r*ish*n*a,
and many more.   In this way the old mythological
gods had not to be discarded altogether ; on the
contrary, devotion to them (Bhakti) was not only
tolerated, but actually enjoined, till true knowledge
or G*ñ*âna had arisen.   *S*iva and Vish*n*u and other
gods were accepted as persons or as faces (Pratîka)

of Brahman. Nay, they were recognised as the phenomena of Brahman, and whosoever worshipped them was led to believe that he worshipped Brahman, though ignorantly. Here lies a wonderful amount of wisdom, from which even we may have something to learn ; and it is not surprising that some of these modern Hindu philosophers and religious teachers should have felt that they had not only to learn from us, but had something also to teach us. This may sound very strange to our ears, and yet what is more natural ? Nay, strange as it sounds to our ears, it is nevertheless a fact, that may have been exaggerated in the American papers, but that is not without some real foundation, namely, that some Vedântist missionaries, such as Vivekânanda, Abhedânanda, Sâradânada, and others, who were sent to America, are lecturing there before large audiences, and have actually made some converts who accept the Vedântic view of the world, and call themselves Theosophists or Vedântists. These missionaries are mostly the disciples and followers of a well-known Indian ascetic, who had spent his life in preaching Vedântic sentiments, and who died as late as 1886[1]. Men of that class are well known in India, and are spoken of as Mahâtmans. They live as much as possible retired from the world, it may be in a cave or a small hut in the forest. They wear hardly anything but rags, bear heat,

[1] A full account of this Saint is to be found in a book lately published by me, " Râmakrishna, his Life and Sayings," by F. M. M., 1898.

cold, and hunger without complaining, and strive
hard to become Vairâgins, men without any passions
and without any desires.   It need hardly be said
that some of them are mere impostors and disrepu-
table characters, well known to the police.   Others,
however, are real religious enthusiasts.   Though
they may know a little Sanskrit, they are not the
recognised depositaries of ancient learning; but,
once filled and fired with the spirit of the Vedânta,
they become very eloquent preachers, and gather
crowds around them, willing to drink in the truths
which never fail to exercise their intoxicating power
on the Indian mind.   Many of these Mahâtmans
know by long practice how to put themselves into
a real trance, and thus to make people believe that
they have been outside their body or beside themselves, and have received inspirations from a divine
source.   If this is a deception, it is certainly a very
old deception.   It is practised by sons, as they had
seen it practised by their fathers, and, as far as
I can see, without any sinister intentions.   Râma-
kri̇shṇa and men of his class are addicted to Bhakti,
devotion or love, rather than to Gñâna, knowledge,
or pure philosophy.   They speak of Kri̇shṇa rather
than of Brahman, nay, Brahman itself becomes with
them Brahmâ, a masculine and active god.   If some
of these men declare their perfect willingness to
adopt the religion of Christ, they can do so with
perfect honesty.   The God of Christianity, the
Creator of the world, the Father of all the children
of man, would be to them but another name,

another face or person of the Godhead. Christ would be to them not simply a manifestation, like Râma or Nârada, but, from a far higher point of view, born of God, one with God, having realised God, as we all are to realise Him in time, in order to attain real brotherhood with Christ and among ourselves, and divine sonship, the long forgotten or forfeited birthright of every son of man. Would not that be enough to make them Christians, truer Christians than even some of the missionaries, who approach them as if they were a degraded race, and who are often satisfied if they can baptize them, even without having really converted them? If we want them to understand us, let us first try to understand them. If that mutual recognition is once achieved, there may be a future for Christianity in store in India such as we hardly venture to dream of as yet. There are Hindus of the highest caste who would be able, like the eunuch, to say with perfect honesty that they believed that Jesus Christ was the son of God, in the highest sense of the word. What then hindereth them from being baptized? No wonder that European visitors who come to see these devotees in India should often be repelled by what they see. They are generally naked, or in rags, with dishevelled hair, emaciated, and not always very clean. Their expression is wild and often half crazy. Even their photographs are enough to frighten us. But for all that, their utterances, partly their own, partly echoes of what they have heard, are sometimes

very powerful and even beautiful, and people of
all classes, educated and uneducated, are willing to
listen to them for hours.   One thing is certainly
to their credit.   Though they accept alms, they
never ask for them; and even the missionaries who
have travelled all the way to America to lecture and
preach, never ask for money.   They do not want it,
and what is given to them is sent to India forthwith
towards a fund for building and endowing what we
should call monasteries, where the style of life is
as simple as it was in the best days of monastic life
in Europe.   The sayings of Râmakrishna have
been published by his disciples, and I cannot resist
the temptation of giving here at least a few of
them :—

" Thou seest many stars at night in the sky, but
findest them not when the sun rises.   Canst thou
say that there are no stars then in the heaven of
day ?   O man, because thou beholdest not the
Almighty in the days of thy ignorance, say not
that there is no God."

" Different creeds are but different paths to reach
the Almighty."

" As from the same gold various ornaments are
made, having different forms and names, so our
God is worshipped in different countries and ages,
and has different forms and names.   Though He
may be worshipped variously, some loving to call
Him Father, others Mother &c., yet it is one God
that is being worshipped in all these various relations
and modes."

" Man is like a cushion-cover. The colour of one may be red, another blue, another black, but all contain the same cotton inside. So it is with man; one is beautiful, one is black, another holy, a fourth wicked; but the Divine dwells in all of them."

"God is in all men, but all men are not in God, that is the reason why they suffer."

"As the lamp does not burn without oil, man cannot live without God."

" There are two egos in man, one ripe and the other unripe. The ripe ego thinks, 'Nothing is mine, whatever I see, or feel, or hear, nay, even this body is not mine; I am always free and eternal.' The unripe ego, on the contrary, thinks, ' This is my house, my room, my child, my wife, my body,' &c."

" When the knowledge of Self is obtained, all fetters fall off by themselves. Then there is no distinction of a Brâhmana or a Sûdra, of high caste or low caste. In that case the sacred thread, the sign of caste, falls away of itself. But so long as man has the consciousness of distinction and difference of caste, he should not forcibly throw it away."

" A man after fourteen years of hard asceticism in a lonely forest, obtained at last the power of walking on the waters. Overjoyed at this acquisition, he went to his teacher and told him of his great feat. At this the master replied: ' My poor boy, what thou hast accomplished after fourteen years of arduous labour, ordinary men do the same by paying a penny to the boatman.' "

"Where is God? How can we get at Him? There are pearls in the sea. One must dive again and again till one gets at them. So there is God in the world, but you should persevere in diving."

"The vanities of all others may gradually die out, but the vanity of a saint is hard, indeed, to wear away."

There are hundreds of such sayings, all breathing the same spirituality, the same familiarity with the unseen world. Some of them sound to us trivial and common, but in publishing them I did not like to leave out any, for fear of being suspected of falsifying the record and representing the bright side of the movement only. To our taste there may be too much of that familiarity. Silence in the presence of God seems to us more reverential than words, but to a man of the character of Râma-krishna, and I might say, to Hindus in general, the distance between the human and the Divine, between God and man, has always been very small, till at last it seems to vanish altogether. To their eyes the unseen world and the unseen God are not unseen. The veil formed by what we call the flesh is to them so transparent that it often vanishes altogether. The idea of a distance from God or of a gradual approach to Him after death exists indeed in their exoteric philosophy, but to the true Vedântist such an approach is really unthinkable. To the Vedântist the highest goal has always been to have his humanity taken back into the Godhead, not to put on a new nature,

but to recover his old and true nature, in fact to
become what, in spite of the dreams and fancies
of life, he has always been. Those who cannot
soar so high, may indeed be allowed to worship
a distant God, nay, to approach His throne rever-
entially in another life, and they are taught that
even in that state of mind, they are moving forward
on the right road, the road that may at last bring
them to themselves and make them enjoy the
Divine and the Eternal within them. Hence with
all their strong sense of the imperfections of this
life, with the acknowledgment of their guilt and
their consequent separation from God, they never
use the disparaging language of other religions
which seems to make man the most contemptible
worm on earth. No doubt, they also have imagined
a number of beings intermediate between God and
man, but when these creatures of their own fancy
have been dissolved again, they seem to feel that in
reality there is no class of real beings that can claim
to fill the self-made gap between God and man.
Râmak*r*ish*n*a himself was still in the bonds of the
popular faith of India. He worshipped the gods
created by man, such as Vish*n*u, *S*iva, and others,
he did not shrink even from offering sacrifices to
idols, but he felt and saw that behind them there
is the inexpressible Essence which is more than any
or all of them. The purely human devotion and
love which he expresses for his Divine Mother, for
instance, is sometimes most startling, but one feels
all the time that, if he could only express it, he is

groping for that Godhead which he must find in himself or in his Self before he can find it in the Self of the whole world, in the Self even of the old idols. A distant God like the Jewish Jehovah would be no God at all to the Vedântist, he cannot be too near to his God; nay, to be without Him but for one moment would be death and annihilation to him.

Such ideas are no doubt strange to most of us, but if we cannot as yet make them our own, we should at all events give Râmakrishna and his followers credit for holding them honestly.

MY INDIAN FRIENDS.

III.

Behramji Malabári.

INTIMATELY connected with the reform of religion in India were social reforms, such as the education of women, the recognition of widow-marriages, the fixing of the marriageable age of boys and girls, &c. The burning of widows or of Suttees, had been boldly put down by the English Government years ago; though, as we saw, it was still defended as resting on Vedic authority by so learned and enlightened a man as Râdhâkânta Deva. But, though widows were no longer burnt, their life as widows was in many cases worse than death. Owing to the system of very early, and what has been truly called, child-marriages, the number of child-widows is, and has been for many years, very large in India; and the only means of reducing their number was to prohibit early marriages altogether. The chief actors in this good work were my friend Behramji Malabári, and another dear friend, Râmabâi, both still alive and hard at work in the good cause. The former was chiefly bent on preventing these premature marriages, the latter on taking care of the victims of that pernicious system. We need not enter here

on purely physiological questions, for here the
answer is always ready that marriage at the early
age of seven or eight can mean no more than
betrothal. That in the East, men and women are
more precocious in their physical development is an
assertion rather than an established fact. But it is
not the body only, it is the mind that has to be
considered, and what can be the mental condition
of a child-wife of seven, nay, even of fourteen?
How such a system ever sprang up, it is difficult
to say. It was not the old Indian system. It may
have originated at the time of the Mohammedan
conquest, married women being supposed to be
more respected by the conquerors than unmarried
girls. At present its fatal effects are but too clear,
in the premature decay of the women, in the weakness of their offspring, and, more particularly, in the
large number of child-widows. No wonder therefore
that a man of Malabâri's patriotism and sense of
duty should have devoted himself body and soul,
and purse too, to the abolition of that evil. Though
there were many to sympathise with him and to
help him, still there was also strong opposition, and
from quarters where one would least have expected
it. Malabâri was a Parsi, and the Hindus did not
like to be lectured by an outsider. If their dirty
linen had to be washed at all, they wished to have
it washed at home by their own washerwomen.
Others, though admitting abuses, gave a most
idyllic picture of the first love of young children,
which extended its blessing over the whole of their

lives, while the European system led to endless
misery, to broken hearts, to divided affections, and
sometimes even to a sundering of ties which in the
eyes of the Hindus can never be sundered.

There have been many strong protests from
numbers of well-conducted families in India who
deny altogether that child-widows, or any widows,
are subject to cruel treatment, and who maintain
that early marriages have by no means all the evil
effects which are charged against them.   There are
exceptions, no doubt, to everything, but I doubt
whether these exceptions can make up for the
mischief caused by the system of early marriages
as still prevalent in India.   And what is there that
can be urged in favour of a system which even
its strongest supporters can only defend as less
monstrous than it appears to be.   We are told[1]
that in Bengal a young husband is able to educate
his young wife.   That sounds very well.   But in
a Hindu family a married child is not supposed
even to see her husband during the daytime, so that
the education, whatever that may mean, could only
take place in the stillness of the night, not the most
propitious time after a day of constant work.   We
are likewise told that a child-wife divides her year
in two halves.   One of them she spends with her
parents, this being a sort of vacation time, and the
other she spends at the house of her husband's
parents, this being confessedly the time of daily
drudgery.   In well-ordered families the young wife is

[1] The Interpreter, Nov. 1898, p. 303.

never allowed to live with her husband permanently
till she has reached her fourteenth year.

This defence, however, does not amount to much,
and though we may quite believe that in good
families the evils of the system of child-marriage
are very much mitigated, the system itself is unnatural, full of dangers, and certainly lowering, both
physically and morally, to the mothers of India.

The most unexpected defender of child-marriages
appeared in Ânandibâi Joshee, a young Hindu lady
who had gone to America to study medicine, and,
after taking her medical degree at the Women's
Medical College of Pennsylvania in 1886, was
appointed Physician-in-charge of the Female Ward
of the Albert-Edward Hospital at Kolhapur, and
died in 1887 at the early age of twenty-two. She
was evidently a most enlightened lady, and a great
friend of Râmabâi. But when she had been asked,
in 1884, to lecture on child-marriages, she surprised
her large American audience by defending the
national custom of early marriage. I am sorry
I have never been able to see her lecture, but it
shows at all events that the abolition of that custom
was not so universally desired as it ought to have
been, and by no means so easy in India as it might
appear to us. We are told that the early betrothal
of boys and girls made their mutual affection more
natural and firm, and added the feelings of brother
and sister to those of husband and wife. It was
fondly hoped that under such circumstances the
idea of anybody else ever taking the place of the

first beloved one would be altogether impossible. Many other arguments were adduced in support of what seemed a national, time-hallowed, and almost sacred custom, but they soon crumbled away at the touch of so well-informed and determined a man as my friend Malabâri. I do not know how many voyages he has made to England to insure sympathy and help. He has spent years in travelling all over India and gaining support for his crusade. He has told us that he is a poor man, but whatever he possessed or gained, he seems to have given up for the main object of his life. I am quite willing to believe that in the better families the evil consequences of premature matrimony are guarded against, just as I cannot altogether withhold my belief from those who declare that in good families child-widows, and in fact all widows, are treated with sympathy and respect. But without denying such exceptions, it was the rule or the custom, such as he knew it to exist, that roused the indignation of Malabâri. He may be congratulated on having lived to see some at least of the fruits of his devoted labours. Assisted by his friends, both native and English, he carried at last a Bill which fixed the respective ages of freedom to marry at eighteen and twelve. This was a decided victory; still the battle is by no means over, and probably never will be till the marriageable age of girls is raised at least to sixteen, and that of boys to twenty. It was twenty-four in Vedic times. That every kind of abuse was heaped on Malabâri need not surprise us;

still his own conscience must tell him that he has done a real service to millions of human beings, and removed from his country a slur that had lowered it in the eyes of all civilised nations. It is highly creditable to him that he declined all rewards and honours offered to him at the end of his successful campaign, and we should not be surprised if we met him again on the old battlefield, anxious to win new victories as the defender of a good cause.

The number of widows in India is simply appalling. According to the census of the year 1881 their number of all ages amounted, at that time, to twenty million nine hundred and thirty thousand six hundred and twenty-six. Of these six hundred and sixty-nine thousand one hundred were under nineteen years of age.

From 15 to 19 years of age 382,736
From 10 to 14 years of age 207,388
Under 9 years of age   78,976
                                     _____
                                     669,100

Even native states have taken up the cause of the unhappy children. Some of the Rajput states some years ago declared against premature marriage, and Mysore has now followed their good example, passing a law not only to prevent child-marriages, but to make it penal for an old man to marry a young girl. I doubt whether such a law would pass even our own Parliament. Clause 3 says :—

"Any person who causes the marriage of a girl who has not completed fourteen years of age, with

a man who has completed fifty years of age, and
any person who knowingly aids and abets, within
the meaning of the Indian Penal Code, such marriage,
shall be punished with simple imprisonment for a
term which may extend to six months, or with fine,
or with both."

The Madras Presidency will now have to follow
the example of Mysore, instead of taking the lead,
as it ought to have done. In a Memorandum accompanying the Bill for the Madras Presidency, it is
stated that in 1882 there were 157,466 girls married
under the age of nine, and that there were 5,621
widows under the same age. Think of widows
under nine years of age!

In the census of 1891 it was shown that there
were 23,938 girls married in their fourth year and
under, and 142,606 between five and nine years
of age, giving a total of 166,544 girls married under
nine years of age. There were 988 widows of four
years and under, and 4,147 between five and nine
years, making a total of 5,135. In future, however,
the law is never to recognise any widows under
nine years of age, and there is every hope that the
number of these baby-widows will be considerably
reduced as soon as no girl can be betrothed till
she has reached, at least, the age of eight; the
bridegroom being, as a rule, five or six years older.
This is, of course, much too low an age, but it was
considered the least likely to rouse opposition among
the native population, as some of the law-books of
the Hindus are in favour of that age, while they

actually threaten parents who do not marry their daughter before ten with the hell called Raurava. The greatest living legal authorities in India have declared in favour of a limit of age, fixing it at eight for girls. As their support gives immense strength to the aspirations of the reform party, its leaders have accepted it for the present. Men like Malabâri are of course not satisfied, yet they may be proud to have achieved what they have achieved. They have at all events reduced the number of possible child-widows, by limiting the marriageable age of girls to eight. Much more, however, remains to be done, and Malabâri is not the man to let sleeping dogs lie. He wields a powerful pen in English, and he is the best living writer of Guzerathi. He began life as a Guzerathi poet, but he gave up poetry and everything else to concentrate all his energy on his crusade. He has written several very successful English books, the last being "The Indian Eye on English Life." He is the editor of an influential paper at Bombay, *The Indian Spectator*. He has also undertaken to spread my Hibbert Lectures "On the Origin and Growth of Religion" all over India, by having them translated into Sanskrit and every one of the modern languages of the country. This undertaking also he has carried through successfully, without flinching from considerable trouble and pecuniary risk. All these undertakings require money, and in the present state of things a willingness to spend money is a very good, if not the best, test of a man's sincerity.

Malabâri has stood that test for many years, and
much as he longs for rest, I learn that he is not
likely to stand by with folded arms, and to leave
the fight to others [1].

Râmabâi.

If we admire the boldness and perseverance of
Malabâri, we cannot withhold the same admiration
from a young Indian lady who, though she could
not hope to prevent child-marriages, has done her
very best to ameliorate the lot of the victims of
those unnatural unions.

To be a widow at all is hard enough, but nothing
can be more miserable than the lot of a young
widow in India, whose life may be said to be over
before it has begun.   Widows are looked upon in
their own homes as beings of evil omen, as having
deserved their misfortune by some unknown mis-
deeds in this or, what is worse, in a former life,
and, particularly if childless, they are treated no
better than servants, whether in the house of their
parents-in-law, or even in the house of their real
parents, if they are allowed to return there.   They
are shunned, excluded from all amusements, obliged
to wear coarse garments, deprived of their ornaments, and often condemned to have their heads
shaved, a great indignity in the eyes of every
woman.   What a life to look forward to for a girl,
often, it may be, not yet sixteen years old!   No
wonder that they should often commit suicide, or

[1] See an excellent account of his life by Karkaria.

fall still lower by being driven to lead an immoral life. It is to ameliorate the lot of these unhappy creatures that Râmabâi has been working for years, chiefly at Poonah. She is certainly a most courageous woman, not to be turned away from her purpose by any misfortunes or any threats.

I saw much of her when she stayed with us at Oxford, but the most eventful part of her career belonged to an earlier period. With what she told me then, and what has been published since by Mrs. R. L. Bodley in the Introduction to Râmabâi's account of the "Life of a High-Caste Hindu Woman" (Philadelphia, 1887), we begin to understand the high aims of this truly heroic Hindu lady, in appearance small, delicate, and timid, but in reality strong and bold as a lioness. Her life, so far as we know it from herself and from others, draws away the veil behind which so much that is really of the deepest interest to us, is hidden in the East. Here we see first of all from her own case how carelessly marriages are often arranged in India. Râmabâi's grandfather, who belonged to an old and very illustrious Brâhmanic family, the Kauthumas, was on a religious pilgrimage with his family, that is, his wife and two daughters, one nine, the other seven years of age. One morning, when bathing in the Godâvarî, he saw a fine-looking man in the river, and after inquiring for his caste, his clan, and his home, and finding out that he was a widower, he offered him his eldest daughter, that is, a child of nine, in marriage. All things

being satisfactorily settled in a few hours, the
marriage took place the next day, and the stranger
started with his child-wife for his home, nearly nine
hundred miles away from the child's own home,
while the father continued his pilgrimage, unconcerned any longer about the fate of his daughter.
However, the marriage, though we might call it
hasty and imprudent, turned out well, and her
husband, who was a great Sanskrit scholar, a pupil
of Râmachandra *S*àstri, not only was kind to his
little wife, but was most anxious to teach her the
sacred language. This was a very unusual measure,
in fact, it was against the Brâhmanic law. It seems
that he had made the same experiment with his
first wife, but that it had failed owing to the opposition of her family. When therefore he was met
by a similar opposition in the case of his second
wife, he suddenly left his home and his friends,
and journeyed with his young wife to the forest
of Gungamul, on a remote plateau of the Western
Ghauts, and there founded his new home, where
the world could no longer hinder or trouble him.
Such things are possible in India only, and even
there they are of rare occurrence. Râmabâi was
told by her mother how she and her husband spent
the first night after their flight from home in the
open air without shelter of any kind, she rolled up
in her pasodi or cotton quilt, he watching by her
side. Wild animals were heard howling all around
them, and the young wife lay convulsed with terror ;
and no wonder she did, though her husband kept

watch till daybreak, frightening the wild animals
away as best he could from his bride and his new
home. However, there, in the forest, husband and
wife, like another Yâg*ñ*avalkya and Maitreyî, remained, and there the husband began to teach his
wife Sanskrit. A rude hut was soon constructed,
such as suffices in a forest and in the climate of
India. The wife grew in stature and in knowledge,
and soon became the mother of three children born
in this wilderness, one son and two daughters. As
they grew up the father at once began the instruction of his son and his elder daughter. Soon the
fame of his scholarship began to attract other
students from the neighbourhood, and the hermitage, situated as it was near the source of one of the
rivers, became a place of pilgrimage, and attracted
many visitors.

When the younger daughter, our Râmabâi, grew
up, the father was getting too old and too weary to
teach her also, so that her education fell chiefly
to the share of her mother, Lakshmâbâi.

Soon the household grew, partly by the arrival
of the aged father and mother-in-law, who had to
be taken care of, partly by the arrival of many
pilgrims, who in India have a right to hospitable
entertainment. At last the expenses grew too high,
the little hermitage had to be broken up, and father
and children had to begin a new life, that of a
pilgrim family without any home, wandering about
from place to place, tramping, in fact, as we should
say, and earning a small livelihood by recitations,

whether in palaces or monasteries. When Râmabâi began her career as a prodigy of learning, she had learned ever so many Sanskrit texts by heart, either from her mother or from listening unknown, as she told me, to the lessons given by her father to her brother. Erudition in India means learning by heart. A pupil learns a number of verses every day and repeats them the next day, constantly adding new lines, till at last he can repeat thousands of lines without a hitch. Râmabâi listened at the door while her brother and other students repeated their daily lessons, and in this way she learnt in the end to repeat more lines than most young Brâhmans. For this she received rewards while travelling on foot from place to place with her father, mother, and brother. The elder sister had been married, though not very happily, it would seem, while Râmabâi gladly remained unmarried long after the statutable age. This was really considered as a breach of the law, but as long as her parents were alive she had a recognised support in them. When, however, the father died, and very soon after the mother also, her position became almost desperate. She still had her brother, who then became her natural guardian and protector ; but the whole of the small family property had been spent. There was not even enough left to pay a few Brâhmans for carrying the remains of her mother to the burning-ghat, about three miles distant. At last two Brâh-mans were found who took pity on the bereaved children, and with their assistance son and daughter carried the sacred burden to the place of cremation. Poor Râmabâi's low stature compelled her to carry her share of the dear burden on her head. We can hardly imagine such a state of things, and such suffering; yet what seems to us incredible comes from Râmabâi's own mouth, and, from what I know of her, she may be implicitly trusted. When I once asked her how she knew that she belonged to the famous Brâhmanic clan of the Kauthumas, she replied very simply, "But who would ever doubt it?" And the same remark applies to all that she has told us of the sufferings of her life.

These sufferings were not over yet. She had now no one to look to but her brother, and without some male support the life of a single woman is ·simply impossible in India. For some years brother and sister travelled together on foot all over India, earning what they wanted for their support by their recitations of Sanskrit texts, and afterwards by lecturing on the degraded position of women in India. Arrived in Calcutta Râmabâi's lectures excited great interest. But now followed a new blow. Her brother died, and from sheer necessity she had to take a husband. The marriage turned out perfectly happy, but after nineteen months of quiet married life there followed a new blow. Her husband died, and she was left a widow with one daughter, whom she called Manoramâ, or Heart's Joy.

Her case seemed desperate indeed, but she was upheld by her strong desire to fit herself for useful work among her own countrywomen. Helpless as she was, she resolved to go to England in order to study medicine. This was a bold decision, and required more moral courage than Napoleon's march to Russia.

Member of a high-caste Brâhman family though she was, the mere prejudice against crossing the black water would hardly have affected her, but she was very poor. All she possessed was a small sum of money which she had earned by her lectures and by translations done for Government, and how was she to pay for her passage and to support herself, her child, and a friend who was to accompany her to England? But undeterred by any fears she started with her little daughter and a female friend, and when she arrived in England, almost destitute, she fortunately found shelter for a time with the Sisterhood at Wantage, some members of which she had known at Poonah. But even then her tragedy was not yet ended. She had declared to the Sisters that, grateful as she felt for their kindness, she would never become a Christian, because, as she often said, a good Brâhmani is quite as good as a good Christian. Her friend, however, was frightened by the idea that she and Râmabâi would be made Christians by force; and to save Râmabâi and herself from such a fate, she tried one night to strangle her. Failing in that, she killed herself. It was after this terrible catastrophe at Wantage that Râmabâi came to stay with us at Oxford, and such was her nervous prostration that we had to give her a maidservant to sleep every night in the same room with her. Nor

was this all. After all arrangements had been made
to enable her to attend medical lectures at Oxford,
her hearing became suddenly so much affected that
she had to give up all idea of a medical career.
She then determined to study nursing, and thus fit
herself for useful work in India. Then came an
invitation from America to be present at the con-
ferring of a medical degree on her countrywoman,
Ânandibâi Joshee, of whom I spoke before, and
being once there, she soon succeeded in gaining
many friends, who helped her to start a refuge or
Âsrama for child-widows in India. This is the work
to which at last she has devoted herself, and with
great success, her only difficulty being that in the
meantime she had, after all, become a Christian and
joined her Christian friends; not that she considered
her former religion false or mischievous, but because,
as she told me, she could no longer stand quite
alone, she wanted to belong to somebody, and particularly to be able to worship together with those
whom she loved and who had been so kind to her.
Her having become a Christian has, no doubt,
proved a serious obstacle to her success in her
chosen sphere of usefulness in India. Though we
may trust her that she never made an attempt at
proselytising among the little widows committed to
her care, yet how could it be otherwise than that
those to whom the world had been so unkind, and
Râmabâi so kind, should wish to be what their
friend was, Christian! Her goodness was the real
proselytising power that could not be hidden; but

she lost, of course, the support of her native friends, and has even now to fight her battles alone, in order to secure the pecuniary assistance necessary for the support of her little army of child-widows. She is, indeed, a noble and unselfish woman, and deserves every help which those who sympathise with her objects, can afford to give her.

Ânandibâi Joshee, M.D.

There is another Hindu lady to whom I alluded before as a friend of Râmabâi's, who in fact invited Râmabâi to come to the United States to be present at her taking her degree of M.D. in the Medical College of Pennsylvania, and who thus determined, to a great extent, the future course of Râmabâi's life. She too must have been a young heroine, and it is well that her name should not be forgotten on the roll of martyrs, who have lived, worked, and died in the cause of elevating and regenerating their country. I draw my information chiefly from a sympathetic article, signed Isabel M. Sullivan, in the *Indian Social Reformer*, July 10, 1898. Ânandibâi was different from Râmabâi in one respect. Though free from many prejudices, she remained a true Brâhmanî through life. She fearlessly stood by Râmabâi after her husband's death, and even offered her the shelter of her home. She remained her faithful friend to the end, which took place in 1887, when she was only twenty-two years of age. Though she could not bring herself to go quite so far as Râmabâi in giving up the religion of her childhood, her enthusiasm took another, yet very perilous form. She had seen the untold physical sufferings of girls and women in India, who are almost entirely left to the medical care of uneducated *femmes sages* and inefficient nurses. But for a young girl of eighteen, brought up in the narrowly guarded sphere of an Indian home, to dream of leaving her country, to travel to America, and enter as a medical student at an American University required such an amount of moral courage as we should never have expected from a young and timid Hindu lady who could know little of the world outside her Zenânah, and had probably never spoken to a man except her husband and members of her own family. She was married already, when she conceived her plan of going to America, and such was her strength of character that she succeeded in persuading her husband to accompany her in her voyage of discovery, and to support her in her endeavour to preserve her caste while living abroad. " I will go to America as a Hindu," she said, " and come back and live among my people as a Hindu." And she carried out her resolve in spite of endless difficulties. Yes, she had been married in 1874, at the age of nine. We can hardly believe in such marriages, yet they exist, and in her case this early, nay premature marriage proved certainly most successful. No wonder therefore that, when she was asked to speak about child-marriages before an American audience, she should have stood up for them, even in the presence of her friend Râmabâi, treating them, of course, as what they really are, betrothals, but betrothals binding for life. Accompanied by her husband, Gopalrao Vinayak Joshee, she arrived in the United States, being really the first Brâhman lady who had ever set foot in New York. From thence she went to Philadelphia, where her arrival is described to us by her friend, Dr. Rachel Bodley. " One day in September, 1883," she writes, "there came to my door a little lady in a blue cotton saree, accompanied by her faithful friend, Mrs. B. F. Carpenter of New Jersey, and since that hour, when, speechless for very wonder, I bestowed a kiss of welcome upon the stranger's cheek instead of words, I have loved the women of India. The little lady was Mrs. Ânandibâi Joshee, who had come to study medicine in the Medical College of Pennsylvania." Dr. Bodley proved a true friend in need to the lonely stranger. She tells us that " though from the first Ânandibâi had received a cordial welcome in America, it must have been with some heartsinking that she settled down alone in her college rooms, confronted by the anthracite coal stove, which was the only means of cooking her food, and which she did not know how to manage. She tried faithfully to prosecute her studies, and at the same time keep caste-rules and cook her own food, but the anthracite coal stove in her room was a constant vexation and likewise a source of danger, and the solitude of the individual house-keeping was overwhelming. After a trial of two weeks her health declined to such an alarming extent that I invited

her to pay a short visit to my home, and she never
left it again to dwell elsewhere in Philadelphia during
her student-residence. In the performance of College
duties, going in and out, up and down, always in her
measured, quiet, dignified, patient way, she has filled
every room with memories which now hallow the
home and must continue to do so throughout the
years to come." Ânandibâi's faculties developed
rapidly under Western opportunities, her scientific
acquirements placed her high in rank among her
peers in College, and on March 11, 1886, she took
her medical degree, being the first Hindu woman
to receive the Degree of Doctor of Medicine in any
country. On June 1, 1886, she was appointed to
the position of Physician-in-Charge of the Female
Ward of the Albert Edward Hospital at Kolhapur,
and on October 9 she sailed from New York to
assume the duties of her new official position. But,
alas, the strain of the last three years in a foreign
land had undermined her constitution, perchance the
cold of the American winters had attacked lungs
inured to naught but tropical heat, and when she
landed in Bombay it was found that she was in an
advanced stage of consumption. She had come
home to die, and, after spending three years in the
study of medicine, she must have known very well
the fate that awaited her. After these three years
of voluntary exile, she found herself once more in
the familiar places of her childhood, at Poonah, surrounded by her mother and sisters, and it was her
mother's sad privilege to support her daughter in

her arms when at midnight the end came quickly. This occurred on February 26, 1887, in the home in which she was born.

All this is unspeakably sad. So much silent heroism, so many sacrifices patiently borne for years, and then at the end resignation, and farewell! Mrs. Bodley, who has been such a motherly friend both to Ânandibâi and Râmabâi, and to whom we owe most of what we have been allowed to know of Ânandibâi's last years, when receiving the photograph of her protégée taken on her deathbed, writes: " The pathos of that lifeless form is indescribable. The last of several pictures taken during the brief public career of the little reformer, it is the most eloquent of them all. The mute lips, and the face wan and wasted and prematurely aged in the fierce battle with sorrow and pain alike convey to her American friends this message, not to be forgotten : ' I have done what I could.' "

If we consider all the impediments that barred the way of a young Indian lady when conceiving the plan of studying medicine in a foreign country, we are amazed at Ânandibâi's courage and perseverance, and we shall hesitate before we declare that Hindu women cannot be worthy peers of English women. Our own lady doctors, who have cut their way through the compact phalanx of prejudice and jealousy, can best judge of the heroism of their unknown Hindu colleague, whose name ought to hold its place on the roll of those who have fallen in a noble fight, and whose very death marks a

victory. Though she had so painfully striven to
preserve her caste in a foreign land, it seemed
doubtful at first whether the Brâhmans of Poonah
would receive her as pure, after her long sojourn
among unbelievers. But humanity proved too strong
even for caste. Men and women, old and young,
orthodox and unorthodox, all received the young
doctor with open arms, paid her friendly visits, and
extended to her a most cordial welcome. Her own
friends were astonished at the unprecedented concession made in her favour by the strictly orthodox
party. And when the end came the whole of Poonah
seemed to share in the mourning of the family, and
the fear that the priests might raise objections to
cremating her body according to the sacred rites
of the Hindus, proved perfectly groundless. Not
only on the occasion of her funeral, but earlier,
when her husband offered sacrifices to the gods and
the guardian planets to avert their anger and her
death, the priests showed no sign of any prejudice
against him or her. This, too, is a victory, for it
shows that even the most inveterate social and
religious diseases are not incurable when treated
with unselfish love and generosity. If all this could
be achieved by a frail young daughter of India,
what is there that could be called impossible for
the strong men of that country? Even now her
example has been followed, and Ânandibâi's life has
not been in vain.

National Character of the Hindus.

No wonder that those who look upon the Indian nation as an inferior race should have so often protested against my judgment of them as prejudiced and as far too favourable. I know quite well that the men and women of whom I have here spoken are exceptional beings. They would be exceptional in England also, and anywhere else. But exceptions, after all, represent possibilities, and the good work achieved by such men as Rammohun Roy, Keshub Chunder Sen, and Malabâri, or by Râmabâi, shows how much of real power lies dormant in the people of India. If it is always wise in judging of people to look more to their strong than to their weak points; why should we, in trying to determine the average intellectual and moral stature of the Hindus, take account of their dwarfs rather than of their giants? Is it right, for instance, to say that all Indians are liars? It is a very hackneyed charge, but it is never forgotten, and it often crops up again when least expected. Because culprits before an Indian judge and witnesses before a jury, nay, even cooks and butlers in Anglo-Indian homes, have occasionally, or even frequently, told lies, does it follow that all Indians are liars? It is unfortunate that so many who have spent their lives as civil servants or officers in India should represent the few hundreds or the few thousands of people with whom they have been brought into contact at Calcutta, Benares, Bombay, or Madras as fair specimens of the people

of India at large. It should never be forgotten that
the true home of the Indians is in their villages,
and that those who go to Calcutta or other great
towns to take service in English families are by no
means the best specimens of the Indian population.
They are willing to submit for some time to the
unkind treatment which they not seldom receive
from men, women, and children of alien origin ; but
they can but seldom feel any real attachment or
even respect for their employers, though here, too,
there are most honourable exceptions. From the
earliest times truthfulness has always been mentioned as a national characteristic of the inhabitants
of India, and we are now told that all Indians are
liars ! We cannot open any of the ancient law-books
or epic poems without coming across such sentences
as " Truth is the ladder to heaven and the ship
across the ocean"; "The end of all the Vedas is
Truth "; " Seeking after all the virtues, I have
nowhere found anything so purifying as Truth." We
appeal to the literatures of other nations as records
of their true character, why not in the case of the
Hindus ? It is easy to say that all this is changed
now, and that those who have been magistrates and
judges in India ought to know best.   But do these
judges consider the peculiar difficulties with which
the lower classes in India have to contend, being ruled
by men of a different colour, of a different language,
and a different religion ? Would they expect or find
much regard for truth even in an English sailor if
examined by a French, ay, even by an English

judge ? It is easy to be truthful if you have nothing
to fear, but we must not wonder if, to escape an
oath or a kick, a native servant will now and then
tell a lie to his master.   Anyhow, one case, a hundred, nay, a thousand cases are not sufficient to
condemn a whole nation of more than two hundred
millions.   It has been my rule through life never
to accept any of these sweeping assertions about a
whole nation.   If I hear a man calling all Indians liars,
I generally ask how many he has known, and I do
the same when I hear all Frenchmen called monkeys,
all Italians assassins, all Germans unwashed, all
Russians savages, or even England *Perfide Albion*.
I have never in all my life repented having had
eyes for the bright side rather than the dark side
of nations as well as of individuals.   I hoped I had
exposed the fallacy and folly of such undiscriminating
accusations in the Lectures which I gave at Cambridge, to the candidates for the Indian Civil Service,
Lect. 2, "On the Truthful Character of the Hindus."
But no, the old charge is brought up again and
again.   That some members of the Indian Civil
Service who had for years to deal with native
servants and tradesmen should have had some
painful experiences, who can doubt ?   Even within
the small circle of my own personal acquaintances
I have met with Indians who disregarded the old
commandment of telling the truth; but to generalise
in such matters, from a limited number of instances,
is surely against all the rules of inductive logic.
This prejudice against the inhabitants of India as

being a nation of liars may become really dangerous in its consequences. Even now, as the press is open to the ruled as well as to the rulers of India, the charge of ingrained untruthfulness has been hurled back most savagely by the accused on the accusers. It always is so, and there is in the end but one remedy, even when an inclination towards untruthfulness does exist, and that is trust. I have no doubt that I shall be much abused again for having ventured to say so much, and to stand up for the people of India, and particularly for having produced evidence in support of my opinion, taken from their literature, ancient and modern, from their sacred books, their law-books, and their plilosophical systems. Such evidence is admitted when we judge of any other nation; why should it be ruled out of court in the case of the people of India ?

Missionaries seem to imagine that they have a better chance of spreading their own religion by vilifying the popular religion of India, and trying to show that all the vices of the people are due to it. King Asoka, in the third century B.C., knew better, when he had his edicts engraved all over his kingdom, and declared "that people should never praise their own religion or disparage other religions without a cause ; and that whenever there is a cause, our words should be moderate." Our own missionaries might safely take these words to heart. At all events, no virtue stands higher in the eyes of the founders of the Indian religion than truthfulness, and if religion has any influence in forming the character of a whole nation, no nation should be more truthful than that of India.

I am far from being an indiscriminate admirer of India, and, if I am told that I exaggerate the good qualities of the people, I am quite willing to confess that even among the small number of young men who are now sent every year from India to England, and particularly to Oxford, I have myself had some disappointing experiences. Want of straightforwardness arising from want of moral courage, want of truthfulness arising from a desire to please, hollow pretence amounting in some cases to actual deception, all these I have witnessed among the young men who now come to spend two or three years at Oxford. But may we not look upon these defects as clouds that will pass? And are there never any cases of untruthfulness when there has been a disturbance in college, or when an election has to be carried, *coûte qu'il coûte*. The worst of it is that those who complain of untruthfulness in others, cannot help posing as patterns of truthfulness themselves.

I may mention some curious cases. A young Bengali told me that he came all the way from Benares to Oxford, because he had been told by his friends who had contributed money towards the founding of an Indian Institute there, that he would be received there and enabled to attend lectures in the University. How he had paid his passage money I cannot understand, but I believe the poor boy was actually starving when he came to me, and he was in despair, when I had to tell him that there was no such institution at Oxford, and no scholarships open to him as he had been led to imagine. He told me that he had been to the Indian Institute, but could get no help. He told me that he saw no students or teachers there, but only stuffed animals. "My friends in India," he said, "have been asked to subscribe money for the benefit of Indian students at Oxford, but no one would even speak to me or help me there. If one of your students," he added, "came to Benares, our Pandits would receive him with open arms, teach him all they know, and gladly give him food and lodging." "Yes," I said, "but the laws of Manu do not apply to England." I gave him the little he wanted, but what became of him afterwards I cannot tell, nor how he found the means of returning to his own country. I confess I was at first a little suspicious, but, after all, his story may have been true, and what then?

The manners of the young Indians when they arrive at Oxford are generally excellent, but they soon acquire what they consider English manners, rough and ready, bluff and blunt, and by no means an improvement on their own. The same young man who at first enters your room with folded hands and a graceful salâm, will after a very short time walk in, sit down, stretch out his legs, and address you in the most familiar terms. They imagine that this is English. Some profess to know Sanskrit, and pour out a stream of words which at school they may have learnt by heart, but often with an utter disregard of case and gender. Some who had failed, as we afterwards were informed by the authorities, to even pass their matriculation examination in Sanskrit at the Calcutta University, posed as Pandits at Oxford, expressing at the same time their undisguised contempt for all who professed to know and to teach Sanskrit in the Universities of England. These men have a very curious way of blushing. If you convict them of a downright falsehood, their bright brown colour turns suddenly greyish, but their eloquence in defending themselves never fades or flags.

Altogether the experiment of sending young Hindus to prepare for the Civil Service Examination in England has not, as far as I have been able to judge, proved a great success. At Oxford they find it very hard to make friends among the better class of undergraduates. Most of our undergraduates come from public schools, and have plenty of friends of their own. If they are asked to be kind to any of the Indian students, all they can do, or really be expected to do, is to invite them once or twice to a breakfast party. They have hardly any interests in common with them, and anything like friendship is out of the question. If the young students from India have money to spend, there is danger of their falling into bad company, and even if they pass their examinations, I am afraid that some of them return to India not much improved by their English exile. The worst of it is that they often return désillusionné. At first everything English is grand and perfect in their eyes, an Oxford degree is the highest goal of their ambition. But when they have

obtained it, chiefly by learning by heart, they make
very light of it. And this making light of it is soon
applied to other things English also, which they
hear constantly criticised or abused, particularly in
the newspapers and in Parliament, so that they
often leave England better informed, it may be, but
hardly better affected towards the Government
which they are meant to serve. The present state
of things is certainly discouraging, particularly as it
seems impossible to suggest any real remedy. But
here also there are bright exceptions, and I have
always held that we must judge of things by their
bright rather than by their dark sides. There are,
and there always will be, difficulties in the intercourse between Europeans and Orientals. It is
wonderful to see how well they have been overcome
in the Government of India. Natives in the Civil
Service or at the Bar seem to work quite harmoni-
ously with their English colleagues, and even after
they have reached high employment, and have to
exercise authority, little has been heard of conflicts,
whether caused by arrogance or subserviency. There
are Continental statesmen who, while they cannot
help admiring the English system of governing
India, look upon it as suicidal in the end. They
consider the Russian system of complete repression
as the only right system of dealing with Orientals,
and as far more merciful in the end. Well, we must
wait for the end; but, whatever it may be, it seems
right to treat the inhabitants of India as they have
been hitherto treated by the Government and by the

wisest rulers of India, not as born enemies or as conspirators to be kept under by force, but as loyal subjects to be trusted. Of course, there sometimes will be troubles, for how can it be expected that in two or three hundred millions of conquered subjects there should be no grumbling, no disaffection, no fanaticism? The government of India by a mere handful of Englishmen is, indeed, an achievement unparalleled in the whole history of the world. The suppression of the Indian mutiny shows what stuff English soldiers and statesmen are made of. If people say that ours is not an age for Epic poetry, let them read Lord Roberts' " Forty-one Years in India." When I see in a circus a man standing with out-stretched legs on two or three horses, and two men standing on his shoulders, and other men standing on theirs, and a little child at the top of all, while the horses are running full gallop round the arena, I feel what I feel when watching the government of India. One hardly dares to breathe, and one wishes one could persuade one's neighbours also to sit still and hold their breath. If ever there were an accident, the crash would be fearful, and who would suffer most? Fortunately, by this time the people of India know all this, and they have learnt to appreciate what they owe not only to the *Pax*, but to the *Lux Britannica*. If one could dare to read the mind of three hundred millions, I should say that in the present state of things the people of India, as a whole, want no change except such changes as can be achieved by ordinary constitutional means. It is true that I have not known a large number of Indians, but I have known Indians who could well speak in the name of large numbers, and they speak to me more openly perhaps than to others, looking upon me as a kind of Mle*kkh*a, but at the same time as half an Indian. Some young Indian Râjahs while travelling in Switzerland, found themselves lately in the same railway carriage with some Russian princes and noblemen. They had been discussing among themselves some of their grievances in English, and the Russians, who of course understood English, after listening to them for some time, became very communicative, and began to explain to them the beneficent rule of the Tsar. They even went so far as to hold out a hope to them of an Indian Parliament, as soon as the Russians were settled in Calcutta. On parting they asked the Indian princes, " When shall we see you at St. Petersburg ? " And they were not a little taken aback when the strangers bowed and smiled, and said, "We are going just now to be present at the opening of Parliament in London. We should like very much to see St. Petersburg afterwards, and to be present at the opening of your Parliament there. . . ."

Again and again have I been urged to go to India, and have been told many a time by people who had spent a few months there that I could never hope to know the Indians, to understand Indian literature, or even pronounce Sanskrit properly without having passed a vacation at Calcutta or

Bombay. I would have given anything to go to India when I was young. There was a time when I was on the point of becoming a missionary in order to be able to spend some years in India. But what a strange missionary I should have made! What I cared to know in India were not the Râjahs and Mahârâjahs, the streets of Bombay, the towers of silence, or the temples of Ellora. What I cared to see were the few remaining Srotriyas who still knew their Vedas by heart, who would have talked to me and shaken hands with me, even though I was a Mlekkha. Had they not asked me even at a distance to act as one of the sixteen priests at their Shrâddhs (Srâddhas), their funeral services? Had they not asked me to recite Vedic prayers for the souls of their deceased fathers? Had they not actually sent me the same presents which on those occasions they are bound to give to their priests, because, as they wrote, I knew the Veda better than their own priests? Had they not actually sent me the sacred Brâhmanic thread which I am as proud to wear as any more brilliant decoration?

Here is a letter which I received some years ago beautifully printed in gold :—

"RESPECTED SIR,—On the occasion of my departed father's Shrâddh ceremony, which was celebrated some months ago, amongst the offerings to Adhyâ-paks and Âchâryas (teachers), an offering was made to you in consideration of your eminent services to the laws of Sanskrit literature (sic). I am a believer in the New Dispensation of the Brahmo-Somâj of

India, which teaches reverence to the great and good men of all lands and religions. I trust you will kindly accept the piece of shawl sent in separate parcels, and pronounce your blessing both for me and for the spirit of my honoured father in heaven."

Was it very wrong or sacrilegious that I did so? I extract a few sentences from the letter I wrote in reply :—

" I deeply sympathise with your Shrâddh ceremony; nay, I wish we had something like it in our own religion. To keep alive the memory of our parents, to feel their presence during the great trials of our life, to be influenced by what we know they would have wished us to do, and to try to honour their name by showing ourselves not unworthy bearers of it, that is a Shrâddh ceremony in which we can all partake, nay, ought to partake, whatever our religion may be. There is a real, though unseen bond of union (tantu) that connects us through our parents and ancestors with the Great Author of all things, and the same bond will connect ourselves through our children with the most distant generations. If we know that, and are constantly reminded of it by ceremonies like that of your Shrâddh, we are not likely to forget the responsibility that rests on every one of us. In that sense your Shrâddh is a blessing, on your parents because on yourselves, and whatever the future of your religion may be in India, I hope this communion with the spirits of your ancestors, or Pitris, will always form an essential part of it."

Two or three years in India would certainly have been a delight to me, but short of that I did not care to go. I was quite satisfied with that ideal India which I had built up for myself, whether from their books or from those who had come to see me at Oxford. If my India, as I am often told, is an ideal India, is it more so than Greece as seen through the poems of Homer, or Italy as seen through the verses of Virgil ? What is ideal is not necessarily unreal, it is only like a landscape seen in sunshine. Look at a landscape on a brilliant summer's day bathed in light and verdure, and again on a bleak day of March with its bitter winds and cloudy sky. It is the same landscape, but which of the two is its true aspect ? I shall not speak here of ancient Indian poets, of ancient Indian philosophers, or of ancient Indian heroes. What I feel, and what I wish my friends would feel with me, is that a country which, even in these unheroic days, could produce a Rammohun Roy, a Keshub Chunder Sen, a Malabâri, and a Râmabâi, is not a decadent country, but may look forward to a bright, sunny future, as it can look back with satisfaction and even pride on four thousand years of a not inglorious history.

I have never bestowed excessive praise on Indian literature, nor do I feel answerable for having filled the brains of native scholars with exaggerated ideas about its value. Its value to us is great, but chiefly from a historical point of view, and this is just what native scholars find it so difficult to understand.

No wonder that after Goethe had bestowed such superlative praise on the Sanskrit play of " Sakuntalâ," the Hindus should have spoken of their Kâlidâsa as the equal of Shakespeare. They forget that what surprised Goethe was not only the beauty of Kâlidâsa's poetry, great as it is, but its antiquity, and the fact that such refined poetry should have existed where it was least expected, and at a time when it could not have been matched by the poetry of any other country.

Indian Theosophy.

Empty panegyrics are always to be deprecated, and I am afraid that great and lasting mischief has been wrought, for instance, by Madame Blavatsky and her friends who went to India, ignorant of Sanskrit and Sanskrit literature, and who have for years been proclaiming to the world at large that Hindu philosophy, particularly that of the Vedânta and that of Buddhism, which they did not always distinguish very carefully one from the other, was infinitely superior to all the philosophies of Europe, that the Brâhmans even at the present day were the depositaries of the primeval wisdom of the world, and that by the united efforts of Madame Blavatsky and Dayânanda Sarasvatî a new theosophy would dawn on India and Europe which would eclipse all former systems of thought. Poor Dayânanda Sarasvatî had no idea of what Madame Blavatsky was thinking of; but, though bewildered for a time by the unaccustomed adulation poured on

him and the extravagant veneration paid to him by
Europeans, he soon recovered, and declined to have
anything to do with the Polish prophetess and her
vagaries.

Mme. Blavatsky might certainly have done a good
work if she had joined some really learned Pandits,
familiar with the six systems of Hindu philosophy;
nor would it have been too much for a person
endowed with such extraordinary, if not miraculous,
powers as she was said to have possessed, to have
mastered the grammar of Sanskrit. But what has
been the result of all her labours? Indian philosophy has gained some Corybantic followers, but
the true teaching of Bâdarâyana and Kapila has
been obscured rather than illuminated by being
mixed up with poor and contemptible conjuring
tricks. New prejudices have been roused against
the noble philosophies of Vedânta, Sâmkhya, and
Yoga which it will take many years to remove.
Why not take the authoritative texts of these
systems, many of which have been translated into
English and German, and place their essential
doctrines in a clear and intelligible form before
the philosophic public of Europe? There is no
mystery about that philosophy, or about the Mahâtmans who are versed in it. There is nothing esoteric
in their teaching; all is open to those who are
properly qualified and trustworthy. Their Upanishads and Darsanas can be studied exactly like the
philosophies of Plato or Des Cartes—nay, even better,
because every one of their tenets has been put down

in their Sûtras very clearly and definitely by Indian philosophers far more so than by Plato or Hegel. It is difficult, therefore, not to get angry if one sees the elevated views of these ancient philosophers dragged down to the level of cloudy hallucinations, and rendered absurd by being mixed up with vulgar trickeries. "Corruptio optimi pessima."

I have often been blamed for the hard judgments which I have pronounced against Madame Blavatsky and her friends. I have been told that she and her friends have done good by rousing a new interest in their ancient philosophy among the people of India, and by attracting the attention of European thinkers towards it. If that is so, let it be to their credit; but I feel convinced that no good has ever come from anything that is not perfectly honest and straightforward; and what a lurid light has been thrown on the Theosophist Society at Adyar! There is no excuse for such things, however good the intention may have been, and even now, when I see wellintentioned men like Vivekânanda preaching the doctrines of the Upanishads, of Bâdarâyana and Samkara in America, and gaining, as I read, numerous converts, I still seem to perceive now and then something of the old Blavatsky leaven that has not yet been entirely thrown off. Vedântism requires no bush, no trappings, no tricks. What we want is a historical and critical treatment, just the same as that which has been applied to Plato and Aristotle.

When I saw hundreds of people running after Madame Blavatsky and her apostles, and the texts

and the excellent translations of the philosophical
Sûtras hardly looked at, an old Oriental story often
came into my mind. The story is a mere illustration,
a D*r*ish/ânta, but it is full of truth.

" A certain man had the peculiar power of grunting exactly like a pig, so much so that whenever
he grunted where pigs were grazing they would all
turn round to see if any new member had come into
their fold. This man's fame spread abroad, and he
began a tour to obtain money by means of his art.
Wherever he went he erected a pandal, and issued
tickets for admission, all of which got exhausted
very soon, such was the eagerness of people to hear
him grunt. While he was thus making money in
a village a sage happened to pass by with his
disciples, and it struck him that he could teach
a good lesson to them through this incident.
Accordingly he ordered a small pandal to be
erected, and advertised that even better grunting
would be heard here than in the other pandal, and
that free of cost. The people were naturally very
eager to hear it, and they visited it. The sage
brought a real pig before them, and squeezing it
a little, made it grunt. Really the grunt was much
better than the man's, but the people exclaimed,
' Pooh, is this all ? We hear this every day, but
what is there in it ? It is nothing wonderful,' and
went away. The sage said, ' Here is a splendid
lesson for us. We seldom care for reality, but
always go in for imitation.' That is why even this
world exists, which is a mere imitation, a reflection

in the distorting mirror of Mâyâ, of the great Âtman. No external help is required to see the Self,
but very few care for it, and, even if you eagerly
advertise it, none will go to you except those who
love truth for truth's sake. Reflect on this."

This story is a mere parable, and, as such, cannot
possibly offend anybody. At all events, if anybody
might complain, it would be the showman of the
real pig, not the mere imitator. I have never seen
Madame Blavatsky. She threatened once she would
come to Oxford to face and to confound me, but she
never did. Though she preached to the undergraduates at Balliol, she never came near me. It
is simply my love of genuine Indian philosophy that
induced me to protest against what I knew to be
a mere travesty of Vedânta, Sâmkhya, and Yoga
philosophy. If even in this travestied form Indian
philosophy has found friends, in India and Europe,
owing to her preaching, I am quite content, but
Satyam paramo dharma*h*, " Truth is the highest
religion," or the highest virtue, and nothing, I am
deeply convinced, can prosper for any length of
time that is mixed up with exaggeration or untruth.
If it is right and our bounden duty to protest
against foolish disfigurements of our own religion,
why should misrepresentation of the Hindu religion
and Hindu philosophy be allowed to pass un-
challenged ?

From what I have seen and read of Vivekânanda
and his colleagues, they seem to me honestly bent
on doing good work, and I feel the same about the

propaganda carried on by Dharmapâla in favour of Buddhism. It is honest, it is unselfish, it is free from juggling. Vivekânanda and the other followers of Râmak*ri*sh*n*a ought, however, to teach their followers how to distinguish between the perfervid utterances of their teacher, Râmak*ri*sh*n*a, an enthusiastic Bhakta (devotee), and the clear and dry style of the Sûtras of Bâdarâya*n*a. The Vedânta spirit is there, but the form often becomes too vague and exaggerated to give us an idea of what the true G*ñ*ânin (knower) ought to be. However, as long as these devoted preachers keep true to the Upanishads, the Sûtras, and the recognised commentaries, whether of *Sa*m*k*ara or of Râmânu*g*a, I wish them all the success which they deserve by their unselfish devotion and their high ideals.

My Indian Correspondents.

Were I to publish any of the innumerable letters which I receive from unknown correspondents from every part of India, some written in English, others in Sanskrit, they would surprise many readers by showing how like the present political, philosophic, and religious atmosphere in the higher classes of Indian society is to our own. My Indian friends are interested in the same questions which interest us, and they often refer us to their own ancient philosophers who have discussed the same questions many centuries ago. Many of them read and write English perfectly well, though there is a certain bluntness in their questions which would startle us in England.

While I am writing these lines, a letter signed by a number of Indian gentlemen is lying on my table, as yet unanswered, and, if the nature of the questions be considered, likely to remain unanswered for some time. To us some of these questions sound certainly very startling, but they are nevertheless interesting, because they show us the problems on which the Indian mind is brooding, and which to many of them are like their daily bread. We ourselves are more inclined to suppress questions of this kind, or to say with Sir Philip Sidney, "Reason cannot show itself more reasonable than to leave off reasoning on things above reason." To Indian thinkers, however, there seem to be no regions at all which cannot be approached and penetrated by human reason.

The questions on which my unknown friends want my answer, and probably expect it by return of post, are :—

(1) What is your opinion regarding God and soul ? Is the latter a reflection of the former, or is the one quite separate from the other ?

Athanasius might have answered such a question, but how can I ?

(2) If both God and soul are said to have been separated from the beginning, then how, when, and whence is the latter afflicted with Karman (acts and their results) which cause sad suffering to each individual soul ?

(3) Is the universe eternal and self-abiding, or has it been created by some one ?

(4 A) Taking it for granted that there is some one to be considered the Creator of the universe, we want to know what was the period of the creation, and how long the creation will last; what it was at first, and what will it be hereafter? Did the Creator create all beings (old and young, children and parents) in a moment, or did He create them in succession? Were male and female created at the same time, or one after the other?

(4 B) Did the Creator bestow rewards on the actions of men in a former life, or did He create them freely of His own accord? Is He the Giver of rewards, the Ruler of the Universe, or simply the Creator?

(4 C) How is it, then, that God created rich and poor, happy and sad? What were the acts that could have produced such results?

(5) What is the real matter of the five elements —earth, water, fire, air, and ether, and of the soul? What is the origin of the smallest atoms (paramânu) and of time?

(6) Is there any method which, acted upon, will save us from anxieties and troubles of this world, and by means of which we may reach Nirvâna?

(7) What was the origin of idol-worship? Is it good, or is it contrary to the Sacred Books?

(8) Was Buddhism an offshoot of Gainism, or vice versa? or have both religions arisen separately from time immemorial?

(9) By whom were the Vedas compiled, and what do they treat of?

(10) Where does the soul go to after death? Is there any heaven or hell in which the rewards of actions, both good and bad, are to be enjoyed?

My correspondents, who are evidently men of cultivated minds, describe themselves simply as cloth-merchants. I know nothing more about them, but we may learn from their letter what is the unseen stream of thought running through India. They seem to belong to the Digambara sect of the *G*ain religion. I doubt whether any English cloth-merchants would have appealed to J. S. Mill or to Darwin for a solution of such metaphysical difficulties. We may consider such questions unreasonable, only we must not imagine that because we do not speak of these riddles, we ourselves have solved them. Nay, it may be useful to be reminded from time to time of the limits of our knowledge, so as not to trust too much to the omniscience of our own philosophers.

I often feel ashamed that I cannot answer such letters. But first of all, let me assure my kind correspondents that I am not omniscient, and never pretended to be so. On some of the questions they ask me, their own philosophers have said all that can be said, more even than our own. But let them consider likewise that with the best will on my part, I should have no time left for my own studies, were I to attempt to enter on a discussion of such problems as are set before me by my unknown friends in India and elsewhere. Every one who writes to me seems to imagine that he is the only

person who does so.   If they saw the chaos of unanswered letters on my table they would see that
I do not exaggerate, and would understand that it
would be physically impossible for any human being
to answer all the letters addressed to me.   Life has
its limits, every day has its limits, and one hour out
of the twenty-four might well be left to an old man
for dreaming, for looking back on the years and
the friends that are gone, and forward to that life
to which our stay on.earth forms, as he thinks, but
a short prelude.

In one respect, as I pointed out before, the Indians
differ from us very characteristically.   They give
very free expression to their sentiments, whether of
love or of admiration, and even when they have to
express their disapproval they do it in the gentlest
and least offensive words.   Some of them have expressed to me on several occasions their surprise,
nay, disgust, at the rudeness and coarseness of
certain Sanskrit scholars in their literary controversies.   Some people may call Oriental gentleness
and courtesy flattery, some dishonesty, and it certainly would be so for us.   Even in French and
Italian, however, there are some expressions which
we would not use in English, and which, if translated
into English, sound to us unreal and exaggerated,
while not to use them would amount in French to
a want of politeness.   We are not so easily *enchanted*
or *ravished*, nor are we always *devoted servants*, but
at the same time I must confess that our *yours truly*
sounds almost brutal in answer to the eloquent finish

of the letters of our French friends. But though
I fully admit that considerable deductions must be
made from the panegyrics addressed to us by our
Indian correspondents, it would be wrong to accuse
them of intentional insincerity. If their panegyrics
seem sometimes to come very near to an apotheosis,
we must not forget that their Devas or gods are not
looked upon as anything very extraordinary after all.

I must mention at least one instance when I was
agreeably surprised by the thorough sincerity of one
of my Indian correspondents, who certainly meant
far more than he said. The Mahârâjah of Vizianagram wrote to me some years ago expressing a wish
to possess a copy of my edition of the " Rig-Veda "
in six volumes. It had been published at £15, but
when I applied to a second-hand bookseller he
charged £24, and told me that complete copies of
the book were getting very scarce. Soon after the
Mahârâjah wrote again asking the bookseller to
send him a second copy, but he was informed by his
agent in England that he could not get a complete
set for love or for money. The Mahârâjah wrote to
ask me why I did not bring out a new edition, and
I had to tell him what the expense of printing such
a work would be, and that, though I should gladly
give my labour for nothing, I could not find a
publisher in England, not even a University Press,
to undertake such a work. The Indian Government
had for years used the first edition for making
presents in Europe and in India, and though in this
way it had fully reimbursed itself for the original

outlay, it was not inclined to venture on a second
edition. Upon this the Mahârâjah, who had hitherto
been most lavish in his praises of the work, showed
that the praise he had bestowed on it was not mere
empty praise, but was really meant. After telling
me what his Pandits had said to him, and sending
me some valuable MSS., as a present, which they
had prepared for me, he offered to pay himself for
the printing of a new edition, if I would undertake
the labour of revising the text.

This I readily accepted, and in two years, 1890
to 1892, a new, and I hope more correct edition,
was issued from the Press at Oxford in four large
volumes. The Mahârâjah paid to the Press not
less than £4,000. I found out afterwards that this
Indian nobleman was by no means a student, an
antiquarian, or a theologian ; but, on the contrary,
a man of the world, very fond of racing and hunting.
He distinguished himself on one occasion, as I was
told, by riding up the staircase to the very roof of his
palace. When in one of my last letters I asked him
what had induced him to spend so large a sum on
the Rig-Veda, he replied that India wanted its Bible,
and he added, " It may benefit me hereafter." That
hereafter has come sooner than he expected. He
died a comparatively young man, and as long as the
Veda lives his name will certainly not be forgotten.
The Veda has lived now for four thousand years,
or, according to Indian ideas, it has existed from all
eternity. Four thousand years is but a small slice
of eternity, but are there many books that have

lasted or will last four thousand years ? I ought to
add that his liberality did not stop at paying the
expenses of the work, but that he placed a large
number of copies at my disposal, which was more
than I expected or deserved. Are there many
Mahârâjahs or Zemindârs in Europe who would
have spent so large a sum on a new edition of the
Bible, or, in fact, of any other important book ?
Would any scholar even think of appealing to the
millionaires of England or America to help him in
bringing out an old forgotten book, if it "benefited
them hereafter" only ? Anyhow, I came to learn
that Hindus are not simply grandiloquent, but that
they can do grand things also, when the opportunity
offers.

If I finish here the list of my Indian friends, it is
not because I have no more names to add. We have
lately had a book called "Representative Indians,"
by C. P. Pillai, 1897, containing biographical sketches
of thirty-six distinguished Hindus and Parsis. Many
of them I have known or corresponded with, but of
their sentiments, their hopes and disappointments,
I know but little. The undercurrent of their life,
the deeper motives of their actions, are under a kind
of purdah, and we hardly ever get either autobio-
graphical confessions or outspoken memoirs. This
is a pity, and naturally deprives reminiscences of
Indian friends of much of that human interest which
everybody feels when catching glimpses of the more
intimate life of distinguished persons. We seldom
hear of a good or smart saying from a Hindu, such

as we have in large numbers from English, German, or French statesmen or poets. The people of India are still a deep secret to us, and if I have succeeded in withdrawing the curtain from only a small portion of their inmost thoughts and feelings, if, here and there, I have helped to change mere curiosity about them into a warm human sympathy with them, my reminiscences will have fulfilled their true object. In some respects, and particularly in respect to the greatest things (τὰ μέγιστα), India has as much to teach us as Greece and Rome, nay, I should say more. We must not forget, of course, that we are the direct intellectual heirs of the Greeks, and that our philosophical currency is taken from the capital left to us by them. Our palates are accustomed to the food which they have supplied to us from our very childhood, and hence whatever comes to us now from the thought-mines of India is generally put aside as merely curious or strange, whether in language, mythology, religion, or philosophy. But however foreign Indian thought may appear to us, it has filled an important place in the growth of the human race, and that growth is important, whether it took place on the borders of the Ilissos or on the shores of the Ganges. In India we still see, as it were, the last traces of the primordial surprise at this world. Their earliest thinkers seem still to feel strange in it, while Greeks and Romans are thoroughly at home in their little world. No doubt the Greeks as well as the Indians saw the riddles of the world, were perplexed by them, and tried to solve them.

But while Greeks and Romans, and later on the leading races of Europe also, settled down to their practical work in life, the Indians, at least the leading thinkers among them, never felt quite at ease even in their beautiful forests, by the side of their mighty rivers, or under the shadow of their gigantic snow-mountains in the north. They never cared so intensely for this span of life on earth as the Greeks did. Hence they never brought political life to its full development, like the Greeks and Romans; they never strove to conquer what was not theirs, or to govern the world which they had conquered; nor did they, like the Hebrews, look upon the exact fulfilment of the law as the highest object of their life on earth. Even while passing through this world, their eyes were for ever fixed on the Beyond. They strove to pierce through the dark roof of their forests, to travel to the distant sources of their rivers, and to transcend even the snowy peaks of the Himâlaya Mountains. Their hearts would never forget the life that lay behind them, and their minds were for ever set on the life that was to come.

The old questions of Whence? Why? and Whither? fascinated and enthralled their thoughts. They may have but little of practical wisdom to teach us, for they paid but small attention to the arts of peace and war. But, though they fell in consequence an easy prey to their neighbours, they had something nevertheless which their barbarous conquerors had not. They had their own view of the world, and this view, different as it is from our own, deserves to be looked at carefully and seriously by us. Whatever we may think of the world which they had built up for themselves, and in which they lived, their idea of the Godhead is certainly higher, purer, and more consistent than that of Greeks, Romans, and Hebrews. They passed through polytheism, henotheism, and monotheism, and they arrived at last at what is generally called pantheism, but a pantheism very different from vulgar pantheism. They started with the firm conviction that what we mean by God must be a Being without a second, without beginning or end, without limitations of any kind. Whatever there is or seems to be, call it mind or matter, man or nature, can have one substance only, one and the same, whatever we name it, God, or Brahman, the Absolute, or the Supreme Being. They never say, like other pantheists, that everything in this phenomenal world is God, but that everything has its being in God.

How the change from the real to the phenomenal came about, or, as we say, how the world was created, they can tell us as little as we can tell them. They simply point to the fact that it has come about, that it is there, that it is and can be nothing but phenomenal to us, but that the phenomenal could not even seem to be without the real behind it. In order to restore the phenomenal world to its reality, they hold that all that is wanted is knowledge or philosophy, which destroys that universal Nescience which makes us all take the phenomenal for the real, the objective for the subjective. Their philo-

sophy is chiefly the Vedânta, though other systems
also pursue the same object. Each man is in substance or in self identical with God, for what else
could he be ? If they say that each man is God,
that would, no doubt, offend us, but that man and
everything else has its true being in the Godhead
is a very different kind of pantheism. To regain
that full self-consciousness or God-consciousness, to
return to God, to break down the artificial wall that
seemed to separate man from God, is the highest
object of Indian philosophy, and in some form or
other these thoughts have gradually leavened all
classes of society from the highest to the lowest.

In order to be able to appreciate the true value
of the Vedânta, we have to study its growth in the
Upanishads, and in the minute disquisitions of the
Vedânta-Sûtras and their commentaries. No doubt
these are sometimes very tedious, and to us, in this
age of the world, may often appear childish and
useless. And yet the Vedânta view of the world
has a right to claim the same attention as that of
Heraclitus, Plato, Spinoza, or Kant. It is as true and
as untrue as any of these philosophical intuitions,
but it possesses an attraction of its own which has
held the best minds of India captive for generations,
and will continue to do so for ages to come.

Nay, as we have always had among us Platonists,
Spinozists, and Kantians, the time will come, nay,
has come already, when European philosophers will
try to look at the world through the glasses of the
Vedânta also. It is well known that Schopenhauer,

no mean thinker of modern times, declared the
Vedânta as taught in the Upanishads "the product
of the highest wisdom" (*Ausgeburt der höchsten
Weisheit*). May not these words make other philosophers pause before they reject as childish a
philosophy which Schopenhauer placed above the
philosophy of Giordano Bruno, Malebranche, and
Spinoza ?

India should be known, not from without, but
from within, and it will require a long time and
far abler hands than mine before we really know
what India was meant to be in the development of
mankind. Heinrich Simon remarked very truly,
"Our history is miserable because we have no
biographies. . . . If a man's life lies open before me
from day to day in all his acts and all his thoughts,
so far as they can be represented externally, I gain
a better insight into the history of the time than
by the best general representation of it." What we
want to know is, how the prominent men of India
imbibed the Vedânta, and how the principles they
had imbibed from that source influenced their lives,
their acts, and their thoughts. With us philosophy
remains always something collateral only. Our
mainstay is formed by religion and ethics. But with
the Hindus, philosophy is life in full earnest, it is
but another name for religion, while morality has
a place assigned to it as an essential preliminary
to all philosophy. Most of our greatest philosophers
and of their followers seem to lead two lives, one
as it ought to be, the other as it is. One of our

greatest philosophers, Berkeley, knew quite well what the world is, but he lived as a bishop, unconcerned about the unreal character of all with which he had to deal. There have been cases of true Vedântists, also, who have led useful, active lives as ministers and organisers of states, but he who has grasped the highest truths of the Vedânta, or has been grasped by them, is driven at once into the solitude of the forests, waiting there for the solution of all riddles, for perfect freedom, and in the end for the truest freedom of all, for death— Θανοῦμαι καὶ ἐλευθερήσομαι.

IV.

The Veda.

WE live no longer in times when the head of a great publishing firm would ask a scholar who offered a translation of the Veda, as I know the late Professor H. H. Wilson was asked, " But what in all the world is the Veda, or what you call the Rig-Veda ?" But nevertheless in spite of the years that have passed since, I am still asked from time to time much the same question, and I confess I cannot answer it in two words.

I should not be surprised if even some of those who are doing me the honour of reading my Recollections of Auld Lang Syne, and who in this volume of recollections of my Indian Friends, have so often come across the name of Veda, were to say in their secret heart, What in all the world can that Veda be to which this misguided man has devoted the whole of his life ? I have been asked such a question before now, and it is perhaps not unreasonable that I should try to answer it here. For after all, was not the Veda the first of my Indian friends ? Was it not the bridge that led me from West to East, from Greece and Italy to India, nay,

from Dessau to Oxford, from Germany to England ?
Whatever other people may say about the mis-
guided man who sacrificed everything to the Veda,
I still count the Veda among my best friends, and
I sometimes regret that my duties as Professor of
Comparative Philology in the University of Oxford
should during my later years have withdrawn my
full allegiance from it.   What then is the Veda ?

The Vedas, as we possess them, are four systematically arranged collections of hymns and verses,
and the Veda is often used in the sense of these
four Vedas taken together.   The first and most
important Veda is the Rig-Veda, which has often,
and not without some truth, been called the only
true Veda.   It contains 1,017, or with some additions,
the Vâlakhilya-hymns, 1,028 hymns, each on an average containing about ten verses.   They are all
addressed to Devatâs or deities, and whatever subject is addressed in these hymns, down to bows,
arrows, and stones, is supposed to become, *ipso facto*,
a Devatâ, while the poet is called the seer or Rishi.
The metres are numerous and strictly regulated,
though there is more freedom in them than in the
later artificial poetry of India.

The hymns of the Rig-Veda were meant to be
recited at sacrifices, and this is no doubt the explanation of their careful preservation during many
centuries, by means of a strictly regulated oral
tradition.

The second, the Sâma-Veda, is a much smaller
collection of hymns, most of them borrowed from

the Rig-Veda, but different in character so far as they were meant to be sung at the ancient sacrifices.

The third, the Yagur-Veda, consists of sacrificial formulas and of verses to be repeated in a low voice by a class of priests who were entrusted chiefly with the manual work required for the performance of sacrifices.

The fourth, the Atharva-Veda, probably collected at a later time, contains, besides many hymns from the Rig-Veda, a large number of popular verses used for magical and medicinal purposes, some of them possibly of great antiquity, particularly if we adopt the principle that whatever is very silly is necessarily very old.

Taken as a whole these hymns, particularly those of the Rig-Veda, are certainly older than any other poetry we possess in India, nay, older than any literary composition we possess of any of the Aryan nations in Asia or Europe. Their real interest, however, consists not only in their age, but in the simplicity and naturalness of their poetical addresses to the most striking phenomena of nature by which the Aryan settlers found themselves surrounded in India, and in which and behind which they recognised unseen agents by whom both their physical and their moral life were powerfully influenced.

If all books have their fates, the oldest book of the world, the Veda, has certainly had the most extraordinary fate. It was known to exist and people began to write about it, long before it had been seen or handled by any European. I remember Baron Bunsen telling me how his chief object in arranging to go to India with his pupil, Mr. Astor, was to see whether there really was such a book in existence. By consulting the *Lettres édifiantes* he might have known that it was in existence as a real book, and had been seen and handled by some of the Catholic missionaries in India. But though seen, not a line of it had ever been published, still less translated, because native scholars, willing as they might be to help missionaries and others in reading the Laws of Manu, the Mahâbhârata and Râmâyana, were most decidedly unwilling to help them to an understanding of the Veda. There were, no doubt, many reasons for it, one of them being possibly that there were few, if any, Brâhmans at the beginning of this century who were able to translate the Veda themselves. There were many who knew it or large portions of it by heart, and could recite the hymns at sacrifices and public or private gatherings, but they did not even profess that they understood it. They were proud to know it by heart and by sound, and there were some who actually thought that the hymns would lose their magic power, if recited by one who understood their meaning. Manuscripts were never very numerous, and even when one of them fell into the hands of Europeans, they soon found that, without a commentary, the hymns baffled all endeavours at translation.

During all that time the most exaggerated ideas were spread about the Vedas. The Brâhmans themselves declared that they contained the oldest

divine revelation, that they were not the compositions of human authors, but the work of Brahman,
the Supreme Spirit, who had revealed them to
inspired sages or Rishis, seers. European scholars
were carried away for a time by the hope that they
would find in these Vedas, if not the jabberings of
the Pithecanthropoi, at least the earliest flashes of
thoughts of an awakening humanity, the faint echoes
of a primordial wisdom going back to the very beginning of human life on earth, " when the morning stars
sang together and all the sons of God shouted for joy."

When at last not only the texts but the immense
Sanskrit commentary also of the most important,
the Rig-Veda, had been published, people began to
see that there was little of primeval, mysterious
wisdom to be found in the Vedic hymns, but
only the simplest thoughts that must have passed
through the minds of the Rishis when they began
to ponder on the great phenomena of nature which
every morning and night, every spring and winter
were unfolded before their eyes. No superhuman
revelation was required for that kind of poetry.
Nothing could be clearer than that the constant
themes of these Vedic songs were sunrise and
morning, day and night, earth and the rivers, storms,
lightning, rain, sunset and night. Even this was for
a time stoutly denied by writers who did not know
the Sanskrit alphabet. But what else was there to
interest the ancient Âryas ? It is true that even the
Brâhmans themselves protested against the Western
scholars, whose translations seemed to reduce their

sacred hymns to the low level of mere descriptions
of nature [1]. We are not and never have been, they
said, mere sun-worshippers or fire-worshippers, or
rain-worshippers, but sun, fire, and sky were only
symbols to us of the Godhead, of one and the same
Divine Being in His manifold manifestations. In
one sense they were certainly right, but I doubt
whether many of the much abused Western
scholars had ever denied this. Many things have
to be taken as understood, and Western scholars
evidently took it for granted that when the Vedic
poets addressed their hymns to the dawn, to the
sun, the sky, the storm-winds, the earth, or the rain,
they did not simply mean the fiery ball that rose in
the morning and vanished at night, or the blue sky,
or the soil on which they stood, or the rain that had
fertilised the soil. The very fact that they addressed
these phenomena of nature with the pronoun of the
second person, changed them at once into persons, or
what were called Devatâs, deities, and thus the saying
of one of their old grammarians, Yâska, is justified,
that whatever object is addressed in these Vedic
hymns is to be called its Devatâ—or deity. Later on
it came to be recognised that there was even a deeper
ground for this deification, and that the necessities
of language, that is, of thought, did not allow at first
of any names being formed, except names of agent.
Dyaus, masc., for instance, the lighter, was earlier
than Dyaus, fem., what is lighted up, the sky.

If we take some of the most ancient and most

---

[1] Kâmeʂvar Aiyar, Sandhyâvandana, pp. 58, 105, 113.

popular daily prayers, used in the daily Sandhyâvandana [1], we find that one of them is the famous
Gâyatrî, addressed to Savit*ri*, the sun :—

" We meditate on the adorable light of the divine
Savit*ri*, that he may rouse our thoughts."

This Savit*ri*, the sun, is, of course, more than
the fiery ball that rises from the sea or over the
hills, but nevertheless the real sun serves as a
symbol, and it was that symbol which suggested
to the suppliant the divine power manifested in
the sun.   Hence almost everything that could be
predicated of the sun was predicated of Savit*ri* also,
whatever was true of the sky, Dyaus, fem., was
supposed to be true of Dyaus, masc., Zeus or
Jupiter also.   As early an authority as Kâtyâyana
in his Index to the Rig-Veda declared that all the
gods invoked in the Vedic hymns can be reduced to
three, to Agni, fire and light, on earth, to Vâyu, air,
in the atmosphere, and to Sûrya, sun, in the sky, but
he adds that all three are in the end meant for one,
for Pra*g*âpati, the Lord of creation.   And later on he
says, that there is only one deity, namely the Great
Self, Mahân Âtmâ, and some say that he is the sun,
(Sûrya), or that the sun is he.   One of the prayers

[1] Sandhyâ is derived from Sandhi, literally the joining, the
coming together of day and night, or night and day.   Sandhi-
velâ is twilight, and Sandhyâ has the same meaning.   Sandhyâvandana was originally the twilight-worship, the morning and
evening prayer, to which a third was added (the Mâdhyâhnika) the
noon prayer, when the sun culminated.   These prayers were once
incumbent on every Brâhman, though they have now assumed
a very perfunctory form, or are omitted altogether.

in the Sandhyâvandana begins with Asâv Âdityo
Brahma, that Âditya (sun) is Brahman, and in the
Taitt. Upanishad, VIII, 8, it is said : " He who
dwells in man and he who dwells in the sun, are
one and the same." The same idea may be likewise
deduced from the hymns themselves. In X, 158, 1,
we read : " May the sun (Sûrya) protect us from the
sky, the wind (Vâyu) from mid-air, and fire (Agni)
from the earth ; " whereas in another hymn, 115, 1,
we read : " the Sun is the Self or soul of all that
moves and rests." Here we can clearly watch the
gradual transition from the visible sun to the invisible
agent of the sun which may have taken centuries
to evolve, and if we consider how almost everything
on earth is dependent on the sun for its very life,
we can understand how a perfectly natural road led
from the sun as seen in heaven, to the sun as the
highest, the supreme, nay, in the end, as the only
deity. This religious and philosophical development
of the concept of the sun did not, however, prevent
its simultaneous mythological growth. This is the
famous Solar Theory, which, no doubt, has been
much exaggerated, but which, if properly understood,
admits, we know, of cheap cavil, but never of refutation ; nay, which, if but rightly understood, has really
received more support from its supposed critics than
from its originators and supporters. One of the
most intelligible names given to the sun was Asva,
the racer, or Dadhikrâvan or Vâgin, horse. And
while at one time the sun was a racer, at another the
sun was conceived as approaching men and standing

on a golden chariot which was drawn by horses, as in Greek mythology. Thus we read, Rig-Veda I, 35, 2: " The god Savit*ri* (the sun), approaching on the dark-blue sky, sustaining mortals and immortals, comes on his golden chariot, beholding all the worlds."

I have been assured that the noisy cannonade which was directed for years against this explanation of Vedic and Aryan mythology, was really meant as a kind of salute ; but I should have much preferred a few twenty-pounders to test the solidity of my entrenched position. When at last I was charged with never having taken any notice of certain illustrious critics, it seemed to me but courteous to respond to that appeal. But there was really little to answer because there was so little difference between my critics and myself. They evidently thought that I was opposed to their anthropological theories, whereas on the contrary I rejoiced in them, whenever they rested on scholarly evidence. I had myself dabbled in the grammar of the Mohawk and Hottentot languages, because I considered grammar a *sine quâ non* of mythology, nor was I much disturbed when my Sanskrit scholarship was found fault with by critics who did not know the Sanskrit alphabet. That real Sanskrit scholars should have differed on certain etymologies, was quite another thing, nor was it difficult to come to an understanding with them. Either they were mistaken on certain points or I was, but no real Sanskrit scholar would ever join in the clamour of those who maintained that Greek, Latin, and Teutonic mythology had quite a different origin from that of the Veda. Such things pass and are soon forgotten, and no one who, like myself, remembers the time when Bopp was laughed at by classical scholars for the foolish idea that Greek and Latin grammar should be explained by a comparison with Sanskrit would be much disturbed by those who did not blush to say that there was only one tenable equation be- tween the names of classical and Vedic deities, viz. Dyaus = Zeus. But have those ready writers ever reflected what such an admission would really mean, and how it would disable the whole of their machinery? What would happen if the name of Jehovah, or even of Yahveh, turned up suddenly in the Veda? Thinking is difficult, but it is sometimes useful. Such things will be remembered hereafter among the Curiosities of Literature. No one is infallible, but because we have occasionally a fall on the ice, it does not follow that we must not skate or even cut figures on the ice. There is plenty of work to do for those who are willing to work either at the language of the Rig-Veda, or at that of the Maoris, but without some of that grammatical drudgery, I doubt whether mere assertions, or repeating the opinions of others, will really forward our knowledge of the *origines* of our own race.

It is surely as clear as daylight to anybody who will read a number of the hymns of the Rig-Veda that they refer to the principal phenomena of nature, and that in that respect they require no antecedents, but are intelligible to any child. Yet for a number of years there has been a constant outcry from certain anthropologists, who asserted that the Vedic hymns were modern in spirit, modern in language, and modern in their pantheon, and that this pantheon had nothing whatever to do with the phenomena of nature, and had no relationship whatever with the gods of the other Aryan nations, particularly of Greeks, Romans, and Teutons. They looked upon the Vedic religion as the last phase in a development, the earlier stages of which had to be studied among savage races, such as the *well-known* Kamilaroi, Wiraturei, Waihvun, &c. Have they forgotten this? It is true, no doubt, that the ideas expressed in the Veda presupposed a long development, even a period of savagery, considering that all civilised nations must once have been less civilised, uncivilised, or even savages. There are quite sufficient survivals of savagery even in the Veda itself, only it is Aryan savagery, not savagery of the Pacific Islanders, African negroes, or Dravidians. If only some cases could be produced in which the Australian blacks shared any of the ideas of the Veda, or displayed similar ideas, only more savage, every true scholar would welcome them with open arms. Our expectations have been raised to a very high pitch in that direction, and I still hope that in time they may be fulfilled. In the meantime it is fortunate that the mere clamour against the Veda has at last subsided, so that now people only marvel how it could ever have arisen.

Most of the names of the Vedic deities implied

II.   N

at first activity only, but very soon personality also, and what is most important, some of them were found to be exactly the same in Sanskrit, in Greek, Latin, German, and Slavonic, being only changed in every one of these languages according to the phonetic rules peculiar to each. Such verbal coincidences had to be accounted for, and they could not be accounted for except by the admission that there was once a period, a truly historical period, during which the framers of these mythological names and the believers in these physical powers, or, as we are accustomed to call them, these natural Gods or Devas, were still living together as one language, people or nation. Such an admission, inevitable as it was in the eyes of all true scholars, roused at the time a certain dislike and incredulity among those who like to shrug their shoulders at every new discovery. Forgetful of the fact that proper names in all languages undergo certain phonetic changes which do not apply to ordinary appellatives, they thought they could belittle the value of such equations as Sâramêya = Ἐρμείας, Saranyû = Ἐρινύς, Haritas = Χάριτες by pointing out that strictly speaking the Greek forms should have been Ἐρεμείας and Ἐρινύς, while the Greek Charites, though identical in names, seemed to resist all efforts to trace them back to the same source from which sprang the bright horses of the sun-god.

This cheap scepticism, however, or, as it is now called, this higher criticism, may safely be said to belong to the past. I am old enough to remember the conversion of such giants as Gottfried Hermann, Otfried Müller, and Welcker to the principles of scholarship, as taught by Bopp, Grimm, and others. That was indeed a real triumph. In 1825, Otfried Müller, the real founder of a scientific mythology (*wissenschaftliche Mythologie*), was sighing for a translation of the Rig-Veda. In 1899, when a great part of it has been made accessible by the patient labours of English, French, and German scholars, some writers, who call themselves mythologists, seem to take a pride in ignoring the existence of the Veda. How far we have advanced since 1825, may be gathered from a statement to which I should be very sorry to affix a name, "that the only generally accepted case of similarity between Vedic and classical mythological names was that of Dyaush-pitar, Ζεὺς πατήρ, and Jupiter." Has Benfey taught in vain? Even in 1839, Benfey (*Wörterbuch*, II, 334) knew that Ushas was = Eos, Agni (fire) = ignis, (ibid., II, 217), Sûrya = Helios (ibid., I, 458), to say nothing of later equations which, even if disapproved of, or disproved, would leave the general principles of Comparative Mythology exactly as they were fifty years ago. Has all this been forgotten, or never been learnt?

The discovery of Vedic literature which had retained the clearest traces of a common Aryan mythology, even if no equation besides that of Dyaush-pitar = Ζεὺς πατήρ had survived, was really the discovery of a new world, of a *terra antiquis incognita*, and gave us a glimpse at a whole period of

N 2

thought, of which no relics whatever could be found anywhere else, whether in Greece, Italy, or Germany.

But highly interesting as these Vedic hymns are to us, in spite of, or, I should say, on account of their simplicity and childishness, anybody who came to know them at first hand had to confess that they seem quite unfit to satisfy the religious cravings of a later generation.   They contain praises of the physical gods, they implore their help, they render thanks for benefits supposed to have come from their hands, light and life from Dyaus, rain and food from a closely related power, called Indra, warmth and light from Agni, new life every morning from Ushas or Eos.   All this is historically and psychologically full of interest, but there is little only, except here and there, of exalted religious thought, of poetry or philosophy, still less of any records of historical events.   Besides, their language is so difficult that, as yet, it makes a satisfactory translation of the whole Veda a perfect impossibility. This may seem surprising in the days when hiero-glyphic and cuneiform inscriptions have been so readily translated.   But the fact is that most of those inscriptions are very straightforward, they hardly contain a conditional or a relative sentence. We read of Kings and Kings of Kings, of their battles from year to year, of the towns they founded, of the conquests they made, the captives they led away, the tribute they received and so on, and yet even such simple statements vary very considerably from year to year according as they are translated

by bold or timid scholars. The Vedic hymns on
the contrary, even when we understand every word
of them, remain very obscure in their structure or
construction; and though their texts are very
firmly established from the time they were first
reduced to writing and made the subject of the
most minute grammatical study in India, even
before the spreading of Buddhism, it is clear that
before that time, when the Vedic texts existed in
oral tradition only, they must have been exposed
to many vicissitudes. There are verbal emenda-
tions so palpable that we can hardly understand
how the mistakes could have arisen, and could have
been tolerated for one moment. Besides that, there
are evidently old and new hymns, yet all of them
are recognised as belonging to the Veda, ever since
the Vedic hymns were systematically collected.

The attempts that have been made to translate
the Vedic hymns may be divided into four periods.
The first consisted of those who followed Sâyana's
great Sanskrit commentary. This was the method
followed by Rosen in 1830 and 1838, and again,
in 1850, by H. H. Wilson. It was soon found
out, however, that highly useful, nay indispensable,
as the traditional interpretation of Sâyana might be,
it was in many places quite impossible to follow
him, because the true meaning was too clear, and
that adopted by Sâyana too absurd. Rosen already
used very freely the privilege of the scholar to
choose between what is rational and what is not.
Wilson had a stronger faith in Sâyana, and gave

us in his translation the traditional rendering, even where his own sound sense rebelled against it.

There were others again who went into the other extreme, and from sheer despair at Sâya*n*a's commentary, translated the Veda according to what they thought it ought to mean. Langlois, a professor of eloquence at Paris, carried this principle very far indeed, yet we find that his translation is still followed by some writers on ancient religion and mythology.

In the meantime a new school was slowly gaining ground who held that the only satisfactory way of translating the Veda was to construct, first of all, a complete *Index Verborum* [1], to examine every passage in which the same word occurs, and then to assign that meaning to each word which would satisfy the context wherever it occurred. I published such an *Index Verborum* at the end of my edition of Sâya*n*a's commentary, and it is easy to see the influence which it exercised at once on the translations of the Rig-Veda which we owe to

----

[1] I still have a letter from the late M. Bergaigne, in which he asks when my Index would be published, and adds: " Je m'étais décidé pendant ces vacances à écrire tout le Rig-Véda sur des fiches, et à me composer ainsi un index qui pût me permettre des essais d'interprétation indépendante. Je suis arrivé à la moitié de ce travail, et grâce à la rapidité que je suis parvenu à atteindre, et aussi à une grande puissance de travail, je puis le terminer en moins d'un mois . . . S'il n'était pas trop exiger, je vous prierais de me dire aussi si vous citez tous les emplois de chaque mot *sans aucune exception*, ou si vous êtes départi de cette rigueur pour les mots très usuels, et enfin si vous adoptez l'ordre alphabétique pur et simple." I could answer all these questions in the affirmative.

Grassmann, to Ludwig, and to Ralph T. H. Griffith, and to others who tried their hands on single hymns or single verses. Still greater was the influence exercised by the Sanskrit Dictionary of Boehtlingk and Roth, and the Vedic Vocabulary of Grassmann, though, of course, neither the one nor the other professed to give a complete index of every word and every form in every passage in which it occurred.

The method which I recommended, and which I followed in the specimens published (in 1859, in my "History of Ancient Sanskrit Literature," in 1869, in the "Hymns to the Storm-gods," and again in the "Sacred Books of the East," 1891), was so tedious, however, that few scholars only felt tempted to follow it. Professor Roth, the scholar most qualified, through his lexical labours, to give us a real translation of the Veda, was honest enough to say again and again that such a work belonged to the next generation of Sanskrit scholars, and to the next century. I myself, having accepted the appointment to a new professorship of Comparative Philology at Oxford, had other things to do, and after I had given the best part of my life to supplying the materials necessary for such a task, I hoped that the ambition of younger scholars would have been roused to undertake this no doubt difficult, but very grateful work. I did not go so far as to say, as has been supposed, that every word, whenever it occurred, should again and again be followed by every translator through all its hiding-places. A number of

words have once for all been fixed in their meanings,
and when that was the case, they were naturally
passed, as known to every Sanskrit scholar. Still
the mere physical exertion in collecting all parallel
passages became too much for me, and I had re-
luctantly to give it up to younger and more vigorous
hands.

We are now at the beginning of a new era in Vedic
scholarship whenever the Complete Concordance,
promised by Professors Bloomfield and Lanman,
shall have been published. This will be a gigantic
work, but it is really the *sine quâ non* for the Vedic
exegesis of the future, and we may expect much
help from it. But though many passages may be
unravelled by a more complete intercomparison, my
own impression is that, through the influence of a
long-continued oral tradition a great amount of real
corruption has crept into our texts which no amount
of conjectural emendation will ever entirely remove.
This may sound very discouraging, but fortunately,
after deducting ever so much that is hopeless, there
remains enough of the 1,017 hymns to give us
that insight into the first development of religious
thought in India and indirectly among the Aryan
nations in general, which is so full of interest to us
psychologically, even more than historically. So
many conflicting theories have lately been started
about the origin of religion, that it must seem to
many people as if, like other beginnings, that of
religion also was really beyond our grasp. But this
is to a great extent our own fault, because philoso-

phers are bent on discovering the origin of religion, instead of being satisfied with studying the origin of religions, or of each individual religion with which it is possible to do so, that is of which we possess old literary documents. For that purpose the study of the Veda is invaluable. But who would try to discover the origin of Islam, without studying the Korân? or of Buddhism without knowing the Suttas? Who would offer an opinion about the beginning of Christianity, unless he had read the Gospels? Even then, it is well known how far removed the Gospels are from the Nativity, and the Korân from the Hejrah. But if we approach the religions of Greeks and Romans, where shall we find the Sibylline leaves telling us of their real parentage? If there lived many heroes before Agamemnon, there lived many poets and prophets before Homer; but who can pierce through the cruel darkness that hides them from our sight?

And what shall we do when we have to deal with religious customs and mythological lore of savage, uncivilised, and illiterate tribes? A study of their languages is no doubt an immense help towards a correct understanding of their traditions; and we cannot be sufficiently grateful to men like Hahn, Codrington, Tregear, and others who did not shrink from that drudgery, before writing on the myths or customs of uncivilised tribes. The most useful materials may be found where some popular poetry has been preserved to the present day, as among the Maoris or of some of the Ugro-Finnic tribes.

It is well known how much labour has been spent
on establishing the date and the authenticity of the
Vedic hymns.   Their authenticity is now admitted
by all Sanskrit scholars.   Their date has been fixed
by me in my " History of Ancient Sanskrit Literature " (1859) at about 1200 to 1500 B. C.   But
though this date has met with very general acceptance, I am the very last person to consider it as
firmly established, and I have again and again given
my reasons why I should gladly escape from the
force of my own arguments.   If other scholars have
clamoured for a higher age, for 2000 or 5000 B. C.,
they are quite welcome to these dates if they can
establish them by any kind of historical evidence, and
not merely by their wishes ; but as yet these guesses
are outside the sphere of practical scholarship, quite
as much as the date assigned by a Babylonian
scholar to the immigration of the Âryas into India,
so late as 500 or at the utmost 600 B. C. !

But no literary or traditional documents which we
possess, whether in Greek or Latin or in any other
Oriental language, to say nothing of barbarous
dialects, bring us so near, if not to the origin, at
least to the early historical development of any
of the ancient religions of mankind as the hymns
of the Veda.   If the study of single religions must
precede the study of religion in general, nowhere
can we get so near to the origin of any single religion
as in the hymns of the Rig-Veda.   Other religions
may be older, and religion by itself may be beyond
all conception old, but no single religion, as far as

I know, has been preserved in documents so old, and so near to the very cradle of a religion as that which we see growing before our eyes in the Veda. Let those who want to know the origin of religion, *a priori*, take refuge in metaphysics; but those who care to understand the origin of one single religion will find no better oracle to consult than the poems of the Vedic Rishis.

The chronological date of the Vedic hymns, which has been fixed by some at 1200, by others at 2000, nay at 4500 B. C., are, no doubt, very uncertain, and can be no more than constructive. But though Egyptian and Babylonian dates go far beyond any date in India, we can see more of the real beginnings of religion in India than even in Egypt or Babylon. Nor would anybody accept the principle laid down by students of the religion of savages, that whatever is savage or barbarous in religion, must be old. This is a major premiss that would play fearful havoc with our chronology.

What is quite clear is that, between the Vedic hymns and the next period, that of the prose Brâhmaṇas, there is a great gulf. The hymns of the three Vedas had not only been collected, such as we have them, but had already been invested with a divine authority, such as is seldom ascribed to works of recent date. Besides, it is clear that the language of the hymns had often been completely misunderstood by the authors of the Brâhmaṇas, and that a new style had sprung up in the place of that of the old poetical compositions. From the time of the Brâhma*n*as, which precede the rise of Buddhism (500 B. C.), to the present day, the old hymns of the Veda have retained their unique position in India. Invested with the character of a divine revelation, they have been to the people of India what the Bible has been to us.

And yet how different is this Bible of India from all other Bibles! No doubt we meet in the Veda with some exalted, and some very abstract ideas also, but its general character is very different. It is simple, straightforward, natural, without any attempt at systematic treatment, without any effort for poetical beauty. When we take day and night, spring and winter, as they come and go, we shall find in the hymns thoughts such as would naturally spring up in the minds of any unsophisticated observers who felt that there must be something behind the visible world, some powers or persons directing the course of nature, possibly some power even beyond the powers, whom they called Devas or Bright ones. It was chiefly the phenomena which recurred regularly that impressed themselves on their minds and evoked in time the idea of order and law as pervading the whole of nature, even its very thunderstorms and lightnings.

There is hardly a language in which sun and moon, day and night, dawn and fire have not received their names, many of which, on account of their multiplicity, led almost inevitably to mythological metamorphosis. Anthropology has clearly shown that the idea that exceptional events such as meteors,

earthquakes, hurricanes, lightning, eclipses of sun
or moon, furnished the first impulses to religion and
mythology is no longer tenable, even though it has,
or rather seemed to have, the often quoted support
of Seneca. If we may judge by what has been
observed among uncivilised as well as civilised
races—for even civilised races must once have been
uncivilised—regularity attracts attention first and
irregularity follows, or, as it has been more tersely
expressed, the Gods come first, the Devils second,
though it is quite true that in later times Devil-
worship may have become more important, or, at
least, more prominent than the worship of the Gods.
Of these so-called prehistoric periods of human
thought, however, we must always speak with great
reserve. We must never forget that they are con-
structions of our own, and that we shall never be
able to appeal to historical facts in support of our
theories. Facts are given us for the first time
during the Etymological Period of languages, and
afterwards, but at a much later time, by the scant
remains to be gathered from the Sacred Books of
the East. And here the Vedic hymns will always
hold their foremost place. However late we may
place this systematic collection, their composition
carries us back far beyond the chronological limits
reached by any other documents. And what gives
an additional interest to these Vedic fragments is
that they allow us an insight into the earliest development not only of religion, but of mythology also. We
see superstitions springing up by the side of religion,

demons by the side of gods, agriculture by the side
of the chase, bows and arrows by the side of the
stone-weapons (A*s*ani), such as Indra hurled against
V*ri*tra in his fight against the powers of darkness.
Though the conception of the rainbow being the
bow of the god of the sky is not to be found in
the Rig-Veda, bows and arrows were well known
to the worshippers of the Vedic gods. The Science
of Mythology, after tossing about for centuries on
the ocean of mere conjectures, has at last found its
compass. We no longer see in it, like Bacon, mere
lessons of morality in the disguise of fables, or
broken rays of a primeval revelation, or misunderstood fragments of the Old Testament, still less
recollections of a period of savagery to be studied
in the myths and customs of modern savages, or
survivals of a belief in amulets and magic incantations, generally the very latest outcome of mythology in its historical development, though I believe
there are still survivals of defenders of every one
of these time-hallowed theories. We know now, and
we know it chiefly from the lessons taught us by
the Veda, that our Aryan mythology, and to a
certain extent our ancient Aryan religion also, took
its origin from a poetical interpretation of the great
phenomena of nature, personified and named as the
chief agents of the eternal physical drama, enacted
before us every day, every month, every season,
every year, and we know also that this broad stream
of mythology, when once started, was open to ever
so many tributaries, superstitions, customs, vain gene-

alogies, sorceries, idolatries of every kind, whether springing from fancies and imaginations, or from downright falsehoods and impositions. All these things are apt to be absorbed by mythology, and must be taken into account when we attempt a scientific analysis of it. It must not be supposed, however, that the attempt to find the key of Aryan mythology in fetishism, totemism, shamanism, and wherever it was *not* to be found, have been entirely wasted. A reconnoitring party, even though it return disappointed, has rendered real service by showing where the enemy is not to be found, and that service has certainly been rendered by the exploring parties who thought they could discover in Africa, America, or Australia what was ready to hand in India, Greece, Italy, and among Celtic, Teutonic, and Slavonic races.

People continue to write as if there was still some mystery about the Rig-Veda. There may have been when we began, in the days of Rosen and Burnouf, but there is no longer. The tools are there, all that is now required is honest work, and there is plenty of it, even if there were more real labourers and not merely gleaners than we have at present. It would be by no means difficult to put together a number of hymns which would at once settle the question by showing us the Hindu mind such as it really was during the Vedic period, and impressed by the grand sights of nature that passed before it day and night.

The same story is told again and again, and

wherever we open the Rig-Veda, the same daily drama in its successive stages seems enacted before our eyes. Some people, more particularly the late M. Bergaigne, have been disconcerted by the many allusions not only to the sights of nature, but to the daily sacrifices also which occur in these hymns, but they evidently did not realise that, however complicated and technical the sacrifice had become before the time when these Vedic hymns were collected, there is nothing incongruous between praise and sacrifice. Sacrifice was a very natural occupation for the Vedic savages, as it is among savages at the present day. Whether a man who can describe the daily sunrise in artificial metres belongs to a more primitive humanity than a man who marks the stations of the sun, the phases of the moon, or the return of the seasons to say his prayers and pour out his libations, Sanskrit scholars would gladly leave to members of Ethnological Societies to determine. Whether the Veda is primeval or not, is another question that may likewise be left to those who know what primeval really means.

The grave mistake to be guarded against is to suppose that the Veda is an exclusively liturgical book, monotonous throughout, and belongs therefore to a late liturgical age. Savages, as ethnologists themselves have told us, are often very punctilious ritualists, and if we only consider how essential the Vedic sacrificial system was to the Âryas of India in determining times and seasons, in fact, in laying the first foundations of a well-regulated society, we

shall no longer be surprised at the numerous liturgical allusions which occur in the Vedic hymns, nor
on the other hand see more of liturgy in them than
there really is. Whoever has read if only the first
hymn of the Rig-Veda [1], will know how many words
in it have a liturgical meaning, but nowhere have
those liturgical ideas obscured the original character
of the Vedic gods, as being the agents or actors in
the physical drama of nature which first made the
simple sons of nature ponder on the meaning of day
and night, of sun and moon, of earth and sky, in
fact of all that made them wonder, and turn their
thoughts beyond the horizon of the visible world.

I think it may be best if I give here a few of
those Vedic hymns. They have a right to a place
among my Indian Friends. They have been with
me for many years. They have often roused me in
the morning, they have soothed me in the evening.
I have tried to make them out as one tries to make
out the character of a friend, even when at times
one feels puzzled with him. I have always trusted
them with good intentions, and if some of their
utterances for a long time remained dark and still
remain dark, are there not some dark corners in
most of our friends, nay, even in ourselves?

It has been truly said that books are our best
friends. We see more of them than of any other
friends, and even if we get tired of them at times,
they are always ready to renew their friendship.

[1] Giuseppe Turrini, *Raccolta degli Inni del Veda*, Libro I,
Fascicolo I, Bologna, 1899.

People of the world may wonder what we can see to attract us in such books as the Rig-Veda and to keep us faithful to them to the end. But if they tried, they would find that there are few of the great books of the world which are not worth knowing, and that there are many which deserve our friendship, our love, and our lasting gratitude.

I shall select these Vedic friends at random, following, however, the guidance of an old grammarian, Yâska, who tells us in what succession the Vedic gods appear on the heavenly stage every day, and particularly in the morning. It is in the morning, when light and life return that the bright beings, the Devas, are seen, and the daily revelation of another world takes place, while the various aspects of the new light are personified in the principal gods of the Veda. The order in which they appear, according to Yâska, is: Asvinau, day and night, Ushas, dawn, Sûryâ, wife of the sun, Vrishakapâyî, wife of Vrishakapi, doubtful, Saranyû, early dawn, Erinys, Savitri, the enlivening sun, Bhaga, the sun before sunrise, Sûrya, the risen sun.

We begin with the two Asvins whom Yâska places at the head of the daily procession of the Devas, the Bright Ones.

Hymn to the Asvins, Day and Night.

No Vedic gods have been so completely misunderstood as these heavenly twins, and misunderstood by the Brâhmans themselves. Still even these misunderstandings are instructive. The Asvins were

taken for a pair of horsemen, though it is well known
that riders on horseback occur very seldom in the
Veda, so that some scholars have wrongly maintained
that riding on horseback was altogether unknown in
Vedic times.   The Asvins were taken by native
exegetes for old heroes or kings, and why they
should have formed part of the Vedic gods who
appear in the morning and the evening[1], was never
so much as asked.   Besides, Asvin would be a very
strange name for rider, and would much rather
convey the meaning of a descendant or connection
of Asva, or Asvâ, i. e. the Horse, or the Mare, one
of the many mythological names, as we saw, of the
sun and the dawn.   Being a couple the Asvins were
really the oldest representatives of the couple of
day and night, travelling always on their ordained
path from morning till evening, the same path on
which Agni also travels[2] in his character of the light
of day.   Thus they were very naturally mixed up
with many of the daily adventures of the Sun and
the Dawn[3].   Dyaus is called the father of the
Asvins (Rig-Veda X, 61, 4), the Dawn their mother,
while under another name, as Sûryâ, she is represented as the daughter of Savitri and as the beloved
of the Asvins[4].   Another poet says that the Dawn is
born, when the Asvins have harnessed their chariot,
and that Day and Night, again the Asvins, spring
from Vivasvat[5], the shining sun.   As Saranyû,

[1] Rig-Veda X, 39, 1.
[2] Rig-Veda III, 29, 6.
[3] Rig-Veda III, 20, 1.
[4] Rig-Veda I, 116, 17.
[5] Rig-Veda X, 39, 12.

Erinys, also is called the mother of the Asvins, she must likewise have been another form of the Dawn in her varying aspects.

The stories about the Asvins when they have once become mythological characters, heroes, saviours, and physicians, are endless, but they need not detain us. The important point is to perceive their physical background, and that can always be discovered even behind the thick veil of legend. Nothing is more instructive for the student of mythology than to see how this natural conception of Day and Night, of Light and Darkness, as the Asvins, becomes the germ from which spring in time ever so many half-legendary and even half-historical fables, the so-called Itihâras.

Most of the hymns addressed to the Asvins are very tedious, and repeat again and again the numerous miracles which they performed and the kindnesses which they showed to their friends and worshippers. I give here one short hymn only (V, 76), enough, however, to show what physical background there was for them, a background which in many cases had entirely vanished from the purview of the Vedic Rishis, but which is clear enough to the student of mythology.

I have endeavoured in these translations to keep strictly to the metre of the original, which is not always easy. I must therefore crave the indulgence of my readers for certain infelicities of expression which I could not avoid without departing too much from the original.

Hymn to the Asvins, Day and Night.

1.

Agni shines forth, the shining face of Ushas [1],
The priests' god-loving voices have ascended,
O Asvins, on your chariot hither tending,
Come to our overflowing morn-libation.

2.

The quick do not despise our ready offering;
They have been praised, and are now near
  beside us;
Early and late they hasten to our succour,
The worshipper's best friends against all evil.

3.

Come hither then at milking-time, at breakfast,
Come here at noon, and come at sunset also,
By day, by night, come with your happy succour;
Our draught has always brought the Asvins hither.

4.

This place, forsooth, has always been your dwelling,
The houses here, O Asvins, and this shelter;
Come from high heaven then, and from the
  mountain [2],
Come from the waters, bringing food and vigour.

5.

May we attain the Asvins' newest blessings,
Their happy guidance, health and wealth bestowing;
Immortals, bring us riches, bring us heroes,
And all that here on earth can make us happy.

   [1] Dawn.   [2] The cloud.

If we remember that these twins were originally
meant for morning and evening, the process by
which they gradually became what they are in this
hymn and in other hymns more full of personal
legends, is most instructive to watch. That the
Asvins were originally meant for morning and
evening, or for the two halves of the diurnal twenty-
four hours, cannot be called in question, unless
another germ-idea is first suggested for them. But
then, is it not instructive to see how day and night
simply by being addressed in the second person
became personified, became human and even divine,
and were called by a name which would be unintelligible unless we remembered that the sun had once
been called Asva, the runner, and that Asvâ, the
mare, had been used as a not uncommon name of
the Dawn. These beings who seemed to move on
the same daily path as the sun, or to have been
born of the Dawn, called Asvâ, were then called
the sons or friends of the Dawn, Asvinau, or the
horsemen, as representing the two phases of the
sun, or of the horse ; or, as Yâska says, Nir. XII, 2,
the sun of night and the sun of morning. Their
three-wheeled chariot is golden, and in a single day
goes round heaven and earth. And when that first
metamorphosis had once been effected, when Day
and Night had once become a pair of runners, ever
returning to the same spot in the morning, almost
every blessing that comes from day and night,
particularly health and length of days, would
naturally be ascribed to them. Thus they gradu-

ally assumed the general character of saviours and of physicians, and ever so many beings who were rescued from dangers or from death, whether the setting sun, or the setting moon, or the setting year, were supposed to have been rescued by them. Their chief work is to restore life, and to renew youth, or to give sight to the blind. In many cases the names of the heroes rescued or helped by them speak for themselves, and leave no doubt, in the minds of Sanskrit scholars at least, that they represent physical phenomena, a fact admitted in this case even by so great a sceptic as Bergaigne. Only it must not be supposed that, because we can explain some of their names, we ought to be able to explain them all. The Brâhmans themselves had long forgotten the original purport of these names, and when that was the case, they did not hesitate to give us as facts what were merely their conjectures. As one of the characteristic features of the Asvins was that they always returned, Nâsatya, the returning (*νόστιοι from νόστος, homeward journey) would seem a very applicable name. But ancient grammarians quoted by Yâska, VI, 13, explained it by Na + Asatya, not untrue, or by Nasikâprabhava, born of the nose. Yet Yâska himself had a very just perception of the nature of the Asvins. He quotes various opinions of his predecessors who saw in them heaven and earth, or day and night, or sun and moon, or, lastly, two pious kings. Only this is not a question so much of *aut—aut*, as of *et—et*. They were all this, only from different points of view, and this comprehensiveness is one of the most important features of ancient mythological thought. However startling this may sound to those who form their theories without any reference to historical facts, it is really one of the most important keys for unlocking the riddles of the most ancient periods of mythology, and should be carefully distinguished from what is meant by the syncretism of much later times.

Hymn to Ushas, Dawn.

Next follows Ushas, the Dawn, identical in name, *pace* M. Reinach, with the Greek Eos. She is repre- sented as the most beautiful heavenly apparition among the gods in their procession from East to West. She is called the daughter of Dyaus, the sister of Agni, also his beloved, according to the changing aspects in which the sun of the morning and the dawn presented themselves to the fancy of the Vedic poets. I subjoin the translation of a hymn addressed to Ushas from the first Ma*nd*ala, hymn 123.

I.

Dakshinâ's[1] roomy chariot has been harnessed,
And the immortal gods have mounted on it,
The growing Dawn, free from the dark oppressor,
Stepped forth to spy for the abode of mortals.

---

[1] Name of the Dawn. It requires a considerable acquaintance with phonetic laws to doubt the identity of the names Ushas in Sanskrit and Eos in Greek. Yet I believe that even this has been achieved by those who seem to imagine that scepticism is the best proof of knowledge.

2.

The mighty woke before all other creatures,
She wins the race, and always conquers riches;
The Dawn looks out, young and reviving ever,
She came the first here to our morning prayers.

3.

When thou, O Dawn, to-day dividest treasures,
Thou goddess, nobly born, among all mortals,
May Savit*ri*[1], the god, the friend of homesteads,
Proclaim us innocent before the sun-god!

4.

To every house is Ahanâ[2] approaching,
Giving to every day its name and being,
Dyotanâ[2] came, for ever bent on conquest,
She gets the best of all the splendid treasures.

5.

Varu*na*'s sister, sister thou of Bhaga,
O Sûn*ri*tâ[2], O Dawn, sing first at daybreak;
May he fall back, the man that plotteth mischief,
With Dakshi*nâ* and car let us subdue him.

6.

Let hymns rise up, let pray'rs rise up together,
The fires have risen, clad in flaring splendour,
The brilliant Dawn displays the lovely treasures
Which had been hidden by the night and darkness.

---

[1] Savi*tri*, the sun-god, but distinct from Sûrya, the sun and sun-god.
[2] Name of Dawn.

7.

The one departeth and the other cometh [1],
Unlike in hue the two march close together;
One secretly brought night to earth and heaven,
Dawn sparkled forth on her refulgent chariot.

8.

Alike to-day, alike to-morrow also,
They ever follow Varuna's [2] commandment;
They one by one achieve their thirty Yogans [3],
And without fail achieve their lord's (Varuna's)
    commandment [4].

9.

She knows the first day's name, and brightly
    shining,
White she is born to-day, from out the darkness;
The maiden never breaks th' eternal order [5],
And day by day comes to the place appointed.

10.

Proud of thy beauty, maiden-like thou comest,
O goddess to the god [6] who thee desireth;
A smiling girl, thou openest before him
Thy bosom's splendour, as thou shinest brightly.

---

[1] Day and Night, Dawn and Twilight are conceived as sisters, and spoken of as Ahanî, the two days, one bright, the other dark, like the Asvins.

[2] Varuna, sometimes the highest god, whose laws have to be obeyed by all creatures.

[3] Their appointed course.

[4] Kratu, thought, will, here command.

[5] The order in which the heavenly bodies come and go, which gave the first intimation of order in the universe.

[6] The sun.

11.

Fair as a bride, adorned by loving mother,
Thou showest forth thy form, that they may see it;
Auspicious Dawn, shine forth more wide and
   brightly,
No other dawns[1] have ever reached thy splendour.

12.

With horses, cows, and all delightful treasures,
And striving with the rays of yonder Sûrya,
The Dawns depart and come again with splendour,
Bearing auspicious names and forms auspicious.

13.

Obedient to the reins of law eternal,
Grant us auspicious thoughts for our endeavours,
Shine thou upon us, Dawn, thou swift to listen,
May we and all our liberal chieftains prosper!

In spite of all the angry and ill-natured words of
M. Bergaigne, I ask once more whether this address
to the Dawn is not perfectly natural and intelligible.
Whether it required a priest to compose it, or
whether any father of a family could have done so,
who can tell? And who can tell whether the first
priest was not simply the father of a family, who
had his fire always burning on the domestic hearth,
and who felt grateful for the return of the dawn,
which coincided with the kindling of the fire on his
hearth? If the morning service was called Pûrva-
hûti, what is that more than the early calling, Hûti

---

[1] Dawn is often spoken of in the plural, being conceived as new
every day, or being considered manifold in her wide expanse.

being derived from the same root, Hvê, from which we had before Hot*ri*, the invoker, the priest.

But whatever we may think on that point, it seems perfectly clear that the different names by which the Dawn is here addressed, Ushas, Ahanâ, Dyotanâ, Dakshi*n*â, and Sûn*ri*tâ, were understood as names of the Dawn. But will it be believed, that when the Dawn is addressed in the very first verse by the name of Dakshi*n*â, when her chariot is mentioned, and her stepping forth out of darkness to come to the morning-prayer of the people, Mr. Bergaigne, always on the look-out for priest-craft and ritual, sees in Dakshi*n*â, not the Dawn, but *le salaire du sacrifice?* He thinks it not impossible that *le salaire du sacrifice* might have been the name of the Dawn, *considérée comme le don céleste accordé pour récompense à l'homme pieux.* But he declines even this small concession, and, if I understand him rightly, he actually takes Dakshi*n*â in the first and fifth verses of our hymn as the salary of the priests. Now it is quite true that Dakshi*n*â has this meaning of salary or gift due to the priest who performs that sacrifice, but that meaning is clearly impossible here. Our hymn contains several unusual names of the Dawn, such as Ahanâ, Dyotanâ, Sûn*ri*tâ, all ἄπαξ λεγόμενα, as names of the Dawn, then why not Dakshi*n*â? Dakshi*n*â means right, *dexter*, evidently from Daksha, strength, the right hand being the strong or clever hand. It then means southern. It also means the cow, the strong cow which has calves and gives milk (Dakshi*n*â gâva*h*, Lâ*ty*. VIII, 5), and as such a cow was the most primitive payment (*fee* and *pecu*), it may well have become the regular name for the fee due to the priest. She is celebrated as such in one of the Vedic hymns, X, 107. But however prominent a place may have been assigned to this Dakshi*n*â, the salary of priests, how could the Dawn have been called the salary? We can hardly explain why even that salary was called Dakshi*n*â, unless we suppose that it was meant for the right hand, or *la bonne main*, and in that case Dakshi*n*â, Dawn, might have been meant for the liberal goddess. But whatever the evolution of the meaning of Dakshi*n*â may have been [1], when she was invoked as Dakshi*n*â, she could not have been invoked as Salary. I am glad to see that even M. Bergaigne has not been bold enough to translate "*Le large char du Salaire a été attelé*," but "*Le large char de la Dakshinâ.*" If Dakshi*n*â were really in that sense an ἅπαξ λεγόμενον, surely it is not the only ἅπαξ λεγόμενον in the scanty survivals of Vedic poetry. When we read that Dakshi*n*â was the daughter of Dyaus and the mother of Agni (Rig-Veda III, 58, 1), we need no more to feel convinced that she was meant for the Dawn. Besides, who is the Putro Dakshi*n*âya*h*, the son of Dakshi*n*â, if not Agni, the same who brings Dyotani, Rig-Veda III, 58, 1? Another name of the Dawn is Dyotanâ, and who can doubt that it

---

[1] Perhaps it should be remembered that in the Mahâbhârata the wife of Ka*s*yapa, the mother of the Âdityas, was called Dakshâya*n*î; see Pramatha Nâth Mullick, "Origin of Caste," p. 33.

meant the brilliant, i. e. the Dawn. More difficult are the other names Ahanâ and Sûn*r*itâ.

Ahanâ is clearly connected with Ahan, day, just as our dawn is connected with day. It has long been known that day is not connected with *dies*, as was formerly supposed, but that the root of Goth. dags, day, can only have been dah, or dhah, with double aspirate, to burn, to shine. The loss of an initial d is no doubt quite irregular[1], though it can be matched by Goth. tagr, Gr. δάκρυ, tear, which in Sanskrit appears as A*s*ru, instead of Da*s*ru. I pointed out long ago, and I have never seen any valid reason to retract it, that in the Greek δάφνη, laurel tree, the name of a matutinal goddess, we have the root with its initial d, and that another derivation of the same root, without the initial d, may be recognised in Athanâ or Athênê.

No one, I thought, could have supposed that I meant to see in this Ahanâ one of the grandest Greek goddesses, Athênê. Why will people so often misunderstand, and then place their misunderstanding on the shoulders of those whom they misunderstand? When I said that Zeus is Dyaus, that Eos is Ushas, that Agni is Ignis, surely I could not have meant that these gods and goddesses migrated bodily from India to Greece and from Greece to India. Why must what seems perfectly clear be said again and again, that the Greek and Indian gods were not beings that ever existed in heaven or on earth, but were mere names, mere

[1] Cf. " Chips," IV, p. 385.

creations of the human mind. In all comparative
mythological studies we have to look for the germs
only, and I see in Ahanâ and Athênê a common
germ, that withered on Indian soil, while it assumed
the grandest development in Greece.

Surely not even Deva is the same as Deus; though
it may be the same sound, it does not represent the
same meaning, so that strictly speaking we cannot
translate the one by the other. The Greek
concept of Zeus also was very different from that
of the Vedic Dyaus, as that of Eos from that of
Ushas. I never went so far as to claim for Greek
and Vedic deities what might be called personal
or bodily identity. I was simply looking for germs
which after thousands of years might have developed
into a Sûrya in the Veda, and into a Helios in
Homer. These very modest claims may possibly
surprise my adversaries, for, to judge from their
remarks, they evidently imagined that I recognised
in Zeus a heavenly king who had migrated from
India to Greece, and in the Haritas the horses of the
morning who in their journey to Greece had been
metamorphosed into the brilliant children of Helios
and Aigle. I even begin to see why what some
critics supposed to have been my idea, should have
ruffled their temper so much, and I say once more,
and I hope for the last time, that I never believed
that Athênê lived in the thoughts of Vedic Rishis,
nor Varuna in the prayers of Greek priests. No,
I am and always have been satisfied with far less.
All I stand up for is that, given the sky, the Greeks

raised Dyu, sky, to become their Zeus, while the
Vedic Rishis made the sky their Dyaus. This
Dyaus is superseded in the Veda by his own son,
Indra, whereas Zeus in Greece remained to the
end the θεῶν ὕπατος καὶ ἄριστος. What is common to
both is the word, that is, the concept of Dyaus, or
Greek Zeus, the sky as a person and as an agent.
I may not always have spoken quite guardedly, and
have taken certain things for granted which are
understood by themselves among scholars. The
important lesson is always the same. If Ahanâ is
phonetically identical with Greek Athanâ and if
Ahanâ is a name of the Dawn, it follows that the
first conception of Athênê was the Dawn and that, as
such, she sprang from the East or from the forehead
of Zeus or Dyaus, the sky. If in the Veda she
brings light and wakes and stirs up the thoughts
of men, she became in Homer also the goddess of
wisdom and the τεχνῶν μήτηρ πολύολβος. All this
was perfectly known to Otfried Müller when in
1825 he wrote : " Because the name of the goddess
was originally a word of the language and always
remained so, Charis glided from poem to poem
and preserved by means of the word her general
meaning in every individual manifestation " (p. 249).

Sûnritâ, another name of the Dawn, is more
difficult to explain. Sûnrita in the sense of true,
seems to me to have been formed in mistaken
analogy to An-rita [1], untrue, and to have meant

---

[1] The two words are used together, as ubhayor antaram veda,
sûnritânritayor api, Mahâbh. V, 5667.

originally true, then sincere, gentle, agreeable. As applied to the Dawn it would have meant true, kind, auspicious.

But whatever obscurity there may still be left as to the meaning of single words in our hymn, can any one doubt that the whole of it was simply an address or a prayer to the Dawn, without any reference, as yet, to any complicated ceremonial, as described in the Sûtras and Brâhmanas, and alluded to in some of the hymns also? And why this persistent searching for allusions to ceremonial? No one ever denied the presence of real allusions in the Vedic hymns. But it is a matter of degree, a question of more or less, and these ceremonial details, so far from proving our hymns to be very modern and the work of professed priests, serve only to prove, what was well known from other sources also, that savage or uncivilised races adhere at all times with great punctiliousness to their ceremonial customs and traditions. M. Bergaigne has done excellent work in pointing out traces of the same punctiliousness among Vedic poets, but he has allowed himself to be carried away much too far by his own system, without either paying sufficient attention to native commentaries or allowing sufficient credit to his predecessors, particularly in Germany. To speak of *ces philologues d'outre Rhin*, is entirely out of place in the republic of letters, and encourages a literary *chauvinisme* which will never find favour with the best scholars of France.

Leaving out Sûryâ, the female representative of

II.   P

the sun, and more or less a Dawn again, and Vrishâ-
kapâyî, because her character is not quite clear as
yet, and Saranyû = Erinys, because she is only
mentioned in a few verses, we proceed now to
Savitri, the rising sun. Though Savitri is a name
applied to the sun in general, it is most frequently
used as the name of the rising and life- and light-
giving sun. Nor must it be supposed that Savitri
is simply an appellative of the solar globe. Savitri
has become a divine name or a divine *numen* as full
of life and personality as any other Deva. He can
therefore be asked, as he is in verse 9, to hale and
bring back the real sun. We shall easily recognise
his character in the following hymn (Rig-Veda I,
35, 2) :—

Hymn to Savitri, Sun.

I.

I first call Agni [1] hither for our happiness,
I then call Mitra-Varuna [2] to shield us here,
I call on Râtrî [3], sending all the world to rest,
I call for help on Savitri, the brightest god.

2.

Approaching on the darkest path of heaven,
Setting to rest both mortal and immortal,
God Savitri, on golden chariot standing,
Comes hither and beholdeth all creation.

---

[1] Agni, fire, is here, as often, taken for the light of day.

[2] Mitra and Varuna stand for morning and evening, or day
and night.

[3] Râtrî, night, sometimes called the black day, Krishnam ahar,
opposed to Argunam ahar, the bright day. Cf. Rig-Veda VI, 9, 1.

3.

The brilliant god moves upward and moves down-
     ward,
The worshipful, drawn by his brilliant racers,
And from afar god Savitri approaches,
Driving away from us all that is evil[1].

4.

God Savitri stepped on his jewelled chariot,
The strong, the many-hued, its pins all golden[2],
And he, the worshipful, in brightest splendour,
Displays his strength across the darkest welkin.

5.

Black with white hoofs the horses shone upon us,
Dragging along the golden-shafted chariot;
All men, all creatures here for ever rested,
Safe in the lap of Savitri in heaven.

6.

Three skies are there of Savitri, two places,
And one in Yama's realm that holds our heroes[3],
Immortals[4] mounted on the chariot's axle,—
Let him speak out who understands this saying.

7.

The glorious bird[5] has lighted-up the heaven,
The guide divine, whose wings are deeply sounding;
Where is the sun? Who knows it now, to tell us,
Which of the heavens his ray may have illumined?

---

[1] Evil, physically darkness, morally sin.   [2] Pins of the chariot.
[3] The departed.   [4] Explained as stars.   [5] The sun.

8.

The earth's eight quarters has the sun illumined,
Three miles of land, and all the seven rivers,
God Savit*ri*, the golden-eyed, has neared us,
And brought choice treasures to the liberal mortals.

9.

The golden Savit*ri*, who never rested,
Is moving forward, straight 'tween earth and
    heaven,
He strikes disease, and hales the sun from yonder;
Through darkest clouds up to the sky he hastens.

10.

The guide divine, with golden arms appearing,
May come to us, the rich and gracious giver,
Praised every night, the god did come towards us,
Chasing away the noxious evil spirits.

11.

O Savit*ri*, come hither on thy pathways,
The old, well-made ones, dustless in the heavens,
And on those paths be thou our sure protector,
And grant to us to-day thy gracious blessing!

Is there one verse in this hymn that is not perfectly clear and intelligible, as belonging to a hymn
addressed to the personified deity of the sun? Let
us once understand that Savit*ri* was a name of the
sun, and why should he not be invoked for pro-
tection and for every kind of blessing? Of course,
as soon as the sun was addressed by a poet, he

ceased to be a mere sight. He became subjective,
personal, and human, whether we like it or not.
After that it does not require a great effort of
imagination to address him as standing on a golden
chariot, drawn by brilliant horses and all the rest.
Surely the Vedic poets stood not alone in indulging
in such imagery.

The sixth verse is no doubt difficult to understand in its minute detail, but its general sense is
clear, and we must remember that the whole verse
was really meant as a kind of riddle, a kind of
amusement in which uncivilised races all over the
world seem to have delighted.

Everything else is exactly what any poet might say
of the sun. The sun might well be called a bird with
golden wings, and if he is thanked for the treasures
which he brings, surely the mere light of the
morning and the warmth of the day are treasures
sufficient for those whose very life must often have
depended on the return of light and warmth after a
cold and dark night, or on the return of spring after
a severe winter. I cannot think that even native
scholars could discover anything beyond what we ourselves see in this hymn, and as to M. Bergaigne, he
must surely have been dazzled by his own system if
he could perceive many, nay, any allusions to a highly
developed system of sacrifice in any hymn like this.
That such allusions exist in other hymns, I am very
far from denying; what I deny is that liturgical
thoughts ever obscured the broad physical features
which formed the background of the ancient Vedic

religion[1], nay, of the Vedic ceremonial also, built up
at first for the sake of regulating the times and
seasons of the year.   I am the very last to deny
to M. Bergaigne and his pupils the merit of having
made the sacrificial system of the Vedic hymns more
intelligible, but they have not sufficiently resisted
the temptation of trying the key that opened one
drawer, on all the drawers that still remained to be
unlocked.

These hymns would suffice for the gods of the
morning, and may help to open the eyes of our
mythological Parâv*rig*as, who cannot see the light
because there is too much of it.

I shall, however, add one more matutinal hymn
addressed to Agni, not simply as the fire, but as
the god of light which brightens the world every
morning, and is in fact very difficult to distinguish
from the sun.   This Agni is sometimes called the
first of all the gods.   The word itself is the general
name of fire in Sanskrit.   It is phonetically the
same as the Latin *ignis*, though the change of a
into i is phonetically irregular.   No one, however,
is likely to be so bold an agnostic as to deny that
the Âryas, before they separated, had made the discovery of fire, and given a name to it, such as Agni
or *ignis*.   What is most interesting in the development of this word is that while in India it entered

---

[1] Bergaigne, Vol. II, p. 277: 'Les interprétations purement
naturalistes, appliquées à l'analyse des mythes du Rig-Véda, laissent
toujours, ou presque toujours, un résidu liturgique, et ce résidu,
le plus souvent négligé jusqu'alors, en est précisément la partie
la plus importante pour l'exégèse des hymnes.'

into a very rich, religious, and mythological career,
it remained a simple appellative in Italy, and was
almost entirely lost and forgotten among the other
Aryan nations. Should we be justified then in
saying that the Latin *ignis* cannot possibly be the
same word as Agni, because the latter is one of
the greatest gods in the Veda, while *ignis* is no
god at all? In the Veda Agni is a most prominent
deity, though his character has often been misunderstood. Agni was, no doubt, the fire on the hearth
and on the altar, and as such had his own development in India[1]. But Agni was also light in general,
and more especially the light of the sun, whether
in the morning, or at noon, or in the evening.
Thus we read, Rig-Veda III, 28, 1 :—

Agni, accept our offering, the cake, at the *morning
libation !*

Agni, eat the cake offered to thee when the *day
is over !*

Agni, accept here the cake at the *midday libation !*

Here Agni is clearly the sun, or the sunlight, or
some power dwelling in the sun, all of which are
very natural ideas with people in a nomadic or
even agricultural state of society, nor do the three
daily libations seem to me to point to any elaborate
ceremonial. They are hardly more than the beginnings of the Sandhyâvandana and they could
easily be matched among Semitic, nay, even among
savage races.

---

[1] See M. M., " Physical Religion," p. 120.

In many hymns the solar character of Agni is merged in his domestic character, as the fire on the domestic hearth, as the centre of each family. Thus we read, Rig-Veda X, 1 :—

Hymn to Agni, Fire.

1.

High [1], at the head of Dawn, he stood, the mighty,
With light he came, emerging from the darkness,
Fair-bodied Agni with his radiant splendour
Has filled, when born, all human habitations.

2.

Thou, being born, art child of Earth and Heaven,
Agni, the fair one, spread among the flowers [2];
The brilliant child by night and through the
    darkness,
Shouts for the cows [3] from far, above his mothers.

3.

Then knowing well the highest place in heaven,
As Vishnu, he, when born, protects the third place [4].
And when their milk [5] has in his mouth been offered,
They sing to him with one accord their praises.

---

[1] I have tried to preserve some of the Vedic rhythm in these translations, but I must apologise for these poetic efforts of mine in English. I have consulted, of course, the translations of Grassmann, Ludwig, Griffiths, and Bergaigne, and others where accessible, and have adopted some of the renderings which seemed to me particularly happy.

[2] Flowers and plants in general are supposed to be supported by warmth within them.

[3] The clouds that give their milk, the rain.

[4] The culminating point of the sun, between sunrise and sunset.

[5] The milk of the clouds, or the rain.

4.

And then the mothers, bringing food, approach him,
They bring him viands and they watch his increase;
Though they have changed, thou goest again to
    see them
And art a priest[1] among the tribes of mortals.

5.

Then hail to Agni, as the guest of mortals[1],
The priest of holy rites on glittering chariot,
The brilliant signal[1] of all sacrifices,
Of any god, by might divine, the equal.

6.

Then, dressed in raiment beautiful, and standing
In morning light, a priest on earth's old centre,
Thou, born in Iḍâ's place[2], a king and high priest,
Shalt hither bring the gods to our oblation.

7.

For thou hast ever spread both earth and heaven[3],
Again our friend, a true son to thy parents
Come hither, youthful god, to us who call thee,
And bring the gods, O son of strength[4], to
    usward!

[1] The fire on the hearth, in which oblations were offered.
[2] On the altar or the omphalos of the earth.
[3] Made visible.
[4] The rubbing of the fire-sticks required great strength and skill
to bring out the fire that was supposed to be hidden in the wood.
The fire, when lighted on the hearth, was supposed to bring the
gods to their offerings; nay, by a change of cause and effect the
fire kindled on the hearth was identified with the light kindled in
the sky at the approach of the dawn.

Now, I ask once more, can anything be more
simple and natural? And can we not, without any
great effort on our part, transport ourselves into the
position of the Vedic poet who uttered these words,
and follow his thoughts, as he gazed on the rising
sun? No one would suppose that this poet was the
first on earth who ever addressed the rising sun, and
that it was he who coined all the names by which
the sun is addressed in these short songs. We can
easily see what a long distance lies behind him,
behind his words and behind his ideas. He was
certainly not the first who invented priests and their
sacrificial work. Only let us remember that, if we
use such terms as priest or high priest, or king,
we must not allow ourselves to assign to these
terms, however unconsciously, all the meanings
these words have with us.

These are very important cautions for people
ignorant of Sanskrit, who have been led to imagine
that the Vedic Âryas had kings like Solomon or
Louis Quatorze, or High Priests like Samuel or
Bossuet. The word which I translate by priest,
is hotri, which meant originally no more than
shouter or invoker, and which in due time became
the technical name of one of the sixteen Ritvigas
or Season-priests. The other word Purohita means
praepositus, or provost, and was at first no more
than the priest who had to assist or to replace the
father of a family, and had to see that all the offerings to the gods were made at the proper times and
seasons, which probably was in the beginning no

more than a contrivance for marking the essential
divisions of the year.

Much depends here, as elsewhere, on the words
which we use. Every act of worship may be called
a sacrifice, and every sacred poet a high priest. To
us these are very grand names and full of meaning.
But let us look at some of the hymns addressed to
Agni which are called sacrificial, and it seems to me
that any peasant in his own cottage could have performed what is called a sacrifice, as presupposed, for
instance, in the following hymn (Rig-Veda II, 6).

Hymn to Agni, Fire.

1.

Agni, accept this log of wood,
This service which I bring to thee,
Hear graciously these prayers and songs!

2.

With this log let us honour thee,
Thou son of strength, the horse's friend,
And with this hymn, thou nobly born.

3.

And let us servants with our songs
Serve thee, the lover of our songs,
Wealth-lover, giver of our wealth!

4.

Be thou our mighty, generous lord,
Thou lord and giver of our wealth,
And drive all hatred far from us!

5.

He gives us rain from heaven above,
He gives inviolable strength,
He gives us food a thousandfold.

6.

Come here, most youthful messenger,
To him who lauds and craves thy help,
Most holy priest[1], called by our song.

7.

Agni, between both worlds[2], O sage,
Thou passest, as a messenger
Between two hamlets, kind and wise,

8.

Thou hast befriended us before,
Bring hither always all the gods,
And sit thou on this sacred turf[3].

But whether these so-called sacrifices were in the beginning as complicated as they certainly were in the end, they are perfectly intelligible, and probably will become much more so when we know more of the literature in which they are described. How much of their development is presupposed in the Vedic hymns, I tried to explain, however shortly, as long ago as 1859 in my 'History of Ancient Sanskrit Literature,' p. 468, and much has been added by others during the last forty years; but when we speak of Vedic sacrifices, we must not think of the temple at Jerusalem, or of St. Peter's, but of a small plot of grass, on which a fire was kindled within the walls of piled up turf, and kept alive by pouring butter or fat upon it.

What is far more instructive in these hymns is the general attitude of the poet towards the sights

---

[1] The fire on the altar was supposed to call the gods, like a priest.　　　　　[2] Heaven and earth, gods and men.

[3] The place where the fire was kept.

of nature which attracted his attention, and the
transition from a mere description of nature such
as he saw it, to its being peopled with persons whom
we call either divine or mythological. Here it is
where the Veda has proved so useful, and has given
quite a new character to the study of ancient religion
and ancient mythology in every part of the world.

How much ingenuity was spent in former days
to discover the origin of Zeus and the Greek
dwellers on Olympus! After opening the Veda
all becomes clear. What doubt can there remain
that Zeus was Dyaus, originally the sky, but not
the sky as the blue vault of heaven, but the sky
as active, as personified and divine ? We cannot
expect to find many such cases as that of Dyaus =
Zeus, where an Aryan god has preserved not
only his old character in India and Greece and
Italy, but his name, and that almost unchanged.
We saw how the name of Agni was altogether lost
in Greece, though preserved as an appellative in
Italy. Yet the Greeks also had their god of fire,
and their gods of light, such as Hephaestos, Apollon,
Dionysos, Hermes and others, each developed in
his own way. And here we come across some
curious reminiscences among the Aryan nations.
We saw how Agni, as morning sun, was called the
son of heaven and earth. In other hymns he is
actually called Dvimâtâ, having two mothers. This
strange name meets us again in Greek Dimêtôr,
in Latin as Bimatris. The child of two mothers
or parents, a name quite intelligible, as we saw, in

Sanskrit, as the son of heaven and earth, had become
unintelligible in Greek and Latin, so that every
kind of myth was invented to account for so strange a
name. To say that the deity called Dvimâtâ in the
Veda was the same as the Greek Dimêtôr or the
Latin Bimatris would be going too far; but to say
that Dimêtôr, i.e. Dionysos (*Dyu-ni*sya) was originally a god of light, as much as Agni, as much as
Apollon, and Hermes, the son of heaven and earth,
is perfectly right and helps us to account for a
number of myths in classical mythology.

These more hidden influences of ancient Aryan
mythology on that of Greeks and Romans, are often
the most interesting. We have a similar case in
Jupiter Stator, which is generally explained as the
stopper, stopping the soldiers from running away.
That may be the Roman explanation, but in the
Veda we have the same word Sthâtâ, applied to Indra,
first as Sthâtâ hari*n*âm, i.e. holder of horses, when
he comes in his chariot; then as Sthâtâ rathasya,
holder or governor of his chariot. When this origin
was once forgotten, it would be not unlikely that
a new meaning was discovered in Stator, viz. the
preserver of law and order, or the keeper in battle.

If Agni, as in hymn X, 1, is identified with
Vish*n*u, i.e. the sun in the zenith, we see how
pliant the ideas of gods still were in the Veda. This
Vish*n*u in India became in time as independent a
deity as Apollon and Dionysos ever were in Greece,
but they were all conceived as in the beginning
sons of heaven and earth, and as closely allied

with the sun in its various manifestations. The Vedic poet saw no difficulty in recognising the same elementary power in the sun rising in the morning, culminating at noon, and vanishing at night, nay in the fire on the hearth, and in the fire of the sacrifice, as the divine guest, the friend of the family, the priest on the altar. All this is not the Solar Theory, it is the Solar Fact, and not easily to be disposed of by an ignorant smile. Though Sanskrit scholars differ as much as other scholars, the broad facts of the Solar Theory have never been called in question by any competent authority, I mean, by anybody acquainted with Greek and Latin, and a little of Vedic Sanskrit.

While Agni here appears before us as the god of light in general, and often begins the procession of the daily gods as the light of the morning, as chasing away the dark night, as holding aloft the radiant sun, as leading forth the daughter of Dyaus (Διὸς θυγάτηρ), that is the Dawn, he being represented sometimes as the brother of the Dawn, sometimes as her lover [1], once even as kissing her [2], there are other deities, equally representative of light, but more specialised in their functions. Sûrya himself, the Greek Helios, appears among the Vedic deities, and Ushas (Eos), the dawn, is called Sûrya-prabhâ or sunshine.

We have so far watched the daily procession of the Vedic gods as reflected in the hymns, beginning with Agni, as god of light, especially the

[1] X, 3, 3.   [2] X, 4, 4.

light of the morning, and in many respects the
alter ego of the sun. We saw that in one sense
the Dawn also is only a female repetition of the
auroral Agni (Agnir aushasya), and we met with
a third personification of the morning sun in the
shape of Savit*ri*, who is perhaps the most dramatic
among the solar heroes, such as Mitra, Âditya,
Vish*n*u and others.

The procession of the matutinal gods, which
we have followed so far under the guidance of
our old grammarian, Yâska, can be shown to rest
on even earlier authority. Thus we read in one
of the hymns themselves, Rig-Veda I, 157, 1 :—

Agni awoke, from earth arises Sûrya,
Ushas, the great and bright, throws heaven open,
The pair of A*s*vins yoked their car to travel,
God Savit*ri* has roused the world to labour.

There are other hymns, of course, that refer
to the light of day or to the sun in his later stages
also, culminating as Vish*n*u, or setting with T*ri*ta,
till at last Râtrî, night, appears, and Varu*n*a, the
coverer, reigns once more supreme in heaven.
When we see Varu*n*a together with Mitra, the
sun-god, they represent a divine couple, dividing
between them the sovereignty of the whole world,
heaven and earth, very much like the A*s*vins. They
are not so much in opposition to each other, as
partners in a common work.

Just as the night, the sister of the Dawn, is sometimes conceived as a dawn or day (Ahan) herself,

Mitra and Varu*n*a also seem often to be charged with the same duties. They hold heaven and earth asunder, they support heaven and earth and are the common guardians of the whole world. Varu*n*a as well as Mitra is represented as sun-eyed. Still the contrast between the two becomes gradually more and more pointed, and we can clearly see that, while light and day become the portion of Mitra, night and darkness fall more and more to the share of Varu*n*a. The sun is said to rise from the abode of Mitra and Varu*n*a, but night, moon, and stars are mentioned in the hymns already, as more closely related to Varu*n*a. Thus we read, Rig-Veda I, 27, 10 :—

The stars fixed high in heaven and shining
      brightly
By night, Oh say, where have they gone by day-
      time ?
The laws of Varu*n*a are everlasting,
The moon moves on by night in brilliant splendour.

In Rig-Veda VIII, 41, 10, we ought surely to translate, "He made the white-clothed black-clothed," and not, as proposed, "He made the black-clothed white-clothed," a change which is never ascribed to Varu*n*a.

This explains why some scholars went so far as to recognise in Varu*n*a the original represen-tative of the moon or of the evening star, a far too narrow conception, however, of that supreme deity, though true, no doubt, so far as Varu*n*a, like the sky, comprehends within his sphere of influence night and stars as well as sun and dawn. The almost perfect identity of name between Varu*n*a and Ouranos shows that Varu*n*a was not only a Vedic or Indian deity, but had been named already in the Aryan period. There are phonetic difficulties, but how should we account for the coincidences in the name and character of these two gods?

These few specimens of Vedic poetry will suffice, I hope, to show what is meant by the Solar Theory. It means that most of the physical phenomena which impressed the mind of primitive races, like those that have left us their religious utterances in the Veda, were connected with the sun, with the light of the morning, with day and night succeeding each other, and regulating the whole life of an agricultural population. What else was there to interest such people and to draw away their thoughts from a visible to an invisible world? If I have sometimes called that population uncivilised, what I meant was that we come across customs, such as the selling of children or offering them as victims, polygamy, possibly even polyandry, which are generally considered as signs or survivals of savagery. Such general terms, however, are often very misleading, and because in the Râgasûya sacrifice, for instance, there are remnants of disgusting customs, we must not allow ourselves to indulge with certain so-called missionaries in a general condemnation of the Vedic ceremonial. We should rather learn the lesson that ceremonial is generally the accumulation of centuries, and contains, besides much that may be useful, a large quantity of old rubbish, mostly misunderstood, muddled, and complicated, till the meaning of it, if it ever had any, is lost beyond the hope of recovery.

If anybody, after reading these few hymns, selected quite at random, can still doubt whether the Solar Theory is the only possible theory to account for these Vedic deities, and in consequence, for the Aryan deities connected with them by name or character, I have nothing more to say. I doubt the existence of such a person. He must in very truth be a solar myth. Let me say once more that I have never looked upon all Vedic deities as solar or matutinal, but that other physical phenomena also, such as rivers, clouds, earth, night, storms, and rain had been personified or deified before these hymns could have been composed. It is true there is one hymn only addressed exclusively to the Night (X, 127), two only addressed to the Earth, but I pointed out before why such statistics, though very tempting, are altogether untrustworthy and have nothing whatever to do with the real importance or popularity of these deities. Does the ninth Man*d*ala of the Rig-Veda, with its 114 hymns almost entirely addressed to Soma, prove the supreme popularity of Soma as a member of the Vedic Pantheon? However, to guard against all possibility of misapprehending my purpose, here follows the hymn to Râtrî or Night; which can hardly be called solar in the usual sense of that word.

Hymn to Râtrî, Night.

1.

The Night comes near and looks about,
The goddess with her many eyes,
She has put on her glories all.

2.

Immortal, she has filled the space,
Both far and wide, both low and high,
She conquers darkness with her light[1].

3.

She has undone her sister, Dawn[2],
The goddess Night, as she approached,
And utter darkness[3] flies away.

4.

For thou art she in whose approach
We seek to-day for rest, like birds
Who in the branches seek their nest.

5.

The villages have sought for rest,
And all that walks and all that flies,
The falcons come, intent on prey.

6.

Keep off the she-wolf, keep the wolf,
Keep off the thief, O kindly Night,
And be thou light for us to pass.

[1] The darkness of the night is lighted by the light of the moon and stars.

[2] The dawn or bright day that lasts from morning till evening.

[3] The darkness, caused by the retreat of Dawn or Day, is lighted up by the brilliant Night.

7.

Black darkness came, yet bright with stars,
It came to us, with brilliant hues;
Dawn, free us as from heavy debt!

8.

Like cows, I brought this hymn to thee,
As to a conqueror, child of Dyaus,
Accept it graciously, O Night!

We must remember that the night to the Vedic
poet was not the same as darkness, but that on the
contrary, when the night had driven away the
day, she was supposed to lighten the darkness, and
even to rival her sister, the bright day, with her
starlight beauty.   The night, no doubt, gives peace
and rest, yet the Dawn is looked upon as the
kindlier light, and is implored to free mortals from
the dangers of the night, as debtors are freed from
a debt. Many conjectural alterations have been
proposed in this hymn, but it seems to me to be
intelligible even as it stands.

One more hymn to show how the belief in and
the worship of these physical gods, the actors behind
the phenomena of nature, could grow naturally into
a belief in and a worship of moral powers, endowed
with all the qualities essential to divine beings.
Moral ideas are not so entirely absent from the
Veda, as has sometimes been asserted, and nothing
can be more instructive than to watch the process
by which they spring naturally from a belief in the

gods of nature. I give the hymn to Varuna from Rig-Veda VII, 86, which I translated for the first time in my " History of Ancient Sanskrit Literature" in the year 1859, and which, with the help of other translations published in the meantime, I have now tried to improve and to clothe in the metrical form of the original.

Hymn to Varuna.

1.

Wise, surely, through his might is his creation,
Who stemmed asunder spacious earth and heaven;
He pushed the sky, the bright and glorious, upward,
And stretched the starry sky and earth asunder.

2.

With my own heart I commune, how I ever
Can now approach Varuna's sacred presence;
Will he accept my gift without displeasure?
When may I fearless look and find him gracious?

3.

Fain to discover this my sin, I question,
I go to those who know, and ask for counsel.
The same reply I get from all the sages,
'Tis Varuna indeed whom thou hast angered.

4.

What was my chief offence that thou wilt slay me,
Thy oldest friend who always sang thy praises?
Tell me, unconquered Lord, and I shall quickly
Fall down before thee, sinless with my homage.

5.

Loose us from sins committed by our fathers,
From others too which we ourselves committed,
As from a calf, take from us all our fetters,
Loose us as thieves are loosed that lifted cattle.

6.

'Twas not our own free will, 'twas strong temptation,
Or thoughtlessness, strong drink, or dice, or passion,
The old was near to lead astray the younger,
Nay, sleep itself suggests unrighteous actions.

7.

Let me do service to the bounteous giver,
The angry god, like to a slave, but sinless;
The gracious god gave wisdom to the foolish,
And he, the wiser, leads the wise to riches.

8.

O let this song, god Varuna, approach thee,
And let it reach thy heart, O Lord and Master!
Prosper thou us in winning and in keeping,
Protect us, gods, for evermore with blessings!

I wish I could have introduced a larger number
of my so-called Indian friends, the poets of sacred
songs who may have lived thousands of years ago.
But I am afraid I have already tired out the patience
of my readers with these very ancient friends of
mine. The only excuse I can plead is that my own
friends in England and in Germany have so often
wondered how I could have fallen in love with the

Veda, and actually left my own country in order
to rescue this forgotten Bible from utter oblivion.
It is fortunate that people have different tastes and
that we are not all devoted to the same beauty.

One more hymn I must add, however, for I am
afraid if I do not, I shall be accused of having mis-
represented the character of the Veda, as reflecting
only the simplest thoughts of shepherds and culti-
vators of the land.   I have remarked several times
before that the Rig-Veda contains some very striking
philosophical passages, and how far some of the
Vedic poets must have been carried by purely metaphysical speculations may be seen by a hymn which
I translated for the first time in my " History of
Ancient Sanskrit Literature," 1859.   In putting it
into a metrical form I was helped at the time by
my departed friend, the late Archbishop of York,
then Mr. Thomson, and I am glad to say I find
little to alter in his translation even now.

Hymn X, 129.

Nor aught nor naught existed; yon bright sky
Was not, nor heaven's broad woof outstretched
        above;
What covered all? what sheltered? what concealed?
Was it the waters' fathomless abyss?
There was not death, hence was there naught
        immortal,
There was no light of night, no light of day,
The only One breathed breathless in itself,
Other than it there nothing since has been.

Darkness there was, and all at first was veiled
In gloom profound, an ocean without light;
The germ that still lay covered in the husk,
Burst forth, one nature, from the fervent heat.
Then first came Love upon it, the new germ,
Of mind; yea, poets in their hearts discerned
Pondering this bond between created things
And uncreated. Came this ray from earth
Piercing and all-pervading, or from heaven?
Then seeds were sown, and mighty powers arose,
Nature below, and Power and Will above';
Who knows the secret? who proclaimed it here,
Whence, whence this manifold creation sprang?
The gods themselves came later into being,
Who knows from whence this great creation
    sprang?
He from whom all this great creation came,
Whether his will created or was mute,
The most high Seer that is in highest heaven,
He knows it—or perchance e'en He knows not.

This hymn is important, not only by what it says,
but by what it presupposes. Whatever date we
may ascribe to it as incorporated in the Rig-Veda,
many generations of thinkers must have passed
before such questions could have been asked or
could have been answered. As yet we see the
Vedic age only as through a glass darkly. The
first generation of Vedic scholars is passing away.
It has done its work bravely, though well aware
of its limits. Let the next generation dig deeper

and deeper. What is wanted is patient, but independent and original work. There is so much new ground still to be broken, that the time has hardly come as yet for going again and again over the same ploughed field.

I must now part with my Vedic Friends. I can hardly hope that I have persuaded many of my English friends to share my feelings for my antediluvian acquaintances. All I care for is to make others understand how my heart was caught, and what I' saw in my Indian love, not only in her Vedântic dreams and aspirations, but in the simplicity of her earliest utterances of trust in powers invisible, yet present behind what is visible, and in her faith in a law that rules both the natural and the supernatural world.

A Prime Minister and a Child-wife.

I HAVE often had to give expression to a certain disappointment at not being able, when speaking of my Indian friends, to reveal more of their inner life. That life, we may be certain, is not absent, but it is kept hidden, just as Indian women are kept behind their purdahs or curtains and hidden under veils, more or less transparent. Some of our own distinguished men and women are perhaps too much given to perform their confessions and moral ablutions in public, while in India such books as Rousseau's *Confessions*, or the *Confessions of St. Augustine*, nay, of Amiel or Marie Bashkirtseff, to mention some well-known instances only, can hardly be imagined. Introspection or self-examination exists no doubt among the men and women of India as well as anywhere else. But unless such inward searchings take a definite form in words, nay, in written and published words, they can hardly be said to exist. A man may enter into a dark cave and see visions, but unless he can find his way back into the bright light of day, unless he can find words for what was

vaguely passing through the twilight of his memory,
all vanishes again and leaves nothing behind but
a nameless sentiment, like the feeling that is left
by a dream, when we know indeed that we have
been dreaming, but cannot recall what we saw in
our dreams.

Even in the prayers which we possess of the
people in India we find no very deep delvings into
the soul of man.   They consist chiefly of praises of
the greatness of the gods or of God, of general
confessions of human weakness or sin, but we hardly
ever come across the agonised sufferings of self-
reproachful saints, and we see little of that moral
vivisection which, painful as it is to witness, often
reveals to us some of the most secret springs of
human nature which nothing else will bring to our
view.

I cannot, therefore, even in the two cases of
Indian friends which I have selected for my purpose
here, promise anything like that minute moral and
spiritual analysis which we find in the works of
St. Augustine, of Rousseau, or Marie Bashkirtseff.
One of my friends belonged to the highest, the
other to the lowest ranks of Indian life; the one
was a Prime Minister, the other what we should
call a poor peasant-girl.   I was brought into contact
with them, not indeed face to face, but by correspondence only.   The Prime Minister was the well-known
Gaurishankar Udayshankar Ozá, Minister of Bhavnagar.   I am afraid that when people see these long
and unpronounceable names they will at once put

down the book. Names such as Rudyard Kipling, Bashkirtseff, or Pobedonostzeff may be mastered in time, but Gaurîshankar Udayshankar Ozâ is too much for most people's memories; and how can people, even if they manage to pronounce such a name, attach any meaning whatever to it? It might be better, perhaps, to give the name in its Sanskrit form, viz. Gaurî-*samkara*; we could then see some kind of meaning in it, provided we knew a little of Sanskrit. So far as one may guess the meaning of any proper names, Gaurî-*samkara* would be the name of the divine couple, *Siva*, sometimes called *Samkara*, and Gaurî, better known under the name of Pârvatî, his wife. Of course the name may be interpreted differently also, but when we know that Gaurî stands for Pârvatî, and Shankar for *Siva*, we move at once in more or less familiar spheres, and we may look on the name as something like the Christian name Joseph Maria, which is not unusual as a Christian name in Roman Catholic countries. But when I call Gaurî-*samkara* the well-known Prime Minister of Bhavnagar, I anticipate another shrugging of the shoulders. What is Bhavnagar, where is it, and what is there really known about its "well-known" Prime Minister? Here are our difficulties, when we want to rouse the sympathies of our readers for anything connected with India. Yes, if Gaurî-*samkara* of Bhavnagar were Fergus McIvor, chief of Glennaquoich, all would go well. But to most people, except those who have been in India, Bhavnagar is almost a *terra incognita*, and as there are

now no separate postage-stamps for the independent
states of India, even children would say that there
is no such state as Bhavnagar anywhere. Still there
is a native state of that name in Kathiawar, with
about 500,000 inhabitants, and there is a Râjah,
who is called the Thakur Sahib of Bhavnagar.
There is also a town of Bhavnagar, the capital of
the state. Like most of the protected Rajput states,
Bhavnagar enjoys as much freedom as is compatible
with the welfare of its neighbours and the imperial
interests of India. Under such conditions conflicts
are, no doubt, inevitable, and it required no little
statesmanship in the Râjah, and in his Dewân, or
Prime Minister, to reconcile the interests of their
subjects with those of their neighbours and with
those of the British Empire. Quite a new class of
native statesmen seems to have sprung up of late
in these various dependent states, who are enabled,
through the moral support which they receive from
the Central Government, to reform the abuses of
a personal and autocratic *régime*, to revive education, and to improve the sanitary condition of the
towns and villages, to open commercial communications, and altogether to raise the political and moral
status and character of the people committed to their
charge. In many cases they had at the same time
to keep on good terms with the English residents,
who are not always the most amiable, and to protect
the Râjahs themselves against the corrupting influences of their little courts and harems. Taking
all this together, it is not difficult to see that their

position was by no means an easy one, and that it required high qualities indeed in these native states-men to enable them to hold their own, to satisfy the claims of all the parties with whom they had to deal, and at the same time not to stifle the voice of their own conscience.

But when an opening had once been made for native talent in this direction, native talent was not wanting. The names of such men as Sir Salar Jung in Hyderabad, Sir T. Madao Rao in Travancore, Indore, and Baroda, Sir Dinkar Rao in Gwalior, are well known, not in India only, but in England also, and not the least successful among them was our friend Gaurî-saṃkara.

With all the narrow prejudices of Oriental society, particularly in India, there was always a *carrière ouverte aux talents*. Gaurî-saṃkara was the son of a poor man, though he belonged to a good Brâh-manic family. His education would not, perhaps, have enabled him to pass the Indian Civil Service Examination, and yet what an excellent Civil servant would he have made. Examinations prevent many evils, but they cannot create or even discover the qualities necessary for a ruler of men.

Like Mr. Gladstone, Gaurî-saṃkara became known in India as the Grand Old Man, or, better still, as the Good Old Man, and, like Mr. Gladstone, he represented in himself a striking combination of the thinker and the doer, of the meditative and the active man. His deepest interest lay with the great problems of human life on earth, but this did not prevent him from taking a most active part in the great and small concerns of the daily life and the daily cares of a small state. He acted as Minister to four generations of the rulers of Bhavnagar, and he was a constant referee on intricate political questions to successive Political agents of Kathiawar. He could remember the first establishment of British authority in the Bombay Presidency, and he had been the contemporary and fellow-worker of Mountstuart Elphinstone at the time when the settlement of Guzarat and Kathiawar had to be worked out between the Gaikwar on one side and the English Government, as successor of the Peshwa, on the other. He came in contact not only with Mountstuart Elphinstone, who visited Kathiawar in 1821, but with Sir John Malcolm also, with Lord Elphinstone and Sir Bartle Frere—nay, as late as 1886, with Lord Reay, then Governor of the Bombay Presidency. After a conference with the old man— he was then eighty-one years of age, having been born in 1805—Lord Reay declared that he was struck as much by the clearness of his intellect as by the simplicity and fairness and openness of his mind; "and if we admire administrators," he added, "we also admire straightforward advisers—those who tell their chiefs the real truth about the condition of their country and their subjects. In seeing the man who freed this State from all encumbrances, who restored civil and criminal jurisdiction to their villages, who settled grave disputes with Junaghad, who got rid of refractory Jemadars, I could not help thinking what could be done by such men of purpose and strength of character.

These words contain a rapid survey of the work of a whole life, and if we were to enter here into the details of what was actually achieved by this native statesman we should find that few Prime Ministers even of the greatest states in Europe had so many tasks on their hands, and performed them so boldly and so well. The clock on the tower of the Houses of Parliament strikes louder than the repeater in our waistcoat pocket, but the machinery, the wheels within wheels, and particularly the spring, have all the same tasks to perform as in Big Ben himself. Even men like Disraeli or Gladstone, if placed in the position of these native statesmen, could hardly have been more successful in grappling with the difficulties of a new state, with rebellious subjects, envious neighbours, a weak sovereign, and an all-powerful suzerain, to say nothing of court intrigues, religious squabbles, and corrupt officials. We are too much given to measure the capacity of ministers and statesmen by the magnitude of the results which they achieve with the immense forces placed at their disposal. But most of them are very ordinary mortals, and it is not too much to say that for making a successful marriage-settlement a country solicitor stands often in need of the same vigilance, the same knowledge of men and women, the same tact, and the same determination or bluff which Bismarck displayed in making the treaty of Prague or of Frankfurt. Nay, there are mistakes

made by the greatest statesmen in history which,
if made by our solicitor, would lead to his instant
dismissal. If Bismarck made Germany, Gaurî-*sam*-
kara made Bhavnagar. The two achievements are
so different that even to compare them seems absurd,
but the methods to be followed in either case are,
after all, the same; nay, it is well known that the
making or regulating of a small watch may require
more nimble and careful fingers than the large clock
of a cathedral. We are so apt to imagine that the
man who performs a great work is a great man,
though from revelations lately made we ought to
have learnt how small—nay, how mean—some of
these so-called great men have really been.

Gaurî-*sam*kara found nothing to begin with—or
rather, less than nothing, for he found not only an
unorganised but a disorganised state. General
Keatinge, who was Political Agent of Kathiawar
during the years 1863 to 1867, found the trans-
formation that had been wrought by Gaurî-*sam*kara
so complete that he could hardly believe that Bhavnagar was the same town which he had known in
former days. Splendid buildings had arisen, devoted
either to education or to the relief of the sick, the
poor, and the needy. The harbour had been improved, and roads for trade and communications
of every kind had been newly laid out or made
serviceable. There was a large reservoir to supply
the town with water; there were paddocks, a new
jail, two medical dispensaries, and an immense
hospital; there were telegraph and post offices, a

High School, and a High Court of Justice. A railway had been built from Bhavnagar to Gondal, and so well was it administered, without syndicates or any other kind of jobbery, that it yielded annually a fair revenue to the state. The responsibility for all these undertakings rested on the shoulders of one man, and the credit for them should rest there also.

All this, however, is not what interested me in the old man, nor will it, I fear, interest many of my readers. He is after all but one of the many unknown ants that build up hills which, for all we know, one stroke of a stick may destroy again. Nor was it his moral character, noble and pure as it doubtless must have been, that riveted my attention chiefly. A man could hardly have achieved what he did, unless he stood high above the reach of the vulgar vices and failings of mankind. In that direction, I may quote a few more judgments from the mouths of those who had known him during his long active life. " His chief strength," as one of his friends writes, " was to be found in his exemplary private character—

" His words were bonds, his oaths were oracles,
  His love sincere, his thoughts immaculate ;
  His tears pure messengers sent from his heart ;
  His heart as far from fraud as heaven from earth."

This is beautifully expressed; but does it give us an image of the man himself ? Even the strongest words seem so colourless when they are meant to give us the picture of a living man. It may be quite true that he enjoyed in private and domestic life a veneration that was due to his noble and patriarchal character, and that his influence was, as we are told, invariably and unerringly exerted in putting an extinguisher on private feuds and dis-agreements among a wide and ever-widening circle of relations, friends, and members of his caste. We read that "in order to promote harmony among them he often made personal sacrifices, and that he proved himself a friend of the needy and the helpless, of genius and talent struggling to rise. If it was not to be a blessing to others, life seemed to him not worth living."

All this is very strong testimony; and yet of how many people has the same been said, particularly by mourners at the grave of one whom they loved, and who had loved them! Funeral eloquence has its bright, but it also has its very dark side. It is delightful to see how much can be forgotten and forgiven at the grave, how gently all faults can be passed over or accounted for, how none but the noblest motives can then be imputed. But all is spoiled at once if rhetorical exaggeration comes in, so that even the truth contained in the panegyrics is hidden and choked by a rank growth of adulation and untruthfulness.

But though I was quite prepared to believe all that we were told about the private as well as public character of Gauri-samkara, what attracted me most in him was that the same man should through life have been a true philosopher, nay, what men of the world would call a dreamer of dreams; and should yet have proved so excellent a man of business. Plato's dictum, which has so often been ridiculed, that philosophers are the true rulers of men, has indeed been signally vindicated in Gaurī-*sam*kara's case. And his philosophy was not what may be called useful philosophy—a knowledge of nature and its laws. This might be tolerated in a Prime Minister, even in Europe. No; it consisted in the most abstruse metaphysics which would turn even the hardened brains of some of our best philosophers perfectly giddy. And yet that very philosophy, so far from unfitting Gaurī-*sam*kara for his arduous work, gave him the proper strength for doing and doing well whatever from day to day his hands found to do. He felt the importance of his official work to the fullest extent, but he always felt that there was something more important still. Though devoting all his powers to this life and its duties, he felt convinced that this life would soon pass away, that there was no true reality in it, that it was Mâyâ, illusion, arising from Avidyâ, nescience, and that there was behind, beneath, and above, another and higher life which alone was worth living. It was his faith in, or his knowledge of, that higher life which best fitted him to perform his work in the turmoil of the world. Thus it was that when any of his schemes ended in failure, disappointment never upset him, and that though he was often deceived in the friends he had trusted, he never became a pessimist.

It is very difficult to describe what was the faith
or the philosophy which supported him throughout
his busy life. From his early youth he was impressed with certain views of the Vedânta philosophy,
which form the common spiritual property, so to say,
of all the inhabitants of India. That philosophy
seems to have entered into the very life-blood of the
nation, but it assumed, of course, very different
forms as believed in by men of talent and education,
and by the drudging tillers of the soil throughout
the land. The number of those who study the
Vedânta in the works of such minute philosophers as
Bâdarâya*n*a and *S*a*m*kara is naturally very small, but
the number of those who have drunk in the spirit
of it, it may be in a few sayings only, is legion.

It seems almost impossible to give a short and
clear account of that ancient philosophy, though, when
once known, it can be, and has been, described and
epitomised in a few very short lines. The approaches
to it are very various, but anybody accustomed to
Greek or European forms of thought is sorely perplexed how to find an entrance into it from exactly
the same point as the Hindus themselves. The
Vedânta philosophy is meant to be an interpretation
of the world, different from all other interpretations,
whether philosophical or religious. It was to lead
to a new birth, and therefore remained unintelligible
and unmeaning to souls that will not be regenerated.
It is partly an advantage, partly a disadvantage, that
for several of their most important tenets the
Vedântists simply appeal to the Vedas, their Bible,

as containing the absolute truth, as being the highest seat of authority, or the last Court of Appeal on questions which with us would require very different arguments to prove that, given our reasoning powers, such as they are, and the world, such as it is, certain doctrines are inevitable, or that at all events their opposites are unthinkable. To make the results at which the Vedântists arrive intelligible, it is best for us to start with a few maxims which seem to underlie their philosophy, and which, whether true in themselves or not, do not at all events offend against our own rules of reasoning.

If, then, we start with the idea of the Godhead, which is never quite absent in any system of philosophy or religion, we may, excluding all poly-theistic forms of faith, allow our friends, the Vedântists, to lay it down that before all things the Godhead must be one, so that it may not be limited or conditioned by anything else. This is the Vedânta tenet which they express by the ever-recurring formula that the Sat, the true Being or Brahman, must be Ekam, one, and Advitîyam, without any second whatsoever. If, then, it is once admitted that in the beginning, in the present, and in the future, the Godhead must be one, all, and every-thing, it follows that nothing but that Godhead can be conceived as the true, though distant cause of everything material as well as spiritual, of our body as well as of our soul. Another maxim of the Vedântist, which likewise could hardly be gain-said by any thinker, is that the Godhead, if it exists

at all in its postulated character, must be unchangeable, because it is perfect and cannot possibly be
interfered with by anything else, there being nothing
beside itself.   On this point also all the advanced
religions seem agreed.   But then arises at once
the next question, If the Godhead is one without
a second, and if it is unchangeable, whence comes
change or development into the world; nay, whence
comes the world itself, or what we call creation—
whence comes nature with its ever-changing life and
growth and decay?

Here the Vedântist answer sounds at first very
strange to us, and yet it is not so very different from
other philosophies.   The Vedântist evidently holds,
though this view is implied rather than enunciated,
that, as far as we are concerned, the objective world
is, and can only be, *our knowledge* of the objective
world, and that everything that is objective is *ipso
facto* phenomenal.   Objective, if properly analysed,
is to the Vedântist the same as phenomenal, the
result of what *we* see, hear, and touch.   Nothing
objective could exist objectively, except as perceived
by us, nor can we ever go beyond this, and come
nearer in any other way to the hidden, subjective
part of the objective world, to the *Ding an sich*
supposed to be without us.   If, then, we perceive
that the objective world—that is, whatever we know
by our senses, call it nature or anything else—is
always changing, whilst on the other hand, the one
Being that exists, the Sat, can be one only, without
a second, and without change, the only way to escape

from this dilemma is to take the world when known to us as purely phenomenal, i. e. as created by our knowledge of it, only that what we call knowledge is called from a higher point of view not knowledge, but Avidyâ, i.e. Nescience. Thus the Godhead, though being that which alone supplies the reality underlying the objective world, is never itself objective, still less can it be changing. This is illustrated by a simile, such as are frequently used by the Vedântists, not to prove a thing, but to make things clear and intelligible. When the sun is reflected in the running water it seems to move and to change, but in reality it remains unaffected and unchanged. What our senses see is phenomenal, but it evidences a reality sustaining it. It is, therefore, not false or illusory, but it is phenomenal. It is fully recognised that there could not be even a phenomenal world without that postulated real Sat, that power which we call the Godhead, as distinguished from God or the gods, which are its phenomenal manifestations, known to us under different names.

The Sat, or the cause, remains itself, always one and the same, unknowable and nameless. And what applies to external nature applies likewise to whatever name we may give to our internal, eternal, or subjective nature. Our true being—call it soul, or mind, or anything else—is the Sat, the Godhead, and nothing else, and that is what the Vedântists call the Self or the Âtman. That Âtman, however, as soon as it looks upon itself, becomes *ipso facto*

phenomenal, at least for a time; it becomes the I,
and that I may change. The I is not one, but
many. It is the Âtman in a state of Nescience,
but when that Nescience is removed by Vidyâ, or
philosophy, the phenomenal I vanishes in death,
or even before death, and becomes what it always
has been, Âtman, which Âtman is nothing but the
Sat, the Brahman, or, in our language, the Godhead.

These ideas, though not exactly in this form or
in this succession, seem to me to underlie all Vedântic philosophy, and they will, at all events, form
the best and easiest introduction to its sanctuary.
And, strange as some of these ideas may sound
to us, they are really not so very far removed from
the earlier doctrines of Christianity. The belief in
a Godhead beyond the Divine Persons is clearly
enunciated in the much-abused Athanasian Creed,
of which in my heart of hearts I often feel inclined
to say: "Except a man believe it faithfully, he
cannot be saved." There is but one step which the
Vedântists would seem inclined to take beyond
us. The Second Person, or what the earliest
Christians called the Word—that is, the divine idea
of the universe, culminating in the highest concept,
the Logos of Man—would be with them the *Thou*,
i. e. the created world. And while the early
Christians saw that divine ideal of manhood realized
and incarnate in one historical person, the Vedântist
would probably not go beyond recognising that
highest Logos, the Son of God and the Son of man,
as Man, as everyman, whose manhood, springing from

the Godhead, must be taken back into the Godhead. And here is the point where the Vedântist differs from all other so-called mystic religions which have as their highest object the approach of the soul to God, the union of the two, or the absorption of the one into the other. The Vedântist does not admit any such approach or union between God and man, but only a recovery of man's true nature, a remembrance or restoration of his divine nature or of his godhead, which has always been there, though covered for a time by Nescience. After this point has once been reached, there would be no great difficulty in bringing on an agreement between Christianity, such as it was in its original form, and Vedântism, the religious philosophy of India. What seems to us almost blasphemy—a kind of *apotheosis* of man, is with the Vedântist an act of the highest reverence. It is taken as man's *anatheosis*, or return to his true Father, a recovery of his true godlike nature. And what is or can be the meaning of God-like? Can anything be godlike that is not originally divine, though hidden for a time by Nescience? After all, though Nescience may represent Manhood as the very opposite of Godhead, what beings are there, or can be imagined to be, that could fill the artificial interval that has been established long ago between God and man, unless we allow our poets to people that interval with angels and devils? The real difficulty is how that interval, that abyss between God and man, was ever created, and if the Vedântist

says by Nescience, is that so different from what
we say " By human ignorance"?

It was necessary to give these somewhat abstruse
explanations—though in reality they are not abstruse,
but intelligible to every unsophisticated and childlike
mind.   These, then, were the ideas that supported
our friend Gaurî-*sam*kara, and which support, under
different disguises, millions of human beings in
India—men, women, and children.   On such simple
but solid foundations it is easy to erect ever so
many religions, to build ever so many temples, and
to find room for the most elevated and the most
superstitious minds, all yearning for the same Peace
of God, and for the same Giver of Peace and Rest.
Names may differ and truth may adopt different disguises.   But, after all, the peace which Gaurî-*sam*kara
enjoyed amid the daily cares of his official life, and
which arose from his forgetting himself and finding
himself in God, or, as he would say, forgetting his
phenomenal in his real Âtman, could it have been
so very different from what we call the peace of God
that passes all understanding?   Such a view of the
world as his was, is generally supposed to unfit a man
for all practical work, but this, as we see, is by no
means a necessary consequence.   One thought of
Brahman was sufficient to refresh and strengthen
him for the battle of life, like a header taken into the
waves of an unfathomable ocean.   He knew where
he was and what he was, and that was enough to
keep him afloat.

And here we come across another curious feature

of Hindu life, which shows how thoroughly their philosophy had leavened and shaped their social institutions in ancient times. As soon as we know anything of these institutions we read that the passage through life of a twice-born man was divided into four periods—one of the pupil, Brahma*k*ârin, the next of the married man or the householder, G*ri*hastha. Then followed the third stage, after a man had fulfilled all his duties, had performed all necessary sacrifices, and had seen the children of his children. Then and then only came the time when he might retire from his house, give up all that belonged to him, and settle somewhere in the forest near, with or without his wife, but still accessible to his relations, and chiefly occupied in overcoming all passions by means of ascetic exercises, and withdrawing his affections more and more from all the things of this life. During that third station, that of the Vânaprastha or the ὑλόβιος, the mind of the hermit became more and more concentrated on that higher philosophy which we call religion, and more particularly on the Vedânta, as contained in the Upanishads, and similar but later works. Instead of merely dipping into the waters, the philosophical baptism became then a complete submergence, an entrance into life with Brahman, where alone perfect peace and a perfect satisfaction of man's spiritual desires could be found. This third station was followed by a fourth—the last chapter of life, when the old and decrepit man dragged himself away into the deep solitude of the forest, forgetting all that had once troubled or delighted his heart, and falling at last into the arms of his last friend, Death.

Such a conception and division of life seems quite natural from a Hindu point of view, and there was no necessity therefore for explaining it, as some anthropologists have done, by a circuitous appeal to savage customs, as is now the fashion. It is well known, no doubt, that both savage and half-civilised races get rid of their old people by either killing them or by causing them to be killed by wild animals. This inhuman cruelty may, no doubt, have been an act of necessity, particularly during a nomadic state of life. But in India the third station of life is quite different. It is based on a voluntary act, and it is followed by a fourth and final station, equally chosen by a man's own free will. Besides, all this was meant for the higher classes only, without a hint of its ever having been considered as inhuman or cruel. These anthropological explanations are very amusing, no doubt; their only drawback is that most of them can neither be proved nor disproved.

At present the four stations of life in India seem to possess an archaeological interest only, they are no longer of any practical importance. In the case of Gaurî-saṃkara it was no doubt his love of the ancient customs of his country, combined with a true desire for rest at the end of a most laborious and most successful career, that made him think of reviving in his own case the old custom, though even then

in a milder form only. He gave up his post as
Prime Minister, and entered into private life in
January, 1879. His mind, we are told, when he was
bordering upon eighty, was as bright and active
as ever, but he then directed all his mental energies
to one subject only, to a constant contemplation of
the great problems of life. His presence had
attracted many itinerant anchorites, many eminent
teachers and students of the Vedânta to Bhavnagar,
which became for a time the home of Indian philosophical speculation. He himself now devoted his
time to a serious study of Sanskrit, for which his
incessantly busy career had left him little time in
youth. He published in 1884 *The Svarûpânusandhâna* in Sanskrit, being considerations on the nature
of the Âtmâ (Self), and on the unity of the Âtmâ
with the Paramâtmâ (the Highest Self). He still
saw some friends, and, living in what we should
call a garden house, he remained in touch with
the outer world, though no longer affected by any
of the conflicting interests which had occupied
him for so many years. When, in 1886, Lord and
Lady Reay wished to see him once more, he con-
sented to receive them, but in the dress, or rather
uniform, of his Order, with his Dhoti, his frock, and
his cap all covered with ochre. Their interview
lasted for an hour, and Lord Reay declared that
of all the happy moments he spent in India, those
spent in the presence of that remarkable man remain
engraved on his memory.

A few letters which I received from the old man

after his retirement from the world may be interesting. He had sent me a copy of his book which
contained, as he said, a collection of Vedântic
sentences, forming, as it were, a chain of precious
jewels or pearls. I thanked him in the same spirit,
and as my letter has been published in his Life,
I may as well repeat it here :—

"OXFORD, *December* 3, 1884.

" I have to thank you for your kind letter and for
your valuable present, the Svarûpânusandhâna. If
you had sent me a real necklace of precious stones
it might have been called a magnificent present,
but it would not have benefited myself, my true
Âtman. The necklace of precious sentences which
you have sent me has, however, benefited myself,
my true Âtman, and I, therefore, consider it a far
more precious present than mere stones or pearls.
Besides, in accepting it, I need not be ashamed,
for they become only my own, if I deserve them,
that is, if I truly understand them. While we are
still in our first and second Âsrama (station of life)
we cannot help differing from one another according
to the country in which we are born, according to
the language we speak, and according to the Dharma
(religion) in which we have been educated. But
when we enter into the third and fourth Âsrama,
into which you have entered and I am entering, we
differ no longer, *Gñâtvâ* Deva*m* sarvapâsâpahâni*h*,
'When God has become really known, all fetters fall.'

" Though in this life we shall never meet, I am
glad to have met you in spirit."

I received another letter from him when he was just on the point of retiring from the world altogether and becoming a Samnyâsin, as far as that is possible in modern India.   By taking this step he showed that he was indeed a Vedântist in good earnest. What with us is but one of the many theories of life, was to him the only saving faith ; and while with us an old Prime Minister clings to the end to his political interests, and loves to be surrounded and amused by those who belong to him, we see here a real hero of thought who, freed from all desires, turns his eyes away from the whole pheno-menal world to dwell only on what is eternal and unchangeable, the Paramâtman—the Highest Self. To most of us this intellectual atmosphere, which he breathed to the very last, would prove too ex-hausting.   We can never drop all fetters—nay, many of us glory in them to the very end.   But whatever we may think of his philosophy, there can be no doubt that his life was consistent throughout.   He tried to live up to the standard which had been handed down to him from remote antiquity, and which he fully believed to be the best and the truest.   This last letter is dated July 11, 1886.   In it he says :—

" I had sent you a book which is the result of my long study of the Vedânta Philosophy.   You can easily imagine that I, being a Hindu Brâhman, can be said to have fully realized the truth of the doctrine therein discussed, when I can give you patent proofs of the effect which that study has had

on me.   There are, as you well know, four Â*s*ramas
prescribed by our *S*âstras, and the Brâhmans are
required to successively pass through them all, if
they can do so.   But in this Kaliyuga people are
not very particular about it.   The second Â*s*rama,
namely that of G*ri*hastha (householder), is more
or less enjoyed by all, and there are some who
enter into the third or fourth order.   Fortunately
for myself I have attained an old age by which
I was enabled to fulfil the requirements of the
*S*âstras, and thus lead a life of the third order after
I left public life.

   " Now my health is failing fast, and to finish the
whole I have made up my mind to enter into the
fourth order or Â*s*rama—namely, that of Sa*m*nyâsin.
Thereby I shall attain that stage in life when I shall
be free from all the cares and anxieties of this world,
and shall have nothing to do with my present circumstances in life.

   " After leading a public life for more than sixty
years, I think there is nothing left for me to desire
except the life of a Sa*m*nyâsin, which will enable
my Âtman (Self) to be one with Paramâtman (highest
Self), as shown to us by the enlightened of old.
When this is accomplished a man is free from births
and rebirths ; and what can I wish more than that
which will free me from births and rebirths, and
give me means to attain Moksha (freedom) ?

   " My learned friend, in a few days I shall be a
Sa*m*nyâsin, and thus there will be a total change
of life.   I shall no more be able to address you

in this style, so I send you this letter to convey my best wishes for your success in life, and my regards, which you so well deserve.

"After this, as you have so well said in your note, you and I will be not two persons, and as the Âtman which, being all-pervading, is one, there is total absence of duality. I shall end this note with the same words which you have mentioned, *Gñâtvâ Devam* sarvapâsâpahâni*h*, 'When God has been known, all fetters fall.'"

I heard no more of him except indirectly, when his son sent me a copy of the Bhagavad-gîtâ as a present from his father, who was no longer Gaurî-sa*m*kara then, but Sa*kk*idânanda, that is, the Supreme Spirit, i.e. he "who is, who perceives, and is blessed."

It would be a mistake to imagine that a life such as was lived by Gaurî-sa*m*kara is usual in modern India. On the contrary, it is now quite exceptional, and Gaurî-sa*m*kara was in every respect an exceptional character. Still we must guard against a mistake made by many biographers, who represent their hero as standing alone on a high pedestal without any other people around him with whom he could be compared. We have of late had a number of biographies that would make us believe that in England great men differed by their whole stature from their contemporaries. It is but seldom, however, that we find one man a whole head taller in physical stature than the majority; and so it is in intellectual and moral height also. It is true that it is the head that makes the whole difference, and sometimes a very great difference, still we must never forget that, as a mountain peak seldom stands up by itself, even our greatest men are surrounded in history by their equals, and should be measured accordingly.

Thus in our case, though in Gaurî-*sam*kara we see a rare union of the man of the world and the man out of the world, of the Prime Minister and the philosopher, it so happens that there were several other statesmen living at the same time who, if they had not actually become hermits, were, all their life, devoted students and followers of the Vedânta. The Minister of the neighbouring state of Junagadh, Gokulaji Zâlâ, who had likewise made his way from poverty to the highest place in his little kingdom, was all his life devoted to the study of the Vedânta. He was the personal friend of Gaurî-*sam*kara, and in the reports of the Political Agent he is spoken of as the equal of Gaurî-*sam*kara [1]. Lord Lytton conferred on him the title of Râo Bahâdur, in recognition of his loyal conduct and services. When he died, in 1878, too young to have become a Sa*m*nyâsin, it was said that "having done his task, he became, through the true self-knowledge, free from the three forces—causal, subtile, and gross—which disguise the Self, and that his Self, absorbed in the highest Self, became all happiness, just as space, enclosed in a vessel, becomes one with infinite space and force, as soon as the vessel is broken." Everywhere we

[1] See "A Sketch of the Life of Gokulaji Zâlâ and of the Vedânta." By Manassukharâma Sûryarâma Tripâthi. 1881.

come across the same Vedântic thoughts in India, though, no doubt, under various forms, according to the comprehension of different classes, but in their essence they all mean the same. Gokulaji himself, if we may judge by his biographer, was an assiduous student of the Vedânta all his life, perhaps more even than Gaurî-*samkara* had been ; and, while the latter rejoiced more in the ancient abrupt Vedântic utterances of the Upanishads, Gokulaji had evidently taken an interest in the modern Vedânta also, which enters more minutely into many of the problems which are but started or hinted at in the ancient Upanishads.

In the case of the two Prime Ministers of Bhavnagar and Junagadh there can be little doubt that the Vedântic spirit which filled their minds and guided their steps in life was drawn from a study of the classical works in which that ancient philosophy has been preserved to us. They were Vedântists, as even with us Prime Ministers may be Platonists or Darwinians. But the same philosophical spirit has entered into the language of the people also, into their proverbs and popular maxims, into their laws and poetry. If people, instead of saying " Know thyself," can only say " Know Âtman by Âtman " (know self by self) they are reminded at once of the identity of the ordinary and higher Self. If they meet with people who called themselves Âtmârâma, i. e. self-pleased, they are easily led on to see that the name was really meant for delighting in the Self, i. e. God ; if they are taught that he who sees himself in all creatures, and all creatures in himself, is a self-sacrificer and obtains the heavenly kingdom, they learn at least that this Self is meant for something more than the material body or the Ego, though it can no doubt be used in that sense also.

This Vedânta spirit pervades the whole of India. It is not restricted to the higher classes, or to men so exceptional as the Prime Minister of Bhavnagar. It lives in the very language of the people, and is preached in the streets and in the forests by mendicant Saints. Even behind the coarse idol-worship of the people some Vedântic truth may often be discovered. The "Sayings of Râmakrishna," which I lately published (" Râmakrishna, His Life and Sayings," 1898), are steeped in Vedântic thought, and the life-spring of the reforms inaugurated by such men as Rammohun Roy, Debendranâth Tagore, and Keshub Chunder Sen, must be sought for in the Vedântic Upanishads, though quickened, no doubt, by the spirit of the New Testament.

How omnipresent the influence of the old Vedânta is, even in the lower strata of Indian society, I can, perhaps, show best if I repeat here a story which I have told once before, the story of a poor little girl and her boyish husband. I came to hear that story through her friends who were the friends of Keshub Chunder Sen. We must try to understand, first of all, that it is possible in India for a girl of nine and a boy of twelve to fall in love and to be married, or, rather, to be betrothed. To us such

a state of things seems most unnatural; but as long
as the custom prevails and is looked upon with
favour rather than with disapproval, we can hardly
blame a young peasant boy and a still younger peasant
girl for following the example set them by their
father, mother, and all their friends.   That hearts
so young are capable of mutual affection and devotion we know from the biographies of some of our
own most distinguished men.   Nay, we are told
by the people of India that the years of their boyish
love form the happiest years of their life.   As a
rule, these young couples remain for some time
with their relations—they are like brother and sister;
and as they grow up they have the feeling that,
like their father and mother, brothers and sisters,
husband and wife also are given, not chosen, and
the idea that the bonds of their betrothal could ever
be severed never enters their minds.   The custom
itself is no doubt both objectionable and mischievous,
and those who have laboured to get it abolished by law
deserve our strongest sympathy.   All I wish to say
here is that we must not make an innocent, ignorant
couple, living in an Indian village, responsible for
the perversity of a whole nation.

How perverse a nation can be may be seen from
an Indian newspaper calling itself *The Indian Nation*,
which first denies that Hindu widows are unhappy,
and then adds " that, according to Hindu ideas, they
ought to be unhappy, because the end of life is not
happiness, nor the gratification of dreams, but the
regulation, or, if possible, the extinction of them."

The widow's life, we are told, was not meant to be joyful, nor should it be rendered joyful or useful, because Hindu ethics are not utilitarian like ours.

These two, Srîmatî and her husband Kedar Nâth, were as happy as children all day long; but what is even more surprising than their premature marriage is the premature earnestness with which they looked on life. Their thoughts were engaged on questions which with us would seem but rarely to form the subject of conversation, even of far more mature couples. They felt dissatisfied with their religion which, much as we hear about it in Indian news-papers, occupies after all a very small portion only of the daily life of a poor Hindu family. Their priest may come to say a few prayers before their uncouth idol, provided they possess one, there may be some popular rather than religious festivals to attend, and charitable contributions may be extorted by the priests even from those who have barely enough to eat themselves. They wear their sectarian mark on the forehead, and they may repeat a few simple prayers learnt from their mothers. But of religion, in our sense of the word, they know little indeed. Even when there is a sacred book for their own form of faith, Vedas, Purâ*n*as, or Tantras, they probably have never seen or handled it. They are surrounded, however, by temples and idols, and repulsive idolatrous practices are apt to sicken the heart and to excite doubts even in the least inquisi-tive minds. Thus when Srîmatî's young husband arrived at the conclusion that stones could not be gods (nay, in their hideousness, not even symbols of the Godhead), he took refuge in the Vedânta as preached by Keshub Chunder Sen. This was a bold step. But when he told his young wife what had happened to him, and explained to her his reasons, serious as the consequences of such a step were in India, she, as a faithful and devoted wife, at once followed his example. Even then their creed was indeed very simple. It was not pure Vedânta, it was rather devotional Vedânta-Bhakti, a belief in a phenomenal and personal God, not yet in the Godhead that lends substance and reality to all individual beings, whether gods or men. They held that God was one, without a second, that He existed in the beginning and created the universe. They believed Him to be intelligent, infinite, benevolent, eternal, governor of the universe, all-knowing, all-powerful, the refuge of all, devoid of parts, immutable, self-existent, and beyond all comparison. They also believed that in worshipping Him, and Him alone, they could obtain the highest good in this life and in the next, and that true worship consisted in loving Him and doing His will. There is not much heresy, it would seem, in such a simple creed, but to adopt it meant for the young husband and his wife degradation and complete social isolation. They might easily have kept up an appearance of orthodoxy, while holding in their hearts those simple, pure, and enlightened convictions. The temptation was great, but they resisted. The families to which she and her husband belonged occupied a highly respected position in Hindu society, which in India is fortunately quite compatible with extreme poverty. Much as both she and her husband had been loved and respected before, they were now despised, avoided, excommunicated. Even the allowance which they had received from their family was ordered to be reduced to a minimum, and in order to fit himself to earn an independent livelihood, the husband had to enter as a student in one of the Government colleges, while his little wife had to look after their small household. Soon there came a new trial. Her husband's father, who had renounced his son when he joined Keshub Chunder Sen's church, died broken-hearted, and the duty of performing the funeral rites (*Srâddha*) fell on his son. To neglect to perform these rites is considered something awful, because it is supposed to deprive the departed of all hope of eternal life. The son was quite ready to perform all that was essential in such rites, but he declared that he would never take part in any of the usual idolatrous ceremonies. In spite of the prayers of his relatives and the protestations of the whole village, he would not yield. He fled the very night that the funeral ceremony was to take place, accompanied again by no one except his brave little wife. Thereupon his father's brothers stopped all allowances due to him, and he was left with eight rupees per month to support his wife and mother. *Srimati* however managed, with this small pittance, to maintain not only herself and her husband but her husband's mother also, who had become insane, his little sister, and a nurse. Under these changed circumstances her husband found it impossible to continue his career at the Presidency College, and had to migrate to Dacca to prosecute his studies there. Here they all lived together again, and though they were sometimes almost starving, Srîmatî considered these years the happiest of her life. She herself tried to perfect her education by attending an Adult Female School, and so rapid was her progress, that on one occasion she was chosen to read an address to Lord Northbrook when he visited the school at Dacca.

The rest of their lives was not very eventful. The husband, after a time, secured a small income; but their life was always a struggle. Srîmatî, blessed with healthy children, thought that she had all that her heart desired, though she deeply felt the unkindness of their relatives. Her servants loved her and would never leave her, and when her husband complained of certain irregularities in the household and thought she was too lenient to her maids, she would but sigh and say: "Why should I lose patience, and thereby my peace of mind? Is it not better that I should suffer a little by their conduct than that they should be unhappy?" Her love of her children was most ardent. Yet her highest desire was always the happiness of her husband. She twined round him, as her friends used to say, like a creeper, but it was often the creeper that had to give strength to him and uphold him in his many trials and unfulfilled aspirations. Religion was the never-failing support for both of them, and their conversation constantly turned on the unseen life here and hereafter. The life which they lived together may seem to us uneventful, uninteresting, unsatisfying; but it was not so to them. This quiet couple, breathing the keen, wholesome air of poverty, and drinking from the well of homely life, performing their daily round of duty in the village which had been the home of their ancestors, were happy and perfectly satisfied with their lot on earth. When at last the wife's health began to fail, young and happy as she was, she was quite willing to go. She complained but little on her sick-bed, and her only fear was lest she might disturb her husband's slumber and deprive him of the rest which was so necessary for him. She watched and prayed, and when the end came she looked at him whom she had loved from her early childhood, and quietly murmured: "O, All-merciful" (Dayâmaya), and passed away.

Thus she lived and died: a true child-wife, pure as a child, devoted as a wife, and always yearning for that Spirit whom she had sought for, if, haply, she might feel after Him and find Him. And surely He was not far from her, nor she from Him!

INDEX.

—+—

Abhedânanda, 105.
Ádi Brâhma-Samâj, 89.
Agni, son of Dakshinâ, 205.
— first of all the gods, 214.
— fire, hymns to, 214, 216, 219.
Ahanâ, Dawn, 201, 204, 206, 208.
Ânandibâi Joshee, 116, 129; defends child-marriages, 116.
— — her American Degree, 132.
An-*ri*ta, 208.
Arnold, Dr., and the French master, 100.
Árya-Samâj, 93.
— — hold to the Veda, 94. .
Aryan mythology derived from natural phenomena, 190.
Asoka, King,·138.
Aśva, racer, or Vâgin, horse, 174.
Aśvins, Day and Night, hymn to, 194–197.
— the pair of, 224.
Atharva-Veda, 28, 169.
Athênê, first conception of, the Dawn, 208.

Babu Debendranâth Tagore, threw over the Veda, 82.
Bâdarâyana, 149, 153.
Bashkirtseff, Marie, 235, 236.
Bergaigne, M., 192, 203.
— letter from, 182 *n.*
Bhavnagar, 237.
Blavatsky, Madame, 96, 148–152.
Bloomfield's Concordance of the Veda, 184.
Bodley, Dr., and Ânandibâi Joshee, 131.

Bopp, 4, 176.
Brâhma-dharma, the, 101.
Brâhmanas, 187.
Brâhmanical thread, 91.
Brâhmans, and the published Rig-Veda, 23.
Brahmo Samâj, 17.
— — gave up the Veda, 82.
Brockhaus, Professor, 3.
Bunsen, his wish to see the Rig-Veda, 170.
Burnouf, Eugène, 4.

Chaitanya, fifteenth century, 66.
— his followers, 67.
— his teaching, 68 et seq.
Charis, 208.
Charites, Gk., 178.
Child-marriages, 113.
Child-wife, a, 262.
Codrington, 185.

Dakshâyanî, 205 *n.*
Dakshinâ, the Dawn, 200, 200 *n.*, 204, 205.
Dawn, names for, 204.
Dayânanda Sarasvatî, 93, 148.
Debendranâth Tagore, 6, 13, 14, 92.
— — never declared against the Veda, 101.
Dessau, 2.
Devas, 20.
Digambara sect of the Gains, 156.
Dimêtôr, a god of light, 222.
Dvârkanâth Tagore, 5–14, 97.
— — his hospitality, 12.
Dyaus, fem., the sky, 173.

Dyaus, masc.=Zeus, 173.
Dyaush-pitar, Ζεὺς πατήρ, and Jupiter, 179.
Dyotanâ, Dawn, 204, 205.

English translation of a prayer to Vish*n*u, 100.
Erasmus, 98.

Gaurîshankar Udayshankar Ozâ, 236.
— interview with Lord Reay, 240.
— his work in Bhavnagar, 242.
— his belief, 245.
— his retirement into private life, 255.
— letter from, 256.
— change of name, 259.
Gâyatrî, prayer addressed to Savit*ri*, the sun, 173.
Gods chiefly invoked in the Veda, Agni, fire, Vâyu, air, Sûrya, sun, 173.
Gokulaji Zâlâ, minister of Junagadh, 260.
Granth, the, 69, 70.
Gudrun, 46.
Guido d'Arezzo, 9.

Hahn, 185.
Hare, David, 90.
Haritas=Χάριτες, 178.
Hindu life, four periods of, 253.
Hindus, national character of, 135.
— are they truthful? 136.
— entering the Civil Service of India, 141.
Hot*ri*, priest, 218.

Index Verborum of the Rig-Veda, 182.
India, people of, still a secret to us, 161.
— deep thinkers in, 162.
Indian correspondents, 15.
— literature, the ancient, mnemonic, 25.
— Music, 7-9.
— Theosophy, 148.
Inspiration claimed for the Veda, 83.
— — for Buddha, 8.

Jayapura, Mahârâjah of, 96.
Jupiter Stator, 222.

Kabîr, "the Great," 71.
Kapila, 149.
Kâtyâyana on the Vedic gods, 173.
Keshub Chunder Sen, 15, 42, 43, 65, 72, 75-90, 95.
— his feelings about Christianity, 76, 79.
— his visit to England, 85-88.
— his study of various religions, 99.
— selections from the Bibles of the world, 101.

Mahân Âtmâ, the Great Self, 173.
Mahâtmans, 105.
Malabâri, B., 113, 117-121.
Mâyâ, illusion, 104.
Mitra-Varu*n*a, 210.
Mookerjee, H. C., 90.
More, Dr. Henry, 64.
Mozoomdar, 89.
Muir, J., 13, 51.
Müller, Otfried, 208.

Names identical, of deities in Sk., Gk., Latin, &c., 178.
Nânak, 69.
— his teaching, 74.
Nehemiah Goreh, 47.
— — his life in England, 49, 57.
— — his book against Christianity, 51.
— — became a Christian, 51.
Nescience, 103.

Oriental courtesy, 157.
Oxford, young Hindus in, 139-141.

Pig, fable of the man who grunted like a, 151.
Pillai, "Representative Indians," 160.
Prime Minister and child-wife, 235.
Purohita, provost, 218.

Râdhâkânta Deva, 23, 113.
— — recognition of the printed Rig-Veda, 27.
— — his letters, 30, 38.
— — a conservative, 43.
Râmabâi, 113, 121.

Râmabâi, her parents, 123.
— her lectures, 126.
— her life in England, 127.
— her present work, 128.
Râmakrishna, 105 n.
— his views, 106, 111, 112.
— his sayings, 108-110, 153.
Râmânuga, commentary of, 153.
Rammohun Roy, 5, 42, 75.
— — his feeling for Christianity, 77, 78.
Rânitonoo Lahari, 90.
Râtrî, night, 210, 210, n. 3, 224.
— hymn to, 228.
Reformers, Hindu, 66.
Rig-Veda, 168, 170, 171.
— publication of the, 14, 16, 22, 23.
— — considered profane, 27, 33.
Roberts, Lord, "Forty-one Years in India," 143.
Rosen, 181.
Roth, Professor, letter from, 22.
— on translating the Veda, 183.
Rozario, D., 91.
Russians and Indians, 144.

Sacrifices, 220.
Samâjes in India, 89 n.
Sâma-Veda, 168.
— Benfey's edition, 28.
Samkara's commentary, 153.
Sandhyâ, twilight, 173 n.
Sandhyâvandana, 215.
Sâradânada, 105.
Sâramêya = Ἑρμείας, 178.
Saranyû = Ἑρινύς, 178.
Sat, the cause, 249.
Satyendranâth Tagore, 6.
Savitrî, 224.
— the Sun, 173.
— distinct from Sûrya, 201.
— Sun, hymn to, 210.
Sâyana's commentary, 181.
Schopenhauer, on the Vedânta, 165.
Shrâddh ceremonies, 145, 146.
— presents to M. M., 145.
Simon, Heinrich, 165.
Solar Fact, not Theory, 223.
Solar Theory, 174, 226.
Soma, hymns to, 227.
Srîmatî and her husband, 264.

Srîmatî and her husband, their belief in the Vedânta, 265.
— her life and death, 267, 268.
Sûnritâ, Dawn, 201, 204, 208.
Sutti, 29, 45.

Tagore family, 6.
Tawney, C. H., 61, n. 1.
Theosophist Society, 150.
Tregear, 185.
Trita, 224.
Truthfulness of Hindus, 136, 137.

Upanishads, 153, 164, 262.
Ushas, 200-210.
— Dawn, hymn to, 200.

Vairâgya-Sataka, the translations from, 61.
Varuna, 224, 225.
— hymn to, 230.
Varuna and Mitra, 224, 225.
Veda, the, 167.
— four collections of hymns, 168.
Vedânta system, 102, 164, 248 et seq.
— Schopenhauer on the, 165.
— objective world is phenomenal, 248.
Vedânta spirit pervades India, 262.
Vedântists, modern, 105.
Vedic hymn, translated by Abp. Thomson, 232.
— hymns, translations of, 181.
— — their date, 186.
— literature, discovery of, 179.
Vishnu, identified with Agni, 216.
— an independent deity, 222.
Vivekânanda, 105, 150, 153.
Vizianagram, Mahârâjah of, 158.
— — pays for the reprint of the Rig-Veda, 159-160.

Widows in India, 118, 119, 121, 263-264.
Wilson, Professor, 9, 181.
Women, influence of, in India, 84, 85.

Yagur-Veda, 28, 169.
Yâska, on the Devatâs of the Rig-Veda, 172, 224.

Zeus, Dyaus, &c., 221.

OXFORD: HORACE HART
PRINTER TO THE UNIVERSITY

WORKS

BY

The Right Hon. F. MAX MÜLLER.

—>·<—

AULD LANG SYNE. First Series. 8vo, 10s. 6d.
CONTENTS.—Musical Recollections—Literary Recollections—
Recollections of Royalties—Beggars.

RÂMAKR*I*SHN*A*: his Life and Sayings. Crown 8vo, 5s.

DEUTSCHE LIEBE (GERMAN LOVE): Fragments
from the Papers of an Alien. Collected by F. MAX MÜLLER.
Translated from the German by G. A. M. Crown 8vo, 5s.

THE SIX SYSTEMS OF INDIAN PHILOSOPHY.

THE SCIENCE OF THOUGHT. 8vo, 21s.

CONTRIBUTIONS TO THE SCIENCE OF MYTH-
OLOGY. 2 vols. 8vo, 32s.

THREE LECTURES ON THE VEDÂNTA PHILO-
SOPHY, delivered at the Royal Institution in March, 1894. 8vo, 5s.

———

COLLECTED EDITION OF WORKS.

14 vols. Crown 8vo, price 5s. each.

THE ORIGIN AND GROWTH OF RELIGION, as
illustrated by the Religions of India. Hibbert Lectures. Crown
8vo, 5s.

NATURAL RELIGION. The Gifford Lectures, de-
livered before the University of Glasgow in 1888. Crown 8vo, 5s.

PHYSICAL RELIGION. The Gifford Lectures, delivered
before the University of Glasgow in 1890. Crown 8vo, 5s.

ANTHROPOLOGICAL RELIGION. The Gifford
Lectures, delivered before the University of Glasgow in 1891.
Crown 8vo, 5s. [Continued.

———

LONGMANS, GREEN, AND CO.,
LONDON, NEW YORK, AND BOMBAY.

COLLECTED EDITION OF WORKS

[Continued.

14 vols. Crown 8vo, price 5*s.* each.

THEOSOPHY OR PSYCHOLOGICAL RELIGION.
The Gifford Lectures, delivered before the University of Glasgow in 1892. Crown 8vo, 5*s.*

THE SCIENCE OF LANGUAGE. Founded on
Lectures delivered at the Royal Institution in 1861 and 1863. 2 vols. Crown 8vo, 10*s.*

INTRODUCTION TO THE SCIENCE OF RELI-
GION : Four Lectures delivered at the Royal Institution in 1870 ; with Notes and Illustrations on the Vedic Literature, Polynesian Mythology, the Sacred Books of the East, &c. Crown 8vo, 5*s.*

INDIA : WHAT CAN IT TEACH US? A Course of
Lectures delivered before the University of Cambridge. Crown 8vo, 5*s.*

BIOGRAPHIES OF WORDS, AND THE HOME
OF THE ÂRYAS. Crown 8vo, 5*s.*

CHIPS FROM A GERMAN WORKSHOP.

Vol. I. RECENT ESSAYS AND ADDRESSES. Crown 8vo, 5*s.*

Vol. II. BIOGRAPHICAL ESSAYS. Crown 8vo, 5*s.*

Vol. III. ESSAYS ON LANGUAGE AND LITERATURE. Crown 8vo, 5*s.*

Vol. IV. ESSAYS ON MYTHOLOGY AND FOLK-LORE. Crown 8vo, 5*s.*

HANDBOOKS FOR THE STUDY OF SANSKRIT.

THE SANSKRIT TEXT OF THE FIRST BOOK
OF THE HITOPADESA. 3*s.* 6*d.*

THE SECOND, THIRD AND FOURTH BOOKS
OF THE HITOPADESA ; containing that Sanskrit Text, with Interlinear Translation. 7*s.* 6*d.*

A SANSKRIT GRAMMAR FOR BEGINNERS.
New and Abridged Edition. By A. A. MACDONELL. Crown 8vo, 6*s.*

LONGMANS, GREEN, AND CO.,

LONDON, NEW YORK, AND BOMBAY.

THE GERMAN CLASSICS, FROM THE FOURTH
TO THE NINETEENTH CENTURY. With Biographical
Notices, Translations into Modern German, and Notes. By F.
MAX MÜLLER, M.A. A New Edition, Revised, Enlarged, and
Adapted to WILHELM SCHERER'S ' History of German Literature,'
by F. LICHTENSTEIN. 2 vols. Crown 8vo, 21*s*.

Or, separately, 10*s*. 6*d*. each volume.

A HISTORY OF GERMAN LITERATURE BY
WILHELM SCHERER. Translated from the Third German
Edition by Mrs. F. C. CONYBEARE. Edited by F. MAX MÜLLER.
2 vols. 8vo, 21*s*.

Or, separately, 10*s*. 6*d*. each volume.

A HISTORY OF GERMAN LITERATURE, FROM
THE ACCESSION OF FREDERICK THE GREAT TO
THE DEATH OF GOETHE. By the same. Crown 8vo, 5*s*.

ANECDOTA OXONIENSIA.

III. ARYAN SERIES.

I. BUDDHIST TEXTS FROM JAPAN. 1. Vagra-
*kkh*edikâ. Edited by F. MAX MÜLLER. 3*s*. 6*d*.

II. BUDDHIST TEXTS FROM JAPAN. 2. Sukhâ-
vatî-Vyûha. Edited by F. MAX MÜLLER, M.A., and BUNYIU
NANJIO. 7*s*. 6*d*.

III. BUDDHIST TEXTS FROM JAPAN. 3. The
Ancient Palm-Leaves containing the Prag*ñ*â-Pâramitâ-H*ri*daya-
Sûtra and the Ushnisha-Vig*a*ya-Dhâra*nî*. Edited by F. MAX
MÜLLER, M.A., and BUNYIU NANJIO, M.A. With an Appendix
by G. BÜHLER. 10*s*.

V. THE DHARMA-SA*M*GRAHA. Edited by KENJIU
KASAWARA, F. MAX MÜLLER and H. WENZEL. 7*s*. 6*d*.

THE SACRED BOOKS OF THE EAST. Translated
by various Oriental Scholars, and edited by F. MAX MÜLLER.

FIRST SERIES, Vols. I-XXIV. 8vo.
SECOND SERIES, Vols. XXV–XLIX. 8vo.

** *Complete Lists sent on Application.*

OXFORD: AT THE CLARENDON PRESS.

𝔄 Classifieð Catalogue
OF WORKS IN
GENERAL LITERATURE
PUBLISHED BY
LONGMANS, GREEN, & CO.
39 PATERNOSTER ROW, LONDON, E.C.
91 AND 93 FIFTH AVENUE NEW YORK. AND 32 HORNBY ROAD, BOMBAY.

CONTENTS.

	PAGE		PAGE
BADMINTON LIBRARY (THE) -	10	MENTAL, MORAL, AND POLITICAL	
BIOGRAPHY, PERSONAL ME-		PHILOSOPHY - · · · -	14
MOIRS, &c. · · · · ·	7	MISCELLANEOUS AND CRITICAL	
CHILDREN'S BOOKS · · ·	25	WORKS · · · · · ·	29
CLASSICAL LITERATURE TRANS-		MISCELLANEOUS THEOLOGICAL	
LATIONS, ETC. · · · ·	18	WORKS · · · · · ·	32
COOKERY, DOMESTIC MANAGE-		POETRY AND THE DRAMA · ·	19
MENT, &c. · · · · ·	28	POLITICAL ECONOMY AND ECO-	
EVOLUTION, ANTHROPOLOGY,		NOMICS · · · · · ·	16
&c. · · · · · · ·	17	POPULAR SCIENCE · · · ·	24
FICTION, HUMOUR, &c. · · ·	21	*SILVER LIBRARY (THE)* · ·	27
FUR, FEATHER AND FIN SERIES	12	SPORT AND PASTIME · · ·	10
HISTORY, POLITICS, POLITY,		*STUDIES IN ECONOMICS AND*	
POLITICAL MEMOIRS, &c. · ·	3	*POLITICAL SCIENCE* · · ·	17
LANGUAGE, HISTORY AND		TRAVEL AND ADVENTURE, THE	
SCIENCE OF · · · · ·	16	COLONIES, &c. · · · ·	8
LONGMANS' SERIES OF BOOKS		VETERINARY MEDICINE, &c. ·	10
FOR GIRLS · · · · ·	26	WORKS OF REFERENCE · · ·	25
MANUALS OF CATHOLIC PHIL-			
OSOPHY · · · · · ·	16		

INDEX OF AUTHORS AND EDITORS.

	Page		Page		Page		Page
Abbott (Evelyn) ·	3, 18	Bain (Alexander) ·	14	Browning (H. Ellen)	9	Coolidge (W. A. B.)	8
—— (T. K.) · ·	14	Baker (Sir S. W.) ·	8, 10	Buck (H. A.) · ·	11	Corbett (Julian S.) ·	3
—— (E. A.) · ·	14	Balfour (A. J.) ·	11, 32	Buckland (Jas.) ·	25	Corder (Annie)	19
Acland (A. H. D.) ·	3	Ball (John) · ·	8	Buckle (H. T.) ·	3	Coutts (W.) · ·	18
Acton (Eliza) · ·	28	—— (J. T.) · ·	3	Buckton (C. M.) ·	28	Coventry (A.) · ·	11
Adeane (J. H.) · ·	7	Baring-Gould (Rev.		Bull (T.) · · ·	28	Cox (Harding) · ·	10
Æschylus · · ·	18	S.) · · ·	27, 29	Burke (U. R.) · ·	3	Crake (Rev. A. D.) ·	25
Ainger (A. C.) · ·	11	Barraud (C. W.) ·	19	Burrows (Montagu) ·	4	Creighton (Bishop) ·	3, 4
Albemarle (Earl of) ·	10	Baynes (T. S.) · ·	29	Butler (E. A.) · ·	24	Crozier (J. B.) · ·	7, 14
Allen (Grant) · ·	24	Beaconsfield (Earl of)	21	—— (Samuel) · ·	18, 29	Cuningham (G. C.) ·	3
Allingham (F.) · ·	21	Beaufort (Duke of) ·	10, 11			Curzon of Kedleston	
Amos (S.) · · ·	3	Becker (W. A.) · ·	18	Cameron of Lochiel	12	(Lord) · · ·	3
André (R.) · · ·	12	Beddard (F. E.) ·	24	Campbell (Rev. Lewis)	32	Custance (Col. H. ·	12
Anstey (F.) · · ·	21	Bell (Mrs. Hugh) ·	19	Camperdown (Earl of)	7	Cutts (Rev. E. L.) ·	4
Archer (W.) · · ·	8	—— (Mrs. Arthur) ·	7	Cannan (E.) · ·	17		
Aristophanes · · ·	18	Bent (J. Theodore) ·	8	Channing (F. A.) ·	16		
Aristotle · · ·	14, 18	Besant (Sir Walter)·	3	Chesney (Sir G.) ·	3	Dallinger (F. W.) ·	4
Armstrong (G. F.		Bickerdyke (J.) ·	11	Chisholm (G. G.) ·	25	Davidson (W. L.) 14, 16, 32	
Savage) · ·	19	Bicknell (A. C.) ·	8	Cholmondeley-Pennell		Davies (J. F.) · ·	18
—— (E. J. Savage) 7, 19, 29		Bird (R.) · · ·	32	(H.) · · · ·	11	Deland (Mrs.) · ·	21, 26
Arnold (Sir Edwin)·	8, 19	Bland (Mrs. Hubert)	20	Churchill (W. Spencer)	9	Dent (C. T.) · ·	11
—— (Dr. T.) · ·	3	Boase (Rev. C. W.)·	4	Cicero · · · ·	18	Deploige (S.) · ·	17
Ashbourne (Lord) ·	3	Boedder (Rev. B.) ·	16	Clarke (Rev. R. F.) ·	16	De Salis (Mrs.) ·	28, 29
Ashby (H.) · · ·	28	Bosvey (A. W. Crawley-)	7	Clodd (Edward) ·	17	De Tocqueville (A.)·	3
Ashley (W. J.) · ·	16	Bosanquet (B.) · ·	14	Clutterbuck (W. J.)·	9	Devas (C. S.) · ·	16
Atelier du Lys (Author of) 29		Boyd (Rev. A. K. H.) 29, 32		Coleridge (S. T.) ·	19	Dickinson (G. L.) ·	4
Ayre (Rev. J.) · ·	25	Brassey (Lady) · ·	9	Comparetti (D.) ·	30	Diderot · · · ·	21
		—— (Lord) · 3, 8, 11, 16		Comyn (L. N.) · ·	26	Dougall (L.) · ·	21
Bacon · · · 7, 14		Bray (C. and Mrs.) ·	14	Conington (John) ·	18	Douglas (Sir G.) ·	19
Baden-Powell (B. H.)	3	Bright (Rev. J. F.) ·	3	Conway (Sir W. M.)	11	Dowden (E.) · ·	31
Bagehot (W.) · 7, 16, 29		Broadfoot (Major W.)	10	Conybeare (Rev. W. J.)		Doyle (A. Conan) ·	21
Bagwell (R.) · ·	3	Brögger (W. C.) ·	8	& Howson (Dean)	27	Dreyfus (Irma) ·	30

Du Bois (W. E. B.) - 4
Dufferin (Marquis of) 11
Dunbar (Mary F.) - 20
Eardley-Wilmot (Capt. S.) - 8
Ebrington (Viscount) 12
Ellis (J. H.) - 12
—— (R. L.) - 14
Evans (Sir John) - 30
Farrar (Dean) - 16, 21
Fitzwygram (Sir F.) 10
Folkard (H. C.) - 12
Ford (H.) - 12
Fowler (Edith H.) - 21
Foxcroft (H. C.) - 7
Francis (Francis) - 12
Freeman (Edward A.) 4
Freshfield (D. W.) - 11
Frothingham (A. L.) 30
Froude (James A.) 4, 7, 9, 21
Furneaux (W.) - 24
Galton (W. F.) - 17
Gardiner (Samuel R.) 4
Gathorne-Hardy (Hon. A. E.) - 12
Gerard (Dorothea) - 26
Gibbons (J. S.) - 12
Gibson (Hon. H.) - 13
—— (C. H.) - 14
—— (Hon. W.) - 32
Gilkes (A. H.) - 21
Gleig (Rev. G. R.) - 8
Goethe - 19
Gore-Booth (Eva) - 19
—— (Sir H. W.) - 11
Graham (P. A.) - 13, 21
—— (G. F.) - 16
Granby (Marquis of) 12
Grant (Sir A.) - 14
Graves (R. P.) - 7
Green (T. Hill) - 14
Greener (E. B.) - 4
Greville (C. C. F.) - 11
Grey (Maria) - 26
Grose (T. H.) - 14
Gross (C.) - 4
Grove (F. C.) - 11
—— (Mrs. Lilly) - 10
Gurdon (Lady Camilla) 12
Gwilt (J.) - 25
Haggard (H. Rider) 21, 22
Hake (O.) - 11
Halliwell-Phillipps (J.) 8
Hamlin (A. D. F.) - 30
Hammond (Mrs. J. H.) 4
Harding (S. B.) - 4
Harte (Bret) - 26
Harting (J. E.) - 12
Hartwig (G.) - 24
Hassall (A.) - 6
Haweis (Rev. H. R.) 7, 30
Heath (D. D.) - 14
Heathcote (J. M. and C. G.) - 11
Helmholtz (Hermann von) - 24
Henderson (Lieut-Col. G. F.) 7
Henry (W.) - 11
Henty (G. A.) - 26
Herbert (Col. Kenney) 12
Hewins (W. A. S.) - 17
Hill (Sylvia M.) - 21
Hillier (G. Lacy) - 10
Hime (Lieut.-Col. H. W. L.) - 30
Hodgson (Shadworth H.) 14
Holroyd (Maria J.) - 7
Homer - 18
Hope (Anthony) - 22
Horace - 18
Hornung (E. W.) - 22
Houston (D. F.) - 4
Howell (G.) - 16
Howitt (W.) - 9
Hudson (W. H.) - 24
Hullah (J.) - 30
Hume (David) - 14

Hunt (Rev. W.) - 4
Hunter (Sir W.) - 5
Hutchinson (Horace G.) 11
Ingelow (Jean - 19, 26
James (W.) - 14
Jefferies (Richard) - 30
Jerome (Jerome K.) - 22
Johnson (J. & J. H.) 30
Jones (H. Bence) - 25
Jordan (W. L.) - 16
Jowett (Dr. B.) - 17
Joyce (P. W.) - 5, 22, 30
Justinian : - 14
Kant (I.) - 14
Kaye (Sir J. W.) - 5
Kerr (Rev. J.) - 11
Killick (Rev. A. H.) - 14
Kingsley (Rose G.) - 30
Kitchin (Dr. G. W.) 4
Knight (E. F.) - 9, 11
Köstlin (J.) - 7
Ladd (G. T.) - 15
Lang (Andrew) 5, 10, 11, 13, 17, 18, 19, 20, 22, 26, 30, 32
Lascelles (Hon. G.) 10, 11, 12
Laughton (J. K.) - 8
Laurence (F. W.) - 17
Lawley (Hon. F.) - 11
Layard (Nina F.) - 19
Leaf (Walter) - 31
Lear (H. L. Sidney) - 29
Lecky (W. E. H.) - 5, 19
Lees (J. A.) - 9
Lejeune (Baron) - 7
Leslie (T. E. Cliffe) - 16
Lester (L. V.) - 7
Levett-Yeats (S.) - 22
Lillie (A.) - 13
Lindley (J.) - 25
Lodge (H. C.) - 4
Loftie (Rev. W. J.) - 4
Longman (C. J.) 10, 12, 30
—— (F. W.) - 13
—— (G. H.) - 11, 12
Lowell (A. L.) - 5
Lubbock (Sir John) - 17
Lucan - 18
Lutoslawski (W.) - 15
Lyall (Edna) - 22
Lyttelton (Hon. R. H.) 10
—— (Hon. A.) - 11
Lytton (Earl of) - 19
Macaulay (Lord) 5, 6, 19
MacColl (Canon) - 6
Macdonald (G.) - 9
—— (Dr. G.) - 20, 32
Macfarren (Sir G. A.) 30
Mackail (J. W.) - 18
Mackinnon (J.) - 6
Macleod (H. D.) - 16
Macpherson (Rev. H. A.) 12
Madden (D. H.) - 13
Maher (Rev. M.) - 16
Malleson (Col. G. B.) 5
Marbot (Baron de) - 7
Marquand (A.) - 30
Marshman (J. C.) - 7
Martineau (Dr. James) 32
Maskelyne (J. N.) - 13
Maunder (S.) - 25
Max Müller (F.) - 7, 8, 15, 16, 22, 30, 32
—— (Mrs.) - 9
May (Sir T. Erskine) 6
Meade (L. T.) - 26
Melville (G. J. Whyte) 22
Merivale (Dean) - 6
Merriman (H. S.) - 22
Mill (James) - 16
—— (John Stuart) - 15, 17
Milner (G.) - 30
Miss Molly (Author of) 26
Moffat (D.) - 13
Molesworth (Mrs.) - 26
Monck (W. H. S.) - 15
Montague (F. C.) - 6

Montagu (Hon. John Scott) - 12
Moore (T.) - 25
—— (Rev. Edward) - 14
Morgan (C. Lloyd) - 17
Morris (W.) - 20, 22, 31
—— (Mowbray) - 11
Mulhall (M. G.) - 17
Nansen (F.) - 9
Nesbit (E.) - 20
Nettleship (R. L.) - 14
Newdigate - Newdegate (Lady) - 8
Newman (Cardinal) - 22
Ogle (W.) - 18
Oliphant (Mrs.) - 22
Oliver (W. D.) - 9
Onslow (Earl of) - 11
Orchard (T. N.) - 31
Osbourne (L) - 23
Park (W.) - 13
Parr (Louisa) - 26
Payne-Gallwey (Sir R.) - 11, 13
Peek (Hedley) - 11
Pembroke (Earl of) - 11
Phillipps-Wolley (C.) 10, 22
Pitman (C. M.) - 11
Pleydell-Bouverie (E. O.) 11
Pole (W.) - 13
Pollock (W. H.) - 11
Poole (W. H. and Mrs.) 29
Poore (G. V.) - 31
Potter (J.) - 16
Praeger (S. Rosamond) 26
Prevost (C.) - 11
Pritchett (R. T.) - 11
Proctor (R. A.) 13, 24, 28
Quill (A. W.) - 18
Raine (Rev. James) - 4
Ransome (Cyril) - 3, 6
Rauschenbusch-Clough (Emma) - 8
Rawlinson (Rev. Canon) 8
Rhoades (J.) - 18
Rhoscomyl (O.) - 23
Ribblesdale (Lord) - 13
Rich (A.) - 18
Richardson (C.) - 12
Richman (I. B.) - 6
Richmond (Ennis) - 31
Richter (J. Paul) - 31
Rickaby (Rev. John) - 16
—— (Rev. Joseph) - 16
Ridley (Sir E.) - 18
Riley (J. W.) - 20
Roget (Peter M.) - 16, 25
Rolfsen (N.) - 8
Romanes (G. J.) 8, 15, 17, 20, 32
—— (Mrs.) - 8
Ronalds (A.) - 13
Roosevelt (T.) - 4
Rossetti (Maria Francesca) - 31
—— (W. M.) - 20
Rowe (R. P. P.) - 11
Russell (Bertrand) - 17
—— (Alys) - 17
—— (Rev. M.) - 20
Saintsbury (G.) - 12
Samuels (E.) - 20
Sandars (T. C.) - 14
Sargent (A. J.) - 17
Schreiner (S. C. Cronwright) - 10
Seebohm (F.) - 6, 8
Selous (F. C.) - 10
Sewell (Elizabeth M.) 23
Shakespeare - 20
Shand (A. I.) - 12
Sharpe (R. R.) - 6
Shearman (M.) - 10, 11
Sinclair (A.) - 11
Smith (R. Bosworth) 6
Smith (T. C.) - 4

Smith (W. P. Haskett) 9
Solovyoff (V. S.) - 31
Sophocles - 18
Soulsby (Lucy H.) - 26, 31
Spedding (J.) - 7, 14
Sprigge (S. Squire) - 8
Stanley (Bishop) - 24
Steel (A. G.) - 10
—— (J. H.) - 10
Stephen (Leslie) - 9
Stephens (H. Morse) 6
Stevens (R. W.) - 31
Stevenson (R. L.) - 23, 26
'Stonehenge' - 10
Storr (F.) - 14
Stuart-Wortley (A. J.) 11, 12
Stubbs (J.) - 6
Suffolk & Berkshire (Earl of) - 11
Sullivan (Sir E.) - 11
—— (J. F.) - 26
Sully (James) - 15
Sutherland (A. and G.) 6
—— (Alex.) - 15, 31
Suttner (B. von) - 23
Swinburne (A. J.) - 15
Symes (J. E.) - 17
Tacitus - 18
Taylor (Col. Meadows) 26
Tebbutt (C. G.) - 11
Thornhill (W. J.) - 18
Thornton (T. H.) - 8
Todd (A.) - 6
Toynbee (A.) - 17
Trevelyan (Sir G. O.) 6, 7
—— (C. P.) - 17
—— (G. M.) - 6
Trollope (Anthony) - 23
Tupper (. L.) - 20
Turner (H. G.) - 31
Tyndall (J.) - 7, 9
Tyrrell (R. Y.) - 18
Tyszkiewicz (M.) - 31
Upton (F. K. and Bertha) 26
Van Dyke (J. C.) - 31
Verney (Frances P. and Margaret M.) 8
Virgil - 18
Vivekananda (Swami) 32
Vivian (Herbert) - 9
Wakeman (H. O.) - 6
Walford (L. B.) - 23
Walker (Jane H.) - 29
Wallas (Graham) - 8
Walpole (Sir Spencer) 6
Walrond (Col. H.) - 10
Walsingham (Lord) - 11
Walter (J.) - 8
Warwick (Countess of) 31
Watson (A. E. T.) 10, 11, 12, 13, 23
Webb (Mr. and Mrs. Sidney) - 17
—— (T. E.) - 15, 19
Weber (A.) - 15
Weir (Capt. R.) - 11
Weyman (Stanley) - 23
Whately (Archbishop) 14, 15
—— (E. Jane) - 16
Whishaw (F.) - 23
White (W. Hale) - 20, 31
Whitelaw (R.) - 18
Wilcocks (J. C.) - 13
Wilkins (G.) - 18
Willard (A. R.) - 31
Willich (C. M.) - 25
Witham (T. M.) - 11
Wood (Rev. J. G.) - 25
Wood-Martin (W. G.) 6
Woods (Margaret L.) 23
Wordsworth (Elizabeth) 26
—— (William) - 20
Wyatt (A. J.) - 20
Wylie (J. H.) - 6
Youatt (W.) - 10
Zeller (E.) - 15

History, Politics, Polity, Political Memoirs, &c.

Abbott.—*A HISTORY OF GREECE.* By EVELYN ABBOTT, M.A., LL.D.
Part I.—From the Earliest Times to the Ionian Revolt. Crown 8vo., 10s. 6d.
Part II.—500-445 B.C. Crown 8vo., 10s. 6d.

Acland and Ransome.—*A HAND-BOOK IN OUTLINE OF THE POLITICAL HISTORY OF ENGLAND TO 1896.* Chronologically Arranged. By the Right Hon. A. H. DYKE ACLAND, M.P., and CYRIL RANSOME, M.A. Crown 8vo., 6s.

Amos.—*PRIMER OF THE ENGLISH CONSTITUTION AND GOVERNMENT.* For the Use of Colleges, Schools, and Private Students. By SHELDON AMOS, M.A. Cr. 8vo., 6s.

ANNUAL REGISTER (THE). A Review of Public Events at Home and Abroad, for the year 1897. 8vo., 18s.
Volumes of the ANNUAL REGISTER for the years 1863-1896 can still be had. 18s. each.

Arnold.—*INTRODUCTORY LECTURES ON MODERN HISTORY.* By THOMAS ARNOLD, D.D., formerly Head Master of Rugby School. 8vo., 7s. 6d.

Ashbourne.—*PITT: SOME CHAPTERS ON HIS LIFE AND TIMES.* By the Right Hon. EDWARD GIBSON, LORD ASHBOURNE, Lord Chancellor of Ireland. With 11 Portraits. 8vo., 21s.

Baden-Powell. — *THE INDIAN VILLAGE COMMUNITY.* Examined with Reference to the Physical, Ethnographic, and Historical Conditions of the Provinces; chiefly on the Basis of the Revenue-Settlement Records and District Manuals. By B. H. BADEN-POWELL, M.A., C.I.E. With Map. 8vo., 16s.

Bagwell.—*IRELAND UNDER THE TUDORS.* By RICHARD BAGWELL, LL.D. (3 vols.) Vols. I. and II. From the first invasion of the Northmen to the year 1578. 8vo., 32s. Vol. III. 1578-1603. 8vo., 18s.

Ball.—*HISTORICAL REVIEW OF THE LEGISLATIVE SYSTEMS OPERATIVE IN IRELAND,* from the Invasion of Henry the Second to the Union (1172-1800). By the Rt. Hon. J. T. BALL. 8vo., 6s.

Besant.—*THE HISTORY OF LONDON.* By Sir WALTER BESANT. With 74 Illustrations. Crown 8vo., 1s. 9d. Or bound as a School Prize Book, 2s. 6d.

Brassey (LORD).—PAPERS AND ADDRESSES.
NAVAL AND MARITIME. 1872-1893. 2 vols. Crown 8vo., 10s.

Brassey (LORD) PAPERS AND ADDRESSES—*continued.*
MERCANTILE MARINE AND NAVIGATION, from 1871-1894. Crown 8vo., 5s.
IMPERIAL FEDERATION AND COLONISATION FROM 1880-1894. Cr. 8vo., 5s.
POLITICAL AND MISCELLANEOUS. 1861-1894. Crown 8vo., 5s.

Bright.—*A HISTORY OF ENGLAND.* By the Rev. J. FRANCK BRIGHT, D.D.
Period I. *MEDIÆVAL MONARCHY:* A.D. 449-1485. Crown 8vo., 4s. 6d.
Period II. *PERSONAL MONARCHY.* 1485-1688. Crown 8vo., 5s.
Period III. *CONSTITUTIONAL MONARCHY.* 1689-1837. Crown 8vo., 7s. 6d.
Period IV. *THE GROWTH OF DEMOCRACY.* 1837-1880. Crown 8vo., 6s.

Buckle.—*HISTORY OF CIVILISATION IN ENGLAND.* By HENRY THOMAS BUCKLE. 3 vols. Crown 8vo., 24s.

Burke.—*A HISTORY OF SPAIN* from the Earliest Times to the Death of Ferdinand the Catholic. By ULICK RALPH BURKE, M.A. 2 vols. 8vo., 32s.

Chesney.—*INDIAN POLITY:* a View of the System of Administration in India. By General Sir GEORGE CHESNEY, K.C.B. With Map showing all the Administrative Divisions of British India. 8vo., 21s.

Corbett.—*DRAKE AND THE TUDOR NAVY,* with a History of the Rise of England as a Maritime Power. By JULIAN S. CORBETT. With Portraits, Illustrations and Maps. 2 vols. 8vo., 36s.

Creighton. — *A HISTORY OF THE PAPACY FROM THE GREAT SCHISM TO THE SACK OF ROME,* 1378-1527. By M. CREIGHTON, D.D., Lord Bishop of London. 6 vols. Crown 8vo., 6s. each.

Cuningham. — *A SCHEME FOR IMPERIAL FEDERATION:* a Senate for the Empire. By GRANVILLE C. CUNINGHAM, of Montreal, Canada. With an Introduction by Sir FREDERICK YOUNG, K.C.M.G. Crown 8vo., 3s. 6d.

Curzon.—*PERSIA AND THE PERSIAN QUESTION.* By the Right Hon. LORD CURZON of Kedleston. With 9 Maps, 96 Illustrations, Appendices, and an Index. 2 vols. 8vo., 42s.

De Tocqueville.—*DEMOCRACY IN AMERICA.* By ALEXIS DE TOCQUEVILLE. Translated by HENRY REEVE, C.B., D.C.L. 2 vols. Crown 8vo., 16s.

History, Politics, Polity, Political Memoirs, &c.—*continued.*

Dickinson.—*THE DEVELOPMENT OF PARLIAMENT DURING THE NINETEENTH CENTURY.* By G. LOWES DICKINSON, M.A. 8vo., 7s. 6d.

Froude (JAMES A.).

THE HISTORY OF ENGLAND, from the Fall of Wolsey to the Defeat of the Spanish Armada.

   Popular Edition. 12 vols. Crown 8vo., 3s. each.
   '*Silver Library*' *Edition.* 12 vols. Crown 8vo., 3s. 6d. each.

THE DIVORCE OF CATHERINE OF ARAGON. Crown 8vo., 3s. 6d.

THE SPANISH STORY OF THE ARMADA, and other Essays. Cr. 8vo., 3s. 6d.

THE ENGLISH IN IRELAND IN THE EIGHTEENTH CENTURY. 3 vols. Cr. 8vo., 10s. 6d.

ENGLISH SEAMEN IN THE SIXTEENTH CENTURY. Cr. 8vo., 6s.

THE COUNCIL OF TRENT. Crown 8vo., 3s. 6d.

SHORT STUDIES ON GREAT SUBJECTS. 4 vols. Cr. 8vo., 3s. 6d. each.

CÆSAR : a Sketch. Cr. 8vo, 3s. 6d.

Gardiner (SAMUEL RAWSON, D.C.L., LL.D.).

HISTORY OF ENGLAND, from the Accession of James I. to the Outbreak of the Civil War, 1603-1642. 10 vols. Crown 8vo., 6s. each.

A HISTORY OF THE GREAT CIVIL WAR, 1642-1649. 4 vols. Cr. 8vo., 6s. each.

A HISTORY OF THE COMMONWEALTH AND THE PROTECTORATE. 1649-1660. Vol. I. 1649-1651. With 14 Maps. 8vo., 21s. Vol. II. 1651-1654. With 7 Maps. 8vo., 21s.

WHAT GUNPOWDER PLOT WAS. With 8 Illustrations. Crown 8vo., 5s.

CROMWELL'S PLACE IN HISTORY. Founded on Six Lectures delivered in the University of Oxford. Cr. 8vo., 3s. 6d.

Gardiner (SAMUEL RAWSON, D.C.L., LL.D.)—*continued.*

THE STUDENT'S HISTORY OF ENGLAND. With 378 Illustrations. Crown 8vo., 12s.

   Also in Three Volumes, price 4s. each.
   Vol. I. B.C. 55—A.D. 1509. 173 Illustrations.
   Vol. II. 1509-1689. 96 Illustrations.
   Vol. III. 1689-1885. 109 Illustrations.

Greville.—*A JOURNAL OF THE REIGNS OF KING GEORGE IV., KING WILLIAM IV., AND QUEEN VICTORIA.* By CHARLES C. F. GREVILLE, formerly Clerk of the Council. 8 vols. Crown 8vo., 3s. 6d. each.

HARVARD HISTORICAL STUDIES.

THE SUPPRESSION OF THE AFRICAN SLAVE TRADE TO THE UNITED STATES OF AMERICA, 1638-1870. By W. E. B. Du Bois, Ph.D. 8vo., 7s. 6d.

THE CONTEST OVER THE RATIFICATON OF THE FEDERAL CONSTITUTION IN MASSACHUSETTS. By S. B. HARDING, A.M. 8vo., 6s.

A CRITICAL STUDY OF NULLIFICATION IN SOUTH CAROLINA. By D. F. HOUSTON, A.M. 8vo., 6s.

NOMINATIONS FOR ELECTIVE OFFICE IN THE UNITED STATES. By FREDERICK W. DALLINGER, A.M. 8vo., 7s. 6d.

A BIBLIOGRAPHY OF BRITISH MUNICIPAL HISTORY, INCLUDING GILDS AND PARLIAMENTARY REPRESENTATION. By CHARLES GROSS, Ph.D. 8vo., 12s.

THE LIBERTY AND FREE SOIL PARTIES IN THE NORTH WEST. By THEODORE C. SMITH, Ph.D. 8vo, 7s. 6d.

THE PROVINCIAL GOVERNOR IN THE ENGLISH COLONIES OF NORTH AMERICA. By EVARTS BOUTELL GREENER. 8vo., 7s. 6d.

   *** *Other Volumes are in preparation.*

Hammond.—*A WOMAN'S PART IN A REVOLUTION.* By Mrs. JOHN HAYS HAMMOND. Crown 8vo., 2s. 6d.

Historic Towns.—Edited by E. A. FREEMAN, D.C.L., and Rev. WILLIAM HUNT, M.A. With Maps and Plans. Crown 8vo., 3s. 6d. each.

Bristol. By Rev. W. Hunt.	Oxford. By Rev. C. W. Boase.
Carlisle. By Mandell Creighton, D.D.	Winchester. By G. W. Kitchin, D.D.
Cinque Ports. By Montagu Burrows.	York. By Rev. James Raine.
Colchester. By Rev. E. L. Cutts.	New York. By Theodore Roosevelt.
Exeter. By E. A. Freeman.	
London. By Rev. W. J. Loftie.	Boston (U.S.) By Henry Cabot Lodge.

History, Politics, Polity, Political Memoirs, &c.—*continued.*

Hunter.—*A History of British India.* By Sir WILLIAM WILSON HUNTER, K.C.S.I., M.A., LL.D.; a Vice-President of the Royal Asiatic Society. In 5 vols. Vol. I.—Introductory to the Overthrow of the English in the Spice Archipelago, 1623. 8vo., 18s.

Joyce (P. W., LL.D.).

A Short History of Ireland, from the Earliest Times to 1603. Crown 8vo., 10s. 6d.

A Child's History of Ireland. From the Earliest Times to the Death of O'Connell. With specially constructed Map and 160 Illustrations, including Facsimile in full colours of an illuminated page of the Gospel Book of Mac-Durnan, A.D. 850. Fcp. 8vo., 3s. 6d.

Kaye and Malleson.—*History of the Indian Mutiny,* 1857-1858. By Sir JOHN W. KAYE and Colonel G. B. MALLESON. With Analytical Index and Maps and Plans. 6 vols. Crown 8vo., 3s. 6d. each.

Lang (ANDREW).

Pickle the Spy: or, The Incognito of Prince Charles. With 6 Portraits. 8vo., 18s.

The Companions of Pickle: Being a Sequel to ' Pickle the Spy '. With 4 Plates. 8vo., 16s.

St. Andrews. With 8 Plates and 24 Illustrations in the Text by T. HODGE. 8vo., 15s. net.

Lecky (The Rt. Hon. WILLIAM E. H.)

History of England in the Eighteenth Century.
Library Edition. 8 vols. 8vo. Vols. I. and II., 1700-1760, 36s.; Vols. III. and IV., 1760-1784, 36s.; Vols. V. and VI., 1784-1793, 36s.; Vols. VII. and VIII., 1793-1800, 36s.
Cabinet Edition. ENGLAND. 7 vols. Crown 8vo., 6s. each. IRELAND. 5 vols. Crown 8vo., 6s. each.

History of European Morals from Augustus to Charlemagne. 2 vols. Crown 8vo., 12s.

History of the Rise and Influence of the Spirit of Rationalism in Europe. 2 vols. Crown 8vo., 12s.

Democracy and Liberty.
Library Edition. 2 vols. 8vo., 36s.
Cabinet Edition. 2 vols. Cr. 8vo., 12s.

Lowell.—*Governments and Parties in Continental Europe.* By A. LAWRENCE LOWELL. 2 vols. 8vo., 21s.

Macaulay (LORD).

The Life and Works of Lord Macaulay. 'Edinburgh' Edition. 10 vols. 8vo., 6s. each.

Complete Works.
Cabinet Edition. 16 vols. Post 8vo. £4 16s.
Library Edition. 8 vols. 8vo., £5 5s.
'Edinburgh' Edition. 8 vols. 8vo., 6s. each.
'Albany' Edition. With 12 Portraits. 12 vols. Large Crown 8vo., 3s. 6d. each.

History of England from the Accession of James the Second.
Popular Edition. 2 vols. Cr. 8vo., 5s.
Student's Edition. 2 vols. Cr. 8vo., 12s.
People's Edition. 4 vols. Cr. 8vo., 16s.
'Albany' Edition. With 6 Portraits. 6 vols. Large Crown 8vo., 3s. 6d. each.
Cabinet Edition. 8 vols. Post 8vo., 48s.
'Edinburgh' Edition. 4 vols. 8vo., 6s. each.
Library Edition. 5 vols. 8vo., £4.

Critical and Historical Essays, with Lays of Ancient Rome, etc., in 1 volume.
Popular Edition. Crown 8vo., 2s. 6d.
Authorised Edition. Crown 8vo., 2s. 6d., or gilt edges, 3s. 6d.
'Silver Library' Edition. With Portrait and 4 Illustrations to the 'Lays'. Cr. 8vo., 3s. 6d.

Critical and Historical Essays.
Student's Edition. 1 vol. Cr. 8vo., 6s.
People's Edition. 2 vols. Cr. 8vo., 8s.
'Trevelyan' Edition. 2 vols. Cr. 8vo., 9s.
Cabinet Edition. 4 vols. Post 8vo., 24s.
'Edinburgh' Edition. 3 vols. 8vo., 6s. each.
Library Edition. 3 vols. 8vo., 36s.

Essays, which may be had separately, sewed, 6d. each; cloth, 1s. each.

Addison and Walpole.	Ranke and Gladstone.
Croker's Boswell's Johnson.	Milton and Machiavelli.
Hallam's Constitutional History.	Lord Byron.
	Lord Clive.
Warren Hastings.	Lord Byron, and The
The Earl of Chatham (Two Essays).	Comic Dramatists of the Restoration.
Frederick the Great.	

Miscellaneous Writings.
People's Edition. 1 vol. Cr. 8vo., 4s. 6d.
Library Edition. 2 vols. 8vo., 21s.

History, Politics, Polity, Political Memoirs, &c.—*continued.*

Macaulay (LORD)—*continued.*

MISCELLANEOUS WRITINGS, SPEECHES AND POEMS.
Popular Edition. Crown 8vo., 2s. 6d.
Cabinet Edition. 4 vols. Post 8vo., 24s.
SELECTIONS FROM THE WRITINGS OF LORD MACAULAY. Edited, with Occasional Notes, by the Right Hon. Sir G. O. Trevelyan, Bart. Crown 8vo., 6s.

MacColl.—*THE SULTAN AND THE POWERS.* By the Rev. MALCOLM MACCOLL, M.A., Canon of Ripon. 8vo., 10s. 6d.

Mackinnon.—*THE UNION OF ENGLAND AND SCOTLAND: A STUDY OF INTERNATIONAL HISTORY.* By JAMES MACKINNON. Ph.D. Examiner in History to the University of Edinburgh. 8vo., 16s.

May.—*THE CONSTITUTIONAL HISTORY OF ENGLAND* since the Accession of George III. 1760-1870. By Sir THOMAS ERSKINE MAY, K.C.B. (Lord Farnborough). 3 vols. Cr. 8vo., 18s.

Merivale (CHARLES, D.D.), sometime Dean of Ely.

HISTORY OF THE ROMANS UNDER THE EMPIRE. 8 vols. Crown 8vo., 3s. 6d. each.

THE FALL OF THE ROMAN REPUBLIC: a Short History of the Last Century of the Commonwealth. 12mo., 7s. 6d.

GENERAL HISTORY OF ROME, from the Foundation of the City to the Fall of Augustulus, B.C. 753-A.D. 476. With 5 Maps. Crown 8vo, 7s. 6d.

Montague. — *THE ELEMENTS OF ENGLISH CONSTITUTIONAL HISTORY.* By F. C. MONTAGUE, M.A. Crown 8vo., 3s. 6d.

Ransome.—*THE RISE OF CONSTITUTIONAL GOVERNMENT IN ENGLAND:* being a Series of Twenty Lectures on the History of the English Constitution delivered to a Popular Audience. By CYRIL RANSOME, M.A. Crown 8vo., 6s.

Richman.—*APPENZELL: PURE DEMOCRACY AND PASTORAL LIFE IN INNER-RHODEN.* A Swiss Study. By IRVING B. RICHMAN, Consul-General of the United States to Switzerland. With Maps. Crown 8vo., 5s.

Seebohm (FREDERIC).

THE ENGLISH VILLAGE COMMUNITY Examined in its Relations to the Manorial and Tribal Systems, etc. With 13 Maps and Plates. 8vo., 16s.

THE TRIBAL SYSTEM IN WALES: Being Part of an Inquiry into the Structure and Methods of Tribal Society. With 3 Maps. 8vo., 12s.

Sharpe.—*LONDON AND THE KINGDOM:* a History derived mainly from the Archives at Guildhall in the custody of the Corporation of the City of London. By REGINALD R. SHARPE, D.C.L., Records Clerk in the Office of the Town Clerk of the City of London. 3 vols. 8vo. 10s. 6d. each.

Smith.—*CARTHAGE AND THE CARTHAGINIANS.* By R. BOSWORTH SMITH, M.A., With Maps, Plans, etc. Cr. 8vo., 3s. 6d.

Stephens.—*A HISTORY OF THE FRENCH REVOLUTION.* By H. MORSE STEPHENS. 8vo. Vols. I. and II. 18s. each.

Stubbs.—*HISTORY OF THE UNIVERSITY OF DUBLIN*, from its Foundation to the End of the Eighteenth Century. By J. W. STUBBS. 8vo., 12s. 6d.

Sutherland.--*THE HISTORY OF AUSTRALIA AND NEW ZEALAND*, from 1606-1890. By ALEXANDER SUTHERLAND, M.A., and GEORGE SUTHERLAND, M.A. Crown 8vo., 2s. 6d.

Taylor.—*A STUDENT'S MANUAL OF THE HISTORY OF INDIA.* By Colonel MEADOWS TAYLOR, C.S.I., etc. Cr. 8vo., 7s. 6d.

Todd. — *PARLIAMENTARY GOVERNMENT IN THE BRITISH COLONIES.* By ALPHEUS TODD, LL.D. 8vo., 30s. net.

Trevelyan.—*THE AMERICAN REVOLUTION.* Part I. 1766-1776. By the Rt. Hon. Sir G. O. TREVELYAN, Bart. 8vo., 16s.

Trevelyan.—*ENGLAND IN THE TIME OF WYCLIFFE.* By GEORGE MACAULAY TREVELYAN, M.A. 8vo. [In the Press.

Wakeman and Hassall.—*ESSAYS INTRODUCTORY TO THE STUDY OF ENGLISH CONSTITUTIONAL HISTORY.* By Resident Members of the University of Oxford. Edited by HENRY OFFLEY WAKEMAN, M.A., and ARTHUR HASSALL, M.A. Crown 8vo., 6s.

Walpole.—*HISTORY OF ENGLAND FROM THE CONCLUSION OF THE GREAT WAR IN 1815 TO 1858.* By Sir SPENCER WALPOLE, K.C.B. 6 vols. Crown 8vo., 6s. each.

Wood-Martin.—*PAGAN IRELAND: AN ARCHÆOLOGICAL SKETCH.* A Handbook of Irish Pre-Christian Antiquities. By W. G. WOOD-MARTIN, M.R.I.A. With 512 Illustrations. Crown 8vo., 15s.

Wylie. — *HISTORY OF ENGLAND UNDER HENRY IV.* By JAMES HAMILTON WYLIE, M.A., one of H.M. Inspectors of Schools. 4 vols. Crown 8vo. Vol. I., 1399-1404, 10s. 6d. Vol. II., 1405-1406, 15s. Vol. III., 1407-1411, 15s. Vol. IV., 1411-1413, 21s.

Biography, Personal Memoirs, &c.

Armstrong.—*THE LIFE AND LETTERS OF EDMUND J. ARMSTRONG.* Edited by G. F. SAVAGE ARMSTRONG. Fcp. 8vo., 7s. 6d.

Bacon.—*THE LETTERS AND LIFE OF FRANCIS BACON, INCLUDING ALL HIS OCCASIONAL WORKS.* Edited by JAMES SPEDDING. 7 vols. 8vo., £4 4s.

Bagehot.—*BIOGRAPHICAL STUDIES.* By WALTER BAGEHOT. Crown 8vo., 3s. 6d.

Boevey.—'*THE PERVERSE WIDOW*': being passages from the Life of Catharina, wife of William Boevey, Esq., of Flaxley Abbey, in the County of Gloucester. Compiled by ARTHUR W. CRAWLEY-BOEVEY, M.A. With Portraits. 4to., 42s. net.

Carlyle.—*THOMAS CARLYLE*: A History of his Life. By JAMES ANTHONY FROUDE.
1795-1835. 2 vols. Crown 8vo., 7s.
1834-1881. 2 vols. Crown 8vo., 7s.

Crozier.—*MY INNER LIFE*: being a Chapter in Personal Evolution and Autobiography. By JOHN BEATTIE CROZIER, Author of ' Civilisation and Progress,' etc. 8vo., 14s.

Digby.—*THE LIFE OF SIR KENELM DIGBY, by one of his Descendants,* the Author of ' Falklands,' etc. With 7 Illustrations. 8vo., 16s.

Duncan.—*ADMIRAL DUNCAN.* By THE EARL OF CAMPERDOWN. With 3 Portraits. 8vo., 16s.

Erasmus.—*LIFE AND LETTERS OF ERASMUS.* By JAMES ANTHONY FROUDE. Crown 8vo., 6s.

FALKLANDS. By the Author of 'The Life of Sir Kenelm Digby,' etc. With 6 Portraits and 2 other Illustrations. 8vo., 10s. 6d.

Faraday.—*FARADAY AS A DISCOVERER.* By JOHN TYNDALL. Crown 8vo., 3s. 6d.

FOREIGN COURTS AND FOREIGN HOMES. By A. M. F. Crown 8vo., 6s.
. This book deals with Hanoverian and French society under King Ernest and the Emperor Napoleon III.

Fox.—*THE EARLY HISTORY OF CHARLES JAMES FOX.* By the Right Hon. Sir G. O. TREVELYAN, Bart.
Library Edition. 8vo., 18s.
Cabinet Edition. Crown 8vo., 6s.

Halifax.—*THE LIFE AND LETTERS OF SIR GEORGE SAVILE, BARONET, FIRST MARQUIS OF HALIFAX.* With a New Edition of his Works, now for the first time collected and revised. By H. C. FOXCROFT. 2 vols. 8vo., 36s.

Hamilton.—*LIFE OF SIR WILLIAM HAMILTON.* By R. P. GRAVES. 8vo. 3 vols. 15s. each. ADDENDUM. 8vo., 6d. sewed.

Harper.—*A MEMOIR OF HUGO DANIEL HARPER, D.D.,* late Principal of Jesus College, Oxford, and for many years Head Master of Sherborne School. By L. V. LESTER, M.A. Crown 8vo., 5s.

Havelock.—*MEMOIRS OF SIR HENRY HAVELOCK, K.C.B.* By JOHN CLARK MARSHMAN. Crown 8vo., 3s. 6d.

Haweis.—*MY MUSICAL LIFE.* By the Rev. H. R. HAWEIS. With Portrait of Richard Wagner and 3 Illustrations. Crown 8vo., 7s. 6d.

Holroyd.—*THE GIRLHOOD OF MARIA JOSEPHA HOLROYD (Lady Stanley of Alderley).* Recorded in Letters of a Hundred Years Ago, from 1776-1796. Edited by J. H. ADEANE. With 6 Portraits. 8vo., 18s.

Jackson.—*STONEWALL JACKSON AND THE AMERICAN CIVIL WAR.* By Lieut.-Col. G. F. R. HENDERSON, Professor of Military Art and History, the Staff College. With 2 Portraits and 33 Maps and Plans. 2 vols. 8vo., 42s.

Lejeune.—*MEMOIRS OF BARON LEJEUNE,* Aide-de-Camp to Marshals Berthier, Davout, and Oudinot. Translated and Edited from the Original French by Mrs. ARTHUR BELL (N. D'ANVERS). With a Preface by Major-General MAURICE, C.B. 2 vols. 8vo., 24s.

Luther.—*LIFE OF LUTHER.* By JULIUS KÖSTLIN. With 62 Illustrations and 4 Facsimilies of MSS. Translated from the German. Crown 8vo., 3s. 6d.

Macaulay.—*THE LIFE AND LETTERS OF LORD MACAULAY.* By the Right Hon. Sir G. O. TREVELYAN, Bart.
Popular Edition. 1 vol. Cr. 8vo., 2s. 6d.
Student's Edition. 1 vol. Cr. 8vo., 6s.
Cabinet Edition. 2 vols. Post 8vo., 12s.
'*Edinburgh*' *Edition.* 2 vols. 8vo., 6s. each.
Library Edition. 2 vols. 8vo., 36s.

Marbot.—*THE MEMOIRS OF THE BARON DE MARBOT.* Translated from the French. 2 vols. Crown 8vo., 7s.

Max Müller.—*AULD LANG SYNE.* By the Right Hon. F. MAX MÜLLER. With Portrait. 8vo, 10s. 6d.
CONTENTS.—Musical Recollections—Literary Recollections—Recollections of Royalties—Beggars.

Biography, Personal Memoirs, &c.—*continued.*

Meade. — *GENERAL SIR RICHARD MEADE AND THE FEUDATORY STATES OF CENTRAL AND SOUTHERN INDIA;* a Record of Forty-three Years' Service as Soldier, Political Officer and Administrator. By THOMAS HENRY THORNTON, C.S.I., D.C.L. With Portrait, Map and Illustrations. 8vo., 10s. 6d. net.

Nansen.—*FRIDTJOF NANSEN,* 1861-1893. By W. C. BRÖGGER and NORDAHL ROLFSEN. Translated by WILLIAM ARCHER. With 8 Plates, 48 Illustrations in the Text, and 3 Maps. 8vo., 12s. 6d.

Newdegate.—*THE CHEVERELS OF CHEVEREL MANOR.* By Lady NEWDIGATE-NEWDEGATE, Author of 'Gossip from a Muniment Room'. With 6 Illustrations from Family Portraits. 8vo., 10s. 6d.

Place.—*THE LIFE OF FRANCIS PLACE,* 1771-1854. By GRAHAM WALLAS, M.A. With 2 Portraits. 8vo., 12s.

RÁMAKRISHNA: HIS LIFE AND SAYINGS. By the Right Hon. F. MAX MÜLLER, K.M.; Foreign Member of the French Institute; Fellow of All Souls College, Oxford. Crown 8vo, 5s.

Rawlinson.—*A MEMOIR OF MAJOR-GENERAL SIR HENRY CRESWICKE RAWLINSON, BART., K.C.B., F.R.S., D.C.L., F.R.G.S., ETC.* By GEORGE RAWLINSON, M.A., F.R.G.S., Canon of Canterbury. With 3 Portraits and a Map, and a Preface by Field-Marshal Lord ROBERTS of Kandahar, V.C. 8vo., 16s.

Reeve.—*MEMOIRS OF THE LIFE AND CORRESPONDENCE OF HENRY REEVE, C.B.,* late Editor of the 'Edinburgh Review,' and Registrar of the Privy Council. By JOHN KNOX LAUGHTON, M.A. With 2 Portraits. 2 vols. 8vo., 28s.

Romanes.—*THE LIFE AND LETTERS OF GEORGE JOHN ROMANES, M.A., LL.D., F.R.S.* Written and Edited by his WIFE. With Portrait and 2 Illustrations. Cr. 8vo., 6s.

Seebohm.—*THE OXFORD REFORMERS—JOHN COLET, ERASMUS AND THOMAS MORE:* a History of their Fellow-Work. By FREDERIC SEEBOHM. 8vo., 14s.

Shakespeare. — *OUTLINES OF THE LIFE OF SHAKESPEARE.* By J. O. HALLIWELL-PHILLIPPS. With Illustrations and Fac-similes. 2 vols. Royal 8vo., 21s.

Shakespeare's *TRUE LIFE.* By JAMES WALTER With 500 Illustrations by GERALD E. MOIRA. Imp. 8vo., 21s.

Verney. —*MEMOIRS OF THE VERNEY FAMILY.* Compiled from the Letters and Illustrated by the Portraits at Clayden House.

Vols. I. & II., *DURING THE CIVIL WAR.* By FRANCES PARTHENOPE VERNEY. With 38 Portraits, Woodcuts and Fac-simile. Royal 8vo., 42s.

Vol. III., *DURING THE COMMONWEALTH.* 1650-1660. By MARGARET M. VERNEY. With 10 Portraits, etc. Royal 8vo., 21s.

Vol. IV., *FROM THE RESTORATION TO THE REVOLUTION.* 1660 to 1696. By MARGARET M. VERNEY. With Ports. Royal 8vo., 21s.

Wakley.—*THE LIFE AND TIMES OF THOMAS WAKLEY,* Founder and First Editor of the 'Lancet'. By S. SQUIRE SPRIGGE. With 2 Portraits. 8vo., 6s.

Wellington.—*LIFE OF THE DUKE OF WELLINGTON.* By the Rev. G. R. GLEIG, M.A. Crown 8vo., 3s. 6d.

Wollstonecraft.—*A STUDY OF MARY WOLLSTONECRAFT, AND THE RIGHTS OF WOMAN.* By EMMA RAUSCHENBUSCH-CLOUGH, Ph.D. 8vo., 7s. 6d.

Travel and Adventure, the Colonies, &c.

Arnold.—*SEAS AND LANDS.* By Sir EDWIN ARNOLD. With 71 Illustrations. Crown 8vo., 3s. 6d.

Baker (SIR S. W.).
EIGHT YEARS IN CEYLON. With 6 Illustrations. Crown 8vo., 3s. 6d.
THE RIFLE AND THE HOUND IN CEYLON. With 6 Illustrations. Crown 8vo., 3s. 6d.

Ball.—*THE ALPINE GUIDE.* By the late JOHN BALL, F.R.S., etc. A New Edition, Reconstructed and Revised on behalf of the Alpine Club, by W. A. B. COOLIDGE.
Vol. I., *THE WESTERN ALPS:* the Alpine Region, South of the Rhone Valley, from the Col de Tenda to the Simplon Pass. With 9 New and Revised Maps. Crown 8vo., 12s. net.

Bent.—*THE RUINED CITIES OF MASHONALAND:* being a Record of Excavation and Exploration in 1891. By J. THEODORE BENT. With 117 Illustrations. Crown 8vo., 3s. 6d.

Bicknell.—*TRAVEL AND ADVENTURE IN NORTHERN QUEENSLAND.* By ARTHUR C. BICKNELL. With 24 Plates and 22 Illustrations in the Text. 8vo., 15s.

Brassey.—*VOYAGES AND TRAVELS OF LORD BRASSEY, K.C.B., D.C.L.,* 1862-1894. Arranged and Edited by Captain S. EARDLEY-WILMOT. 2 vols. Cr. 8vo., 10s.

Travel and Adventure, the Colonies, &c.—*continued.*

Brassey (THE LATE LADY).

A VOYAGE IN THE 'SUNBEAM'; OUR HOME ON THE OCEAN FOR ELEVEN MONTHS.
Cabinet Edition. With Map and 66 Illustrations. Crown 8vo., 7s. 6d.
'*Silver Library*' Edition. With 66 Illustrations. Crown 8vo., 3s. 6d.
Popular Edition. With 60 Illustrations. 4to., 6d. sewed, 1s. cloth.
School Edition. With 37 Illustrations. Fcp., 2s. cloth, or 3s. white parchment.

SUNSHINE AND STORM IN THE EAST.
Cabinet Edition. With 2 Maps and 114 Illustrations. Crown 8vo., 7s. 6d.
Popular Edition. With 103 Illustrations. 4to., 6d. sewed, 1s. cloth.

IN THE TRADES, THE TROPICS, AND THE 'ROARING FORTIES'.
Cabinet Edition. With Map and 220 Illustrations. Crown 8vo., 7s. 6d.
Popular Edition. With 183 Illustrations. 4to., 6d. sewed, 1s. cloth.

THREE VOYAGES IN THE 'SUNBEAM'.
Popular Ed. With 346 Illust. 4to., 2s. 6d.

Browning.—*A GIRL'S WANDERINGS IN HUNGARY.* By H. ELLEN BROWNING. With Map and 20 Illustrations. Crown 8vo., 3s. 6d.

Churchill.—*THE STORY OF THE MALAKAND FIELD FORCE*, 1897. By WINSTON SPENCER CHURCHILL, Lieut., 4th Queen's Own Hussars. With 6 Maps and Plans. Crown 8vo., 3s. 6d.

Froude (JAMES A.).

OCEANA: or England and her Colonies. With 9 Illustrations. Cr. 8vo., 3s. 6d.

THE ENGLISH IN THE WEST INDIES: or, the Bow of Ulysses. With 9 Illustrations. Crown 8vo., 2s. boards, 2s. 6d. cloth.

Howitt.—*VISITS TO REMARKABLE PLACES.* Old Halls, Battle-Fields, Scenes, illustrative of Striking Passages in English History and Poetry. By WILLIAM HOWITT. With 80 Illustrations. Crown 8vo., 3s. 6d.

Knight (E. F.).

THE CRUISE OF THE 'ALERTE': the Narrative of a Search for Treasure on the Desert Island of Trinidad. With 2 Maps and 23 Illustrations. Crown 8vo., 3s. 6d.

WHERE THREE EMPIRES MEET: a Narrative of Recent Travel in Kashmir, Western Tibet, Baltistan, Ladak, Gilgit, and the adjoining Countries. With a Map and 54 Illustrations. Cr. 8vo., 3s. 6d.

Knight (E. F.)—*continued.*

THE 'FALCON' ON THE BALTIC: a Voyage from London to Copenhagen in a Three-Tonner. With 10 Full-page Illustrations. Crown 8vo., 3s. 6d.

Lees and Clutterbuck.—B.C. 1887: *A RAMBLE IN BRITISH COLUMBIA.* By J. A. LEES and W. J. CLUTTERBUCK. With Map and 75 Illustrations. Crown 8vo., 3s. 6d.

Macdonald.—*THE GOLD COAST: PAST AND PRESENT.* By GEORGE MACDONALD, Director of Education and H.M. Inspector of Schools for the Gold Coast Colony and the Protectorate. With 32 Illustrations. Crown 8vo., 7s. 6d.

Max Müller.—*LETTERS FROM CONSTANTINOPLE.* By Mrs. MAX MÜLLER. With 12 Views of Constantinople and the neighbourhood. Crown 8vo., 6s.

Nansen (FRIDTJOF).

THE FIRST CROSSING OF GREENLAND. With 143 Illustrations and a Map, Crown 8vo., 3s. 6d.

ESKIMO LIFE. With 31 Illustrations. 8vo., 16s.

Oliver.—*CRAGS AND CRATERS:* Rambles in the Island of Réunion. By WILLIAM DUDLEY OLIVER, M.A. With 27 Illustrations and a Map. Cr. 8vo., 6s.

Smith.—*CLIMBING IN THE BRITISH ISLES.* By W. P. HASKETT SMITH. With Illustrations by ELLIS CARR, and Numerous Plans.
Part I. *ENGLAND.* 16mo., 3s. 6d.
Part II. *WALES AND IRELAND.* 16mo., 3s. 6d.

Stephen. — *THE PLAY-GROUND OF EUROPE* (The Alps). By LESLIE STEPHEN. With 4 Illustrations. Crown 8vo., 3s. 6d.

THREE IN NORWAY. By Two of Them. With a Map and 59 Illustrations. Crown 8vo., 2s. boards, 2s. 6d. cloth.

Tyndall.—*THE GLACIERS OF THE ALPS:* being a Narrative of Excursions and Ascents. An Account of the Origin and Phenomena of Glaciers, and an Exposition of the Physical Principles to which they are related. By JOHN TYNDALL, F.R.S. With 61 Illustrations. Crown 8vo., 6s. 6d. net.

Vivian.—*SERVIA:* the Poor Man's Paradise. By HERBERT VIVIAN, M.A., Officer of the Royal Order of Takovo. With Map and Portrait of King Alexander. 8vo., 15s.

Veterinary Medicine, &c.

Steel (JOHN HENRY, F.R.C.V.S., F.Z.S., A.V.D.), late Professor of Veterinary Science and Principal of Bombay Veterinary College.

A TREATISE ON THE DISEASES OF THE DOG; being a Manual of Canine Pathology. Especially adapted for the use of Veterinary Practitioners and Students. With 88 Illustrations. 8vo., 10s. 6d.

A TREATISE ON THE DISEASES OF THE OX; being a Manual of Bovine Pathology. Especially adapted for the use of Veterinary Practitioners and Students. With 2 Plates and 117 Woodcuts. 8vo., 15s.

A TREATISE ON THE DISEASES OF THE SHEEP; being a Manual of Ovine Pathology for the use of Veterinary Practitioners and Students. With Coloured Plate and 99 Woodcuts. 8vo., 12s.

OUTLINES OF EQUINE ANATOMY; a Manual for the use of Veterinary Students in the Dissecting Room. Cr. 8vo., 7s. 6d.

Fitzwygram. — *HORSES AND STABLES.* By Major-General Sir F. FITZWYGRAM, Bart. With 56 pages of Illustrations. 8vo., 2s. 6d. net.

Schreiner. — *THE ANGORA GOAT* (published under the auspices of the South African Angora Goat Breeders' Association), and a Paper on the Ostrich (reprinted from the *Zoologist* for March, 1897). With 26 Illustrations. By S. C. CRONWRIGHT SCHREINER. 8vo., 10s. 6d.

'Stonehenge.' — *THE DOG IN HEALTH AND DISEASE.* By 'STONEHENGE'. With 78 Wood Engravings. 8vo., 7s. 6d.

Youatt (WILLIAM).

THE HORSE. Revised and Enlarged by W. WATSON, M.R.C.V.S. With 52 Wood Engravings. 8vo., 7s. 6d.

THE DOG. Revised and Enlarged. With 33 Wood Engravings. 8vo., 6s.

Sport and Pastime.

THE BADMINTON LIBRARY.

Edited by HIS GRACE THE DUKE OF BEAUFORT, K.G., and A. E. T. WATSON.

Complete in 28 Volumes.   Crown 8vo., Price 10s. 6d. each Volume, Cloth.

*** *The Volumes are also issued half-bound in Leather, with gilt top.   The price can be had from all Booksellers.*

ARCHERY. By C. J. LONGMAN and Col. H. WALROND. With Contributions by Miss LEGH, Viscount DILLON, etc. With 2 Maps, 23 Plates and 172 Illustrations in the Text. Crown 8vo., 10s. 6d.

ATHLETICS. By MONTAGUE SHEARMAN. With Chapters on Athletics at School by W. BEACHER THOMAS ; Athletic Sports in America by C. H. SHERRILL ; a Contribution on Paper-chasing by W. RYE, and an Introduction by Sir RICHARD WEBSTER, Q.C., M.P. With 12 Plates and 37 Illustrations in the Text. Cr. 8vo., 10s. 6d.

BIG GAME SHOOTING. By CLIVE PHILLIPPS-WOLLEY.

Vol. I. AFRICA AND AMERICA. With Contributions by Sir SAMUEL W. BAKER, W. C. OSWELL, F. C. SELOUS, etc. With 20 Plates and 57 Illustrations in the Text. Crown 8vo., 10s. 6d.

Vol. II. EUROPE, ASIA, AND THE ARCTIC REGIONS. With Contributions by Lieut.-Colonel R. HEBER PERCY, Major ALGERNON C. HEBER PERCY, etc. With 17 Plates and 56 Illustrations in the Text. Cr. 8vo., 10s. 6d.

BILLIARDS. By Major W. BROADFOOT, R.E. With Contributions by A. H. BOYD, SYDENHAM DIXON, W. J. FORD, etc. With 11 Plates, 19 Illustrations in the Text, and numerous Diagrams. Cr. 8vo., 10s. 6d.

COURSING AND FALCONRY. By HARDING COX and the Hon. GERALD LASCELLES. With 20 Plates and 56 Illustrations in the Text. Crown 8vo., 10s. 6d.

CRICKET. By A. G. STEEL and the Hon. R. H. LYTTELTON. With Contributions by ANDREW LANG, W. G. GRACE, F. GALE, etc. With 13 Plates and 52 Illustrations in the Text. Crown 8vo., 10s. 6d.

CYCLING. By the EARL OF ALBEMARLE and G. LACY HILLIER. With 19 Plates and 44 Illustrations in the Text. Crown 8vo., 10s. 6d.

DANCING. By Mrs. LILLY GROVE, F.R.G.S. With Contributions by Miss MIDDLETON, The Hon. Mrs. ARMYTAGE, etc. With Musical Examples, and 38 Full-page Plates and 93 Illustrations in the Text. Crown 8vo., 10s. 6d.

DRIVING. By His Grace the DUKE of BEAUFORT, K.G. With Contributions by A. E. T. WATSON the EARL OF ONSLOW, etc. With 12 Plates and 54 Illustrations in the Text. Crown 8vo., 10s. 6d.

Sport and Pastime—*continued.*

THE BADMINTON LIBRARY—*continued.*

FENCING, BOXING, AND WRESTLING. By WALTER H. POLLOCK, F. C. GROVE, C. PREVOST, E. B. MITCHELL, and WALTER ARMSTRONG. With 18 Plates and 24 Illust. in the Text. Cr. 8vo., 10s. 6d.

FISHING. By H. CHOLMONDELEY-PENNELL.

Vol. I. SALMON AND TROUT. With Contributions by H. R. FRANCIS, Major JOHN P. TRAHERNE, etc. With 9 Plates and numerous Illustrations of Tackle, etc. Crown 8vo., 10s. 6d.

Vol. II. PIKE AND OTHER COARSE FISH. With Contributions by the MARQUIS OF EXETER, WILLIAM SENIOR, G. CHRISTOPHER DAVIS, etc. With 7 Plates and numerous Illustrations of Tackle, etc. Crown 8vo., 10s. 6d.

FOOTBALL. By MONTAGUE SHEARMAN. [*In preparation.*]

GOLF. By HORACE G. HUTCHINSON. With Contributions by the Rt. Hon. A. J. BALFOUR, M.P., Sir WALTER SIMPSON, Bart., ANDREW LANG, etc. With 32 Plates and 57 Illustrations in the Text. Cr. 8vo., 10s. 6d.

HUNTING. By His Grace the DUKE OF BEAUFORT, K.G., and MOWBRAY MORRIS. With Contributions by the EARL OF SUFFOLK AND BERKSHIRE, Rev. E. W. L. DAVIES, G. H. LONGMAN, etc. With 5 Plates and 54 Illustrations in the Text. Cr. 8vo., 10s. 6d.

MOUNTAINEERING. By C. T. DENT. With Contributions by Sir W. M. CONWAY, D. W. FRESHFIELD, C. E. MATTHEWS, etc. With 13 Plates and 95 Illustrations in the Text. Cr. 8vo., 10s. 6d.

POETRY OF SPORT (THE).—Selected by HEDLEY PEEK. With a Chapter on Classical Allusions to Sport by ANDREW LANG, and a Special Preface to the BADMINTON LIBRARY by A. E. T. WATSON. With 32 Plates and 74 Illustrations in the Text. Crown 8vo., 10s. 6d.

RACING AND STEEPLE-CHASING. By the EARL OF SUFFOLK AND BERKSHIRE, W. G. CRAVEN, the Hon. F. LAWLEY, ARTHUR COVENTRY, and A. E. T. WATSON. With Frontispiece and 56 Illustrations in the Text. Crown 8vo., 10s. 6d.

RIDING AND POLO. By Captain ROBERT WEIR, THE DUKE OF BEAUFORT, THE EARL OF SUFFOLK AND BERKSHIRE, THE EARL OF ONSLOW, etc. With 18 Plates and 41 Illustrations in the Text. Crown 8vo., 10s. 6d.

ROWING. By R. P. P. ROWE and C. M. PITMAN. With Chapters on Steering by C. P. SEROCOLD and F. C. BEGG; Metropolitan Rowing by S. LE BLANC SMITH; and on PUNTING by P. W. SQUIRE. With 75 Illustrations. Crown 8vo., 10s. 6d.

SEA FISHING. By JOHN BICKER-DYKE, Sir H. W. GORE-BOOTH, ALFRED C. HARMSWORTH, and W. SENIOR. With 22 Full-page Plates and 175 Illustrations in the Text. Crown 8vo., 10s. 6d.

SHOOTING.

Vol. I. FIELD AND COVERT. By Lord WALSINGHAM and Sir RALPH PAYNE-GALLWEY, Bart. With Contributions by the Hon. GERALD LASCELLES and A. J. STUART-WORTLEY. With 11 Plates and 94 Illusts. in the Text. Cr. 8vo., 10s. 6d.

Vol. II. MOOR AND MARSH. By LORD WALSINGHAM and Sir RALPH PAYNE-GALLWEY, Bart. With Contributions by LORD LOVAT and Lord CHARLES LENNOX KERR. With 8 Plates and 57 Illustrations in the Text. Crown 8vo., 10s. 6d.

SKATING, CURLING, TOBOG-GANING. By J. M. HEATHCOTE, C. G. TEBBUTT, T. MAXWELL WITHAM, Rev. JOHN KERR, ORMOND HAKE, HENRY A. BUCK, etc. With 12 Plates and 272 Illustrations in the Text. Crown 8vo., 10s. 6d.

SWIMMING. By ARCHIBALD SINCLAIR and WILLIAM HENRY, Hon. Secs. of the Life-Saving Society. With 13 Plates and 106 Illustrations in the Text. Cr. 8vo., 10s. 6d.

TENNIS, LAWN TENNIS, RACKETS AND FIVES. By J. M. and C. G. HEATHCOTE, E. O. PLEYDELL-BOUVERIE, and A. C. AINGER. With Contributions by the Hon. A. LYTTELTON, W. C. MARSHALL, Miss L. DOD, etc. With 12 Plates and 67 Illustrations in the Text. Cr. 8vo., 10s. 6d.

YACHTING.

Vol. I. CRUISING, CONSTRUCTION OF YACHTS, YACHT RACING RULES, FITTING-OUT, etc. By Sir EDWARD SULLIVAN, Bart., THE EARL OF PEMBROKE, LORD BRASSEY, K.C.B., C. E. SETH-SMITH, C.B., G. L. WATSON, R. T. PRITCHETT, E. F. KNIGHT, etc. With 21 Plates and 93 Illustrations in the Text. Crown 8vo., 10s. 6d.

Vol. II. YACHT CLUBS, YACHTING IN AMERICA AND THE COLONIES, YACHT RACING, etc. By R. T. PRITCHETT, THE MARQUIS OF DUFFERIN AND AVA, K.P., THE EARL OF ONSLOW, JAMES McFERRAN, etc. With 35 Plates and 160 Illustrations in the Text. Crown 8vo., 10s. 6d.

Sport and Pastime—*continued.*

FUR, FEATHER, AND FIN SERIES.

Edited by A. E. T. WATSON.

Crown 8vo., price 5s. each Volume, cloth.

. *The Volumes are also issued half-bound in Leather, with gilt top. The price can be had from all Booksellers.*

THE PARTRIDGE. Natural History, by the Rev. H. A. MACPHERSON; Shooting, by A. J. STUART-WORTLEY; Cookery, by GEORGE SAINTSBURY. With 11 Illustrations and various Diagrams in the Text. Crown 8vo., 5s.

THE GROUSE. Natural History, by the Rev. H. A. MACPHERSON; Shooting, by A. J. STUART-WORTLEY; Cookery, by GEORGE SAINTSBURY. With 13 Illustrations and various Diagrams in the Text. Crown 8vo., 5s.

THE PHEASANT. Natural History, by the Rev. H. A. MACPHERSON; Shooting, by A. J. STUART-WORTLEY; Cookery, by ALEXANDER INNES SHAND. With 10 Illustrations and various Diagrams. Crown 8vo., 5s.

THE HARE. Natural History, by the Rev. H. A. MACPHERSON; Shooting, by the Hon. GERALD LASCELLES; Coursing, by CHARLES RICHARDSON; Hunting, by J. S. GIBBONS and G. H. LONGMAN; Cookery, by Col. KENNEY HERBERT. With 9 Illustrations. Crown 8vo, 5s.

RED DEER.—Natural History, by the Rev. H. A. MACPHERSON; Deer Stalking, by CAMERON OF LOCHIEL; Stag Hunting, by Viscount EBRINGTON; Cookery, by ALEXANDER INNES SHAND. With 10 Illustrations. Crown 8vo., 5s.

THE SALMON. By the Hon. A. E. GATHORNE-HARDY. With Chapters on the Law of Salmon Fishing by CLAUD DOUGLAS PENNANT; Cookery, by ALEXANDER INNES SHAND. With 8 Illustrations. Cr. 8vo., 5s.

THE TROUT. By the MARQUESS OF GRANBY. With Chapters on the Breeding of Trout by Col. H. CUSTANCE; and Cookery, by ALEXANDER INNES SHAND. With 12 Illustrations. Crown 8vo., 5s.

THE RABBIT. By JAMES EDMUND HARTING. With a Chapter on Cookery by ALEXANDER INNES SHAND. With 10 Illustions. Crown 8vo., 5s.

WILDFOWL. By the Hon. JOHN SCOTT MONTAGU, etc. With Illustrations, etc.   [*In preparation.*]

André.—*COLONEL BOGEY'S SKETCH-BOOK.* Comprising an Eccentric Collection of Scribbles and Scratches found in disused Lockers and swept up in the Pavilion, together with sundry After-Dinner Sayings of the Colonel. By R. ANDRÉ, West Herts Golf Club. Oblong 4to., 2s. 6d.

BADMINTON MAGAZINE (THE) OF SPORTS AND PASTIMES. Edited by ALFRED E. T. WATSON (" Rapier "). With numerous Illustrations. Price 1s. monthly.

Vols. I.-VI. 6s. each.

DEAD SHOT (THE): or, Sportsman's Complete Guide. Being a Treatise on the Use of the Gun, with Rudimentary and Finishing Lessons in the Art of Shooting Game of all kinds. Also Game-driving, Wildfowl and Pigeon-shooting, Dog-breaking, etc. By MARKSMAN. With numerous Illustrations. Crown 8vo., 10s. 6d.

Ellis.—*CHESS SPARKS;* or, Short and Bright Games of Chess. Collected and Arranged by J. H. ELLIS, M.A. 8vo., 4s. 6d.

Folkard.—*THE WILD-FOWLER :* A Treatise on Fowling, Ancient and Modern, descriptive also of Decoys and Flight-ponds, Wild-fowl Shooting, Gunning-punts, Shooting-yachts, etc. Also Fowling in the Fens and in Foreign Countries, Rock-fowling, etc., etc., by H. C. FOLKARD. With 13 Engravings on Steel, and several Woodcuts. 8vo., 12s. 6d.

Ford.—*THE THEORY AND PRACTICE OF ARCHERY.* By HORACE FORD. New Edition, thoroughly Revised and Re-written by W. BUTT, M.A. With a Preface by C. J. LONGMAN, M.A. 8vo., 14s.

Francis.—*A BOOK ON ANGLING :* or, Treatise on the Art of Fishing in every Branch; including full Illustrated List of Salmon Flies. By FRANCIS FRANCIS. With Portrait and Coloured Plates. Crown 8vo., 15s.

Sport and Pastime—*continued.*

Gibson.—*TOBOGGANING ON CROOKED RUNS.* By the Hon. HARRY GIBSON. With Contributions by F. DE B. STRICKLAND and 'LADY-TOBOGANNER'. With 40 Illustrations. Crown 8vo., 6s.

Graham.—*COUNTRY PASTIMES FOR BOYS.* By P. ANDERSON GRAHAM. With 252 Illustrations from Drawings and Photographs. Crown 8vo., 3s. 6d.

Lang.—*ANGLING SKETCHES.* By ANDREW LANG. With 20 Illustrations. Crown 8vo., 3s. 6d.

Lillie.—*CROQUET:* its History, Rules and Secrets. By ARTHUR LILLIE, Champion, Grand National Croquet Club, 1872; Winner of the 'All-Comers' Championship,' Maidstone, 1896. With 4 Full-page Illustrations by LUCIEN DAVIS, 15 Illustrations in the Text, and 27 Diagrams. Crown 8vo., 6s.

Longman.—*CHESS OPENINGS.* By FREDERICK W. LONGMAN. Fcp. 8vo., 2s. 6d.

Madden.—*THE DIARY OF MASTER WILLIAM SILENCE:* a Study of Shakespeare and of Elizabethan Sport. By the Right Hon. D. H. MADDEN, Vice-Chancellor of the University of Dublin. 8vo., 16s.

Maskelyne.—*SHARPS AND FLATS:* a Complete Revelation of the Secrets of Cheating at Games of Chance and Skill. By JOHN NEVIL MASKELYNE, of the Egyptian Hall. With 62 Illustrations. Crown 8vo., 6s.

Moffat.—*CRICKETY CRICKET:* Rhymes and Parodies. By DOUGLAS MOFFAT, with Frontispiece by Sir FRANK LOCKWOOD, Q.C., M.P., and 53 Illustrations by the Author. Crown 8vo, 2s. 6d.

Park.—*THE GAME OF GOLF.* By WILLIAM PARK, Jun., Champion Golfer, 1887-89. With 17 Plates and 26 Illustrations in the Text. Crown 8vo., 7s. 6d.

Payne-Gallwey (Sir RALPH, Bart.).

LETTERS TO YOUNG SHOOTERS (First Series). On the Choice and use of a Gun. With 41 Illustrations. Crown 8vo., 7s. 6d.

Payne-Gallwey (Sir RALPH, Bart.) —*continued.*

LETTERS TO YOUNG SHOOTERS (Second Series). On the Production, Preservation, and Killing of Game. With Directions in Shooting Wood-Pigeons and Breaking-in Retrievers. With Portrait and 103 Illustrations. Crown 8vo., 12s. 6d.

LETTERS TO YOUNG SHOOTERS. (Third Series.) Comprising a Short Natural History of the Wildfowl that are Rare or Common to the British Islands, with complete directions in Shooting Wildfowl on the Coast and Inland. With 200 Illustrations. Crown 8vo., 18s.

Pole—*THE THEORY OF THE MODERN SCIENTIFIC GAME OF WHIST.* By WILLIAM POLE, F.R.S. Fcp. 8vo., 2s. 6d.

Proctor.—*HOW TO PLAY WHIST: WITH THE LAWS AND ETIQUETTE OF WHIST.* By RICHARD A. PROCTOR. Crown 8vo., 3s. 6d.

Ribblesdale.—*THE QUEEN'S HOUNDS AND STAG-HUNTING RECOLLECTIONS.* By LORD RIBBLESDALE, Master of the Buckhounds, 1892-95. With Introductory Chapter on the Hereditary Mastership by E. BURROWS. With 24 Plates and 35 Illustrations in the Text. 8vo., 25s.

Ronalds.—*THE FLY-FISHER'S ENTOMOLOGY.* By ALFRED RONALDS. With 20 coloured Plates. 8vo., 14s.

Watson.—*RACING AND 'CHASING:* a Collection of Sporting Stories. By ALFRED E. T. WATSON, Editor of the 'Badminton Magazine'. With 16 Plates and 36 Illustrations in the Text. Crown 8vo, 7s. 6d.

Wilcocks.—*THE SEA FISHERMAN:* Comprising the Chief Methods of Hook and Line Fishing in the British and other Seas, and Remarks on Nets, Boats, and Boating. By J. C. WILCOCKS. Illustrated. Cr. 8vo., 6s.

Mental, Moral, and Political Philosophy.

LOGIC, RHETORIC, PSYCHOLOGY, &C.

Abbott.—*THE ELEMENTS OF LOGIC.*
By T. K. ABBOTT, B.D.   12mo., 3s.

Aristotle.

THE ETHICS: Greek Text, Illustrated
with Essay and Notes. By Sir ALEXAN-
DER GRANT, Bart. 2 vols. 8vo., 32s.

*AN INTRODUCTION TO ARISTOTLE'S
ETHICS.* Books I.-IV. (Book X. c. vi.-ix.
in an Appendix). With a continuous
Analysis and Notes. By the Rev. E.
MOORE, D.D. Crown 8vo. 10s. 6d.

Bacon (FRANCIS).

COMPLETE WORKS. Edited by R. L.
ELLIS, JAMES SPEDDING and D. D.
HEATH. 7 vols. 8vo., £3 13s. 6d.

LETTERS AND LIFE, including all his
occasional Works. Edited by JAMES
SPEDDING. 7 vols. 8vo., £4 4s.

THE ESSAYS: with Annotations. By
RICHARD WHATELY, D.D. 8vo., 10s. 6d.

THE ESSAYS : with Notes. By F.
STORR and C. H. GIBSON. Cr. 8vo, 3s. 6d.

THE ESSAYS : with Introduction,
Notes, and Index. By E. A. ABBOTT, D.D.
2 Vols. Fcp. 8vo., 6s. The Text and Index
only, without Introduction and Notes, in
One Volume. Fcp. 8vo., 2s. 6d.

Bain (ALEXANDER).

MENTAL SCIENCE. Cr. 8vo., 6s. 6d.
MORAL SCIENCE. Cr. 8vo., 4s. 6d.
*The two works as above can be had in one
volume, price 10s. 6d.*

SENSES AND THE INTELLECT. 8vo., 15s.
EMOTIONS AND THE WILL. 8vo., 15s.
LOGIC, DEDUCTIVE AND INDUCTIVE.
Part I. 4s. Part II. 6s. 6d.
PRACTICAL ESSAYS. Cr. 8vo., 2s.

Bray.—*THE PHILOSOPHY OF NECES-
SITY:* or, Law in Mind as in Matter. By
CHARLES BRAY. Crown 8vo., 5s.

Crozier (JOHN BEATTIE).

CIVILISATION AND PROGRESS : being
the Outlines of a New System of Political,
Religious and Social Philosophy. 8vo.,14s.

*HISTORY OF INTELLECTUAL DE-
VELOPMENT :* on the Lines of Modern
Evolution.

Vol. I. Greek and Hindoo Thought ; Græco-
Roman Paganism ; Judaism ; and Christianity down to the Closing of the Schools
of Athens by Justinian, 529 A.D. 8vo., 14s.

Davidson.—*THE LOGIC OF DEFINI-
TION,* Explained and Applied. By WILLIAM
L. DAVIDSON, M.A. Crown 8vo., 6s.

Green (THOMAS HILL).—THE WORKS
OF. Edited by R. L. NETTLESHIP.
Vols. I. and II. Philosophical Works. 8vo.,
16s. each.
Vol. III. Miscellanies. With Index to the
three Volumes, and Memoir. 8vo., 21s.

*LECTURES ON THE PRINCIPLES OF
POLITICAL OBLIGATION.* With Preface
by BERNARD BOSANQUET. 8vo., 5s.

Hodgson (SHADWORTH H.).

TIME AND SPACE : A Metaphysical
Essay. 8vo., 16s.

THE THEORY OF PRACTICE : an
Ethical Inquiry. 2 vols. 8vo., 24s.

THE PHILOSOPHY OF REFLECTION.
2 vols. 8vo., 21s.

THE METAPHYSIC OF EXPERIENCE.
Book I. General Analysis of Experience ;
Book II. Positive Science ; Book III.
Analysis of Conscious Action ; Book IV.
The Real Universe. 4 vols. 8vo., 36s. net.

Hume.—*THE PHILOSOPHICAL WORKS
OF DAVID HUME.* Edited by T. H. GREEN
and T. H. GROSE. 4 vols. 8vo., 28s. Or
separately, ESSAYS. 2 vols. 14s. TREATISE
OF HUMAN NATURE. 2 vols. 14s.

James.—*THE WILL TO BELIEVE,* and
Other Essays in Popular Philosophy. By
WILLIAM JAMES, M.D., LL.D., etc. Crown
8vo., 7s. 6d.

Justinian.—*THE INSTITUTES OF
JUSTINIAN :* Latin Text, chiefly that of
Huschke, with English Introduction, Trans-
lation, Notes, and Summary. By THOMAS
C. SANDARS, M.A. 8vo., 18s.

Kant (IMMANUEL).

*CRITIQUE OF PRACTICAL REASON,
AND OTHER WORKS ON THE THEORY OF
ETHICS.* Translated by T. K. ABBOTT,
B.D. With Memoir. 8vo., 12s. 6d.

*FUNDAMENTAL PRINCIPLES OF THE
METAPHYSIC OF ETHICS.* Translated by
T. K. ABBOTT, B.D. Crown 8vo, 3s.

*INTRODUCTION TO LOGIC, AND HIS
ESSAY ON THE MISTAKEN SUBTILTY OF
THE FOUR FIGURES..* Translated by T.
K. ABBOTT. 8vo., 6s.

Killick.—*HANDBOOK TO MILL'S
SYSTEM OF LOGIC.* By Rev. A. H.
KILLICK, M.A. Crown 8vo., 3s. 6d.

Mental, Moral and Political Philosophy—*continued.*
LOGIC, RHETORIC, PSYCHOLOGY, &C.

Ladd (GEORGE TRUMBULL).

PHILOSOPHY OF KNOWLEDGE: an Inquiry into the Nature, Limits and Validity of Human Cognitive Faculty. 8vo., 18s.

PHILOSOPHY OF MIND : An Essay on the Metaphysics of Psychology. 8vo., 16s.

ELEMENTS OF PHYSIOLOGICAL PSY-CHOLOGY. 8vo., 21s.

OUTLINES OF DESCRIPTIVE PSYCHO-LOGY: a Text-Book of Mental Science for Colleges and Normal Schools. 8vo., 12s.

OUTLINES OF PHYSIOLOGICAL PSY-CHOLOGY. 8vo., 12s.

PRIMER OF PSYCHOLOGY. Cr. 8vo., 5s. 6d.

Lutoslawski.—*THE ORIGIN AND GROWTH OF PLATO'S LOGIC.* With an Account of Plato's Style and of the Chronology of his Writings. By WINCENTY LUTOSLAWSKI. 8vo., 21s.

Max Müller.—*THE SCIENCE OF THOUGHT.* By F. Max Müller. 8vo., 21s.

Mill.—*ANALYSIS OF THE PHENOMENA OF THE HUMAN MIND.* By JAMES MILL. 2 vols. 8vo., 28s.

Mill (JOHN STUART).

A SYSTEM OF LOGIC. Cr. 8vo., 3s. 6d.

ON LIBERTY. Crown 8vo., 1s. 4d.

CONSIDERATIONS ON REPRESENTA-TIVE GOVERNMENT. Crown 8vo., 2s.

UTILITARIANISM. 8vo., 2s. 6d.

EXAMINATION OF SIR WILLIAM HAMILTON'S PHILOSOPHY. 8vo., 16s.

NATURE, THE UTILITY OF RELIGION, AND THEISM. Three Essays. 8vo., 5s.

Monck. — *AN INTRODUCTION TO LOGIC.* By WILLIAM HENRY S. MONCK, M.A. Crown 8vo., 5s.

Romanes.—*MIND AND MOTION AND MONISM.* By GEORGE JOHN ROMANES, LL.D., F.R.S. Cr. 8vo., 4s. 6d.

Stock.—*LECTURES IN THE LYCEUM ;* or, Aristotle's Ethics for English Readers. Edited by ST. GEORGE STOCK. Crown 8vo., 7s. 6d.

Sully (JAMES).

THE HUMAN MIND: a Text-book of Psychology. 2 vols. 8vo., 21s.

OUTLINES OF PSYCHOLOGY. Crown 8vo., 9s.

THE TEACHER'S HANDBOOK OF PSY-CHOLOGY. Crown 8vo., 6s. 6d.

STUDIES OF CHILDHOOD. 8vo., 10s. 6d.

CHILDREN'S WAYS: being Selections from the Author's ' Studies of Childhood '. With 25 Illustrations. Crown 8vo., 4s. 6d.

Sutherland. — *THE ORIGIN AND GROWTH OF THE MORAL INSTINCT.* By ALEXANDER SUTHERLAND, M.A. 2 vols. 8vo, 28s.

Swinburne. — *PICTURE LOGIC :* an Attempt to Popularise the Science of Reasoning. By ALFRED JAMES SWINBURNE, M.A. With 23 Woodcuts. Cr. 8vo., 2s. 6d.

Webb.—*THE VEIL OF ISIS :* a Series of Essays on Idealism. By THOMAS E. WEBB, LL.D., Q.C. 8vo., 10s. 6d.

Weber.—*HISTORY OF PHILOSOPHY.* By ALFRED WEBER. Professor in the University of Strasburg. Translated by FRANK THILLY, Ph.D. 8vo., 16s.

Whately (ARCHBISHOP).

BACON'S ESSAYS. With Annotations. 8vo., 10s. 6d.

ELEMENTS OF LOGIC. Cr. 8vo., 4s. 6d.

ELEMENTS OF RHETORIC. Cr. 8vo., 4s. 6d.

LESSONS ON REASONING. Fcp. 8vo., 1s. 6d.

Zeller (Dr. EDWARD).

THE STOICS, EPICUREANS, AND SCEPTICS. Translated by the Rev. O. J. REICHEL, M.A. Crown 8vo., 15s.

OUTLINES OF THE HISTORY OF GREEK PHILOSOPHY. Translated by SARAH F. ALLEYNE and EVELYN ABBOTT, M.A., LL.D. Crown 8vo., 10s. 6d.

PLATO AND THE OLDER ACADEMY Translated by SARAH F. ALLEYNE and ALFRED GOODWIN, B.A. Crown 8vo., 18s.

SOCRATES AND THE SOCRATIC SCHOOLS. Translated by the Rev. O. J. REICHEL, M.A. Crown 8vo., 10s. 6d.

ARISTOTLE AND THE EARLIER PERI-PATETICS. Translated by B. F. C. COS-TELLOE, M.A., and J. H. MUIRHEAD, M.A. 2 vols. Crown 8vo., 24s.

Mental, Moral, and Political Philosophy—*continued.*

MANUALS OF CATHOLIC PHILOSOPHY.

(Stonyhurst Series.)

A MANUAL OF POLITICAL ECONOMY. By C. S. DEVAS, M.A. Crown 8vo., 6s. 6d.

FIRST PRINCIPLES OF KNOWLEDGE. By JOHN RICKABY, S.J. Crown 8vo., 5s.

GENERAL METAPHYSICS. By JOHN RICKABY, S.J. Crown 8vo., 5s.

LOGIC. By RICHARD F. CLARKE, S.J. Crown 8vo., 5s.

MORAL PHILOSOPHY (ETHICS AND NATURAL LAW). By JOSEPH RICKABY, S.J. Crown 8vo., 5s.

NATURAL THEOLOGY. By BERNARD BOEDDER, S.J. Crown 8vo., 6s. 6d.

PSYCHOLOGY. BY MICHAEL MAHER, S.J. Crown 8vo., 6s. 6d.

History and Science of Language, &c.

Davidson.—LEADING AND IMPORTANT ENGLISH WORDS: Explained and Exemplified.   By WILLIAM L. DAVIDSON, M.A. Fcp. 8vo., 3s. 6d.

Farrar.—LANGUAGE AND LANGUAGES: By F. W. FARRAR, D.D., Dean of Canterbury. Crown 8vo., 6s.

Graham. — ENGLISH SYNONYMS, Classified and Explained : with Practical Exercises. By G. F. GRAHAM. Fcp. 8vo., 6s.

Max Müller (F.).

THE SCIENCE OF LANGUAGE.—Founded on Lectures delivered at the Royal Institution in 1861 and 1863. 2 vols. Crown 8vo., 10s.

BIOGRAPHIES OF WORDS, AND THE HOME OF THE ARYAS. Crown 8vo., 5s.

Roget.—THESAURUS OF ENGLISH WORDS AND PHRASES. Classified and Arranged so as to Facilitate the Expression of Ideas and assist in Literary Composition. By PETER MARK ROGET, M.D. F.R.S. With full Index. Crown 8vo., 10s. 6d.

Whately.—ENGLISH SYNONYMS. By E. JANE WHATELY. Fcp. 8vo., 3s.

Political Economy and Economics.

Ashley.—ENGLISH ECONOMIC HISTORY AND THEORY. By W. J. ASHLEY, M.A. Cr. 8vo., Part I., 5s. Part II., 10s. 6d.

Bagehot.—ECONOMIC STUDIES. By WALTER BAGEHOT. Crown 8vo., 3s. 6d.

Brassey.—PAPERS AND ADDRESSES ON WORK AND WAGES. By Lord BRASSEY. Edited by J. POTTER, and with Introduction by GEORGE HOWELL, M.P. Crown 8vo., 5s.

Channing.— THE TRUTH ABOUT AGRICULTURAL DEPRESSION: an Economic Study of the Evidence of the Royal Commission. By FRANCIS ALLSTON CHANNING, M.P., one of the Commission. Crown 8vo., 6s.

Devas.—A MANUAL OF POLITICAL ECONOMY. By C. S. DEVAS, M.A. Cr. 8vo., 6s. 6d. (Manuals of Catholic Philosophy.)

Jordan.—THE STANDARD OF VALUE. By WILLIAM LEIGHTON JORDAN. Cr. 8vo., 6s.

Leslie.—ESSAYS ON POLITICAL ECONOMY. By T. E. CLIFFE LESLIE, Hon. LL.D., Dubl. 8vo, 10s. 6d.

Macleod (HENRY DUNNING).

BIMETALISM. 8vo., 5s. net.

THE ELEMENTS OF BANKING. Cr. 8vo., 3s. 6d.

THE THEORY AND PRACTICE OF BANKING. Vol. I. 8vo., 12s. Vol. II. 14s.

THE THEORY OF CREDIT. 8vo. In 1 Vol., 30s. net; or separately, Vol. I., 10s. net. Vol. II., Part I., 10s. net. Vol. II., Part II., 10s. net.

A DIGEST OF THE LAW OF BILLS OF EXCHANGE, BANK-NOTES, &c. 8vo., 5s. net.

THE BANKING SYSTEM OF ENGLAND. [In preparation.

Political Economy and Economics—*continued.*

Mill.—*POLITICAL ECONOMY.* By JOHN STUART MILL.
Popular Edition. Crown 8vo., 3*s.* 6*d.*
Library Edition. 2 vols. 8vo., 30*s.*

Mulhall.—*INDUSTRIES AND WEALTH OF NATIONS.* By MICHAEL G. MULHALL, F.S.S. With 32 full-page Diagrams. Crown 8vo., 8*s.* 6*d.*

Symes.—*POLITICAL ECONOMY:* a Short Text-book of Political Economy. With Problems for Solution, and Hints for Supplementary Reading; also a Supplementary Chapter on Socialism. By Professor J. E. SYMES, M.A., of University College, Nottingham. Crown 8vo., 2*s.* 6*d.*

Toynbee.—*LECTURES ON THE INDUSTRIAL REVOLUTION OF THE 18TH CENTURY IN ENGLAND:* Popular Addresses, Notes and other Fragments. By ARNOLD TOYNBEE. With a Memoir of the Author by BENJAMIN JOWETT, D.D. 8vo., 10*s.* 6*d.*

Webb (SIDNEY and BEATRICE).
THE HISTORY OF TRADE UNIONISM. With Map and full Bibliography of the Subject. 8vo., 18*s.*
INDUSTRIAL DEMOCRACY: a Study in Trade Unionism. 2 vols. 8vo., 25*s.* net.
PROBLEMS OF MODERN INDUSTRY: Essays.

STUDIES IN ECONOMICS AND POLITICAL SCIENCE.
Issued under the auspices of the London School of Economics and Political Science.

GERMAN SOCIAL DEMOCRACY. By BERTRAND RUSSELL, B.A. With an Appendix on Social Democracy and the Woman Question in Germany by ALYS RUSSELL, B.A. Crown 8vo., 3*s.* 6*d.*

SELECT DOCUMENTS ILLUSTRATING THE HISTORY OF TRADE UNIONISM.
1. The Tailoring Trade. Edited by W. F. GALTON. With a Preface by SIDNEY WEBB, LL.B. Crown 8vo., 5*s.*

THE REFERENDUM IN SWITZERLAND. By SIMON DEPLOIGE, Advocate. With a Letter on the 'The Referendum in Belgium' by M. J. VAN DEN HEUVEL, Professor of International Law at the University of Louvain. Translated into English by C. P. TREVELYAN, M.A. Edited, with Notes, Introduction and Appendices, by LILIAN TOMN. Crown 8vo., 7*s.* 6*d.*

THE HISTORY OF LOCAL RATES IN ENGLAND: Five Lectures. By EDWIN CANNAN, M.A. Crown 8vo., 2*s.* 6*d.*

LOCAL VARIATIONS OF RATES OF WAGES. By F. W. LAURENCE, B.A. Trinity College, Cambridge; Adam Smith Prizeman, Cambridge, 1896. [*Shortly.*

THE ECONOMIC POLICY OF COLBERT. By A. J. SARGENT, B.A. Brasenose College, Oxford; Hulme Exhibitioner and Whately Prizeman, Trinity College, Dublin, 1897. [*Shortly.*

SELECT DOCUMENTS ILLUSTRATING THE STATE REGULATION OF WAGES. Edited, with Introduction and Notes, by W. A. S. HEWINS, M.A. [*In preparation.*

Evolution, Anthropology, &c.

Clodd (EDWARD).
THE STORY OF CREATION: a Plain Account of Evolution. With 77 Illustrations. Crown 8vo., 3*s.* 6*d.*
A PRIMER OF EVOLUTION: being a Popular Abridged Edition of 'The Story of Creation'. With Illustrations. Fcp. 8vo., 1*s.* 6*d.*

Lang (ANDREW).
CUSTOM AND MYTH: Studies of Early Usage and Belief. With 15 Illustrations. Crown 8vo., 3*s.* 6*d.*
MYTH, RITUAL AND RELIGION. 2 vols. Crown 8vo., 7*s.*

Lubbock.—*THE ORIGIN OF CIVILISATION,* and the Primitive Condition of Man. By Sir J. LUBBOCK, Bart., M.P. With 5 Plates and 20 Illustrations in the Text. 8vo., 18*s.*

Romanes (GEORGE JOHN).
DARWIN, AND AFTER DARWIN: an Exposition of the Darwinian Theory, and a Discussion on Post-Darwinian Questions.
Part I. THE DARWINIAN THEORY. With Portrait of Darwin and 125 Illustrations. Crown 8vo., 10*s.* 6*d.*
Part II. POST-DARWINIAN QUESTIONS: Heredity and Utility. With Portrait of the Author and 5 Illustrations. Cr. 8vo., 10*s.* 6*d.*
Part III. Post-Darwinian Questions: Isolation and Physiological Selection. Crown 8vo., 5*s.*

AN EXAMINATION OF WEISMANNISM. Crown 8vo., 6*s.*

ESSAYS. Edited by C. LLOYD MORGAN, Principal of University College. Bristol. Crown 8vo., 6*s.*

Classical Literature, Translations, &c.

Abbott.—*HELLENICA.* A Collection of Essays on Greek Poetry, Philosophy, History, and Religion. Edited by EVELYN ABBOTT, M.A., LL.D. Crown 8vo., 7s. 6d.

Æschylus.—*EUMENIDES OF ÆSCHYLUS.* With Metrical English Translation. By J. F. DAVIES. 8vo., 7s.

Aristophanes. — *THE ACHARNIANS OF ARISTOPHANES*, translated into English Verse. By R. Y. TYRRELL. Crown 8vo., 1s.

Aristotle.—*YOUTH AND OLD AGE, LIFE AND DEATH, AND RESPIRATION.* Translated, with Introduction and Notes, by W. OGLE, M.A., M.D. 8vo., 7s. 6d.

Becker (W. A.), Translated by the Rev. F. METCALFE, B.D.

GALLUS: or, Roman Scenes in the Time of Augustus. With Notes and Excursuses. With 26 Illustrations. Post 8vo., 3s. 6d.

CHARICLES: or, Illustrations of the Private Life of the Ancient Greeks. With Notes and Excursuses. With 26 Illustrations. Post 8vo., 3s. 6d.

Butler—*THE AUTHORESS OF THE ODYSSEY, WHERE AND WHEN SHE WROTE, WHO SHE WAS, THE USE SHE MADE OF THE ILIAD, AND HOW THE POEM GREW UNDER HER HANDS.* By SAMUEL BUTLER, Author of 'Erewhon,' etc. With Illustrations and 4 Maps. 8vo., 10s. 6d.

Cicero.—*CICERO'S CORRESPONDENCE.* By R. Y. TYRRELL. Vols. I., II., III., 8vo., each 12s. Vol. IV., 15s. Vol. V., 14s.

Homer.—*THE ILIAD OF HOMER.* Rendered into English Prose for the use of those who cannot read the original. By SAMUEL BUTLER, Author of 'Erewhon,' etc. Crown 8vo., 7s. 6d.

Horace.—*THE WORKS OF HORACE, RENDERED INTO ENGLISH PROSE.* With Life, Introduction and Notes. By WILLIAM COUTTS, M.A. Crown 8vo., 5s. net.

Lang.—*HOMER AND THE EPIC.* By ANDREW LANG. Crown 8vo., 9s. net.

Lucan.—*THE PHARSALIA OF LUCAN.* Translated into Blank Verse. By Sir EDWARD RIDLEY. 8vo., 14s.

Mackail.—*SELECT EPIGRAMS FROM THE GREEK ANTHOLOGY.* By J. W. MACKAIL. Edited with a Revised Text, Introduction, Translation, and Notes. 8vo., 16s.

Rich.—*A DICTIONARY OF ROMAN AND GREEK ANTIQUITIES.* By A. RICH, B.A. With 2000 Woodcuts. Crown 8vo., 7s. 6d.

Sophocles.—Translated into English Verse. By ROBERT WHITELAW, M.A., Assistant Master in Rugby School. Cr. 8vo., 8s. 6d.

Tacitus. — *THE HISTORY OF P. CORNELIUS TACITUS.* Translated into English, with an Introduction and Notes, Critical and Explanatory, by ALBERT WILLIAM QUILL, M.A., T.C.D. 2 vols. Vol. I. 8vo., 7s. 6d. Vol. II. 8vo., 12s. 6d.

Tyrrell. — *DUBLIN TRANSLATIONS INTO GREEK AND LATIN VERSE.* Edited by R. Y. TYRRELL. 8vo., 6s.

Virgil.

THE ÆNEID OF VIRGIL. Translated into English Verse by JOHN CONINGTON. Crown 8vo., 6s.

THE POEMS OF VIRGIL. Translated into English Prose by JOHN CONINGTON. Crown 8vo., 6s.

THE ÆNEID OF VIRGIL, freely translated into English Blank Verse. By W. J. THORNHILL. Crown 8vo., 7s. 6d.

THE ÆNEID OF VIRGIL. Translated into English Verse by JAMES RHOADES. Books I.-VI. Crown 8vo., 5s. Books VII.-XII. Crown 8vo., 5s.

THE ECLOGUES AND GEORGICS OF VIRGIL. Translated into English Prose by J. W. MACKAIL, Fellow of Balliol College, Oxford. 16mo., 5s.

Wilkins.—*THE GROWTH OF THE HOMERIC POEMS.* By G. WILKINS. 8vo., 6s.

Poetry and the Drama.

Armstrong (G. F. SAVAGE).

POEMS : Lyrical and Dramatic. Fcp. 8vo., 6s.

KING SAUL. (The Tragedy of Israel, Part I.) Fcp. 8vo., 5s.

KING DAVID. (The Tragedy of Israel, Part II.) Fcp. 8vo., 6s.

KING SOLOMON. (The Tragedy of Israel, Part III.) Fcp. 8vo., 6s.

UGONE : a Tragedy. Fcp. 8vo., 6s.

A GARLAND FROM GREECE : Poems. Fcp. 8vo., 7s. 6d.

STORIES OF WICKLOW : Poems. Fcp. 8vo., 7s. 6d.

MEPHISTOPHELES IN BROADCLOTH : a Satire. Fcp. 8vo., 4s.

ONE IN THE INFINITE : a Poem. Crown 8vo., 7s. 6d.

Armstrong.—*THE POETICAL WORKS OF EDMUND J. ARMSTRONG.* Fcp. 8vo., 5s.

Arnold.—*THE LIGHT OF THE WORLD :* or, The Great Consummation. By Sir EDWIN ARNOLD. With 14 Illustrations after HOLMAN HUNT. Crown 8vo., 6s.

Barraud. — *THE LAY OF THE KNIGHTS.* By the Rev. C. W. BARRAUD, S.J., Author of 'St. Thomas of Canterbury, and other Poems'. Crown 8vo., 4s.

Bell (MRS. HUGH).

CHAMBER COMEDIES : a Collection of Plays and Monologues for the Drawing Room. Crown 8vo., 6s.

FAIRY TALE PLAYS, AND HOW TO ACT THEM. With 91 Diagrams and 52 Illustrations. Crown 8vo., 6s.

Coleridge.—*SELECTIONS FROM.* With Introduction by ANDREW LANG. With 18 Illustrations by PATTEN WILSON. Crown 8vo., 3s. 6d.

Douglas.—*POEMS OF A COUNTRY GENTLEMAN.* By Sir GEORGE DOUGLAS, Bart., Author of 'The Fireside Tragedy'. Crown 8vo., 3s. 6d.

Goethe.

THE FIRST PART OF THE TRAGEDY OF FAUST IN ENGLISH. By THOS. E. WEBB, LL.D., sometime Fellow of Trinity College ; Professor of Moral Philosophy in the University of Dublin, etc. New and Cheaper Edition, with *THE DEATH OF FAUST,* from the Second Part. Crown 8vo., 6s.

Gore-Booth.—*POEMS.* By EVA GORE-BOOTH. Fcp. 8vo., 5s.

Ingelow (JEAN).

POETICAL WORKS. Complete in One Volume. Crown 8vo., 7s. 6d.

POETICAL WORKS. 2 vols. Fcp. 8vo., 12s.

LYRICAL AND OTHER POEMS. Selected from the Writings of JEAN INGELOW. Fcp. 8vo., 2s. 6d. cloth plain, 3s. cloth gilt.

Lang (ANDREW).

GRASS OF PARNASSUS. Fcp. 8vo., 2s. 6d. net.

THE BLUE POETRY BOOK. Edited by ANDREW LANG. With 100 Illustrations. Crown 8vo., 6s.

Layard and Corder.—*SONGS IN MANY MOODS.* By NINA F. LAYARD ; *THE WANDERING ALBATROSS,* etc. By ANNIE CORDER. In One Volume. Crown 8vo., 5s.

Lecky.—*POEMS.* By the Right Hon. W. E. H. LECKY. Fcp. 8vo., 5s.

Lytton (THE EARL OF), (OWEN MEREDITH).

THE WANDERER. Cr. 8vo., 10s. 6d.

LUCILE. Crown 8vo., 10s. 6d.

SELECTED POEMS. Cr. 8vo., 10s. 6d.

Macaulay.—*LAYS OF ANCIENT ROME, WITH 'IVRY' AND 'THE ARMADA'.* By Lord MACAULAY.

Illustrated by G. SCHARF. Fcp. 4to., 10s. 6d.

———————————— Bijou Edition. 18mo., 2s. 6d. gilt top.

———————————— Popular Edition. Fcp. 4to., 6d. sewed, 1s. cloth.

Illustrated by J. R. WEGUELIN. Crown 8vo., 3s. 6d.

Annotated Edition. Fcp. 8vo., 1s. sewed, 1s. 6d. cloth.

Poetry and the Drama—*continued*.

MacDonald (GEORGE, LL.D.).

A BOOK OF STRIFE, IN THE FORM OF THE DIARY OF AN OLD SOUL : Poems. 18mo., 6s.

RAMPOLLI : GROWTHS FROM A LONG-PLANTED ROOT : being Translations, New and Old (mainly in verse), chiefly from the German ; along with 'A Year's Diary of an Old Soul '. Crown 8vo., 6s.

Moffat.—*CRICKETYCRICKET :* Rhymes and Parodies.   By DOUGLAS MOFFAT. With Frontispiece by Sir FRANK LOCKWOOD, Q.C., M.P., and 53 Illustrations by the Author. Crown 8vo, 2s. 6d.

Morris (WILLIAM).

POETICAL WORKS—LIBRARY EDITION. Complete in Eleven Volumes.   Crown 8vo., price 6s. each.

THE EARTHLY PARADISE.   4 vols. 6s. each.

THE LIFE AND DEATH OF JASON. 6s.

THE DEFENCE OF GUENEVERE, and other Poems. 6s.

THE STORY OF SIGURD THE VOLSUNG, AND THE FALL OF THE NIBLUNGS. 6s.

LOVE IS ENOUGH ; or, the Freeing of Pharamond: A Morality ; and *POEMS BY THE WAY.* 6s.

THE ODYSSEY OF HOMER.   Done into English Verse. 6s.

THE ÆNEIDS OF VIRGIL.   Done into English Verse. 6s.

THE TALE OF BEOWULF, SOMETIME KING OF THE FOLK OF THE WEDERGEATS. Translated by WILLIAM MORRIS and A. J. WYATT. Crown 8vo., 6s.

Certain of the POETICAL WORKS may also be had in the following Editions :—

THE EARTHLY PARADISE.

Popular Edition. 5 vols. 12mo., 25s. ; or 5s. each, sold separately. The same in Ten Parts, 25s.; or 2s. 6d. each, sold separately. Cheap Edition, in 1 vol. Crown 8vo., 7s. 6d.

POEMS BY THE WAY. Square crown 8vo., 6s.

. For Mr. William Morris's Prose Works, see pp. 22 and 31.

Nesbit.—*LAYS AND LEGENDS.*   By E. NESBIT (Mrs. HUBERT BLAND).   First Series. Crown 8vo., 3s. 6d. Second Series. With Portrait. Crown 8vo., 5s.

Riley (JAMES WHITCOMB).

OLD FASHIONED ROSES : Poems. 12mo., 5s.

A CHILD-WORLD : POEMS.   Fcp. 8vo., 5s.

RUBÁIYÁT OF DOC SIFERS.   With 43 Illustrations by C. M RELYEA. Crown 8vo.

THE GOLDEN YEAR.   From the Verse and Prose of JAMES WHITCOMB RILEY. Compiled by CLARA E. LAUGHLIN. Fcp. 8vo., 5s.

Romanes.—*A SELECTION FROM THE POEMS OF GEORGE JOHN ROMANES, M.A., LL.D., F.R.S.* With an Introduction by T. HERBERT WARREN, President of Magdalen College, Oxford. Crown 8vo., 4s. 6d.

Russell.—*SONNETS ON THE SONNET :* an Anthology. Compiled by the Rev. MATTHEW RUSSELL, S.J. Crown 8vo., 3s. 6d.

Samuels.—*SHADOWS, AND OTHER POEMS.* By E. SAMUELS. With 7 Illustrations by W. FITZGERALD, M.A. Crown 8vo., 3s. 6d.

Shakespeare.—*BOWDLER'S FAMILY SHAKESPEARE.* With 36 Woodcuts. 1 vol. 8vo., 14s. Or in 6 vols. Fcp. 8vo., 21s.

THE SHAKESPEARE BIRTHDAY BOOK. By MARY F. DUNBAR. 32mo., 1s. 6d.

Tupper.—*POEMS.*   By JOHN LUCAS TUPPER. Selected and Edited by WILLIAM MICHAEL ROSSETTI. Crown 8vo., 5s.

Wordsworth. — *SELECTED POEMS.* By ANDREW LANG. With Photogravure Frontispiece of Rydal Mount. With 16 Illustrations and numerous Initial Letters. By ALFRED PARSONS, A.R.A. Crown 8vo., gilt edges, 3s. 6d.

Wordsworth and Coleridge.—*A DESCRIPTION OF THE WORDSWORTH AND COLERIDGE MANUSCRIPTS IN THE POSSESSION OF MR. T. NORTON LONGMAN.* Edited, with Notes, by W. HALE WHITE. With 3 Facsimile Reproductions. 4to., 10s. 6d.

Fiction, Humour, &c.

Allingham.—*CROOKED PATHS.* By FRANCIS ALLINGHAM. Crown 8vo., 6s

Anstey.—*VOCES POPULI.* Reprinted from 'Punch'. By F. ANSTEY, Author of 'Vice Versâ'. First Series. With 20 Illustrations by J. BERNARD PARTRIDGE. Crown 8vo., 3s. 6d.

Beaconsfield (THE EARL OF).

NOVELS AND TALES. Complete in 11 vols. Crown 8vo., 1s. 6d. each.

Vivian Grey.	Sybil.
The Young Duke, etc.	Henrietta Temple.
Alroy, Ixion, etc.	Venetia.
Contarini Fleming, etc.	Coningsby.
	Lothair.
Tancred.	Endymion.

NOVELS AND TALES. The Hughenden Edition. With 2 Portraits and 11 Vignettes. 11 vols. Crown 8vo., 42s.

Deland (MARGARET).

PHILIP AND HIS WIFE. Crown 8vo., 2s. 6d.

THE WISDOM OF FOOLS. Stories. Crown 8vo., 5s.

Diderot. — *RAMEAU'S NEPHEW:* a Translation from Diderot's Autographic Text. By SYLVIA MARGARET HILL. Crown 8vo., 3s. 6d.

Dougall.—*BEGGARS ALL.* By L. DOUGALL. Crown 8vo., 3s. 6d.

Doyle (A. CONAN).

MICAH CLARKE: A Tale of Monmouth's Rebellion. With 10 Illustrations. Cr. 8vo., 3s. 6d.

THE CAPTAIN OF THE POLESTAR, and other Tales. Cr. 8vo., 3s. 6d.

THE REFUGEES: A Tale of the Huguenots. With 25 Illustrations. Cr. 8vo., 3s. 6d.

THE STARK MUNRO LETTERS. Cr. 8vo, 3s. 6d.

Farrar (F. W., DEAN OF CANTERBURY).

DARKNESS AND DAWN: or, Scenes in the Days of Nero. An Historic Tale. Cr. 8vo., 7s. 6d.

GATHERING CLOUDS: a Tale of the Days of St. Chrysostom. Cr. 8vo., 7s. 6d.

Fowler (EDITH H.).

THE YOUNG PRETENDERS. A Story of Child Life. With 12 Illustrations by PHILIP BURNE-JONES. Crown 8vo., 6s.

THE PROFESSOR'S CHILDREN. With 24 Illustrations by ETHEL KATE BURGESS. Crown 8vo., 6s.

Froude.—*THE TWO CHIEFS OF DUNBOY:* an Irish Romance of the Last Century. By JAMES A. FROUDE. Cr. 8vo., 3s. 6d.

Gilkes.—*KALLISTRATUS:* an Autobiography. A Story of Hannibal and the Second Punic War. By A. H. GILKES, M.A., Master of Dulwich College. With 3 Illustrations by MAURICE GREIFFENHAGEN. Crown 8vo., 6s.

Graham.—*THE RED SCAUR:* A Story of the North Country. By P. ANDERSON GRAHAM. Crown 8vo., 6s.

Gurdon.—*MEMORIES AND FANCIES:* Suffolk Tales and other Stories; Fairy Legends; Poems; Miscellaneous Articles. By the late LADY CAMILLA GURDON, Author of 'Suffolk Folk-Lore'. Crown 8vo., 5s.

Haggard (H. RIDER).

DR. THERNE. Crown 8vo., 3s. 6d.

HEART OF THE WORLD. With 15 Illustrations. Crown 8vo., 3s. 6d.

JOAN HASTE. With 20 Illustrations. Crown 8vo., 3s. 6d.

THE PEOPLE OF THE MIST. With 16 Illustrations. Crown 8vo., 3s. 6d.

MONTEZUMA'S DAUGHTER. With 24 Illustrations. Crown 8vo., 3s. 6d.

SHE. With 32 Illustrations. Crown 8vo., 3s. 6d.

ALLAN QUATERMAIN. With 31 Illustrations. Crown 8vo., 3s. 6d.

MAIWA'S REVENGE: Cr. 8vo., 1s. 6d.

COLONEL QUARITCH, V.C. With Frontispiece and Vignette. Cr. 8vo., 3s. 6d.

CLEOPATRA. With 29 Illustrations. Crown 8vo., 3s. 6d.

Fiction, Humour, &c.—*continued.*

Haggard (H. RIDER)—*continued.*
BEATRICE. With Frontispiece and Vignette. Cr. 8vo., 3s. 6d.
ERIC BRIGHTEYES. With 51 Illustrations. Crown 8vo., 3s. 6d.
NADA THE LILY. With 23 Illustrations. Crown 8vo., 3s. 6d.
ALLAN'S WIFE. With 34 Illustrations. Crown 8vo., 3s. 6d.
THE WITCH'S HEAD. With 16 Illustrations. Crown 8vo., 3s. 6d.
MR. MEESON'S WILL. With 16 Illustrations. Crown 8vo., 3s. 6d.
DAWN. With 16 Illustrations. Cr. 8vo., 3s. 6d.

Harte.—*IN THE CARQUINEZ WOODS.* By BRET HARTE. Crown 8vo., 3s. 6d.

Hope.—*THE HEART OF PRINCESS OSRA.* By ANTHONY HOPE. With 9 Illustrations. Crown 8vo., 6s.

Hornung.—*THE UNBIDDEN GUEST.* By E. W. HORNUNG. Crown 8vo., 3s. 6d.

Jerome.—*SKETCHES IN LAVENDER: BLUE AND GREEN.* By JEROME K. JEROME. Crown 8vo., 3s. 6d.

Joyce.—*OLD CELTIC ROMANCES.* Twelve of the most beautiful of the Ancient Irish Romantic Tales. Translated from the Gaelic. By P. W. JOYCE, LL.D. Crown 8vo., 3s. 6d.

Lang.—*A MONK OF FIFE*; a Story of the Days of Joan of Arc. By ANDREW LANG. With 13 Illustrations by SELWYN IMAGE. Crown 8vo., 3s. 6d.

Levett-Yeats (S.).
THE CHEVALIER D'AURIAC. Crown 8vo., 3s. 6d.
A GALAHAD OF THE CREEKS, and other Stories. Crown 8vo., 6s.
THE HEART OF DENISE, and other Stories. Crown 8vo., 6s.

Lyall (EDNA).
THE AUTOBIOGRAPHY OF A SLANDER. Fcp. 8vo., 1s., sewed.
Presentation Edition. With 20 Illustrations by LANCELOT SPEED. Crown 8vo., 2s. 6d. net.
THE AUTOBIOGRAPHY OF A TRUTH. Fcp. 8vo., 1s., sewed; 1s. 6d., cloth.
DOREEN. The Story of a Singer. Crown 8vo., 6s.
WAYFARING MEN. Crown 8vo., 6s.
HOPE THE HERMIT: a Romance of Borrowdale. Crown 8vo., 6s.

Max Müller. — *DEUTSCHE LIEBE (GERMAN LOVE):* Fragments from the Papers of an Alien. Collected by F. MAX MÜLLER. Translated from the German by G. A. M. Crown 8vo., 5s.

Melville (G. J. WHYTE).
The Gladiators. | Holmby House.
The Interpreter. | Kate Coventry.
Good for Nothing. | Digby Grand.
The Queen's Maries. | General Bounce.
Crown 8vo., 1s. 6d. each.

Merriman.—*FLOTSAM:* A Story of the Indian Mutiny. By HENRY SETON MERRIMAN. Crown 8vo., 3s. 6d.

Morris (WILLIAM).
THE SUNDERING FLOOD. Cr. 8vo., 7s. 6d.
THE WATER OF THE WONDROUS ISLES. Crown 8vo., 7s. 6d.
THE WELL AT THE WORLD'S END. 2 vols. 8vo., 28s.
THE STORY OF THE GLITTERING PLAIN, which has been also called The Land of the Living Men, or The Acre of the Undying. Square post 8vo., 5s. net.
THE ROOTS OF THE MOUNTAINS, wherein is told somewhat of the Lives of the Men of Burgdale, their Friends, their Neighbours, their Foemen, and their Fellows-in-Arms. Written in Prose and Verse. Square crown 8vo., 8s.
A TALE OF THE HOUSE OF THE WOLFINGS, and all the Kindreds of the Mark. Written in Prose and Verse. Square crown 8vo., 6s.
A DREAM OF JOHN BALL, AND A KING'S LESSON. 12mo., 1s. 6d.
NEWS FROM NOWHERE; or, An Epoch of Rest. Being some Chapters from an Utopian Romance. Post 8vo., 1s. 6d.
⁂ For Mr. William Morris's Poetical Works, see p. 20.

Newman (CARDINAL).
LOSS AND GAIN: The Story of a Convert. Crown 8vo, Cabinet Edition, 6s.; Popular Edition, 3s. 6d.
CALLISTA: A Tale of the Third Century. Crown 8vo. Cabinet Edition, 6s.; Popular Edition, 3s. 6d.

Oliphant.—*OLD MR. TREDGOLD.* By Mrs. OLIPHANT. Crown 8vo., 2s. 6d.

Phillipps-Wolley.—*SNAP:* a Legend of the Lone Mountain. By C. PHILLIPPS-WOLLEY. With 13 Illustrations. Crown 8vo., 3s. 6d.

Fiction, Humour, &c.—*continued.*

Raymond.—*TWO MEN O' MENDIP:* a Novel. By WALTER RAYMOND, Author of 'Gentleman Upcott's Daughter,' etc. Cr. 8vo., 6s.

Rhoscomyl (OWEN).

THE JEWEL OF YNYS GALON: being a hitherto unprinted Chapter in the History of the Sea Rovers. With 12 Illustrations by LANCELOT SPEED. Cr. 8vo., 3s. 6d.

FOR THE WHITE ROSE OF ARNO: a Story of the Jacobite Rising of 1745. Crown 8vo., 6s.

Sewell (ELIZABETH M.).

A Glimpse of the World.	Amy Herbert
Laneton Parsonage.	Cleve Hall.
Margaret Percival.	Gertrude.
Katharine Ashton.	Home Life.
The Earl's Daughter.	After Life.
The Experience of Life	Ursula. Ivors.

Cr. 8vo., 1s. 6d. each cloth plain. 2s. 6d. each cloth extra, gilt edges.

Stevenson (ROBERT LOUIS).

THE STRANGE CASE OF DR. JEKYLL AND MR. HYDE. Fcp. 8vo., 1s. sewed. 1s. 6d. cloth.

THE STRANGE CASE OF DR. JEKYLL AND MR. HYDE; WITH OTHER FABLES. Crown 8vo., 3s. 6d.

MORE NEW ARABIAN NIGHTS—THE DYNAMITER. By ROBERT LOUIS STEVENSON and FANNY VAN DE GRIFT STEVENSON. Crown 8vo., 3s. 6d.

THE WRONG BOX. By ROBERT LOUIS STEVENSON and LLOYD OSBOURNE. Crown 8vo., 3s. 6d.

Suttner.—*LAY DOWN YOUR ARMS (Die Waffen Nieder):* The Autobiography of Martha von Tilling. By BERTHA VON SUTTNER. Translated by T. HOLMES. Cr. 8vo., 1s. 6d.

Trollope (ANTHONY).

THE WARDEN. Cr. 8vo., 1s. 6d.

BARCHESTER TOWERS. Cr. 8vo., 1s. 6d.

Walford (L. B.).

THE INTRUDERS. Crown 8vo., 6s.

LEDDY MARGET. Crown 8vo., 6s.

IVA KILDARE: a Matrimonial Problem. Crown 8vo., 6s.

MR. SMITH: a Part of his Life. Crown 8vo., 2s. 6d.

Walford (L. B.)—*continued.*

THE BABY'S GRANDMOTHER. Cr. 8vo., 2s. 6d.

COUSINS. Crown 8vo., 2s. 6d.

TROUBLESOME DAUGHTERS. Cr 8vo., 2s. 6d.

PAULINE. Crown 8vo., 2s. 6d.

DICK NETHERBY. Cr. 8vo., 2s. 6d.

THE HISTORY OF A WEEK. Cr. 8vo. 2s. 6d.

A STIFF-NECKED GENERATION. Cr. 8vo. 2s. 6d.

NAN, and other Stories. Cr. 8vo., 2s. 6d.

THE MISCHIEF OF MONICA. Cr. 8vo., 2s. 6d.

THE ONE GOOD GUEST. Cr. 8vo. 2s. 6d.

'*PLOUGHED,*' and other Stories. Crown 8vo., 2s. 6d.

THE MATCHMAKER. Cr. 8vo., 2s. 6d.

Watson.—*RACING AND 'CHASING:* a Collection of Sporting Stories. By ALFRED E. T. WATSON, Editor of the 'Badminton Magazine'. With 16 Plates and 36 Illustrations in the Text. Crown 8vo., 7s. 6d.

Weyman (STANLEY).

THE HOUSE OF THE WOLF. With Frontispiece and Vignette. Crown 8vo., 3s. 6d.

A GENTLEMAN OF FRANCE. With Frontispiece and Vignette. Cr. 8vo., 6s.

THE RED COCKADE. With Frontispiece and Vignette. Crown 8vo., 6s.

SHREWSBURY. With 24 Illustrations by CLAUDE A. SHEPPERSON. Cr. 8vo., 6s.

Whishaw (FRED.).

A BOYAR OF THE TERRIBLE: a Romance of the Court of Ivan the Cruel, First Tzar of Russia. With 12 Illustrations by H. G. MASSEY, A.R.E. Crown 8vo., 6s.

A TSAR'S GRATITUDE: A Story of Modern Russia. Crown 8vo., 6s.

Woods.—*WEEPING FERRY,* and other Stories. By MARGARET L. WOODS, Author of 'A Village Tragedy'. Crown 8vo., 6s.

Popular Science (Natural History, &c.).

Beddard. — *THE STRUCTURE AND CLASSIFICATION OF BIRDS.* By FRANK E. BEDDARD, M.A., F.R.S., Prosector and Vice-Secretary of the Zoological Society of London. With 252 Illustrations. 8vo., 21s. net.

Butler.—*OUR HOUSEHOLD INSECTS.* An Account of the Insect-Pests found in Dwelling-Houses. By EDWARD A. BUTLER, B.A., B.Sc. (Lond.). With 113 Illustrations. Crown 8vo., 3s. 6d.

Furneaux (W.).

THE OUTDOOR WORLD; or The Young Collector's Handbook. With 18 Plates (16 of which are coloured), and 549 Illustrations in the Text. Crown 8vo., 7s. 6d.

BUTTERFLIES AND MOTHS (British). With 12 coloured Plates and 241 Illustrations in the Text. Crown 8vo., 7s. 6d.

LIFE IN PONDS AND STREAMS. With 8 coloured Plates and 331 Illustrations in the Text. Crown 8vo., 7s. 6d.

Hartwig (DR. GEORGE).

THE SEA AND ITS LIVING WONDERS. With 12 Plates and 303 Woodcuts. 8vo., 7s. net.

THE TROPICAL WORLD. With 8 Plates and 172 Woodcuts. 8vo., 7s. net.

THE POLAR WORLD. With 3 Maps, 8 Plates and 85 Woodcuts. 8vo., 7s. net.

THE SUBTERRANEAN WORLD. With 3 Maps and 80 Woodcuts. 8vo., 7s. net.

THE AERIAL WORLD. With Map, 8 Plates and 60 Woodcuts. 8vo., 7s. net.

HEROES OF THE POLAR WORLD. With 19 Illustrations. Cr. 8vo., 2s.

WONDERS OF THE TROPICAL FORESTS. With 40 Illustrations. Cr. 8vo., 2s.

WORKERS UNDER THE GROUND. With 29 Illustrations. Cr. 8vo., 2s.

MARVELS OVER OUR HEADS. With 29 Illustrations. Cr. 8vo., 2s.

SEA MONSTERS AND SEA BIRDS. With 75 Illustrations. Cr. 8vo., 2s. 6d.

DENIZENS OF THE DEEP. With 117 Illustrations. Cr. 8vo., 2s. 6d.

Hartwig (DR. GEORGE)—*continued.*

VOLCANOES AND EARTHQUAKES. With 30 Illustrations. Cr. 8vo., 2s. 6d.

WILD ANIMALS OF THE TROPICS. With 66 Illustrations. Cr. 8vo., 3s. 6d.

Helmholtz.—*POPULAR LECTURES ON SCIENTIFIC SUBJECTS.* By HERMANN VON HELMHOLTZ. With 68 Woodcuts. 2 vols. Cr. 8vo., 3s. 6d. each.

Hudson (W. H.).

BRITISH BIRDS. With a Chapter on Structure and Classification by FRANK E. BEDDARD, F.R.S. With 16 Plates (8 of which are Coloured), and over 100 Illustrations in the Text. Cr. 8vo., 7s. 6d.

BIRDS IN LONDON. With 17 Plates and 15 Illustrations in the Text, by BRYAN HOOK, A. D. McCORMICK, and from Photographs from Nature, by R. B. LODGE. 8vo., 12s.

Proctor (RICHARD A.).

LIGHT SCIENCE FOR LEISURE HOURS. Familiar Essays on Scientific Subjects. 3 vols. Cr. 8vo., 5s. each.

ROUGH WAYS MADE SMOOTH. Familiar Essays on Scientific Subjects. Crown 8vo., 3s. 6d.

PLEASANT WAYS IN SCIENCE. Crown 8vo., 3s. 6d.

NATURE STUDIES. By R. A. PROCTOR, GRANT ALLEN, A. WILSON, T. FOSTER and E. CLODD. Crown 8vo., 3s. 6d.

LEISURE READINGS. By R. A. PROCTOR, E. CLODD, A. WILSON, T. FOSTER and A. C. RANYARD. Cr. 8vo., 3s. 6d.

** For Mr. Proctor's other books see pp. 13, 28 and 31, and Messrs. Longmans & Co.'s Catalogue of Scientific Works.

Stanley. — *A FAMILIAR HISTORY OF BIRDS.* By E. STANLEY, D.D., formerly Bishop of Norwich. With 160 Illustrations. Cr. 8vo., 3s. 6d.

Popular Science (Natural History, &c.)—*continued.*

Wood (Rev. J. G.).

HOMES WITHOUT HANDS: A Description of the Habitations of Animals, classed according to the Principle of Construction. With 140 Illustrations. 8vo., 7s. net.

INSECTS AT HOME : A Popular Account of British Insects, their Structure, Habits and Transformations. With 700 Illustrations. 8vo., 7s. net.

OUT OF DOORS; a Selection of Original Articles on Practical Natural History. With 11 Illustrations. Cr. 8vo., 3s. 6d.

STRANGE DWELLINGS: a Description of the Habitations of Animals, abridged from ' Homes without Hands '. With 60 Illustrations. Cr. 8vo., 3s. 6d.

Wood (Rev. J. G.)—*continued.*

PETLAND REVISITED. With 33 Illustrations. Cr. 8vo., 3s. 6d.

BIRD LIFE OF THE BIBLE. With 32 Illustrations. Cr. 8vo., 3s. 6d.

WONDERFUL NESTS. With 30 Illustrations. Cr. 8vo., 3s. 6d.

HOMES UNDER THE GROUND. With 28 Illustrations. Cr. 8vo., 3s. 6d.

WILD ANIMALS OF THE BIBLE. With 29 Illustrations. Cr. 8vo., 3s. 6d.

DOMESTIC ANIMALS OF THE BIBLE. With 23 Illustrations. Cr. 8vo., 3s. 6d.

THE BRANCH BUILDERS. With 28 Illustrations. Cr. 8vo., 2s. 6d.

SOCIAL HABITATIONS AND PARASITIC NESTS. With 18 Illustrations. Cr. 8vo., 2s.

Works of Reference.

Gwilt.—AN ENCYCLOPÆDIA OF ARCHITECTURE. By JOSEPH GWILT, F.S.A. Illustrated with more than 1100 Engravings on Wood. Revised (1888), with Alterations and Considerable Additions by WYATT PAPWORTH. 8vo, £2 12s. 6d.

Longmans' GAZETTEER OF THE WORLD. Edited by GEORGE G. CHISHOLM, M.A., B.Sc. Imp. 8vo., £2 2s. cloth, £2 12s. 6d. half-morocco.

Maunder (Samuel).

BIOGRAPHICAL TREASURY. With Supplement brought down to 1889. By Rev. JAMES WOOD. Fcp. 8vo., 6s.

TREASURY OF GEOGRAPHY, Physical, Historical, Descriptive, and Political. With 7 Maps and 16 Plates. Fcp. 8vo., 6s.

THE TREASURY OF BIBLE KNOWLEDGE. By the Rev. J. AYRE, M.A. With 5 Maps, 15 Plates, and 300 Woodcuts. Fcp. 8vo., 6s.

TREASURY OF KNOWLEDGE AND LIBRARY OF REFERENCE. Fcp. 8vo., 6s.

HISTORICAL TREASURY. Fcp. 8vo., 6s.

Maunder (Samuel)—*continued.*

SCIENTIFIC AND LITERARY TREASURY. Fcp. 8vo., 6s.

THE TREASURY OF BOTANY. Edited by J. LINDLEY, F.R.S., and T. MOORE, F.L.S. With 274 Woodcuts and 20 Steel Plates. 2 vols. Fcp. 8vo., 12s.

Roget. — THESAURUS OF ENGLISH WORDS AND PHRASES. Classified and Arranged so as to Facilitate the Expression of Ideas and assist in Literary Composition. By PETER MARK ROGET, M.D., F.R.S. Recomposed throughout, enlarged and improved, partly from the Author's Notes, and with a full Index, by the Author's Son, JOHN LEWIS ROGET. Crown 8vo., 10s. 6d.

Willich.--POPULAR TABLES for giving information for ascertaining the value of Lifehold, Leasehold, and Church Property, the Public Funds, etc. By CHARLES M. WILLICH. Edited by H. BENCE JONES. Crown 8vo., 10s. 6d.

Children's Books.

Buckland.—TWO LITTLE RUNAWAYS. Adapted from the French of LOUIS DESNOYERS. By JAMES BUCKLAND. With 110 Illustrations by CECIL ALDIN. Cr. 8vo., 6s.

Crake (Rev. A. D.).

EDWY THE FAIR; or, The First Chronicle of Æscendune. Cr. 8vo., 2s. 6d.

ALFGAR THE DANE; or, The Second Chronicle of Æscendune. Cr. 8vo. 2s. 6d.

Crake (Rev. A. D.)—*continued.*

THE RIVAL HEIRS : being the Third and Last Chronicle of Æscendune. Cr. 8vo., 2s. 6d.

THE HOUSE OF WALDERNE. A Tale of the Cloister and the Forest in the Days of the Barons' Wars. Crown 8vo., 2s. 6d.

BRIAN FITZ-COUNT. A Story of Wallingford Castle and Dorchester Abbey. Cr. 8vo., 2s. 6d.

Children's Books.—*continued.*

Henty.— *YULE LOGS :* A Story-Book for Boys. Edited by G. A. HENTY. With 61 Illustrations. Crown 8vo., cloth, gilt edges, 6s.

Lang (ANDREW).—EDITED BY.
THE BLUE FAIRY BOOK. With 138 Illustrations. Crown 8vo., 6s.
THE RED FAIRY BOOK. With 100 Illustrations. Crown 8vo., 6s.
THE GREEN FAIRY BOOK. With 99 Illustrations. Crown 8vo., 6s.
THE YELLOW FAIRY BOOK. With 104 Illustrations. Crown 8vo., 6s.
THE PINK FAIRY BOOK. With 67 Illustrations. Crown 8vo., 6s.
THE BLUE POETRY BOOK. With 100 Illustrations. Crown 8vo., 6s.
THE BLUE POETRY BOOK. School Edition, without Illustrations. Fcp. 8vo., 2s. 6d.
THE TRUE STORY BOOK. With 66 Illustrations. Crown 8vo., 6s.
THE RED TRUE STORY BOOK. With 100 Illustrations. Crown 8vo., 6s.
THE ANIMAL STORY BOOK. With 67 Illustrations. Crown 8vo., 6s.
THE ARABIAN NIGHTS ENTERTAIN-MENTS. With 66 Illustrations. Crown 8vo., 6s.

Meade (L. T.).
DADDY'S BOY. With 8 Illustrations. Crown 8vo., 3s. 6d.
DEB AND THE DUCHESS. With 7 Illustrations. Crown 8vo., 3s. 6d.
THE BERESFORD PRIZE. With 7 Illustrations. Crown 8vo., 3s. 6d.
THE HOUSE OF SURPRISES. With 6 Illustrations. Crown 8vo. 3s. 6d.

Praeger (ROSAMOND).
THE ADVENTURES OF THE THREE BOLD BABES : HECTOR, HONORIA AND ALISANDER. A Story in Pictures. With 24 Coloured Plates and 24 Outline Pictures. Oblong 4to., 3s. 6d.
THE FURTHER DOINGS OF THE THREE BOLD BABIES. With 24 Coloured Pictures and 24 Outline Pictures. Oblong 4to., 3s. 6d.

Stevenson.—*A CHILD'S GARDEN OF VERSES.* By ROBERT LOUIS STEVENSON. Fcp. 8vo., 5s.

Sullivan.—*HERE THEY ARE !* More Stories. Written and Illustrated by JAS. F. SULLIVAN. Crown 8vo., 6s.

Upton (FLORENCE K. AND BERTHA).
THE ADVENTURES OF TWO DUTCH DOLLS AND A 'GOLLIWOGG'. With 31 Coloured Plates and numerous Illustrations in the Text. Oblong 4to., 6s.
THE GOLLIWOGG'S BICYCLE CLUB. With 31 Coloured Plates and numerous Illustrations in the Text. Oblong 4to., 6s.
THE GOLLIWOGG AT THE SEASIDE. With 31 Coloured Plates and numerous Illustrations in the Text. Oblong 4to., 6s.
THE VEGE-MEN'S REVENGE. With 31 Coloured Plates and numerous Illustrations in the Text. Oblong 4to., 6s.

Wordsworth.—*THE SNOW GARDEN, AND OTHER FAIRY TALES FOR CHILDREN.* By ELIZABETH WORDSWORTH. With 10 Illustrations by TREVOR HADDON. Crown 8vo., 3s. 6d.

Longmans' Series of Books for Girls.
Price 2s. 6d. each.

ATELIER (THE) DU LYS : or, an Art Student in the Reign of Terror. BY THE SAME AUTHOR.
MADEMOISELLE MORI : a Tale of Modern Rome.
IN THE OLDEN TIME : a Tale of the Peasant War in Germany.
A YOUNGER SISTER.
THAT CHILD.
UNDER A CLOUD.
HESTER'S VENTURE
THE FIDDLER OF LUGAU.
A CHILD OF THE REVOLUTION.
ATHERSTONE PRIORY. By L. N. COMYN.
THE STORY OF A SPRING MORNING, etc. By Mr. MOLESWORTH. Illustrated.
THE PALACE IN THE GARDEN. By Mrs. MOLESWORTH. Illustrated.
NEIGHBOURS. By Mrs. MOLESWORTH.

THE THIRD MISS ST. QUENTIN. By Mrs. MOLESWORTH.
VERY YOUNG ; AND QUITE ANOTHER STORY. Two Stories. By JEAN INGELOW.
CAN THIS BE LOVE ? By LOUISA PARR.
KEITH DERAMORE. By the Author of 'Miss Molly'.
SIDNEY. By MARGARET DELAND.
AN ARRANGED MARRIAGE. By DOROTHEA GERARD.
LAST WORDS TO GIRLS ON LIFE AT SCHOOL AND AFTER SCHOOL. By MARIA GREY.
STRAY THOUGHTS FOR GIRLS. By LUCY H. M. SOULSBY. 16mo., 1s. 6d. net.

The Silver Library.

CROWN 8VO.   3s. 6d.   EACH VOLUME.

Arnold's (Sir Edwin) Seas and Lands. With 71 Illustrations.   3s. 6d.

Bagehot's (W.) Biographical Studies.   3s. 6d.

Bagehot's (W.) Economic Studies.   3s. 6d.

Bagehot's (W.) Literary Studies. With Portrait. 3 vols, 3s. 6d. each.

Baker's (Sir S. W.) Eight Years in Ceylon. With 6 Illustrations.   3s. 6d.

Baker's (Sir S. W.) Rifle and Hound in Ceylon. With 6 Illustrations.   3s. 6d.

Baring-Gould's (Rev. S.) Curious Myths of the Middle Ages.   3s. 6d.

Baring-Gould's (Rev. S.) Origin and Development of Religious Belief. 2 vols.   3s. 6d. each.

Becker's (W. A.) Gallus: or, Roman Scenes in the Time of Augustus. With 26 Illus.   3s. 6d.

Becker's (W. A.) Charicles: or, Illustrations of the Private Life of the Ancient Greeks. With 26 Illustrations.   3s. 6d.

Bent's (J. T.) The Ruined Cities of Mashonaland. With 117 Illustrations.   3s. 6d.

Brassey's (Lady) A Voyage in the 'Sunbeam'. With 66 Illustrations.   3s. 6d.

Churchill's (W. S.) The Story of the Malakand Field Force, 1897. With 6 Maps and Plans. 3s. 6d.

Clodd's (E.) Story of Creation: a Plain Account of Evolution. With 77 Illustrations.   3s. 6d.

Conybeare (Rev. W. J.) and Howson's (Very Rev. J. S.) Life and Epistles of St. Paul. With 46 Illustrations.   3s. 6d.

Dougall's (L.) Beggars All: a Novel.   3s. 6d.

Doyle's (A. Conan) Micah Clarke. A Tale of Monmouth's Rebellion. With 10 Illusts. 3s. 6d.

Doyle's (A. Conan) The Captain of the Polestar, and other Tales.   3s. 6d.

Doyle's (A. Conan) The Refugees: A Tale of the Huguenots. With 25 Illustrations.   3s. 6d.

Doyle's (A. Conan) The Stark Munro Letters.   3s. 6d.

Froude's (J. A.) The History of England, from the Fall of Wolsey to the Defeat of the Spanish Armada.   12 vols.   3s. 6d. each.

Froude's (J. A.) The English in Ireland. 3 vols. 10s. 6d.

Froude's (J. A.) The Divorce of Catherine of Aragon.   3s. 6d.

Froude's (J. A.) The Spanish Story of the Armada, and other Essays.   3s. 6d.

Froude's (J. A.) Short Studies on Great Subjects.   4 vols.   3s. 6d. each.

Froude's (J. A.) Oceana, or England and Her Colonies. With 9 Illustrations.   3s. 6d.

Froude's (J. A.) The Council of Trent.   3s. 6d.

Froude's (J. A.) Thomas Carlyle: a History of his Life.

1795-1835. 2 vols. 7s. 1834-1881. 2 vols. 7s.

Froude's (J. A.) Cæsar: a Sketch.   3s. 6d.

Froude's (J. A.) The Two Chiefs of Dunboy: an Irish Romance of the Last Century.   3s. 6d.

Gleig's (Rev. G. R.) Life of the Duke of Wellington. With Portrait.   3s. 6d.

Greville's (C. C. F.) Journal of the Reigns of King George IV., King William IV., and Queen Victoria. 8 vols., 3s. 6d. each.

Haggard's (H. R.) She: A History of Adventure. With 32 Illustrations.   3s. 6d.

Haggard's (H. R.) Allan Quatermain. With 20 Illustrations.   3s. 6d.

Haggard's (H. R.) Colonel Quaritch, V.C. : a Tale of Country Life. With Frontispiece and Vignette.   3s. 6d.

Haggard's (H. R.) Cleopatra. With 29 Illustrations.   3s. 6d.

Haggard's (H. R.) Eric Brighteyes. With 51 Illustrations.   3s. 6d.

Haggard's (H. R.) Beatrice. With Frontispiece and Vignette.   3s. 6d.

Haggard's (H. R.) Allan's Wife. With 34 Illustrations.   3s. 6d.

Haggard (H. R.) Heart of the World. With 15 Illustrations.   3s. 6d.

Haggard's (H. R.) Montezuma's Daughter. With 25 Illustrations.   3s. 6d.

Haggard's (H. R.) The Witch's Head. With 16 Illustrations.   3s. 6d.

Haggard's (H. R.) Mr. Meeson's Will. With 16 Illustrations.   3s. 6d.

Haggard's (H. R.) Nada the Lily. With 23 Illustrations.   3s. 6d.

Haggard's (H. R.) Dawn. With 16 Illusts.   3s. 6d.

Haggard's (H. R.) The People of the Mist. With 16 Illustrations.   3s. 6d.

Haggard's (H. R.) Joan Haste. With 20 Illustrations.   3s. 6d.

Haggard (H. R.) and Lang's (A.) The World's Desire. With 27 Illustrations.   3s. 6d.

Harte's (Bret) In the Carquinez Woods and other Stories.   3s. 6d.

Helmholtz's (Hermann von) Popular Lectures on Scientific Subjects. With 68 Illustrations. 2 vols.   3s. 6d. each.

Hornung's (E. W.) The Unbidden Guest.   3s. 6d.

Howitt's (W.) Visits to Remarkable Places. With 80 Illustrations.   3s. 6d.

Jefferies' (R.) The Story of My Heart: My Autobiography. With Portrait.   3s. 6d.

Jefferies' (R.) Field and Hedgerow. With Portrait.   3s. 6d.

Jefferies' (R.) Red Deer. With 17 Illusts.   3s. 6d.

Jefferies' (R.) Wood Magic: a Fable. With Frontispiece and Vignette by E. V. B.   3s. 6d.

Jefferies (R.) The Toilers of the Field. With Portrait from the Bust in Salisbury Cathedral. 3s. 6d.

Kaye (Sir J.) and Malleson's (Colonel) History of the Indian Mutiny of 1857-8. 6 vols. 3s. 6d. each.

Knight's (E. F.) The Cruise of the 'Alerte': the Narrative of a Search for Treasure on the Desert Island of Trinidad. With 2 Maps and 23 Illustrations.   3s. 6d.

Knight's (E. F.) Where Three Empires Meet: a Narrative of Recent Travel in Kashmir, Western Tibet, Baltistan, Gilgit. With a Map and 54 Illustrations.   3s. 6d.

Knight's (E. F.) The 'Falcon' on the Baltic: a Coasting Voyage from Hammersmith to Copenhagen in a Three-Ton Yacht. With Map and 11 Illustrations.   3s. 6d.

Köstlin's (J.) Life of Luther. With 62 Illustrations and 4 Facsimiles of MSS.   3s. 6d.

Lang's (A.) Angling Sketches. With 20 Illustrations.   3s. 6d.

Lang's (A.) Custom and Myth: Studies of Early Usage and Belief.   3s. 6d.

Lang's (A.) Cock Lane and Common-Sense. 3s. 6d.

The Silver Library—*continued.*

Lang's (A.) A Monk of Fife: a Story of the Days of Joan of Arc. With 13 Illusts. 3s. 6d.

Lang's (A.) Myth, Ritual and Religion. 2 vols. 7s.

Lees (J. A.) and Clutterbuck's (W. J.) B. C. 1887, A Ramble in British Columbia. With Maps and 75 Illustrations. 3s. 6d

Levett-Yeats' (S.) The Chevalier D'Auriac. 3s. 6d.

Macaulay's (Lord) Complete Works. With 12 Portraits. 12 vols. 3s. 6d. each.

Macaulay's (Lord) Essays and Lays of Ancient Rome, etc. With Portrait and 4 Illustrations to the ' Lays '. 3s. 6d.

Macleod's (H. D.) Elements of Banking. 3s. 6d.

Marbot's (Baron de) Memoirs. Translated. 2 vols. 7s.

Marshman's (J. C.) Memoirs of Sir Henry Havelock. 3s. 6d.

Merivale's (Dean) History of the Romans under the Empire. 8 vols. 3s. 6d. each.

Merriman's (H. S.) Flotsam: A Tale of the Indian Mutiny. 3s. 6d.

Mill's (J. S.) Political Economy. 3s. 6d.

Mill's (J. S.) System of Logic. 3s. 6d.

Milner's (Geo.) Country Pleasures: the Chronicle of a Year chiefly in a Garden. 3s. 6d.

Nansen's (F.) The First Crossing of Greenland. With 142 Illustrations and a Map. 3s. 6d.

Phillipps-Wolley's (C.) Snap: a Legend of the Lone Mountain With 13 Illustrations. 3s. 6d.

Proctor's (R. A.) The Orbs Around Us. 3s. 6d.

Proctor's (R. A.) The Expanse of Heaven. 3s. 6d.

Proctor's (R. A.) Light Science for Leisure Hours. First Series. 3s. 6d.

Proctor's (R. A.) The Moon. 3s. 6d.

Proctor's (R. A.) Other Worlds than Ours. 3s.6d.

Proctor's (R. A.) Our Place among Infinities: a Series of Essays contrasting our Little Abode in Space and Time with the Infinities around us. 3s. 6d.

Proctor's (R. A.) Other Suns than Ours. 3s. 6d.

Proctor's (R. A.) Rough Ways made Smooth. 3s. 6d.

Proctor's (R.A.) Pleasant Ways in Science. 3s.6d.

Proctor's (R. A.) Myths and Marvels of Astronomy. 3s. 6d.

Proctor's (R. A.) Nature Studies. 3s. 6d.

Proctor's (R. A.) Leisure Readings. By R. A. PROCTOR, EDWARD CLODD, ANDREW WILSON, THOMAS FOSTER, and A. C. RANYARD. With Illustrations. 3s. 6d.

Rossetti's (Maria F.) A Shadow of Dante. 3s. 6d.

Smith's (R. Bosworth) Carthage and the Carthaginians. With Maps, Plans, etc. 3s. 6d.

Stanley's (Bishop) Familiar History of Birds. With 160 Illustrations. 3s. 6d.

Stephen's (L.) The Playground of Europe (The Alps). With 4 Illustrations. 3s. 6d.

Stevenson's (R. L.) The Strange Case of Dr. Jekyll and Mr. Hyde; with other Fables. 3s.6d.

Stevenson (R. L.) and Osbourne's (Ll.) The Wrong Box. 3s. 6d.

Stevenson (Robert Louis) and Stevenson's (Fanny van de Grift) More New Arabian Nights.—The Dynamiter. 3s. 6d.

Weyman's (Stanley J.) The House of the Wolf: a Romance. 3s. 6d.

Wood's (Rev. J. G.) Petland Revisited. With 33 Illustrations. 3s. 6d.

Wood's (Rev. J. G.) Strange Dwellings. With 60 Illustrations. 3s. 6d.

Wood's (Rev. J. G.) Out of Doors. With 11 Illustrations. 3s. 6d.

Cookery, Domestic Management, &c.

Acton. — *MODERN COOKERY.* By ELIZA ACTON. With 150 Woodcuts. Fcp. 8vo., 4s. 6d.

Ashby.—*HEALTH IN THE NURSERY.* By HENRY ASHBY, M.D., F.R.C.P., Physician to the Manchester Children's Hospital, and Lecturer on the Diseases of Children at the Owens College. With 25 Illustrations. Crown 8vo., 3s. 6d.

Buckton.—*COMFORT AND CLEANLINESS:* The Servant and Mistress Question. By Mrs. CATHERINE M. BUCKTON, late Member of the Leeds School Board. With 14 Illustrations. Crown 8vo., 2s.

Bull (THOMAS, M.D.).

HINTS TO MOTHERS ON THE MANAGEMENT OF THEIR HEALTH DURING THE PERIOD OF PREGNANCY. Fcp. 8vo., 1s. 6d.

THE MATERNAL MANAGEMENT OF CHILDREN IN HEALTH AND DISEASE. Fcp. 8vo., 1s. 6d.

De Salis (MRS.).

CAKES AND CONFECTIONS à LA MODE. Fcp. 8vo., 1s. 6d.

DOGS: A Manual for Amateurs. Fcp. 8vo., 1s. 6d.

De Salis (MRS.).—*continued.*

DRESSED GAME AND POULTRY à LA MODE. Fcp. 8vo., 1s. 6d.

DRESSED VEGETABLES à LA MODE. Fcp. 8vo., 1s 6d.

DRINKS à LA MODE. Fcp. 8vo., 1s.6d.

ENTRÉES à LA MODE. Fcp. 8vo., 1s. 6d.

FLORAL DECORATIONS. Fcp. 8vo., 1s. 6d.

GARDENING à LA MODE. Fcp. 8vo. Part I., Vegetables, 1s. 6d. Part II., Fruits, 1s. 6d.

NATIONAL VIANDS à LA MODE. Fcp. 8vo., 1s. 6d.

NEW-LAID EGGS. Fcp. 8vo., 1s. 6d.

OYSTERS à LA MODE. Fcp. 8vo., 1s. 6d.

SOUPS AND DRESSED FISH à LA MODE. Fcp. 8vo., 1s. 6d.

SAVOURIES à LA MODE. Fcp. 8vo., 1s.6d.

PUDDINGS AND PASTRY à LA MODE. Fcp. 8vo., 1s. 6d.

Cookery, Domestic Management, &c.—*continued.*

De Salis (MRS.)—*continued.*

SWEETS AND SUPPER DISHES À LA MODE. Fcp. 8vo., 1s. 6d.

TEMPTING DISHES FOR SMALL INCOMES. Fcp. 8vo., 1s. 6d.

WRINKLES AND NOTIONS FOR EVERY HOUSEHOLD. Crown 8vo., 1s. 6d.

Lear.—*MAIGRE COOKERY.* By H. L. SIDNEY LEAR. 16mo., 2s.

Poole.—*COOKERY FOR THE DIABETIC.* By W. H. and Mrs. POOLE. With Preface by Dr. PAVY. Fcp. 8vo., 2s. 6d.

Walker (JANE H.).

A BOOK FOR EVERY WOMAN. Part I., The Management of Children in Health and out of Health. Crown 8vo., 2s. 6d.

Part II. Woman in Health and out of Health. Crown 8vo., 2s. 6d.

A HANDBOOK FOR MOTHERS : being Simple Hints to Women on the Management of their Health during Pregnancy and Confinement, together with Plain Directions as to the Care of Infants. Crown 8vo., 2s. 6d.

Miscellaneous and Critical Works.

Armstrong.—*ESSAYS AND SKETCHES.* By EDMUND J. ARMSTRONG. Fcp. 8vo., 5s.

Bagehot.—*LITERARY STUDIES.* By WALTER BAGEHOT. With Portrait. 3 vols. Crown 8vo., 3s. 6d. each.

Baring-Gould.—*CURIOUS MYTHS OF THE MIDDLE AGES.* By Rev. S. BARING-GOULD. Crown 8vo., 3s. 6d.

Baynes. — *SHAKESPEARE STUDIES,* and other Essays. By the late THOMAS SPENCER BAYNES, LL.B., LL.D. With a Biographical Preface by Professor LEWIS CAMPBELL. Crown 8vo., 7s. 6d.

Boyd (A. K. H.) ('A.K.H.B.').

And see MISCELLANEOUS THEOLOGICAL WORKS, p. 32.

AUTUMN HOLIDAYS OF A COUNTRY PARSON. Crown 8vo., 3s. 6d.

COMMONPLACE PHILOSOPHER. Cr. 8vo., 3s. 6d.

CRITICAL ESSAYS OF A COUNTRY PARSON. Crown 8vo., 3s. 6d.

EAST COAST DAYS AND MEMORIES. Crown 8vo., 3s. 6d.

LANDSCAPES, CHURCHES, AND MORALITIES. Crown 8vo., 3s. 6d.

LEISURE HOURS IN TOWN. Crown 8vo., 3s. 6d.

LESSONS OF MIDDLE AGE. Crown 8vo., 3s. 6d.

OUR LITTLE LIFE. Two Series. Crown 8vo., 3s. 6d. each.

OUR HOMELY COMEDY: AND TRAGEDY. Crown 8vo., 3s. 6d.

RECREATIONS OF A COUNTRY PARSON. Three Series. Crown 8vo., 3s. 6d. each.

Butler (SAMUEL).

EREWHON. Crown 8vo., 5s.

THE FAIR HAVEN. A Work in Defence of the Miraculous Element in our Lord's Ministry. Cr. 8vo., 7s. 6d.

LIFE AND HABIT. An Essay after a Completer View of Evolution. Cr. 8vo., 7s. 6d.

EVOLUTION, OLD AND NEW. Cr. 8vo., 10s. 6d.

ALPS AND SANCTUARIES OF PIEDMONT AND CANTON TICINO. Illustrated. Pott 4to., 10s. 6d.

LUCK, OR CUNNING, AS THE MAIN MEANS OF ORGANIC MODIFICATION? Cr. 8vo., 7s. 6d.

EX VOTO. An Account of the Sacro Monte or New Jerusalem at Varallo-Sesia. Crown 8vo., 10s. 6d.

SELECTIONS FROM WORKS, with Remarks on Mr. G. J. Romanes' 'Mental Evolution in Animals,' and a Psalm of Montreal. Crown 8vo., 7s. 6d.

THE AUTHORESS OF THE ODYSSEY, WHERE AND WHEN SHE WROTE, WHO SHE WAS, THE USE SHE MADE OF THE ILIAD, AND HOW THE POEM GREW UNDER HER HANDS. With 14 Illustrations. 8vo., 10s. 6d.

THE ILIAD OF HOMER. Rendered into English Prose for the use of those who cannot read the original. Crown 8vo., 7s. 6d.

Miscellaneous and Critical Works—*continued.*

CHARITIES REGISTER, THE ANNUAL, AND DIGEST: being a Classified Register of Charities in or available in the Metropolis, together with a Digest of Information respecting the Legal, Voluntary, and other Means for the Prevention and Relief of Distress, and the Improvement of the Condition of the Poor, and an Elaborate Index. With an Introduction by C. S. LOCH, Secretary to the Council of the Charity Organisation Society, London. 8vo., 4s.

Comparetti. — *THE TRADITIONAL POETRY OF THE FINNS.* By DOMENICO COMPARETTI, Socio dell' Accademia dei Lincei, Membre de l'Académie des Inscriptions, &c. Translated by ISABELLA M. ANDERTON. With Introduction by ANDREW LANG. 8vo., 16s.

Dreyfus.—*LECTURES ON FRENCH LITERATURE.* Delivered in Melbourne by IRMA DREYFUS. With Portrait of the Author. Large crown 8vo., 12s. 6d.

Evans.—*THE ANCIENT STONE IMPLEMENTS, WEAPONS AND ORNAMENTS OF GREAT BRITAIN.* By Sir JOHN EVANS, K.C.B., D.C.L., LL.D., F.R.S., etc. With 537 Illustrations. Medium 8vo., 28s.

Hamlin.—*A TEXT-BOOK OF THE HISTORY OF ARCHITECTURE.* By A. D. F. HAMLIN, A.M. With 229 Illustrations. Crown 8vo., 7s. 6d.

Haweis.—*MUSIC AND MORALS.* By the Rev. H. R. HAWEIS. With Portrait of the Author, and numerous Illustrations, Facsimiles, and Diagrams. Cr. 8vo., 7s. 6d.

Hime.—*STRAY MILITARY PAPERS.* By Lieut.-Colonel H. W. L. HIME (late Royal Artillery). 8vo, 7s. 6d.
CONTENTS.— Infantry Fire Formations -- On Marking at Rifle Matches—The Progress of Field Artillery—The Reconnoitering Duties of Cavalry.

Hullah.—*THE HISTORY OF MODERN MUSIC;* a Course of Lectures. By JOHN HULLAH, LL.D. 8vo., 8s. 6d.

Jefferies (RICHARD).
FIELD AND HEDGEROW: With Portrait. Crown 8vo., 3s. 6d.
THE STORY OF MY HEART: my Autobiography. With Portrait and New Preface by C. J. LONGMAN. Cr. 8vo., 3s. 6d.
RED DEER. With 17 Illustrations by J. CHARLTON and H. TUNALY. Crown 8vo., 3s. 6d.
THE TOILERS OF THE FIELD. With Portrait from the Bust in Salisbury Cathedral. Crown 8vo., 3s. 6d.
WOOD MAGIC: a Fable. With Frontispiece and Vignette by E. V. B. Crown 8vo., 3s. 6d.

Johnson.—*THE PATENTEE'S MANUAL:* a Treatise on the Law and Practice of Letters Patent. By J. & J. H. JOHNSON, Patent Agents, etc. 8vo., 10s. 6d.

Joyce.— *THE ORIGIN AND HISTORY OF IRISH NAMES OF PLACES.* By P. W. JOYCE, LL.D. 2 vols. Crown 8vo., 5s. each.

Kingsley.—*A HANDBOOK TO FRENCH ART.* By ROSE G. KINGSLEY.

Lang (ANDREW).
THE MAKING OF RELIGION. 8vo., 12s.
MODERN MYTHOLOGY: a Reply to Professor Max Müller. 8vo., 9s.
LETTERS TO DEAD AUTHORS. Fcp. 8vo., 2s. 6d. net.
BOOKS AND BOOKMEN. With 2 Coloured Plates and 17 Illustrations. Fcp. 8vo., 2s. 6d. net.
OLD FRIENDS. Fcp. 8vo., 2s. 6d. net.
LETTERS ON LITERATURE. Fcp. 8vo., 2s. 6d. net.
ESSAYS IN LITTLE. With Portrait of the Author. Crown 8vo., 2s. 6d.
COCK LANE AND COMMON-SENSE. Crown 8vo., 3s. 6d.
THE BOOK OF DREAMS AND GHOSTS. Crown 8vo., 6s.

Macfarren. — *LECTURES ON HARMONY.* By Sir GEORGE A. MACFARREN. 8vo., 12s.

Madden.—*THE DIARY OF MASTER WILLIAM SILENCE:* a Study of Shakespeare and Elizabethan Sport. By the Right Hon. D. H. MADDEN, Vice-Chancellor of the University of Dublin. 8vo., 16s.

Marquand and Frothingham.—*A TEXT-BOOK OF THE HISTORY OF SCULPTURE.* By ALLAN MARQUAND, Ph.D., and ARTHUR L. FROTHINGHAM, Junr., Ph.D., Professors of Archæology and the History of Art in Princetown University. With 113 Illustrations. Crown 8vo., 6s.

Max Müller (The Right Hon. F.).
INDIA: WHAT CAN IT TEACH US? Crown 8vo., 3s. 6d.
CHIPS FROM A GERMAN WORKSHOP.
Vol. I. Recent Essays and Addresses. Crown 8vo., 5s.
Vol. II. Biographical Essays. Crown 8vo., 5s.
Vol. III. Essays on Language and Literature. Crown 8vo., 5s.
Vol. IV. Essays on Mythology and Folk Lore. Crown 8vo., 5s.
CONTRIBUTIONS TO THE SCIENCE OF MYTHOLOGY. 2 vols. 8vo., 32s.

Miscellaneous and Critical Works—*continued.*

Milner.—*COUNTRY PLEASURES:* the Chronicle of a Year chiefly in a Garden. By GEORGE MILNER. Crown 8vo., 3s. 6d.

Morris (WILLIAM).
SIGNS OF CHANGE. Seven Lectures delivered on various Occasions. Post 8vo., 4s. 6d.

HOPES AND FEARS FOR ART. Five Lectures delivered in Birmingham, London, etc., in 1878-1881. Cr 8vo., 4s. 6d.

AN ADDRESS DELIVERED AT THE DISTRIBUTION OF PRIZES TO STUDENTS OF THE BIRMINGHAM MUNICIPAL SCHOOL OF ART ON 21ST FEBRUARY, 1894. 8vo., 2s. 6d. net.

Orchard.—*THE ASTRONOMY OF 'MILTON'S PARADISE LOST'.* By THOMAS N. ORCHARD, M.D., Member of the British Astronomical Association. With 13 Illustrations. 8vo., 6s. net.

Poore (GEORGE VIVIAN), M.D., F.R.C.P.
ESSAYS ON RURAL HYGIENE. With 13 Illustrations. Crown 8vo., 6s. 6d.

THE DWELLING HOUSE. With 36 Illustrations. Crown 8vo., 3s. 6d.

Richmond.—*BOYHOOD:* a Plea for Continuity in Education. By ENNIS RICHMOND. Crown 8vo., 2s. 6d.

Richter. — *LECTURES ON THE NATIONAL GALLERY.* By J. P. RICHTER. With 20 Plates and 7 Illustrations in the Text. Crown 4to., 9s.

Rossetti.—*A SHADOW OF DANTE:* being an Essay towards studying Himself, his World and his Pilgrimage. By MARIA FRANCESCA ROSSETTI. With Frontispiece by DANTE GABRIEL ROSSETTI. Crown 8vo., 3s. 6d.

Solovyoff.—*A MODERN PRIESTESS OF ISIS* (MADAME BLAVATSKY). Abridged and Translated on Behalf of the Society for Psychical Research from the Russian of VSEVOLOD SERGYEEVICH SOLOVYOFF. By WALTER LEAF, Litt.D. With Appendices. Crown 8vo., 6s.

Soulsby (LUCY H. M.).
STRAY THOUGHTS ON READING. Small 8vo., 2s. 6d. net.

STRAY THOUGHTS FOR GIRLS. 16mo., 1s. 6d. net.

Soulsby (LUCY H. M.)—*continued.*

STRAY THOUGHTS FOR MOTHERS AND TEACHERS. Fcp. 8vo., 2s. 6d. net.

STRAY THOUGHTS FOR INVALIDS. 16mo., 2s. net.

Southey.—*THE CORRESPONDENCE OF ROBERT SOUTHEY WITH CAROLINE BOWLES.* Edited, with an Introduction, by EDWARD DOWDEN, LL.D. 8vo., 14s.

Stevens.—*ON THE STOWAGE OF SHIPS AND THEIR CARGOES.* With Information regarding Freights, Charter-Parties, etc. By ROBERT WHITE STEVENS, Associate-Member of the Institute of Naval Architects. 8vo., 21s.

Turner and Sutherland.—*THE DEVELOPMENT OF AUSTRALIAN LITERATURE.* By HENRY GYLES TURNER and ALEXANDER SUTHERLAND. With Portraits and Illustrations. Crown 8vo., 5s.

Tyszkiewicz. — *MEMORIES OF AN OLD COLLECTOR.* By COUNT MICHAEL TYSZKIEWICZ. Translated from the French by Mrs. ANDREW LANG. With 9 Plates. Crown 8vo., 6s.

Van Dyke.—*A TEXT-BOOK ON THE HISTORY OF PAINTING.* By JOHN C. VAN DYKE, Professor of the History of Art in Rutgers College, U.S. With 110 Illustrations. Crown 8vo, 6s.

Warwick.—*PROGRESS IN WOMEN'S EDUCATION IN THE BRITISH EMPIRE:* being the Report of Conferences and a Congress held in connection with the Educational Section, Victorian Era Exhibition. Edited by the COUNTESS OF WARWICK. Cr. 8vo. 6s.

White.—*AN EXAMINATION OF THE CHARGE OF APOSTACY AGAINST WORDSWORTH.* By W. HALE WHITE, Editor of the 'Description of the Wordsworth and Coleridge MSS. in the Possession of Mr. T. Norton Longman'. Crown 8vo., 3s. 6d.

Willard. — *HISTORY OF MODERN ITALIAN ART.* By ASHTON ROLLINS WILLARD. With Photogravure Frontispiece and 28 Full-page Illustrations. 8vo., 18s. net.

Miscellaneous Theological Works.

. For Church of England and Roman Catholic Works see MESSRS. LONGMANS & Co.'s
Special Catalogues.

Balfour. — THE FOUNDATIONS OF
BELIEF: being Notes Introductory to the
Study of Theology. By the Right Hon.
ARTHUR J. BALFOUR, M.P. 8vo., 12s. 6d.

Bird (ROBERT).
A CHILD'S RELIGION. Cr. 8vo., 2s.
JOSEPH, THE DREAMER. Crown
8vo., 5s.
JESUS, THE CARPENTER OF
NAZARETH. Crown 8vo., 5s.
To be had also in Two Parts, price 2s. 6d.
each.
Part I. GALILEE AND THE LAKE OF
GENNESARET.
Part II. JERUSALEM AND THE PERÆA.

Boyd (A. K. H.) ('A.K.H.B.').
OCCASIONAL AND IMMEMORIAL DAYS:
Discourses. Crown 8vo., 7s. 6d.
COUNSEL AND COMFORT FROM A
CITY PULPIT. Crown 8vo., 3s. 6d.
SUNDAY AFTERNOONS IN THE PARISH
CHURCH OF A SCOTTISH UNIVERSITY
CITY. Crown 8vo., 3s. 6d.
CHANGED ASPECTS OF UNCHANGED
TRUTHS. Crown 8vo., 3s. 6d.
GRAVER THOUGHTS OF A COUNTRY
PARSON. Three Series. Crown 8vo.,
3s. 6d. each.
PRESENT DAY THOUGHTS. Crown
8vo., 3s. 6d.
SEASIDE MUSINGS. Cr. 8vo., 3s. 6d.
'TO MEET THE DAY' through the
Christian Year: being a Text of Scripture,
with an Original Meditation and a Short
Selection in Verse for Every Day. Crown
8vo., 4s. 6d.

Campbell.—RELIGION IN GREEK LI-
TERATURE. By the Rev. LEWIS CAMPBELL,
M.A., LL.D., Emeritus Professor of Greek,
University of St. Andrews. 8vo., 15s.

Davidson.—THEISM, as Grounded in
Human Nature, Historically and Critically
Handled. Being the Burnett Lectures
for 1892 and 1893, delivered at Aberdeen.
By W. L. DAVIDSON, M.A., LL.D. 8vo., 15s.

Gibson.—THE ABBÉ DE LAMENNAIS.
AND THE LIBERAL CATHOLIC MOVEMENT
IN FRANCE. By the Hon. W. GIBSON.
With Portrait. 8vo., 12s. 6d.

Lang.—THE MAKING OF RELIGION.
By ANDREW LANG. 8vo., 12s.

10,000/1/99.

MacDonald (GEORGE).
UNSPOKEN SERMONS. Three Series.
Crown 8vo., 3s. 6d. each.
THE MIRACLES OF OUR LORD.
Crown 8vo., 3s. 6d.

Martineau (JAMES).
HOURS OF THOUGHT ON SACRED
THINGS: Sermons, 2 vols. Crown 8vo.
3s. 6d. each.
ENDEAVOURS AFTER THE CHRISTIAN
LIFE. Discourses. Crown 8vo., 7s. 6d.
THE SEAT OF AUTHORITY IN RE-
LIGION. 8vo., 14s.
ESSAYS, REVIEWS, AND ADDRESSES.
4 Vols. Crown 8vo., 7s. 6d. each.
HOME PRAYERS, with TWO SERVICES
for Public Worship. Crown 8vo., 3s. 6d.

Max Müller (F.).
THE ORIGIN AND GROWTH OF RELI-
GION, as illustrated by the Religions of
India. The Hibbert Lectures, delivered
at the Chapter House, Westminster
Abbey, in 1878. Crown 8vo., 5s.
INTRODUCTION TO THE SCIENCE OF
RELIGION: Four Lectures delivered at the
Royal Institution. Crown 8vo., 3s. 6d.
NATURAL RELIGION. The Gifford
Lectures, delivered before the University
of Glasgow in 1888. Crown 8vo., 5s.
PHYSICAL RELIGION. The Gifford
Lectures, delivered before the University
of Glasgow in 1890. Crown 8vo., 5s.
ANTHROPOLOGICAL RELIGION. The
Gifford Lectures, delivered before the Uni-
versity of Glasgow in 1891. Cr. 8vo., 5s.
THEOSOPHY, OR PSYCHOLOGICAL RE-
LIGION. The Gifford Lectures, delivered
before the University of Glasgow in 1892.
Crown 8vo., 5s.
THREE LECTURES ON THE VEDÂNTA
PHILOSOPHY, delivered at the Royal
Institution in March, 1894. 8vo., 5s.
RÂMAKRISHNA: HIS LIFE AND SAY-
INGS. Crown 8vo., 5s.

Romanes.—THOUGHTS ON RELIGION.
By GEORGE J. ROMANES, LL.D., F.R.S.
Crown 8vo., 4s. 6d.

Vivekananda.—YOGA PHILOSOPHY:
Lectures delivered in New York, Winter of
1895-96, by the SWAMI VIVEKANANDA,
on Raja Yoga; or, Conquering the Internal
Nature; also Patanjali's Yoga Aphorisms,
with Commentaries. Crown 8vo., 3s. 6d.

www.ingramcontent.com/pod-product-compliance
Lightning Source LLC
Chambersburg PA
CBHW060534030726

47498CB00004B/1195